SHADOWED
LOYALTY

SHADOWED LOYALTY

ROSEANNA M. WHITE

Chrism Press

CHRISM PRESS

SHADOWED LOYALTY

Chrism Press
A division of WhiteFire Publishing
13607 Bedford Rd NE
Cumberland, MD 21502

ISBN: 978-1-941720-79-0 (print)
978-1-941720-80-6 (digital)

ONE

Hope had grown grey hairs,
Hope had mourning on,
Trenched with tears, carved with cares,
Hope was twelve hours gone;

-Gerard Manley Hopkins,
from "The Wreck of the Deutschland"

June, 1922
Chicago

The wind tore down the alley, forcing Sabina Mancari to hold her cloche hat in place with one hand as she stepped around the corner. Another turn and she'd be at her father's office—not a moment too soon. Her gaze flicked to the dark clouds knuckling on the horizon. If she were lucky, she'd beat the storm and be able to hitch a ride home with Papa.

She took the final turn but then halted. Cars littered the street, parked helter-skelter in front of the steps to Papa's building. Men, stationed in formation at regular intervals, clutched guns aimed at the windows. Cops? They wore no uniforms, but her skin prickled.

Every Sicilian, Papa said, was born able to detect a cop from a mile away. And every Sicilian was born with a distrust of them. He said it had come after centuries of government abuse. That kind of instinct, so hard-won, hadn't vanished from their blood just because they immigrated to America.

Sabina took half a step back, eyes skittering in search of cover. *Never cross a cop's path*, her parents had taught her all her life. She lived by that mantra. How many times had she taken one of Little G's hands in hers, gripped Serafina's in the other, and tugged them across the street to avoid a policeman out on his beat?

Her fingers flexed against her palm, the habit of reaching for her siblings so ingrained that her hand still felt empty, years after Little G refused to hold it anymore. Years after Serafina…

No. Don't think about her. The cops, she had to deal with the cops. How could she avoid them? They were everywhere.

The force of it hit her—a dozen policemen, covering every door and window of Papa's office. Her throat closed. Her brows knit together. Plain clothes could mean only one thing—Prohibition Bureau. But that didn't make sense. Everyone knew the Bureau was too corrupt to ever make an arrest.

A tall, fair-haired man raised a megaphone. "Come out, Manny! It's all over! We've got you surrounded!"

Sabina lifted a hand to her throat and retreated another step into the alleyway from which she'd not fully emerged, willing the building at her side to keep her out of the sight of those men. This couldn't be happening. They couldn't be here for her father. That happened to other bosses—she'd heard the stories, she knew it was true—but not Giorgio Mancari. He ran his operation too carefully. He knit his family too tightly. *Omerta*, their code of silence, ruled too strongly—no one would ever turn on a Mancari.

So why were the Bureau boys surrounding Papa's office building?

"Don't waste our time, Manny!"

Without warning, the familiar tattoo of a Betsy sounded from a second-floor window. Papa himself or one of his many underlings? Sabina winced at the shattering glass and peeked around the corner as answering fire rang out from the cops. Bullets ripped through the battered Fords, turning steel into sieves. The men all ducked for cover.

Sabina jolted when a drop of cool rain splashed onto her nose, followed by another and another. The skies unleashed a steady shower that did nothing to drown the thunder of gunfire. She rested a gloved hand on the brick wall at her side and took another step back, Papa's instructions ringing in her memory.

She had to get home, warn Mama and Little G. They would gather everything in the top drawer from the desk in Papa's office—Mama had the key—and flee to the basement. They were not to open the doors to anyone. They were to go into the hidden partition that Sabina had watched the builders install when she was thirteen, with Serafina perched on her hip, and wait. Papa would take the hidden exit out of his office and meet them there, but they'd have to be ready to leave the moment he got home.

He had a series of rendezvous already laid out. All they had to do was get to the right one, and Papa's men would pick them up. They'd get them out of Chicago until the heat was off.

She knew the plan. She'd recited the plan on Papa's knee, then from his side when she outgrew his lap. *Home. Papers. Basement. Hide. Escape.* Words as familiar as the prayer that sprang by rote to her lips, even as her fingers sketched a hurried cross. "Our Father, who art in heaven…"

But she'd never actually had to *use* the plan. Certainly not while guns barked across the alleyway, surely aimed at Papa. "Hallowed be Thy name…" She spun around.

There was no time to waste. She lurched forward—and collided with a male chest. Strong hands gripped her arms, held her captive. She opened her mouth to scream.

"Sabina? What are you doing here?"

Relief left her limp. A prayer answered before she could even finish it— that was new. She blinked against the rain and fell into the arms of the man she loved. "Roman! You have to help. Papa's inside, and they're shooting at him, and—"

"I know." Roman Oliveri's reassuring smile lit hope in her heart as he moved his hands down to her elbows, halting her idiotic babble. Even through the steady rain, his eyes gleamed like emeralds and his teeth shone white as pearls. "Come on."

He used his grip on her elbows to spin her around and guide her forward. Roman would help her get home, help her and Mama execute the plan. She let him tug her a few steps toward the fray—but then reason kicked in. Why was he taking her *toward* the gunfight? She dug in her heels and pulled against his grasp. "Roman?"

His fingers tightened. He gave her a yank, angling a hard, cold look down at her.

Something heavy and terrifying eclipsed her heart—something she hadn't felt since she pressed her shaking fingers to the fever burning up Serafina's forehead and heard the rattle in her chest. It wasn't just terror—it was the absolute certainty that the world was about to come crashing down. "Roman? What are you doing?"

He didn't answer. Didn't even look at her, just tugged her so fiercely that she nearly tripped, pulling her toward the bullets singing out as they kissed pavement and brick. The acrid sting of gunpowder polluted the air.

The Betsy abruptly fell silent when they came into view of the office window; the gunman must have seen her. One of the Prohibition boys shouted out a cease-fire, but they kept their weapons at the ready.

Sabina stumbled along, dreadful certainty swallowing her whole. *Ice.*

Numb. She silently called for it, wishing it could douse the flames consuming her, but it was no use. She could still feel the terror with every stumbling step, every pulse of the veins under Roman's fingers.

Roman was supposed to have been different. He was supposed to have loved her. He was supposed to have seen something in her, more than who her father was and what he owed him. He'd said he did, he had. He'd made her feel, for the first time in too long, like she was worthwhile.

But now he was dragging her straight into the line of fire, straight toward the Bureau boys, his stride sure and fast. She could smell it now on the rain-heavy wind. *Cop.*

Her stomach rebelled at the thought, but she couldn't deny it. Not when Roman, who had waltzed into her life six months ago and brought light back into it, stepped up beside the man who had been shouting and tugged the megaphone to his own lips. "Come out, Manny, or your daughter dies!"

Ice. Numb. For three years she'd been moving through the floes, training herself not to feel the things that would only crush her—why did the ice abandon her now, when she needed it so dearly? But it wouldn't come. All that came was the burning, panicked dread. Sabina tried again to pull free, but Roman's fingers—the fingers that had caressed her cheek two days ago—dug in harder.

A sob wanted to rear up, but she had too much practice fending off tears. *No.* Perhaps the ice wouldn't come, but she still had pride to fall back on. She lifted her chin, straightened her spine, and glared at him.

The fair-haired man beside them shifted, clenched his jaw. "Roman..."

"Shut up, Cliff."

Rain dripped down her face, crying for her. It soaked her new hat and dress, likely ruining them. She'd bought them especially for her dinner with Roman tonight. Roman, who had actually looked at her like she was as beautiful as everyone said. Roman, who had kissed her like he wanted to.

Roman, who thrust her forward now like some kind of sacrificial lamb, still keeping his grip on her elbows. "Get down here, old man! If you love her as much as you say you do, come take her place!"

"Roman..." the man he'd called Cliff said again, his voice heavy with warning as he mopped the moisture from his face. He flicked an uncertain gaze to Sabina. As if he cared about her, this blue-eyed stranger who screamed *Cop!* with his every movement. No. He was only here to ruin her life, her family, all they'd worked for. He was here to steal, like they all were.

Roman snarled. "Give it a rest. Get ready to take him into custody when he comes down."

Finally, that blessed ice drifted over her—first her limbs, then her body, and finally her very soul. But it didn't feel comforting anymore. It didn't insulate her from the pain; it only trapped it inside her.

This was her fault—*all* her fault. Papa…and what would Mama say, and Little G? All the lieutenants and cousins and uncles? The Mancari operation was their world—how they survived, how they fed their children. With Papa pinched, they would *all* suffer. All because she'd trusted Roman Oliveri—because she'd dared to believe that he could actually love her.

Her eyes burned, but she forced herself to look to the door of the building. She knew what she'd see in another moment. Her father wouldn't have had time to escape yet, so he would come down and give himself up for her. Because *he* loved her. But this stranger, this monster beside her… How could she possibly have let herself be used to ruin her own family?

As if sensing her thoughts, Roman looked down at her. His gaze, though softer than a moment before, had never been so cool in their half-year acquaintance. "Look, Sabina, I'm sorry you got dragged into this. You weren't supposed to be here today."

"That's all you have to say to me?" The words burned her tongue as she spat them, flint and spark and fire that melted her hard-won ice from the inside. "I shouldn't have been here *today*? After six months of lying to me, using me—"

"Sabina…"

She had no intention of stopping there. But the front door of the building opened, and her father walked out with his hands held above his head.

She hadn't cried in three years, not since the day of Serafina's funeral. Not since she leaned one last time to press her lips to that precious little cheek and realized that her sweet little sister, the girl she'd given so many years to raising and loving, was gone forever. But a sob heaved its way up now, her tears finally mixing with heaven's. "Papa!"

Giorgio Mancari should not have come to this.

He walked straight toward her and Roman, his chin up and eyes steady. None of the other agents made a move to stop him. Given the gold and gems sparkling on their hands—treasures no one could purchase on a Prohibition agent's salary—she wasn't surprised.

"Get your hands off my daughter." His words were a low growl.

Roman obeyed with a smirk. "Of course. She's free to go, so long as you show yourself into the car without a fuss."

Papa shook his head. "You're a coward and a rat. After you ate at our table, after we gave you our trust, you would do this to us?"

Sabina forced a swallow as guilt ate away at her stomach. Papa never would have looked twice at this newcomer if she hadn't asked him to give Roman a chance. *She* was the one who had trusted him. She was the one who had been duped. Her father's only mistake had been to trust *her* judgment.

Roman's chin went up, his dark, damp hair sticking to his forehead. "I was doing my job." His gaze drifted down to Sabina. "I don't expect you to understand that. I never wanted to hurt you, Sabina, but you can't be the daughter of a mafioso and go through life unscathed."

Unscathed? Her hand slapped his cheek before she was aware of commanding it to do so. The man called Cliff choked on a laugh. Despite the rain eager to lash her face, she rolled back her shoulders and narrowed her eyes. "Neither can a man who would tell a woman he loves her for the sole purpose of using her."

She looked at her father, and his eyes were sad and old. He, too, knew this was all her fault. His darling *principessa* had just brought his kingdom tumbling down. The quaking started somewhere deep inside her and made its way to her limbs.

She had to fix this somehow. Unfortunately, only one recourse sprang to mind. "We'll have you out by the weekend, Papa. I'll call Enzo."

"Not Enzo."

She wanted to agree, to take the out he was clearly offering. But as much as she didn't want to talk to Lorenzo Capecce right now, he *was* a lawyer. A criminal attorney, even. It didn't matter that he'd only just passed the bar—he was in a prestigious firm now. He'd know what to do, or at least who else to turn to.

Papa, the family, was worth it—worth looking into Lorenzo's cool eyes, worth all the questions, all the uncertainties that would plague her. Worth all the shame eating her up at the very thought of him. "I'm calling him."

Papa sighed as Roman let go of Sabina's arm and reached for his instead. "Oh, *principessa*." He didn't say more. But she could hear his unspoken words, and they rang louder than the gunfire.

She should have called Lorenzo long ago.

TWO

Death or distance soon consumes them: wind
What most I may eye after, be in at the end
I cannot, and out of sight is out of mind.

-Gerard Manley Hopkins,
from "The Lantern out of Doors"

The light from the streetlamp barely touched Lorenzo Capecce's heels as he stood on the stoop of the Mancari house. He pinched the bridge of his nose and took a deep breath. Before him stood the door with its familiar stained-glass window, friendly colors glowing. Behind it waited people desperate for good news—Mama Rosa, Little G, Sabina.

Sabina.

An hour ago, he'd stood in front of prison bars with the Mancari patriarch waiting on the other side. Lorenzo had gripped the handle of his leather attaché case and just stared at Manny for a long moment—his godfather. Father not only loved this man like a brother despite no shared blood but respected him enough to treat him as a patriarch, maybe even a king. Manny not only ruled the Mancaris, but the Capecces too. Every aspect of Lorenzo's life had been dictated by this man. He loved him—how could he not? Manny's care for the family couldn't be faulted. He owed him everything.

But *this.*

Lorenzo had only ever demanded one thing. One...blasted...thing. Before he accepted a dime from Manny to go to college or law school, he'd stood in this very house, in the study full of masculine woods and leathers, and made himself stand tall. He'd clenched his hands until they stopped shaking, swallowed back the cough that wanted to rise against the cigar smoke circling the room. He had summoned every last bit of his courage to say, "I want to be a lawyer, not a priest. But I won't work for you, Papa Manny. I need you to know that—I need to know you'd never ask me to. I want out."

To this day, he could still remember the surprise on Manny's face, and the matching expression in his own father's eyes. They'd all assumed for so many years that he felt a call to priesthood just because he took seriously the lessons of their Faith. They'd talked about it, made plans, made connections for him, never bothering to ask if it was what he truly wanted. They'd encouraged him to learn from his cousin Teo, who had taken his vows and was now Brother Judah.

It had only taken one word to explain why the priesthood wasn't his calling. *Sabina.*

But his interest in the law had taken the older men aback. He'd watched the thoughts roll through both sets of eyes—confusion, then calculation, then pleasure. *A lawyer*, he could see them thinking. *That could be handy.*

But he would not be used like that. He would sooner choose another profession, and he'd made that clear from the start. Manny had sworn—*sworn*—that he would never call on him. Yet there he'd stood, opposite his imprisoned godfather, named as his official attorney on the record books. He hadn't been able to work a single word past the fury in his throat.

Manny had sighed and shaken his head. "I told her not to call you."

That did nothing to ease his mind. Because she *had* called. Sabina's voice had filled the phone line and, for one bright moment, lit joy in his heart. One moment, before she sobbed out what had happened to her father and asked him to help. He couldn't refuse. He'd always known he wouldn't be able to, if they asked. That's why he'd made them promise to keep him out of it. But here they were.

And here he was, on the front stoop of the house he knew as well as his own, his second family waiting for him to come and bring them hope. They would expect him to say Manny would be out of prison within days, that the charges couldn't stick, that there would be no trial. He couldn't make those promises.

He'd gone through years of law school, yes, but that didn't give him the ability to rewrite facts. Manny was guilty of all they accused him of and more. How *much* more, Lorenzo had never wanted to know—but the facts were against him.

He squeezed his eyes shut. Why couldn't he have been born into a different family? Or rather, why couldn't his family have lived a different sort of life? One where a Mafia boss wasn't his godfather, where his father wasn't Manny's best friend and lieutenant, where he didn't have to choose between his blood and his convictions?

With a long sigh, Lorenzo rubbed his eyes and finally lifted a hand to the door. He hadn't even finished knocking before the knob turned and the door opened under his fist. Lorenzo smiled down at the teenager standing in the opening. "Hey, G."

Giorgio Jr. dug up a small grin. He was turning into a handsome boy at thirteen, though still gangly and awkward. Unfortunately, if Manny went to prison, Lorenzo suspected Little G would think he had to become the man of the family—a role for which he was still far too young. "Hey, Enzo. Have you talked to Papa?"

Lorenzo nodded and stepped inside, casting his gaze around for Sabina and Mama Rosa. He heard their voices in the parlor directly to his right, where a fire crackled behind its grate despite the warm June day. He and G turned into the room. The women's conversation halted.

When he'd last seen Mama Rosa two weeks before, she had looked young and fresh and as beautiful as ever with her dark hair framing her unlined face. She had aged twenty years in those two weeks—probably in the last two hours. Shadows circled her eyes, her skin had lost its usual glow, and wrinkles he'd barely noticed before now looked as deep as the underworld. She stood when she saw him, eyes pleading and hand outstretched. "Enzo. Tell me he's being released."

Lorenzo went over and gripped her hand, kissed her on the cheek. His apology came out with a sigh. "*Mi dispiaci*, Mama Rosa. Not yet. I'm doing all I can, but it's going to take more than an hour to get him out of this one. O'Reilly did his homework."

Mama Rosa's brows knit together. "O'Reilly?"

"Roman O'Reilly—the Prohibition agent who's been working undercover."

From the corner of his eye, he saw Sabina wince and turn her face toward the fire. Lorenzo tapped his fingers against his leg. There was more going on than he could see, that much had become clear when he met with O'Reilly. He wasn't sure exactly how the man had gotten so deep into the Mancari family, but he had. Lorenzo recognized him, so Sabina had to have known him. She would feel the betrayal just as her father did.

Even in her distress, she was beautiful. So very beautiful. The fire lit her dark bobbed waves with red and cast a glow on her already-golden skin. He had made a work of memorizing her profile, but he never tired of gazing upon the perfect slope of her nose, the purse of her lips, the angle of her jaw. Her beauty always took his breath away, even though he tried not to dwell on it, lest it lead him into trouble—or worse, made Sabina think he only loved her because she was gorgeous.

He moved to the sofa where she sat, took the seat beside her, and reached for her hand. That innocent touch was enough to make emotion pound to life inside him, which was why he didn't allow himself even that much contact very often. "How are you holding up, Bean? I heard O'Reilly used you as a hostage."

Sabina blinked back tears. "I'm…fine."

Mama Rosa snorted, an action so uncharacteristic that Lorenzo's gaze flew her way. He was shocked to see hostility on the elder's face, aimed at her daughter. "I told you from the start that young man was bad news."

Sabina sent what looked like a beseeching glare at her mother and then glanced at him, too. "Mama! You may have had reasons for not liking him, but you never thought he was untrustworthy. None of us did."

Mama Rosa shook her head and turned to leave. "Come, Little G. We'll let your sister explain to Enzo how this Mr. *O'Reilly* came to discover all he did about us."

Lorenzo stared after the two retreating forms, not looking back to Sabina until she tugged her fingers free of his. A furrow dug its way into his brows. "Bean? What's going on?"

She wiped her palms on her skirt and kept her eyes focused on the flames. "Isn't that what you're supposed to tell us?"

He leaned back and studied her. Perspiration gleamed on her forehead, and her pulse skittered in her neck. It wasn't just residual fear—it was something else, something he had no name for. He was missing something. Something vital.

He knew Sabina better than anyone else in the world. They'd been best friends all their lives, whispering and giggling their way through childhood. When he saw how she'd risen up during her mother's illness when she was twelve, the way she'd taken the toddler Serafina under her wing and stepped into the role of "little mama" to her and G while Rosa was recovering in the sanitorium… She was the most remarkable young woman, with a heart so big he couldn't help but want to claim a larger part of it.

Maybe that was what made her so jittery now. Sabina couldn't stand to see her family in pain or in trouble. Every argument, every temper, she'd always tried to soothe away. And she'd always been her papa's girl, his princess. *Principessa*, he'd called her all her life. How horrible it must have been to see him hauled away.

That must be it. Not just residual fear, but current devastation.

"All right." He hooked one ankle over the opposite knee. "Here's what I know so far. Six months ago, Roman O'Reilly was tasked with going undercover for the Prohibition Bureau, his goal to infiltrate the Mancari operation. His superiors wanted him to come away with solid evidence of your father's crimes—bootlegging, bookmaking, murder, anything he could find. He was apparently successful. I know I've seen him at family functions, which means he found an in. His evidence must be solid, or they wouldn't have risked an arrest."

He halted, waited. It took a good five seconds for her to force her eyes to his. Usually when he gazed into those deep sienna irises, his heart pounded. But tonight he saw something unexpected in them—guilt. "This is serious, Bean. They're charging your father with bootlegging, murder, conspiracy to murder, and a handful of lesser charges for good measure. They get their way and he'll go to prison for life."

Assuming he lived that long. Lorenzo wasn't about to say it, but Sabina would know the risk. The other bosses would seize any chance they got to take over Manny's territory.

Her lip quivered as tears spilled onto her cheeks. Poor Sabina. He hadn't seen her cry since the funeral three years ago, and rarely before that. She couldn't—she had to be the strong one for her family. Lorenzo balled his fingers into fists to keep from reaching out and swiping the tears away, which would ignite all sorts of thoughts that he couldn't indulge right now.

Sabina shook her head, one of her wavy locks falling into her face. That was another clue to how upset she was; usually her hair was so carefully sculpted that no strand dared challenge her will.

"It's all my fault." She turned her face down and gripped her hands together, bathing them with her tears. "I…liked him. Roman. I thought he was a nice man, so interesting, with all these fascinating stories about Italy and the rest of Europe. He'd been stationed there in the war. I thought—I thought his experience would be an asset to Papa, so I introduced them. I encouraged Papa and Uncle Franco to take him under their wing."

Lorenzo weighed the risks, then put a hand on her bent shoulder. He wanted to haul her against his chest and hold her tight. He wanted to give comfort, not lead them into temptation, but oh, the touch of her... "You couldn't have known, Bean."

"I should have. All those hours we spent together…"

A knot formed in his gut. "Hours? What, you were…friends?"

It took an eternity for her to look at him. When she finally did, the truth stared back. It hit him so hard he barely heard her whispered words. "He said he loved me."

His hand fell away from her shoulder. The truth he'd thought he'd seen so clearly flew to a million pieces in his mind. Everything he thought he'd known…everything he thought he'd understood…everything he thought he'd been doing for years…

He couldn't breathe. "And you? What did you tell him?"

Her nostrils flared. Her fingers knotted together. All their lives, she'd met his eyes and poured out her heart to him, but now she refused to meet his gaze. Her shoulders sagged. "We…we were going to run away together. Get married."

Lorenzo had always thought it a cliché to say one's heart broke. But right now, he could have sworn he felt his splintering, cracking, falling apart. He wanted to stand, to walk away from this whole situation, to lock himself in his room for the rest of his life. Or better still, to wake up and find this whole day had been nothing but a nightmare. But first he had to get one answer.

Shaking with sudden anger, he wrenched Sabina's left hand from her right and raised it to catch the firelight. The diamond sparkled up at him with cruel mirth. "One question, Sabina. Were you going to bother to give me back my ring?"

THREE

A strangled cry stuck in her throat and forced Sabina awake. Her chest heaved, her breath came out in a panicked gasp. Images of dreams still flickered in front of her eyes like a silent film—except those sorts of images weren't allowed on the silver screen. Death, everywhere she looked. Mama, in her old bed at the sanitorium, unable to be roused no matter how Sabina shook her. Sweet Serafina, lifeless and blue and limp. Papa, imagined bullet holes spilling his blood onto the street. Little G, charging into the fray and jerking to a halt as the bullets found him too.

Lorenzo, a dagger through his heart, gasping and stumbling her way. "How could you? This is all your fault."

She pushed herself up against her headboard and pressed the palms of her hands against her eyes. Lorenzo was always right.

She blinked into the half-darkness of dawn until the dull gray images of her room replaced the ones still trying to flash before her. She willed those others to go away, leave her alone. They weren't real—mostly. She really had seen Mama like that, but she'd eventually woken up. Serafina, though…she hadn't. But God willing, Sabina would never see Papa or G taken down.

She crossed herself against the thought, then again to try to ward off the shame when another face flashed before her. *Roman.* Despite her prayer, the shame only built, crashing over her again and again with each memory that pounded through her mind. She hadn't meant to like him. She hadn't meant for that first walk to turn into a kiss, or to tumble headlong into love. A week ago, she hadn't meant to let his hands wander where they shouldn't have.

But it had been so long since she felt wanted, needed, so long since anyone but her parents had told her she was beautiful. For three years, her soul had been wandering in a desert, and no one had ever offered her a sip of water. Even Lorenzo's affection seemed to have dried up since he proposed. Then Roman had come, and it had felt like he let loose a whole clear spring upon her.

She'd known, probably, that she was doing wrong, sinning against Lorenzo and herself and the Lord. But it had been such a new sin that it tasted sweet on her lips, made her blood tingle in her veins. She'd been too weak to resist it. Even now, the memories were fresh and bright—the rush of slipping out of the house when her parents thought she was asleep, going over to Mary's and putting on one of the new short dresses, painting her lips a bright, vibrant red. The thrill of meeting Roman and Mary's beau Robert without chaperones. They had laughed the whole time as they made their way to one of Papa's speakeasies, fronted by a millinery.

She was a monster. Perhaps it was a blessing that Serafina wasn't here to see what a terrible person her sister had become.

Sabina tossed back the covers and jumped out of bed, needing to wash away the dried sweat and fresh guilt. Sidestepping the squeaky board by her door, she tiptoed out into the hall and down to the water closet, running her fingers along the papered wall so she could find her way without bumping into the stand with the oil lamp. The harsh glow of the bathroom's electric light forced the truth upon her as she looked in the mirror.

She was a wreck.

Bracing her hands on the porcelain of the pedestal sink, she stared into the mirror. She always took care with her appearance—she'd thought she owed it to her family, to Lorenzo, to try to be as pretty as Mama. But what had it ever gotten her?

Lorenzo had only kissed her once. *Once*, in the three years of their engagement. On her eighteenth birthday, the day he proposed. She'd been floating on a cloud that day when he asked to go for a walk, when she'd seen the light in his eyes. She'd hoped…dreamed of marrying him for two years, since the first time he'd held her hand and she realized he didn't intend to join the priesthood.

She had always wanted a chance to be more to him than his best friend, but she hadn't ever dared to imagine that it would happen. Surely it was a grave sin to think such thoughts about someone God had called to serve Him, right?

But then, it had all seemed to come true. Whenever he was home from college, he would drop by to visit, take her on walks, hold her hand. Then that day, he slipped a ring onto her finger and kissed her. She'd thought she could fly straight to heaven with the wings it gave her. She'd come rushing home to tell Serafina, and they'd giggled long into the night, planning the wedding and basking in the joy.

Then the flu had come. Serafina had died. And Lorenzo… He wasn't there. Even when he was with her, he wasn't the friend he had always been, much less the fiancé she needed. He was always a foot away, rarely taking her hand, never kissing her again. He claimed he needed to study instead of drawing her into long conversations like he always used to do. Time he once would have spent at her side he instead spent at daily Mass or adoration.

He would honor the promise he made to her and marry her this August, now that he'd passed the bar, because he was above all a man of his word. But he couldn't have made it any clearer that he regretted choosing her over the Church.

He didn't want her. To make it worse, her family didn't need her anymore. When Prohibition began, the money started pouring in. They'd hired a cook, a maid—people to do all the things Sabina and Mama used to do. Papa said it was so they could enjoy the high life that they'd earned.

Useless, that's what she'd become. No wonder she'd tripped so happily into being used by that Judas.

She shuddered, her stomach threatening to heave.

She ought to have just stayed in her block of ice, let it carry her out to an arctic sea. Better to feel nothing for the rest of her life, to be superfluous, than to be the cause of all this pain.

Tears burned again, but Sabina squeezed her eyes shut against them. She yanked a washcloth from the towel rack and bent over the sink to wash her face. When she straightened again, she jumped to see a second reflection in the mirror.

"Mama! I didn't hear you come in."

Mama gave her a soft, tired smile, and smoothed down Sabina's sleep-frazzled hair. "Bad dreams?"

Sabina nodded, sighing.

"Me too." The stroke of Mama's hand on her hair soothed, despite her anger the night before. "*Mi dispiaci*, Sabina. I shouldn't have judged you so harshly."

A bitter laugh slipped from her throat. "Why not? You were right, Mama. I never should have had anything to do with him."

Mama's breath released in a weary sigh. "No, you shouldn't have. Not while you were engaged to Enzo. But you're young, and you thought your-self in love with him. I remember well enough how that feels. It gets the best of our good sense sometimes."

Sabina blinked rapidly, tried to push aside her rising tears by studying her reflection beside her mother's. On the surface, they looked so much alike—darkest brown hair, though Mama's was still long and worn pinned up most of the time. Deepest brown eyes, made deeper still by Mama's years of illness and that horrible loss of their sweet girl. Sabina's face was still smooth and unlined, but it was Mama's cheekbones that gave it shape, Mama's lips on her own mouth.

All she'd ever wanted was to be like Mama. But her mother never would have done something like this. "I've ruined us, Mama. What am I going to do now?"

"Oh, *cara*. Your papa will get out of this, you'll see. We'll be fine. We'll forget all about Roman, and then you'll marry Enzo in August and work on giving me a *bambino* to dote on."

A sob bent her shoulders with its force. "It's too late for that! Enzo doesn't want me anymore—if he ever really did. You saw how mad he was last night. I've lost him, too. I never thought—I should have known—"

"Hush." Mama folded her into her arms, held her tight, and rocked back and forth, just as she had done for as long as Sabina could remember. "Enzo has loved you all your life, Sabina. He may be mad now, but he'll forgive you."

Sabina lifted her head so that she could look her mother in the eye. They were the same height, but it still felt as though she had to look up to see Mama clearly. In her eyes she saw limitless faith; certainty had overcome the gnawing fear of last night. Confidence brimmed from Mama's smile—the same confidence that had always foretold Sabina's future. She would marry Lorenzo and bear Lorenzo's children. Mama had been the only one who never said he was destined for the Church, who always claimed he was destined for Sabina instead.

Mama had been wrong after all.

Sabina shook her head. "You didn't see him when he found out. It wasn't just anger, Mama. He may forgive me someday"—it would be the righteous thing to do, and Enzo was always righteous—"but he will never give me another chance. And…and maybe that's for the best."

Mama tsked, clearly ready to say something, but Sabina squeezed her eyes shut and shook her head again. "I can't live the rest of my life at his side, knowing I will never be anything but a disappointment to him."

"*Cara*, you don't give either of you enough credit. Enzo will put this in the past. He will be a good husband to you, and you will be his delight and his joy, as you have always been."

Delight? Joy? She hadn't brought him either of those things since they became engaged. "But—"

"Hush." A finger landed on Sabina's lips to make sure she obeyed. "You are still upset. Once you've had time to think things through, I'm sure you'll realize that Lorenzo is the best thing for you. Now, go get dressed. We have a lot to do today, starting with a visit to your father."

She obeyed, because that was what she did when Mama issued a command. But her motions felt distant as she pulled the rags from her hair and combed the curls into waves, as she selected a dress, as she rolled her stockings up her legs. It was as if someone else were completing each step.

She paused mid-reach for a pair of silver earrings, staring at herself in the mirror of her dressing table. Why did she even bother? There was no one to care how she looked, no one to impress. The dress with its embroidery and height-of-fashion lines, the dangling earrings—they would be wasted.

No. No, they were for Papa. Papa needed to know that his *principessa* was standing strong for him, even if she was quaking inside.

"*Arrivederci*, Sabina."

She looked up to see her brother stick his head in the door. His dark hair was slicked back, his smile tight with mutiny. He gave her a wave and made to duck away, but she jumped up and halted him with a sound that meant, "Not so fast, young man!"

He paused in the hallway with a sigh, barely even rolling his eyes as she straightened his collar and smoothed down the cowlick that no amount of pomade could ever tame.

A smile made Sabina's lips twitch before reality blew it away. She'd been fighting that cowlick for thirteen years, but she didn't mind that it always won. The joy was in the smoothing. Her brother was taller than she was now, but she still narrowed her eyes at him like she'd been doing all his life. "No ducking out of work today, G. Papa wouldn't want you skipping out just because of all that's happened."

Little G directed his gaze heavenward in exasperation. "Relax, sis. Mama already gave me the lecture. 'Uncle Franco and Vanni have everything under control. My job is to honor my obligations to cousin Max.'"

He was such a good boy. Love for him made her chest go tight. Maybe she'd failed at everything else in life, but she'd done a good job with him and Serafina while Mama was ill. She could take some comfort in that, even if the prospects of ever having children of her own were suddenly slim. "I'm glad you have it committed to memory."

"But I don't see why *you* get to go see Papa this morning while I—"

"Enough." Sabina raised a hand, and her brother bit off the rest of his complaint. "You wanted a summer job, and now you must bear the responsibilities."

He looked like he wanted to argue, but he pressed his lips against whatever retort he wanted to make, then leaned over to kiss her cheek. "I know. And I will. *Ciao*, Bina." She kissed him back, needing to stand on her toes to accomplish it, and patted his other cheek. Soon, a beard would grow on that smooth skin, and Papa would have to teach him how to shave.

Papa. They had to get him out. He had to come home, show G how to grow into manhood. He *must.*

Her brother moved away, and their mother moved into the hallway from her own bedroom, sighing to a halt beside Sabina. "He has grown too fast. It seems like he should be a little *bambino* still, does it not?"

Sabina could only nod. She was so proud to see the man he was becoming—but she missed the boy he'd once been.

Mama smoothed a piece of Sabina's hair, much like Sabina had just smoothed G's. "You did a good job with him. Much of what he is, we owe to you. You are a good girl, Sabina. And now you will prove yourself anew by supporting your *fidanzata*. We'll be going to see Enzo after we leave your father, if we don't meet him at the jail."

The thought of facing Lorenzo again made panic claw so ferociously, she feared the monster she'd become would roar its way out of her chest. She wanted to argue, to refuse.

She didn't, of course. What was the use? Mama would only override her.

Mama nodded and moved down the hall, out of view. Sabina dragged in a breath and followed her.

On the ground floor, she had to fight the urge to point her feet toward the kitchen. There was no point going in there—she could hear Cook pattering about, mumbling in Sicilian—but she wanted to. She needed the comfort of ingredients before her, dough in her hands. She needed the scents of coffee and toast and sausage.

But the maid, Mia, stood at the door holding a tray with something wrapped in wax paper, and Mama shooed Sabina that direction. "You can eat in the car, *cara*. Hurry now. We do not want to keep your papa waiting."

Sabina took one of the wrapped offerings—an egg sandwich—offered a tight smile to Mia, and followed her mother out the door.

Little G stood from where he'd been tying his shoes, snatched up three of the sandwiches with a grin, and hurried to open the door for them. Sabina slid out into the fresh morning air, wishing it were any other day, that she was heading out for any other errand.

Her brother took off down the street with a wave, heading for their cousin's print shop, leaving her and Mama to move toward the car. Their driver came around to open the Pierce-Arrow's rear door, all decorum and politeness. Sabina noted for the first time the bulge under his jacket. Had he always carried a gun? Probably—but it had never mattered before. Today, it made her heart race as she slid into the back seat with Mama. She had to think about something else, anything else, so she focused on the plush leather of the seat. It should have been an ostentatious car, but her father had specifically requested the less distinctive headlights so that cops wouldn't recognize him easily—or confuse him with Colosimo, who had flaunted his ill-gotten wealth without concern before his death two years ago.

The chauffeur slid behind the wheel, and another bodyguard took the passenger's seat. He looked only vaguely familiar, which made her frown. Who had assigned him? How did they know he could be trusted? What if he was another Roman, set on delivering them into the hands of their enemy?

"Mind your face, Sabina," Mama commanded in quiet Sicilian as they pulled out onto Taylor Street. "If you keep scowling like that, you'll have wrinkles before your time."

Schooling her features, Sabina directed her gaze out the window. She'd been looking at Little Italy all her life, but it seemed different today. The old buildings, huddling together and leaning on each other's shoulders, appeared more tired than charming. The signs, boasting both English and Italian, seemed faded and dirty. The smells coming from the dozens of bakeries and restaurants turned her stomach instead of enticing her taste buds.

She set the fried egg sandwich on the seat between her and Mama and slid her hand into her pocket instead, where her rosary rested. She tangled her fingers in the beads without actually forming the words of a prayer. Her words wouldn't matter—her prayers never seemed to make a difference. No matter how many candles she lit, no matter how many times she said the Our Father or Hail Mary, nothing had gone right, not for years.

Still, there was comfort in the beads.

The miles to the Federal Building passed in silence other than the occasional toot of a horn, the rev of passing motorists, and the oblivious shouts of faceless passers-by. Sabina was glad for the insulating shell of calm.

That shattered when the chauffeur parked outside the courthouse and her mother muttered a quick Latin prayer. Sabina crossed herself by rote on the amen and climbed out, careful to hold her skirt down against a gust of wind. Pedestrians hurried by, unaware that the world had tilted for the Mancari house…and that parts of their world might tip with it. How many of those unconcerned people frequented one of Papa's speakeasies? How many had a bottle of the liquor he smuggled stashed in a cabinet? How many secretly hailed him as a hero?

The Beaux-Arts building leered at her, its looming dome reminding her that it didn't matter *what* the general public thought. It came down to the law, as Lorenzo would say. And to the whims of a government that chose at random when it would work and when it wouldn't, whom it would crush and whom it would spare.

Which would it be today for Papa?

"Hurry up, Sabina." The nerves in Mama's voice matched the lines etching her face again. She held her cashmere sweater closed with a gloved fist, her eyes focused on the main entrance to the courthouse. Sabina picked up her pace, the armed chauffeur and bodyguard bringing up the rear.

A man held the door open for them as he exited and gave Sabina a gleaming smile. What did he see? Mama's cheekbones in her face, Mama's lips on her mouth? Or just the value of the jewelry encircling her wrists and throat, dangling from her ears?

She managed a nod of thanks and slipped past him.

Once inside, they halted and looked around, lost. The building housed the Midwest's federal courts, a post office, and other federal offices Sabina couldn't possibly name. Dwarfed by the sixteen floors of government, she forced a swallow.

The guards stayed outside to flank the door like sentries. When Mama gripped Sabina's hand, the gravity of the situation struck her yet again. Unshakable Mama trembled. Sabina squeezed her fingers, though she wasn't sure she had any strength to offer. "Do you want me to ask somebody where we should go?"

"I suppose we should—oh. No, there's Enzo. Enzo!" Mama lifted her free hand to wave above the people dotting the entrance hall.

Though she had the sudden urge to avert her gaze, Sabina forced herself to look toward her fiancé. Part of her expected him to appear changed by all that had happened the night before. But no—he was the same old Enzo. Of average height, lean, wearing a suit a little too old-fashioned for her tastes. He kept his dark hair conservatively short, and when he was working, he wore a pair of spectacles that hid his sharp eyes. His nose was a little too large—a trait that ran in his family—and his mouth a little too wide. He was handsome, though not quite as handsome as his brother Tony. If he were a stranger walking toward her in a different world, perhaps she would have sent him a smile to see if he'd respond.

But it was Enzo—too serious for flirtation, and so distant these last three years, when they should have been so close. And so furious now.

He usually at least looked at her, but today his gaze only flicked her way once. Then he studiously ignored her and gave his full attention to her mother. She could hardly blame him—but still it cut. Perhaps, when she worked up the courage to go to confession, Father Russo would count this as part of her penance.

"Enzo." Mama stretched up on her toes so Lorenzo could kiss her cheek. She pulled her hand free of Sabina's and put it in his. "Have you seen him? How is he?"

Sabina curled her abandoned fingers into her empty palm.

Lorenzo gave Mama a strained smile. "I just left him. He's in good spirits, still convinced he'll be out by the end of the day. I was just about to go make a few calls for him. He says that the mayor and the governor both, ah, owe him a favor. He expects the charges will all be dropped."

"Oh, that would be wonderful, Enzo."

Enzo's eyes flickered, making Sabina wonder what he was thinking. Five years ago, four even, she would have known. Now…he might as well be a stranger.

He cleared his throat. "In the meantime, you should come to my office this afternoon. We need to discuss the placement of certain assets. The Treasury will try to freeze all they can in preparation for a full investigation, but Manny assures me you have access to some beyond their reach that would cover bail and court expenses, if it comes to that."

"Of course." Rolling her shoulders back, Mama looked more like Mama should. "We are not unprepared, Enzo. Manny has seen to that."

Lorenzo nodded. "I knew he would have. Shall I show you to him?"

"Just point me in the right direction." She patted his arm and smiled. "You can keep Sabina company while I visit with him—I'm sure he'd rather she not see him behind bars."

Sabina's mouth fell open. "But you said—"

Lorenzo looked as panicked as she felt. "I really don't have time to—"

"I won't be but twenty minutes." Mama didn't wait for any more argument. She turned in the direction Lorenzo had come from and headed away at full steam.

Sabina's shoulders slumped. "You don't have to stay with me," she said softly, setting her sights on the space beyond his shoulder. "Our men are right outside. I'll be fine."

Lorenzo sighed and pinched the bridge of his nose. "If I do that, your mother will probably just drag you to my office later and come up with another way of leaving us together."

How had they come to this? What had happened to Enzo and Bean, the inseparable duo? The two who could spend hours gazing up at the stars, talking about everything and nothing? The friends who knew each other's thoughts before they could speak them? How had they been reduced to dreading each other's company, wishing they could avoid it?

That was worth mourning, if Sabina could ever get through the death-throes of the deeper relationship that they obviously never should have attempted. Forcing a swallow past the lump in her throat, she tried to summon a bit of Mama's forthrightness. "So, we might as well get it over with." Willing her hands not to shake, she tugged off her left glove and reached for the diamond on her ring finger. "I guess you want this back."

"Sabina." Frustration laced his voice. "I don't want to do this now, certainly not here. I don't want—I just—I can't think about this yet, all right? I need to concentrate on your father."

Sabina. The word stung like a ruler to her knuckles. He never called her Sabina. He had called her nothing but Bean in all her memory, and the change somehow terrified her. As if he had finally admitted she wasn't the girl he had once loved. Bean was gone, buried with Serafina. Unneeded at home. Unwanted by him.

Who was Sabina, though? Who was she supposed to be in the wake of Bean?

"What happened to us?" he asked softly. His gaze probed her face and seemed to see into her mind, like he used to do so easily. "We used to know each other. We used to be friends. Now, it's as if you're a total stranger, Sabina. I don't know who I've spent so many years loving, but obviously you don't love me back. Why didn't you just tell me you didn't want to marry me? Why go behind my back?"

Spent so many years loving? She pressed her lips together against the words that wanted to tumble free. As a child, yes, she would grant it. As an adolescent, even. But lately? He didn't love her. He didn't really want to marry her. He just couldn't bring himself to say it.

Lorenzo shook his head. His eyes flashed and then extinguished. "Never mind. I know your parents well enough to guess the answer. Mama Rosa said you'd marry me, so you obeyed, like always. Did you ever even *want* to?"

She couldn't bear to see his expression so empty and reached for his hand before she could think better of it. "Enzo, no. Please listen. I've always loved you. You've been one of my dearest friends all my life. I never intended to hurt you. I never meant for this to happen."

"Well, it has." He tugged his fingers free, like he always did. Usually, it felt like an apology. Today, it felt like a slap. "And now you have to figure out what you want. I frankly don't know if I can work through this or not, and I don't intend to waste my time trying if you still love him."

"How could I love him?" Venom rose up, so sharp it astonished her. "He betrayed—"

The arch of his brows silenced her.

She wasn't the only one who had been betrayed.

FOUR

Now no matter, child, the name:
Sórrow's springs áre the same.
Nor mouth had, no nor mind, expressed
What heart heard of, ghost guessed:

-Gerard Manley Hopkins,
from "Spring and Fall"

Whcn he spotted the two burly Italians standing guard at the court-house doors, Roman O'Reilly stopped in his tracks. He recognized Mancari's men, which meant they would recognize him, too. The only question was whether or not Manny had signed his death warrant. He had no doubt they had the gall to gun him down in broad daylight in front of the Federal Building if they had been told to.

Or perhaps if they hadn't been told *not* to.

Since he had no intention of being the next casualty in this war on the Mafia, he spun on his heel and headed for the rear entrance. He was supposed to meet Henry Jennings, the prosecuting attorney, to give him a full deposition on what he'd learned in his months with the Mancaris. But thinking about the coming meeting just made a familiar anger surge, aimed straight at the crooked men he worked with.

"You know he'll be out by next week," Clifford Brewster had said last night as they headed toward their cheap apartments on the fringes of the Levee. "He's got all the big politicians in his pocket."

Roman had shaken his head. "Not this time. We've got him."

"No, buddy. What we've got is evidence gathered by men with diamonds on their fingers and gold in their pockets. One word from the bosses, and they'll either lose all that evidence or forget they ever heard a word to begin with. We'll be left with nothing on him stronger than a first-time violation of the Volstead Act, if that."

Cliff was probably right, and it infuriated him. Most of the Prohibition Bureau was comprised of men with political connections and practically no training, who not only didn't believe in the cause for which they were named but actually enjoyed flaunting it and lining their pockets in the process.

Hunching against the wind, Roman strode around the building. It wasn't that he thought Prohibition was a good idea, or that he was above imbibing. But in the two years since its conception, the new law had poured power into the hands of the Mafia, and *that* he couldn't tolerate. If he could rip them apart on his own, he would. But since one man had no chance of that, he'd joined the Bureau.

Now he had the urge to rip *them* apart, too. They were the most ridiculous, ineffectual, corrupt bunch of bumblers he'd ever met. Cliff, at least, was honest. He had ethics. He also had some independent wealth from his family's railroad legacy that helped keep him away from the temptation of the bribes. They made a good team…even if they were two islands in a treacherous sea.

Although Cliff *had* disapproved of the way he handled things with Sabina. Unable to join him undercover because of his obvious lack of Mediterranean blood, his partner had stood behind the scenes judging for the last six months. He said the distance gave him perspective. Roman figured all it really did was keep him from understanding what he faced every day.

Shoving that thought away, he hurried inside. Jennings had said to meet him here, since he'd be in court off and on all morning, but as to where exactly he would find him…

Roman froze and muttered a curse. There was Sabina, standing with her boyfriend.

Something shriveled up inside. He'd actually kind of liked the middle Capecce son, the few times he'd met him. He seemed like a decent sort, so different from the rest of the family. He reminded him, in some way he never really tried to put his finger on, of Sergeant Brentwood, who had gotten him through plenty of dark times in the Great War. Roman had felt more than a little bad for stealing his girl from him—he deserved a better shake than that.

But maybe he didn't. Because here he was, a leather attaché in hand that said he was working. A criminal defense attorney. Here, now.

Of course. Everything came into focus. Lorenzo Capecce was no different from the rest of the Mancari crew—he'd just been given a different assignment. His role in the family wasn't to tote a gun or ferry bootleg into the city. His job was to go to law school and become the next Clarence Darrow, defending the Mafia against any charges filed against them.

Men like him were the reason Roman was here, drawing a lousy salary instead of climbing the ranks back in the Big Apple. Men like him were why the Mafia kept growing stronger. Men like him had ruined everything.

Well. Men like him could be taken down too.

He was in view only a second when Sabina's gaze homed in on him, as if she sensed his presence instantly. As soon as she spotted him, she flushed. That wasn't unusual—he had always enjoyed the color that stole into her cheeks whenever she saw him—but he could tell from the glint in her eyes that it was fueled by rage this time, not attraction.

In spite of himself, he smiled. Her beauty had stolen his attention from the moment he first staked out the Mancari family. But it was the first conversation with her that had convinced him she could be his in. He'd seen such familiar, hollow pain in her eyes. The same pain he saw in all his friends from the war, the ones who had come back missing limbs or eyes or brothers.

He'd be doing her a favor, he'd told himself, if he could help her see past that. Be a friend. Spending time with her could help her just as it was helping him. She'd never have to know who he really was.

Cliff had warned him he was treading on dangerous ground—wisdom Roman had ignored. He had always been a sucker for a beautiful face, and Sabina's was stunning. As a rule he steered clear of Italian women—no offense intended to his saint of a mother, who was born in Palermo—but he forgot his preference for blonds when Sabina smiled at him.

She now said something to Capecce, who spun around. Roman groaned when the wiry lawyer headed his way. His face was stony, his bearing resolute. Someone must have filled him in on the details last night.

Determined not to flinch, Roman planted his feet, folded his arms across his chest, and glared at the hypocrite striding his way. Representing the law—laughable. Twisting it, bending it. That was what this guy was doing.

"Morning, O'Reilly." Capecce's tone was civil, his smile professional. "Are you here to meet with Jennings?"

That's how they were playing it, was it? Fine. He could play nice too. "I am."

Capecce nodded. "Could you tell him I'll be stopping by his office later this afternoon? I'm going to need the final list of charges, preferably before the weekend. He's still in court right now, though, and I need to head out in a few minutes."

Incredulous, Roman stared at the man for a long minute before flicking his gaze over to Sabina and then back again. "You're kidding me, right? That's all you have to say?" Didn't he care at all about the woman he was supposedly marrying in two months? Where was the anger? He should have been swinging at Roman, ready to defend his girl.

Not just a hypocrite, then. One blind to what was right before his nose. That sort of guy *deserved* to have his girl stolen from him. Sabina would be better off without Lorenzo Capecce.

Not that she was any of his concern anymore.

Capecce cleared his throat. "I see little point in recriminations. I think your actions speak loudly enough about what kind of man you are. I don't need to add my voice to the mix."

Irritation crawled up his spine like a million spiders. "I was just doing my job, which happens to be upholding the law that *you* are supposed to represent."

Capecce breathed a dry laugh and shook his head. His eyes shifted again, dimming. "Nowhere in the law does it say to get to the father by breaking the daughter's heart."

Roman unfolded his arms just to fold them again the opposite way. "Since when do you care about her heart? You know what I saw in my six months undercover, Capecce? I saw Sabina. I saw G. I saw Val and Tony and cousins from both families. But I didn't really see *you*, now did I? Where were you when you should have been at her side?"

Capecce's lips pressed into a thin line. For one blessed second, Capecce looked like he'd haul back his arm and let loose—something Roman found himself itching for. But in the next moment, Capecce relaxed his jaw, uncurled his fingers. "I'm going to do all I can to make sure you get out of Chicago alive. I'm just not sure right now if the desire is genuine or if I only want you to live long enough to regret this."

Coming from a Mafia lawyer, it wasn't much of a guess. "I know which one I'd put money on. I have a feeling before this is over, you and I will settle this score, Capecce."

Capecce's shoulders sank down, making him look suddenly tired. He shook his head. "There is no score, O'Reilly. At this point, I'd say we both lost." He looked back at Sabina to illustrate his point. She stood against the wall, hands clasped in front of her and eyes cast anywhere but at them.

Roman had never wanted to hurt her. He hated the Mafia, but he wasn't so blind that he didn't realize there were innocents caught up in it—like Sabina. He'd known that from their first conversation. She was just a young woman who loved her family, who never saw the evil they were doing. He hadn't wanted to hurt her. But he couldn't have really let himself care about her. Right? He wasn't that big a sap.

When Sabina tried inconspicuously to wipe away a rogue tear, something inside him knotted up and tied his tongue. He had been telling himself all night that he couldn't possibly care for the daughter of a mafioso. Unfortunately, he wasn't so sure his heart had gotten the message.

"Yes, Governor. I'll be sure and tell him." Lorenzo chuckled, mainly because he was expected to. "Have a good weekend, sir, and give your wife Manny's best."

His smile faded as he replaced the tarnished brass receiver of his candlestick phone. That was the last of his scheduled phone calls, thank heavens. He wasn't sure how much more glad-handing he had in him.

He sighed, leaned his forehead onto his hands and closed his eyes. He supposed he should count his afternoon as a victory. It was all but guaranteed that Manny would be out of jail before business halted on Saturday. Between the mayor, the governor, and a few other politicians who had been well paid over the years, the charges weren't going to stick. The more serious charges of murder would be dropped for lack of evidence—though the evidence wasn't so lacking that they would have dropped them for the average joe—and the bootlegging would either be ignored or paid for in fines that would do little damage to Manny's wealth.

O'Reilly hoped to nail him for his holdings in the Levee, but the evidence he had for that truly *was* flimsy. The establishments from which Manny had made his money before Prohibition were screened through several underlings who would take the rap for it before Manny would. And since everyone knew they were underlings, they'd probably be let go, too, unless one of them promised to turn.

But Lorenzo knew that wouldn't happen. *Omerta* wouldn't allow it. It was one thing to kill another Sicilian, to prey on him and destroy his family, but there was a code of honor. One simply didn't rat out a fellow Sicilian to the authorities—a lesson he was raised knowing. Authorities couldn't be trusted because authorities could be bought.

A crushing truth, when you were too poor to do the buying. But Manny wasn't that, not these days. "The government isn't my enemy anymore," he had said to Lorenzo that morning, smiling and leaning back on his thin cot as if it were a luxurious chaise in a resplendent boudoir. "The government is made of men who are easily…persuaded, let us say, to my way of thinking. My only enemy, Enzo, is my competition, and as long as you get me out of here soon, they will be easily managed, too. We all experience these hiccups. We just have to be sure it doesn't turn into more, or they'll see it as weakness and move in on my territory. *That's* when we'd have problems."

With a few phone calls, he had turned the whole situation into a victory for Manny. But certainly not a victory for the law, and Lorenzo couldn't shake the feeling that he'd just sullied his own hands by helping his godfather circumvent justice.

Criminal lawyers were hired all the time to defend the guilty—hadn't he participated in countless debates about that in law school? Everyone was entitled to a defense, rich or poor, guilty or innocent. It was his duty to do whatever he could for a client. Any client.

That didn't make his hands feel any cleaner right now.

A knock sounded on his open door. "Lorenzo? I think we have a problem."

Lorenzo turned weary eyes on his mentor and boss. A frown furrowed Bernard Stein's brows. In a habit Lorenzo had come to know well during his years in Stein's law classes, the older man jammed a hand into the pocket of his suit jacket and jiggled a fistful of loose change.

"What is it, Mr. Stein?"

Stein offset his jaw in contemplation. "Miss Gregory just told me that you're on the Mancari case. Now, son, I know you tend to think the best of people, but don't you know that man's a gangster?"

Oh, boy. He should have realized this would be a problem. Lorenzo cleared his throat, prepared to come clean.

As usual, Stein didn't wait for an answer. "I know everyone's entitled to a defense, but I don't want this to be known as a firm for the Mafia. It can be tempting—don't think I don't know that. Those men pay their lawyers well."

Lorenzo shook his head, not knowing whether to smile or groan. "Mr. Stein, this isn't about money."

Stein's face relaxed. "Good. I didn't think you were that type, Lorenzo. Now we just have to figure out how to get you off this case without making certain dangerous parties angry."

A long exhalation slipped through Lorenzo's lips. His future was falling apart. Yesterday, his engagement had probably come to an end, and now he might lose his job. All because of the clash between the law and the Mafia. "I can't get off the case. I'm sorry—I'd really rather not be working for him, but I don't have much of a choice."

Stein's gray brows pulled together again. He advanced a step into the room and rested a gnarled hand on the back of the client chair across from Lorenzo's desk. "Why? Did he threaten you? I must say I don't understand why he would. You were a brilliant student and you're off to a great start, but the fact remains that you just passed the bar a month ago. Most of these mafioso types go for Darrow or his ilk. Unless it's because you're Sicilian?"

"Sort of." Lorenzo's gaze fell to his desk, where four different files lay in neat stacks. He hadn't opened any of them today—and what he *had* been working on would never get its own folder for his file cabinet. Recognizing it as a nervous habit, Lorenzo drummed his fingers on the ink blotter. "He didn't threaten me. It's just…well." He pulled in a deep breath and forced himself to look back up at Stein. "Giorgio Mancari is Sabina's father."

Stein sank into the chair, never taking his eyes from Lorenzo. Incredulity deepened every line on his visage. "You're engaged to the daughter of a Mafia boss? Did you know that all along?"

Temptation flickered before his eyes. He could say no. He could claim that he just learned it yesterday, that Sabina had come begging him to represent Manny, and that it was the first he had made the connection.

He blinked that hazy idea away—it would never hold up under a cross-examination. Besides, it was time for honesty. Lies had caused enough problems in the last twenty-four hours. "We grew up together." He said it softly, but the implications rang out loud and clear. "My father is Manny's best friend, one of his lieutenants—they immigrated from Sicily together."

Stein's mouth tightened. Creases feathered out from his lips. Usually the German was a cheerful man, all his wrinkles due to smiles. Not today. "Funny. I seem to remember a certain law student arguing ardently about how unfair it was that so many Americans assume all Italians are either Mafia or Camorra or Black Hand. That some of you are just honest men who happened to be born into a Sicilian family."

Lorenzo's fingers fisted. "I *am* an honest man born into a Sicilian family."

"You lied to me about this, didn't you?"

Lorenzo stood up, pushing his chair back with a scrape of its legs. "I didn't tell you. I don't tell anyone my father's one of Manny's men if I can help it, because unlike some of these ridiculous pretenders going around bragging about connections that don't exist, I'm not proud of it. All my life I've been judged because of my father and godfather. I'm sick of it. That's not who I am, and it's not how I wanted to get a job—or *not* get a job. I don't want anything to do with the Mafia."

Stein's eye twitched. "Yet you planned on marrying his daughter."

"I love her." His voice wobbled, and he sank into his chair again. *Loved.* He should have put it in the past tense. Should have spoken it that way so it had a hope of being true. "Mr. Stein, I'm sorry I didn't tell you. I'm sorry I got roped into this case. I understand if you don't want me in your firm. But I also seem to remember a certain law professor telling me that his brother was a general in the Kaiser's army, and that he prayed every day his neighbors wouldn't draw the connection and judge him for it."

"Oh, Lorenzo." Stein folded his hands together and rested his chin on the steeple. "You've put me in a tough spot. But you're right. I understand better than most the position you're in. My wife came from the same type of family I did—but we chose to leave it together. We cut our ties. Is your Sabina willing to do that, too?"

Part of him wished for the release of tears, even though he hadn't given in to such a desire in almost two decades. How many times over the last three years had he started to ask that question, broach that conversation? But he'd been too much a coward. How could he ask her to give up her family? They were her whole world.

So instead he'd said nothing, and the nothing had grown. He'd just blissfully thought that they'd sort it all out when they were married—when he could hold her close without fearing the force of the passion she awoke in his veins.

Blast it all, O'Reilly was right. He hadn't been there for her, not really. He hadn't tried to talk to her about *anything*. He'd been so afraid of losing his control that he'd... just let her drift away. "I don't know. I doubt it matters. The engagement's pretty much off at this point."

Stein shook his head, which sent his fluff of steel-gray hair moving in the breeze. "I'm sorry to hear that. I know how much you care for her."

Lorenzo ran his tongue over his teeth, his insides still too knotted up to want that to be true. But he knew it was. He'd loved her all his life. She was the reason he'd made every single choice that had led him here. How was he ever supposed to get over her? "Perhaps it's for the best. I don't think we really understand each other anymore."

"That doesn't make it hurt any less." Stein pushed himself up again. "I'm guessing this case against Mancari is going to go the way most such cases do?"

Lorenzo nodded. "He's got enough politicians on his side to get it all dismissed in a matter of days."

Stein sighed. "I hate the circumvention of justice, but I can't say I mind that this won't drag out." He turned to the door then paused in the threshold. "I understand why you couldn't say no to him this time. But I trust that you'll steer clear of these sorts of cases as much as possible in the future."

It was on the tip of his tongue to say he'd already tried to make sure of that, but Sabina had dragged him into it. New anger surged up, mixed with the pain. Guilt shot through it too, when he reminded himself that he'd never told her about that promise he'd elicited from her father. Still, shouldn't she have known? Didn't she know him at all?

To his boss, he said, "Yes, sir."

The older man nodded and stepped out the door. "The missus and I are still expecting you for dinner on Monday." He turned his usual sunny smile on him, tinged with mischief. "And since you seem to have the connections, you could always bring a bottle of wine with you."

Lorenzo chuckled as Mr. Stein stepped out of sight. One disaster had been averted, but more waited around the corner. Sooner or later, he was going to have to talk to Sabina again, really talk to her. All those years of saying nothing were going to catch up to them both in the worst possible way.

He made the sign of the cross and whispered a prayer that there'd be enough pieces of them left to pick up afterward. Then he reached for pen and paper to jot a note for Brother Judah.

If ever he could use the council of the older cousin who had long been his mentor, it was now.

FIVE

No worst, there is none. Pitched past pitch of grief,
More pangs will, schooled at forepangs, wilder wring.
Comforter, where, where is your comforting?

-Gerard Manley Hopkins,
from "No worst, there is none. Pitched past pitch of grief."

Dusk had crept over the city by the time Lorenzo left his office on North LaSalle and slid behind the wheel of his new Nash Roadster. As he pulled out into the usual traffic of a Friday evening, he debated for a moment where to go next. Manny was on his way home, and he had invited Lorenzo to join the family for a night of celebration. Everyone would be there. Every Mancari in Chicago, and every Capecce too—or the ones not working elsewhere, anyway. Cousins and aunts and friends he'd known since he was a toddler.

And Sabina. Sabina would be there with her perfect face and her perfect hair and those deep brown eyes that he had no desire to look into right now. Sabina would be there, the devastation of heartbreak in her eyes. All because of that cop who had used her and tossed her aside.

His fingers tightened on the wheel, not sure how he could be so furious with both her and with himself—and with Roman O'Reilly. But he was. He didn't want to go there, he didn't want to talk about O'Reilly...and he didn't want to be alone with his own brooding thoughts, either. With a blustery breath, he made a turn he didn't often make and headed for the shopping district and one of Manny's speakeasies. His brothers would be there, working—if anyone could distract him from himself, it would be Tony and Val. He needed their humor, their perspective. And live music wouldn't hurt his state of mind, either.

He found parking a block away from the dry goods store and joined the pedestrians filling the sidewalks. Heading for the back entrance, he fell in behind a giggling couple dressed for a night on the town. Sequins and beads on the girl, and a glittering band pulled over her forehead. Pin stripes and two-tone shoes on the gent, who walked like he was trying to prove something.

At their approach, the panel in the back door slid open. The man whispered, and the door creaked open wide enough for them to enter. Jazz music spilled out into the street and harmonized perfectly with the shadows of encroaching night. Lorenzo sauntered up to the door, and again the panel opened.

"Password?"

Lorenzo lifted his brows. "Let me in, Valente, or I'm going to tell Mama you're the one who broke her favorite vase."

His little brother laughed and opened the door. "Fancy seeing you here, Enzo. This is, what, the third time you've ever graced our fine establishment?"

Lorenzo stepped into the dim interior, soaking up the anonymity of the busy speakeasy. "I was in the mood for some music."

Val nodded, glanced out the peephole, and then smiled at him. "It's a good group tonight. The female vocals are real smooth, you'll love it. But say, shouldn't you be at Manny's? Pops said there was a big bash over there tonight. I'da thought you'd be a guest of honor, getting him sprung like that."

Lorenzo grunted and loosened his tie. Sometimes Val was such a dunce. He always knew just the wrong thing to say. "Yeah. I'm a real hero."

"One of these days you'll get over yourself, you *babbo*." Val shoved him—too hard, like always, just to prove he could. "Hey, Tony! Get our brother some of the good stuff!"

Lorenzo shook his head and gave the baby of the family a playful cuff on the side of the head for calling him an idiot. And to remind him that shoving had consequences.

Val grinned and waved him away.

As he headed for the bar and one of the few empty stools, Lorenzo arched a brow at his older brother. Tony put down the bottle of gin he held—which had probably been cooked up in a bathtub a few blocks away—and reached instead for a Coca-Cola. Grinning, he popped the top and slid it over. "Thought maybe the events of the last day would give you a thirst for it."

Lorenzo gripped the cool glass bottle. "The idea has a certain allure, but—"

"The law's the law," Tony finished for him. He grabbed a clean mug from a shelf and filled it with beer in response to another patron's demand. "I've heard the lecture. Though technically you wouldn't be doing anything illegal. You neither manufactured, sold, nor transported it."

"But by buying it, I force my brothers to do each of those things. No thanks. I won't contribute to *you* breaking the law, either."

He took a swig of the soda, let the bubbles fizz their way down his throat. And winced. Not at the carbonation, but at the fact that he'd just contributed in a big way to that very thing by helping Manny.

"I swear, Enzo, if you weren't the spitting image of Pops, I'd say you were a foundling."

Lorenzo raised his Coke. "To brotherly love. Where would I be today without your unfailing support?"

Tony laughed, nodded toward the stage where the band prepared for another set, and turned to take an order. Lorenzo swiveled his head to look at the musicians. The lead vocalist was a dark-haired beauty decked out in a low-cut white evening dress, red rose pinned on to draw yet more attention to her décolletage.

"Think I might offer to drop her home tonight," Tony said, leaning onto the bar across from Lorenzo. "Her name's Peggy, I think. Hey, maybe I can convince her to go out with me if you and Bean tag along. Whadaya say?"

He forced his grip on the Coke to relax, reminding himself that his brother had no idea how painful the suggestion was. "I don't know, Tony. I'm not really sure where things stand with me and Sabina right now."

Tony frowned and angled his head so that the dim light caught his strong jaw. Lorenzo had caught him more than once practicing such stances in front of a mirror. He was considered the handsomest of the Capecce brothers, at least since Joey had been killed in the war.

"'Sabina'?" Tony echoed. "You haven't used her full name in…ever. Am I missing something here? 'Cause when I saw you a few days ago, you were talking about the suit you were going to buy for your wedding, and now you sound like…"

"Like it's off?" Lorenzo grunted and pasted his eyes on the scarred bar, liberated from an Irish pub across town when it closed its doors two years ago. He debated for a moment whether to elaborate. On the one hand, he had the urge to coddle his pain a little longer, to protect it from the harsh light of opinion. On the other hand, Tony was the best friend he had, differing views on the world notwithstanding.

He may have told himself he wanted a distraction, but deep down he probably knew that if he came here, his brother would force him to face the situation head on. "I think it is."

"Hey, can I get a beer?"

Tony snarled at the impatient customer three stools down. "Hold your horses or go someplace else. We're having a family crisis here." He smoothed out his features as he turned back to Lorenzo. "What happened? You two have a fight?"

Lorenzo let out a humorless breath of a laugh. "Some might call it that. She doesn't love me, Tony."

His brother straightened, rolling his eyes. "Oh, come on. You two have been joined at the hip since she was old enough to walk."

"She's been seeing someone else."

Though Tony had been reaching for another mug, he froze. "She *what*? Who?"

"You remember Oliveri?"

Tony grabbed the mug and thrust it under a tap while he contemplated. "Maybe. Was he the one that Manny sent to the brewery with Val a month ago? Tall, talks like New York?"

"Mm hm."

Tony shook his head as he slid the beer down the bar. "He's got nothing on you, little bro. Don't worry about him."

"She loves him—she told me so. But it's worse than that." Lorenzo let his eyes flutter shut for a moment. "He's not really Oliveri. He's O'Reilly, the Prohibition agent that took Manny down yesterday."

Tony let fly a few choice expletives in both English and Sicilian. His next words stayed in their parents' native tongue. "*Scioccu!* You think he realizes his life's over?"

With an upward jerk of his head, Lorenzo sent his brother a scorching glare. "I don't want to hear that kind of talk, Antonio." He, too, kept to Sicilian.

The elder bared his teeth, hissed out a breath, and gripped the edge of the counter with both hands. "I promised you years ago I'd keep my hands clean. But Manny has an awful lot of men who don't have kid brothers with your scruples."

"Which is why I made him promise to put out the word that O'Reilly's off limits."

Tony sagged in disbelief. "And he *did* it?"

Lorenzo chuckled again, still without mirth. "He didn't understand why I'd ask it, but I think he figured he owed me for getting him out, especially after what his darling daughter did to me."

Tony spat out a few more ugly words and shook his head. "I don't understand why you'd ask it, either. You could have just kept your mouth shut, you *babbo*, and let someone take care of this for you."

"It wouldn't have changed the fact that Sabina fell in love with him." He waved away a wisp of smoke that drifted over from another patron's fat cigar. "It just would have made me guilty on top of it all."

"It's not like *you* would have—"

"'To him therefore who knoweth to do good, and doth it not, to him it is sin.'"

Tony sent his eyes to the hazy ceiling and shook his head. "You've got one of those for every occasion, don't you?"

"That's the general idea."

His brother muttered one more curse for good measure and turned to fill a few more orders. Lorenzo soaked up the jazz from the stage, content with the pause in the conversation. Sometimes it amazed him how different he and his brothers were, how the same lessons at Holy Guardian Angel could have taken hold in him and not fazed them at all. But, all jokes aside, they were there. They didn't pretend to understand what drove each other, but they'd still be along for the ride. They were family.

As evening edged toward night, the speakeasy came to life. Warm bodies packed every available piece of real estate, the dance floor a writhing mass of shimmies and Charlestons. There were a few flappers present, their faces painted, their dresses short, and their laughter loud, but most of the patrons seemed to be normal folks looking for a diversion from normal life. They kept Tony hopping, and Lorenzo turned on his stool so he could lean against the bar and watch the band.

After about an hour he saw Val relinquish his post at the door to a friend and come over for a drink. Seating was nil, so he just leaned beside Lorenzo and offered a quiet critique of all the people milling around—or at least the female half of them.

"Now *there's* a Sheba." Mischievous grin in place, Val nodded toward a flapper whose skirt ended a scandalous inch below her knee.

Lorenzo chuckled. "Try taking a girl like that home, and Mama would make you the new entryway rug."

Val boomed a laugh. "Got a point there, bro."

Still grinning over the mental image, Lorenzo scanned the crowd again. His smile froze when an inebriated man pushed through to the bar a few spaces down and pounded a fist onto the top.

"Hey, barkeep!" he slurred. "Gimme a gin."

It looked as though he had already had more than enough, but that wasn't what had grabbed Lorenzo's attention.

Following his gaze, Val quirked a brow. "Isn't that Oliveri?"

"O'Reilly," Lorenzo corrected, grinding it out around clenched teeth.

The band kicked up its volume—Val cupped a hand over his ear. "Huh?"

"His name is O'Reilly!"

The shout apparently traveled to more ears than Val's. O'Reilly looked his way. Lorenzo could tell the exact moment when recognition broke through the haze of alcohol. O'Reilly's lips peeled back in a snarl, and he shoved off the bar to stagger over to him.

"Well, well, well." The agent grabbed the counter again to keep from swaying. "If it isn't the self-righteous victor of the day. Here to celebrate?"

Lorenzo almost, *almost* pitied the man. "Not really, no. At the moment I'm just contemplating the irony of a Prohibition agent who claims to be honest drowning his sorrows in the establishment of the man he just failed to put away."

Confusion clouded O'Reilly's eyes briefly. "This one's his too, is it? Here I thought I was avoiding him by not going to the millinery." He looked around as if mentally condemning the place. "Guess I didn't get as much on him as I thought."

Tony sidled up on the other side of the bar, drying out a mug with a white towel. "What was your first clue? When my brother got him released from jail this afternoon?" He set down the clean glass with a thunk. "Do us all a favor and move on, O'Reilly. The likes of you ain't wanted here."

"The likes of me?" O'Reilly narrowed his eyes. "What about the likes of your hypocritical brother here? Claiming to be such a good boy, yet he spends his days getting criminals out of jail and passes his evenings in illegal gin bars."

The words hit their mark. "You really want to talk about pots and kettles, O'Reilly? I'm not the one who's practically falling over drunk. If either of us is a hypocrite, it's you."

O'Reilly poked a finger into Lorenzo's shoulder. "It's the Mafia I hate, not the ridiculous law they're making all their money from. But you—you think Sabina didn't tell me all about your high morals? You claim to be so righteous, but I don't see it. I think you're just a little girl too yellow to do any of the dirty work and too weak-willed to tell your precious Papa Manny no."

Lorenzo pushed himself off his stool and grabbed the suit jacket he had taken off half an hour ago. "You know what? I've lost my desire for music. Val, Tony, I'll see you at home for dinner tomorrow."

Val restrained him with a hand on his shoulder. "Hey, you shouldn't be the one to leave." He tossed the agent a look that usually sent cowards running. "If anyone's going, it ought to be him."

Lorenzo sucked in a deep breath. "No, Val. Let him have his gin. I really ought to go over to Manny's anyway before the evening's through."

O'Reilly loosed a grating chuckle. "Yeah, you do that. And give Sabina a kiss for me, will you? A nice long one, like the last few we shared."

Lorenzo's fingers curled into a fist.

O'Reilly chuckled again. "Bet she didn't mention those, did she? Or that little petting party we had last week?"

Lorenzo didn't say a word. He just pulled back his arm and landed an uppercut on the man's jaw that sent him sprawling flat on the ground, unconscious. The cheer that went up told Lorenzo that his brothers weren't the only ones around who had been listening and piecing together the story.

Tony pressed his lips down on a grin. "Aren't you supposed to turn the other cheek or something?"

Lorenzo flexed his hand. "Fresh out of 'em."

Val laughed and gave him a friendly slap on the back. "Good thing we had older brothers to beat us up, huh? Come on, Enzo, let me buy you another Coke."

"No thanks." Lorenzo punched his arms through the sleeves of his jacket. "I'm going to settle this thing with Sabina while I'm still in the mood."

Tony reached over the bar and grabbed his arm, his brows knit. "You sure, Enzo?"

He pulled his arm free. "I'm sure." She wanted someone else? Then she could have him. He was done, and he'd tell her so while he had the adrenaline giving him the courage.

He took a little too much pleasure in stepping over O'Reilly's limp legs on his way out the door.

◆◈◆

Mancaris and Mancari offshoots packed the dining room, filling it to the brim with talk in two languages, laughter, and the occasional shout across the room. Wine flowed freely, and Little G had set up the new radio, tuning it to KYW—the one station Chicago boasted that played music. Since the opera season had just ended, jazz spilled out, making toes tap under the table.

Sabina tried to celebrate along with her family, but every smile felt forced. Lorenzo hadn't arrived yet. Maybe before he did, she could slink away to her room—as if Mama would let her get away with that. Sighing, she settled in beside her younger cousin, Caterina, and dreaded his arrival. With any luck, he wouldn't come.

Cat, barely seventeen, gave Sabina an innocent, cheerful smile. "Hi, Bina. Bet you're pretty proud of Enzo, huh? I can't believe he got Uncle Manny out so soon!"

"Yeah," Sabina answered with a weak smile. "I never had any doubt he'd be a great lawyer."

She had doubted plenty about him, but never that. Lorenzo had always been the smartest person she knew. He could do anything he set his mind to.

Except love her, apparently.

She focused again on Cat. "So what are you going to get into this summer? Big plans now that school's out?"

"Not much. Mama and I have the latest *Philipsborn Catalog*, and we're going to copy some of the styles and then fancy them up with these great beads we found. After I finish my dress for your wedding, of course. Have you and Aunt Rosa started on yours yet?"

Though she nodded, Sabina tried not to think of the white silk folded carefully in the other room. Who knew when, if ever, they'd finish it?

Her attention was stolen by a figure rushing through the door. It was a more distant cousin, and he went straight to where Papa laughed with Uncle Franco and Vanni Capecce, Lorenzo's father. Though she couldn't hear a word of the exchange, she recognized the look that passed over Papa's face. Seconds later, he stood and pasted on a smile as fake as the ones Sabina had been giving.

"You'll have to excuse us for a minute, ladies." He aimed his words at where Mama, Aunt Luccia, and Fran Capecce chatted in the corner over half-eaten plates of *cannolu* and steaming coffee. "There's a little business matter we need to take care of."

Sabina couldn't count the times her father had excused himself to take care of business. But this was the first time she wondered what business, exactly, it might be. She knew what he was—it had shaped every aspect of their lives—but before, she had never really thought about his crimes. He was only protecting Sicilians and even Italians, providing for the family, circumventing unfair laws.

But the list of charges she'd heard them discussing now marched through her mind like a parade. The bootlegging didn't really bother her—but cold-blooded murder? That had been among the charges, though of course it had been dropped. Still…could Papa really be guilty of something like that?

He dropped a kiss onto her head on his way out and gave her a warm smile. "When Enzo shows up, tell him to hang around until I get back, okay, *principessa*?"

She nodded, her returning smile tight. He *couldn't* be guilty of that. He couldn't—he was Papa. The man who made it clear he'd move heaven and earth for their family. The man who always double-checked Mama's tithe money to make sure enough was going to Holy Guardian Angel. The man who had brushed a tear from his eye at her First Communion, and at Little G's, and at Serafina's.

How could a man like that be all the things Roman *O'Reilly* accused him of?

The three men walked out, though the door no more than closed before opening again. Papa stuck his head back in. "Bina, Isadora and that flapper are heading this way."

Sabina managed her first real smile, partly at the arrival of her friends, and partly because Papa had stridently refused to acknowledge Mary by name since she raised her hems, rolled her stockings, and painted her face. He still hadn't forgiven her for taking Sabina to get her hair bobbed, though he never went as far as to say they couldn't spend time together. "Thanks, Papa." She turned her smile on Cat. "Let's go meet them on the stoop. It's too nice an evening to stay in here."

Her cousin followed her out, and they arrived at the stoop just as Mary and Isadora Bennato reached the steps. Mary was, as usual, dressed to shock. Her garment of choice for the evening was in clashing reds and pinks, cut so low up top that her *bandeau* was visible when she moved the wrong way and so high on the bottom that the hems of her stockings—held up today by flashy garters—showed with every step.

"I can't believe her parents let her out of the house like that," Cat whispered into Sabina's ear.

Sabina's smile faded. Mrs. Bennato was too ill to even notice what Mary was wearing, most days. And it seemed like the sicker she grew, the more outrageous Mary became. And the less Mr. Bennato bothered coming home.

Cat snorted. "Of course, then there's Izzy."

Sabina sighed as she looked at Isadora. The exact opposite of her year-younger sister, she had refused to bob her hair, and her clothes were so Victorian that they looked like she got them straight from her mother's closet.

Come to think of it, maybe she had. Hadn't Mary complained just last month that her father hadn't given them any pocket money for more than a year? Her boyfriend, Robert, was the one who bought her the new clothes. But Isadora had no Robert—she'd been engaged to Joey Capecce, but since he hadn't come home from the war…what did that leave her?

Mary bounded over and wrapped Sabina in a perfume-laden hug. "Oh, Bina. We heard about the whole thing, Robert told us. He got the scoop from the courthouse gossip. It's so *awful*. I can't believe Roman would do that to you—I really can't. He couldn't have been faking his feelings, you know that, right? I bet he'll come back for you." She grabbed Sabina's left hand and let out a loud sigh. "And *still* Enzo hasn't cut you loose?" Subtlety was not one of Mary's strong suits.

"Mary!" Isadora chided her sister with a tone born of much practice. "Have a care, will you? Sabina is upset."

Mary rolled her kohl-rimmed eyes. "Oh, she's fine. Or will be. Listen, pussycat, the only thing for it is to get out and put it all from your mind. Robert and I are going to a party tonight that's going to be the bee's knees. You should come."

The idea did nothing but depress her further. "I really can't, Mary. The whole family's here to celebrate Papa's release."

For just a moment, something flickered in Mary's eyes, something pleading and on the edge of desperate. She clung to Sabina's hand. "Oh, come on. I loved it when you came with me. We had fun, didn't we? And that's what you need right now. Fun."

As if gin-flavored *fun* could make all this go away for her any more than it could make Mary's mother well or her father care. She sighed and squeezed Mary's fingers back. "Why don't you just stay here with me tonight? Please?"

Mary hesitated just long enough to make her think she might agree. But then she shook herself, pasted on a smile, and drew a compact out of her beaded purse. "Not tonight, doll face. Robert's already on his way." Apparently unconcerned with the fact that she was in plain sight of a busy street, she powdered her nose and then reapplied a generous coat of red lipstick.

Cat gasped in disbelief, which made Sabina smile, at least for a second. Most of them wore some makeup—but not many flaunted it. Heaven knew what her cousin might do if Mary drew out one of her cigarettes and lit up.

A brand-new Auburn pulled up, Robert at the wheel. He honked the horn and gave an enthusiastic wave. Mary tossed her compact back into her purse and hugged Sabina again. "I bet you Roman shows up to steal you away, just like you planned. You two will be out with me and Robert again by next week, you'll see."

Sabina shook her head, throat too tight to speak. She could understand that Mary liked having another couple to hit the town with, and they all knew Lorenzo would never be game for a night of carousing. But couldn't she see that Roman was no knight in shining armor? He was the worst kind of guy—a rodent. A mole.

Mary bounded back down the stairs, calling over her shoulder, "If anyone bothers asking, tell them I'm staying the night with Bina, Izzy."

Isadora sighed and sank down on the top step. "I keep trying to tell her that acting this way won't make them ask. Mother's just too ill, and Father..." She pressed her lips together. "I don't want to see her get in trouble. But she will, if she keeps this up. Not with them, maybe, but she will."

Sabina sat beside Isadora when Cat settled in one of the chairs. She'd tried defending Mary plenty in the past, saying she wasn't really doing anything wrong. After all, what did red lipstick and a flashy dress really matter?

But she'd been out with her, on Roman's arm. She knew exactly what Mary did when she was full of "giggle water," and it wasn't as harmless as she'd wanted to think. "The more you warn her, though, the faster she's going to run."

"I know." Isadora flicked a stray curl out of her face and then attempted to tuck it into the knot at the base of her neck. Her eyes, as always, were shadowed and bloodshot. Did she even sleep anymore, or just sit up all night with her mother? Why didn't she make Mary help her?

As if anyone could make Mary do anything.

Turning her gray eyes on Sabina, Isadora probed her for a long moment. "You holding up all right?"

Sabina lifted her shoulder in a shrug. "It's been a tough couple of days."

"If you need to talk about it, I'm here, you know."

She nodded, her eyes on the twilit street. The lamps flicked on as she watched. At the moment their light was barely visible in the rays of the dying sun, but in a matter of minutes they'd be the brightest things on the street.

Sometimes Isadora struck her in the same way—faded in contrast to her vibrant sister, but the one who really shone when darkness fell. And the darkness had been falling for years, it seemed.

Sabina sighed. "I'm just not sure what I'm feeling. Part of me hates Roman for what he did, but another part wants to mourn him. Then there's a part that wants to cling to Enzo because he's familiar, but it's at war with the part that got me into this mess in the first place, the part that wants more than he was ever willing to give." She looked over at Isadora now, fully expecting to see rebuke in her eyes. Instead she saw compassion. "I'm awful, aren't I?"

Isadora smiled and reached over to grip her hand. "I know it's not exactly the same, but when I got the news that Joey had been killed, I had some conflicting feelings, too. I wasn't just upset at losing him—I was furious with him for signing up in the first place, instead of staying here to marry me like he promised. I wanted to go out and find someone else just to spite him, but then if I went to a party or something, I felt so guilty I'd leave in minutes. I think it's pretty normal to be mixed up when you lose someone, Sabina. Even when the loss isn't death."

Sabina angled her body in to reply, but the door opened and more of the family spilled out to enjoy the night. And this wasn't exactly a conversation she wanted every cousin and aunt and uncle to overhear. So she sighed and let her shoulders curl forward, let her mouth shut again, just like always.

Isadora squeezed her hand. "Later."

Chaos ensued as a dozen bodies tried to find places to sit, most overflowing onto the sidewalk to avoid the crush on the porch. Sabina let herself get lost in the hubbub. If nothing else, it insulated her, distracted her from all the questions that still needed to be answered.

Soon darkness fell in earnest. Lorenzo still hadn't shown up, and she began to let herself think he wouldn't. Maybe this day would just whimper to a close, and she could drag herself up to bed and pray no nightmares found her tonight.

Then his Nash pulled up. Her breath came in with a shudder when Lorenzo stepped out and slammed the door behind him. His shoulders were drawn up, his stride long—sure signs of a rare temper. "Oh, boy."

Isadora chuckled at her mumble. "Just be honest with him about everything. I imagine it's the deception really stinging him right now."

He brushed by her as he mounted the stairs, going straight for Mama, who greeted him with a wide smile and a smacking kiss on his cheek. He returned the smile, but one would have had to be blind to miss the strain in it.

Had she thought she stood a chance of getting away, Sabina would have slipped over the railing and made a break for it.

"Giorgio said to stick around until he got back." Mama had apparently overheard the instructions and didn't trust Sabina to convey them.

Lorenzo nodded, but that was all the attention he spared Mama. He turned his face Sabina's way, all but commanding her to get up with his eyes. "Mama Rosa, do you mind if Sabina and I go for a little stroll around the block?"

"Of course I don't mind," Mama said on a laugh. "Go, go."

Sabina moaned, but she forced herself up. The others exchanged brief greetings with Lorenzo. Hoping he'd get distracted, she hung back beside the railing. No such luck—seconds later he put a hand under her elbow to lead her down the steps and halted all the idle chat with a short, "We won't be long."

His fingers scorched her arm, and she clasped her hands together to keep them from shaking. How often had she wished he'd take her arm, her hand, *something*? Now, he finally did, and there wasn't even a sliver of affection in it. She felt like a naughty schoolgirl standing in front of a nun, wondering what punishment might be handed down, and how much it would hurt.

He said nothing as they gained the sidewalk. His tension sang through his hand, and she was about to snap with it. It was somehow even worse when he dropped his grip on her elbow. As if, just like that, he was letting her go.

She ought to be glad. For him, for her, for both of them. It would be for the best, wouldn't it?

But she wasn't ready. She wasn't ready to lose him. She reached for his hand.

When she squeezed his fingers, he let out a hiss of pain, tugging them away. With a single look over her shoulder to make sure they were out of earshot, Sabina grabbed his hand again—by the palm this time. His knuckles were bruised. "What happened to you?"

Lorenzo pulled free again. Not even deigning to look at her, he rolled his shoulders forward. "Had a little run-in with your boyfriend."

For a second she just walked, too stupefied to speak. "You *hit* him?" The idea was ludicrous. Lorenzo wouldn't—couldn't—had *never*—

"I imagine he's still sprawled on the floor of the bar, if you want to go nurse him back to health. Though he was already pretty well medicated when he came in."

A long blink didn't change the impossible image. Lorenzo still stood like Val usually did, on the offensive and ready to brawl. She didn't know if it frightened her or amused her. "If I went over there, I'd probably grind my heel into the first vital part I came across. I'm just surprised, Enzo. You never fight. Tony and Val, sure, and even Joey used to, but you…you're…"

"What?" They turned the corner, and he halted her simply by stopping and crossing his arms over his chest. "What is it, exactly, that you think I am? Boring? Unfeeling? Stoic? Do you think I don't have a heart beating in my chest?"

No. She'd always known he had a heart, one as beautiful as his mind. It was just that he'd closed her out of it. "I don't—"

"I'm through, Sabina." He slashed a hand through the air to illustrate it. "I trusted you. Maybe that makes me stupid, but I don't think *I'm* the one to blame when my supposedly virtuous bride is out necking with the first smooth-talking charlatan who comes along."

Her blood began to boil, a haze over her eyes blocking out the reality of nosy neighbors and other pedestrians. "You *trusted* me? Is that what you call ignoring me for the last three years—trust? Just trusting that I could keep going without you, trusting that you didn't need to do anything? Trusting that I'd just sit around forever, waiting for you to remember that I exist?"

"That's rich. As if I wasn't working every day for us, trying to build a life we could live without strings. Why do you think I worked two jobs while I juggled classes, Sabina? Why do you think I insisted we wait until this summer to get married?"

A question she had asked over and over, time and again inside her own mind. Why was he always, always choosing something else above her? Why did he keep saying "not yet" for so long when she asked him about a date?

The truth had become clear, eventually, and it hissed out now like the accusation it was. "Because you didn't want me, you never really wanted me!"

Funny—she'd meant it to accuse *him*. But it cut her own heart far more deeply than it could have cut his.

He gaped at her like she was an idiot. "It was for you. *Everything* was for you, it was always for you. So I could save enough to have a place of my own. So we wouldn't have to rely on them, on the dirty money. So I could get you away from all this."

Her hands shook. "Away? You want to talk about *away*? You've been 'away' from all this, from me, for years. You may have told yourself it was for me, but if so, why did you never give me a word? Never a touch? You couldn't have made it any clearer—"

"I was *protecting* you! Honoring you."

"You abandoned me!"

For a moment, the words seemed to hit their mark. A million thoughts flashed through his eyes, illuminated by the lamplight. But then a shutter—oh, that familiar shutter—fell over his gaze again.

"Is that your excuse, then, for why you fell into his arms? Instead of talking to me, you just turned to someone else?"

Her nostrils flared, but she couldn't suck in air enough to steady the waves of pain. She'd done wrong—she knew it. But he'd left first. He'd chosen those jobs and school and his high ideals above her. She'd sat at home for three eternal years, silently screaming for someone to see her, to give her something to do, and he hadn't. Whatever he told himself, he *hadn't*.

He took a step away. "You've made your decisions, and now you're going to live with them. I want you to take off my ring. You can keep it, hock it, whatever—I don't want it. But I don't want you wearing it."

She wasn't going to cry. Not again. Not for him. *Ice. Numb.* It was all she had now, all she'd ever have. It had seen her through the last three years, and it would see her through the next thirty. "Well." She drew in a deep breath that betrayed her by catching in her throat. "I guess that's that. Unless there's something else you'd like to say?"

"Yeah." Lorenzo shook his head. "I thought you had more sense than this—but *him*. Never mind that he was a cop—you didn't know that. But you thought he was a mafioso. And that's what you chose? That makes me doubt whether I even knew you. That you'd want to marry some gangster, just like our fathers?"

Her hackles rose. "What's so wrong with our fathers?"

Disgust colored his countenance before he turned away, his legs already stretching into long strides. "Ask me that when a Betsy rips apart your world," he tossed over his shoulder.

She let him go. Stood there simmering and steaming and wanting nothing more than to stomp her foot like a child. Then she realized his march would take him straight to his car in his current mood, so she ran to catch up with him.

Never mind her petulance—Papa had issued an order. "Enzo, wait. Papa wanted to talk to you."

He didn't so much as slow. "You know what, Sabina? I don't really care. If it's important, he can find me later."

And leave her to explain to her father why he'd vanished? Maybe it was a fair punishment, but that didn't mean she wanted to bear it. She could do nothing but dog his steps, though, since any logic would fall on deaf ears.

They hadn't gone all that far, so it didn't take long to reach her house again. As she expected, Lorenzo headed straight for his Nash, though he hadn't quite reached it when the Pierce-Arrow pulled in behind him, Papa and Uncle Franco and Vanni emerging. Sabina let out a relieved breath and slowed down. Papa and Vanni would stop him, and it wouldn't be her problem anymore.

Lorenzo disproved that theory when he ignored the hails from the men and kept his aim true. Sabina picked up her pace again, moving toward her father. She opened her mouth, but a shrill whistle interrupted her thoughts.

Her blood froze. The world slowed. In her periphery, streetlight glinted off of ugly gun barrels. Her father cursed. The air went heavy like right before a lightning strike, filled with the acrid scent of impending disaster. She saw Lorenzo wheel around, eyes wide, and make a charge—not for the relative safety of his car, which was well out of the line of fire. For her.

A second later, the fury of gunfire was unleashed, tripping over the panicked screams of the family still on the stoop. Too stunned to move, Sabina fought for breath as the three men beside her dove for cover and weapons. She was vaguely aware of the growing figure of Lorenzo, who was upon her in another second. His arm caught her mid-chest and wrenched her from her anchored feet, pulling her down and over.

Bullets sliced the air all around her, even as they fell. She braced for impact with the ground, but instead she found that Lorenzo had turned them so that he hit first, softening her landing. Still her breath abandoned her. Pain blazed.

He had gotten them partially covered by the stairs, but their legs were still exposed and bullets bit the ground all around them. Her reflexes finally recovered. She jerked her knees up to her chest and slid off Lorenzo so he could do the same.

He didn't. "Enzo?" She forced her eyes to focus on him and was met with the sight of blood gushing from a wound in his head. His eyelids were closed all but a crack, his mouth slack, his face pale. Terror bubbled through her. "Enzo?" Frantic, she shook him a little. He didn't stir. "No. No, no, no. Come on, Enzo, wake up. Please. Please wake up!"

As quickly as it had started, the barrage of gunfire ceased. Maybe people were screaming—maybe her ears were just ringing. She didn't know. Didn't care. Didn't pay any attention to the pounding footsteps or the flurry of activity. All she could see was the stillness. Enzo's legs, not moving. Enzo's eyelids, not lifting. Enzo's hands, not reaching for hers.

No, that wasn't all. There was the red too. Enzo's blood, gushing out all over her hands.

She hadn't thought she had enough of her heart left to break, not after Serafina's death and Roman's betrayal and Papa's arrest.

She had never been so wrong.

SIX

Not, I'll not, carrion comfort, Despair, not feast on thee;
Not untwist-slack they may be-these last strands of man
    In me or, most weary, cry *I can no more.* I can;

-Gerard Manley Hopkins,
from "Carrion Comfort"

Darkness still reigned when Roman blinked his eyes open. He looked at the unfamiliar ceiling, ran a hand over the nubby sheets beneath him. Street noise poured through an open window along with a cool breeze. He had absolutely no idea where he was and no recollection of how he had gotten there.

A noise from his right caught his attention. He looked over to see a flame flicker onto the end of a cigarette, illuminating a feminine face. The smell of burning tobacco almost made him salivate. "Can I bum one of those?"

The woman turned his way, not seeming surprised to hear his voice. "Sure, champ." Before handing him one, she leaned over and switched on a lamp. Roman became instantly aware of her state of undress. She wore a combination, but the bloomer part was shortened to the top of her thigh, and the chemise part was scooped lower than could possibly be useful under a dress. Teddies, he thought they called them. This one was in a powder blue and ridiculously adorned, telling him that the blond wearing it had intended it to be seen.

"Where am I?"

The woman laughed and leaned over to hand him a ciggie she had lit while he studied her. The action gave him an unobstructed view down her wisp of clothing, which he enjoyed for the moment it lasted. She was obviously a prostitute—but she was a pretty one, young. Her fair hair was bobbed and waved to perfection, her features were fine, and her lips were stained a bright red.

She took another puff of her own smoke. "It ain't the Everleigh, that's for sure."

The reference to the upscale bordello removed any doubt of the woman's profession. He pushed himself up on her lumpy bed—noting that though his shirt was off, his pants were not—and took a long drag of tobacco. "You gotta name?"

She smiled. "A couple of 'em. Most often I go by Sally."

He nodded, though the information didn't help clarify the recent past. "And what am I doing here, Sally?"

A cross between mockery and annoyance flickered in her eyes. "Not much, champ. Not much."

The insult irritated him, and the irritation irritated him even more. "Look, doll—"

"Oh, lighten up." She smiled again and blew out an impressive smoke ring. "I wasn't really expecting much when your buddies dumped you at my feet. Practically had to scrape you off the sidewalk to get you up here, so it was no big surprise when you fell asleep straight away."

"Buddies?" Now that interested him. The last thing he could really remember was stumbling for a speakeasy. As far as he knew, he hadn't had any friends with him.

"Yeah. Couple of Italians, brothers I'd bet. Good looking fellas, strapping like, ya know? One of 'em called the other Tony."

An image flashed in his memory. Lorenzo Capecce sitting on a stool scowling at him, flanked on either side by his "strapping" brothers. He had another flash of Lorenzo's fist heading for his face. Reaching up, he gingerly touched a finger to his bruised jaw.

"Nice colors." Sally chuckled. "Looks like you had quite the evening. Over a dame, I bet."

He grunted his agreement and stewed for a minute, let the anger build up to a satisfying inferno. He was going to bring them down, the whole lot of them. Mancaris and Capecces and anyone else stupid enough to step into the crossfire. He narrowed shrewd eyes on the hooker. He was willing to use any means at his disposal to achieve his goal—and if the Capecces brought him here, it was possibly because they were familiar with the location. "Say, Sally, who's your man?"

She lifted brows that had been drawn on too high. "What's it to ya?"

He affected a disinterested shrug. "Call me curious. Is it Mancari?"

She snorted and ground out her cigarette stub in an ugly glass ashtray. "You kidding? His places have more class than this joint. Nah, these days we're run by a new guy to town, from Brooklyn." It was her turn to narrow her eyes. "You sound pretty New York yourself, champ. You a friend of Al's?"

"Al?"

"Yeah, Al. Capa-something, though he usually goes by Brown."

He searched his mind for who she meant. "Oh—Capone? Torrio's new guy?"

"That's him." Apparently deciding he was becoming lucid enough to make himself useful, she slid over onto the bed and trailed a fingernail down his chest. "Rumor has it Torrio's grooming him to take over while Johnny takes wifey and her mama back to Italy for a while. You ask me, young Al's not likely to step down again once he steps up."

The newcomer to Torrio's ranks really wasn't Roman's concern. "You know any of Mancari's girls?"

Her fingers stilled on his chest. "Why the interest?"

He touched his bruise again. "His daughter's the dame. I'm feeling vindictive."

Sally chuckled and placed a skillful kiss on his shoulder. "Always did like scorned lovers. They make good customers." She set her hand on an exploration of his chest, though she paused when her fingertips brushed over his necklace.

He tugged it away from her, wishing he'd taken the useless thing off a year ago, when he boxed up the rest of his mother's tokens. Somehow it had been easier to pack away the icons and crucifixes than to take off the St. Michael medallion. The archangel was supposed to protect cops, after all.

Right.

"Mancari," he said again, to distract Sally from his reaction.

"Hmm." She set her fingers trailing over his chest again, but contemplation lit her eyes, not seduction. "Let's see. There's Gloria—no, wait, she's over at the Victoria. Hm. Oh! Ava, that's right. She's been his girl for twenty years. Even claims to have his ear, if you know what I'm saying. Nice lady, real upscale. Took me under her wing for a few weeks when I first hit the city. A little old for you, though."

Roman pushed himself up, leaned over to stub out his cigarette in the same ugly ashtray, and brushed Sally's hands away. "Not looking for a roll in the hay with her. No offense, doll, but I'm not looking for one with you, either."

Sally straightened with a shrug, her eyes cold and hard and older than her face. "No skin off my back, champ. But you're paying for the night either way."

He halted with his hands on his filthy shirt, which he had spotted crumpled on the floor beside the bed. "Think so?"

She ran her tongue over teeth that were surprisingly white. "This ain't your mama's house, buster, it's a place of business. You take the bed, you pay for it. Couldn't exactly bring up another john while you were sleeping it off, could I?"

"Fine." Grinding out the word between clenched teeth, he fished his money clip out of his pocket and withdrew a bill, slapped it on the table. "That should cover a night's rent in this dump."

She fingered the payment for a second before tucking it into a book on the table. A Bible, of all things. He snorted at the irony. "Nice reading. Let me guess—you're a good girl under the makeup and perfume."

She didn't bother to answer, though she shut the Bible again with a bit too much force. When he stood, she sat on the bed and leaned against the peeling wallpaper. "Well, nice seeing you, champ. You can sleep in my bed and give me a night off anytime."

He shouldn't let the insult get to him—he knew that. But he'd had a few too many of them lobbed at him in the last twenty-four hours. Who could really blame him for lobbing this one back? He undid that one button again, figuring he might as well take what he had paid for. Cliff always said Roman acted too fast, without thinking things through. But he was tired of thinking. "You clean?"

She folded her arms over her chest. "What a question."

"Well this ain't the Everleigh, doll."

Her chin edged up. "I still take care of myself. Get myself checked. Yeah, I'm clean. Why, you interested after all?"

He flashed a smile and pushed her easily down onto the mattress. "I always did have a thing for blonds."

Pain pressed Lorenzo down, heavy as an anchor. Searing, scraping, suffocating. His dreams were a collection of darkness and bursts of light that scorched his eyes, a continuous roar, and fear. The fear stalked and sprang, released him from its jowls only to toy with him. He wrestled with it, clawing his way up only to fall back down until finally, finally he won.

Lorenzo blinked his eyes open only to let them fall shut again. His head pulsed in time with his heartbeat, and it was enough to make him want to sink back into that horrible darkness. But no. There was a reason he couldn't go there again. Something…there'd been something beyond it, hadn't there? A reason he had to wake up. If only he could peel back the pain, just a little, he would surely remember…

Sabina!

His eyes flew open again and he jerked his head to the side, though he regretted it immediately. His senses swam, but this time flashes of images took shape through the fog. Manny. Father. Mama and Rosa. A lookout's whistle piercing the night. He remembered turning and realizing Sabina was right beside her father, who was undoubtedly the target of the attack.

Panic made him force his eyes open again, pat the surface under which he lay, try to determine where he was so he could get up, find someone to fill in the blanks. What had happened after that whistle? Were his family all right? Mama, Father? Manny?

Sabina. What had happened to Sabina? Had he reached her in time? He had an image of horror on her face, of her body jerking back, of her scream. Was it real? Or was it just part of that nightmare that had been holding him down?

She couldn't be dead—she couldn't be. If those bullets had found her, if he'd lost her—and like that, after he'd said those things… *Father, forgive me. Protect her.* He reached for more words, his fingers looking for familiar beads, but there was no rosary in his hand, and words still darted away like fireflies in the night.

Then he realized that the darkness before his eyes wasn't night—it was a cloud that smelled of Colgate's Brilliantine.

Relief left him numb for one long moment. "Sabina." He tried to form the word, but it came out as nothing more than a croak. The cloud of hair didn't move. After a minute's struggle, he managed to lift his arm and settle his hand on her head, smoothing down the disheveled mass of waves.

Sabina—his precious Bean. She was alive. He was aware, now, of her body rising and falling against his chest. Beyond her hair, in the dim light of an oil lamp turned low, he could make out walls with the expensive paper Mama Rosa had picked out last year for the guest room. He could see the beautiful painting of the Sacred Heart that he'd praised when she had commissioned it.

He kept his gaze fastened on that for a long moment, just taking it in.

The crown of thorns, the cross, the heart of the Savior who had sacrificed everything for them. *Thank you, Jesus.*

Sabina's breath hitched. Her head lifted off his chest. "Enzo?"

He managed a weak smile and another croak that didn't form any words.

She sat up quickly and framed his face in her hands. Hers was swollen and tear-tracked, dark circles shadowing her beautiful eyes. "Enzo! *Grazii Diu.* I was beginning to think you'd never wake up."

He cleared his throat. It was still parched, but he managed a husky, "What happened?"

Sabina gave him a blubbery smile, her eyes filling again. Bean, crying... for him? Or had they lost someone? "An attack. Papa suspects it was Torrio, though he can't be sure. There were three shooters—he thinks we injured at least two of them, but they got away. You were the only one on our side that got shot."

Grazii Diu indeed—the rest of his family was well. But... "Shot?" The question pulled his brows down. How in the world had that happened? The one person in the family who had taken steps to avoid such a fate, and he was the first to take a bullet? Val and Tony would never let him live it down.

"Mm. Grazed your temple. It was the fall that knocked you out—you smacked your head on the step." She swallowed hard. "I thought I'd lost you. There was blood everywhere. You were limp, unconscious." She shook her head and reached over to pour water into a tall glass. He eyed it ravenously, accepting her help as she held it to his mouth, though he added his hand to keep it steady.

He drained the cup but shook his head when she offered more. After setting the glass back down, Sabina clasped her hands together on the edge of the bed and studied him. If her frazzle was any indication, she had been doing the same thing all night. "I thought I'd lost you," she whispered again. "Why did you turn back? You were safe at your car—safer than anywhere else, anyway."

As if he could have sought his own safety when she was in the line of fire.

Her lips pressed together, and she reached up to brush his hair off his forehead, her touch so soft he could barely feel it. "Everyone else scrambled. Some for shelter, some for guns. But not you—you just came straight for me, as if you knew I was too scared to move. You could have gotten away,

Enzo. You could have stayed safe, but instead you saved me, and you got shot in the process. But why? Why did you do it?"

A tired sigh leaked out. "You know why, Bean. I love you."

She picked up one of his hands in both of hers and cradled it against her cheek. He could feel the sticky dampness of her tears, the softness of her skin, the fear in her fingers. "I wasn't so sure. I haven't been sure for so long, and after what I did...and you coming over like that, ready for a fight..."

Letting his eyes slide closed, Lorenzo dragged in a new breath. "I was mad. Maybe I still am. But it doesn't change that I love you." He forced his eyes open again. "How could you ever have doubted that? You know me—or you used to. You *know* I love you." More than breath, more than air, more than life itself.

The eyes she focused on him glistened with tears that magnified years' worth of uncertainty. "How could I know, Enzo? How could I be sure you didn't regret proposing? You were never here. Even when—when Serafina died. You blew in, blew away again. You didn't hold me, you didn't tell me it would be all right. You never kissed me again after that first time—"

"Sabina." He lifted his spare hand and rested it, heavy as the world, on her head. "Because I couldn't trust myself." How could she not have known that? That first kiss—he could still remember the weight of it, the wonder, the fire that had blazed through him and her both, leaving them breathless. But he wasn't going to be like their fathers, like his brothers. He wasn't going to play with that fire before it was right. He couldn't do that to her soul or to his.

But what had he done instead? He'd made her doubt the very love he'd meant to demonstrate. He'd failed her.

And then she'd betrayed him.

She was there now, inches away, and it felt like a canyon yawned between them—his mistakes and hers, three years of pain and misunderstanding. Lorenzo could not shake the haunting thought of another man's lips on that perfect rosy mouth, claiming what he had tried and failed to protect.

How had they destroyed each other like this?

Sabina rested her head on his chest again, right above where his heart thudded its recriminations. Her eyes slid closed. "On Thursday, when I saw the Prohibition cops shooting at Papa, I was terrified. I tried to run away, but I ran into Roman. He dragged me straight into the line of fire. I thought he loved me—yet there he was, deliberately putting my life at risk. Then there's you, deliberately putting your *own* life at risk to save mine."

Lorenzo shifted, telling himself it was because of every ache and pain shooting through his body. He hadn't done it to make her move because she'd compared him to O'Reilly.

Objection, Your Honor. The witness is clearly lying through his teeth. Much as he wished he could allow it, it was sustained. He cleared his throat again. "Hey, I could've told you I was the nicer guy."

She lifted her head to smile at his feeble humor. It faded fast. "I'm sorry, Enzo."

She was. He could hear it in her voice, see it in her eyes.

He sighed. "So am I. I didn't realize…I thought you knew. You'd always understood me so well, I just thought you *knew*. That we didn't need words."

In his classes, even before a judge, he could always find the right words to prove his case—but he'd clearly chosen the wrong ones now. The uncertainty compounded in her eyes, and she shifted away. "I'm sorry. I should have. I guess. I…"

"No. That's not—I didn't mean it was your fault." Blast. He tried to push himself up a little against the mound of pillows, though every inch of altitude made the pounding that much worse.

He must have made some noise of distress, because she fussed over him, moving the pillow, soothing her hands over his face while he waited for the blinding pain to pulse its way back down. When his vision cleared, only worry filled her eyes—the last thing he wanted to see in them. "Oh, Sabina. Everything—everything I did was to keep this from happening. I never wanted you to face the violence of this life our fathers have chosen. I just wanted to rescue you from it. To spare that tender heart of yours any more pain." He hadn't wanted to see her turn into his mother, or hers, so careful about where they looked, so desperate not to see anything they couldn't bear. He didn't want her to be another Mafia wife, so strong and yet so broken.

But he'd broken her anyway.

His eyes drifted back to the Sacred Heart on the wall, the reminder of all Christ had done, His immeasurable love for mankind. He'd thought he understood what God wanted of him. He'd been so sure when he decided to pursue the law, to marry Sabina. He thought they could live out Christ's love together, change things for their families, build one of their own. They could show the next generation that you didn't have to steal and cheat and kill to survive—you could give and serve and love instead.

Maybe he'd been wrong. Maybe he'd been following his own base desires, not what God wanted for him. Maybe that's why everything had fallen apart.

"I miss you." How could words be so soft they barely reached his ears, yet strike his heart like hammers? "I miss talking to you, laughing with you. I know you don't trust me anymore—and you shouldn't—but do you think we could try to get that back? Pretend we're kids again?"

He averted his face, watching the sun's fire spill over the skyline through the window. Light washed over the world, but he felt only darkness, only the questions pounding in time with his head. *What if you were wrong? What if you were wrong? What if you were wrong?*

"Enzo?" Her voice was tight with more tears, stabbing him with new guilt.

If he *had* been wrong, then this was his fault. He'd destroyed something precious and beautiful by trying to force it into what was never meant to be. He'd hurt them both, and he didn't know if it could be undone. "Sure, Bean. We can be friends again."

He must have sounded about as convinced as he felt. She shifted away, and the mattress lifted when she stood. "Never mind. I'll just..."

"Sabina." She sounded so hollow, so hopeless that he couldn't help but look her way. He couldn't stop his hand from snagging hers to keep her from fleeing the room. If she left now, like this, it would be over. He'd thought last night that was what he wanted. But he couldn't, *couldn't* let her just walk away so upset. He would sort out later which step had been the biggest mistake, but right now he just wanted to keep from making another.

He linked their fingers together and met her eyes. "I want to be your friend."

If it brought her any joy, the message didn't reach her eyes. "But... nothing else?"

Did it even matter what he wanted? He didn't know if it was *right*. He didn't know if she still loved that cop who'd used her so ill, didn't know if he'd ever be able to look at her again without imagining her in O'Reilly's arms. And some invisible hand was driving an invisible spike through his skull. "What is it you want, Bean?"

She sat on the mattress again, but on the edge, barely perching. A timid little bird, ready to fly away at the first sign of danger. "What do *you* want?"

Despite himself, he smiled. It had been an endless game when they were kids. *What do you want to do? I don't know, what do* you *want? I don't know, what do* you *want?* He wanted to reclaim that—the beauty of it, the innocence. "I asked you first."

She drew in a breath so long it surely filled her lungs to bursting. "I…" The way she pulled out that single syllable told him that whatever came next was difficult. Heavy. "I want to keep your ring on. I want to keep making our plans for August thirteenth. And in the meantime, I want to start over with you. If *you* want to—if you can forgive me."

Did he? Could he? He didn't know. But admitting it was too cruel. So he nodded.

SEVEN

...wáre of a wórld where bút these |
twó tell, each off the óther; of a rack
Where, selfwrung, selfstrung, sheathe- and shelterless, |
thóughts against thoughts ín groans grind.

-Gerard Manley Hopkins,
from "Spelt from Sibyl's Leaves"

After making sure that Lorenzo was sleeping peacefully, Sabina padded into the hall and eased the spare room door closed behind her.
She jumped a foot in the air when she turned around and found
herself inches away from her mother. She threw a hand over her mouth to
cover the instinctive squeal. "Mama!" She kept her voice a whisper. "You
scared a year off my life."

Mama chuckled and patted Sabina's cheek. She, too, spoke in a bare
murmur. "I thought I heard talking and was coming to check on Enzo. Did
he wake up?"

"Briefly." Her shoulders slumped. "He's asleep again now. I figured I'd
go get the coffee started."

Mama nodded and turned to lead the way down to the kitchen. Sabina
followed, talking at a normal volume once they'd gained the cozy room and
turned on a light. She missed it in here—the well-worn workbench and the
old, scratched table, the comforting feel of the percolator's handle as she
pulled it from the cabinet. She missed the knowledge that she could create
a meal at the stove to satisfy the people she loved and make them smile.

This was home—the one room in the house that hadn't been completely remodeled, with more expensive furniture moved in. Sabina might resent
that the stalwart Sicilian woman whose one English word was "Cook" had
taken over, but she had at least given Papa an earful when he'd suggested
updating this room. Cook had made it clear that if his construction crew
touched her space, she'd take a wooden spoon to the lot of them.

Mama didn't seem to share Sabina's regard for the old, worn fixtures.

She scowled at the stove as if it offended her sensibilities and reached for the coffee beans. "How is Enzo?"

"He's still pale, and I could tell he had a splitting headache, but I imagine he'll be ready for breakfast in a few hours."

"Ah, good." As she cranked the handle on the grinder, Mama lifted her brows. "So? You talked to him?"

Sabina filled the metal carafe with water and put it on the stove, then picked up a box of matches. "Yeah."

"You told him you still want to marry him?"

It had taken every ounce of courage she had to say those words. "Mm hm." She struck the match and put it under the pot to light the burner.

Mama's motion stopped. Sabina could feel her steady gaze. "And? Did he agree?"

She squeezed her eyes shut, but that only made the look on his face that much clearer in her mind's eye. He loved her; he'd proven that last night. But would he ever trust her again, ever really forgive her? "He didn't *disagree*." She sighed, set down the spent match, and leaned against the counter. Exhausted didn't begin to describe her current state. She had snatched a few minutes of sleep here and there as she held vigil over Lorenzo through the night, but the quality had been as lacking as the quantity. Nightmares had stalked her, filled with blood and bullets and an empty, yawning future. "He isn't convinced it's a good idea."

"Of course it is. You've learned your lesson." Mama turned the crank again, stopped again, pierced her with those eagle eyes. "You *have* learned your lesson, right?"

"I have." The rising smell of fresh-ground coffee tried to comfort her, but even its magic could only do so much. Sabina slid over to the table and pulled out a chair. Her nostrils flared. "Mama, are you in love with Papa?"

The sound of grinding filled the kitchen again. "If I didn't love your father, I wouldn't be here."

"I know you love him. But I mean *in* love. You know, passion and fire and racing heartbeats."

"Ah, *cara*. I outgrew such fleeting feelings long ago. They don't last long in this world. Had I let myself be ruled by them, our family would be in tatters."

Sabina rested her forehead on the table, its cool surface too inviting to pass up. She felt like crying again and wasn't sure why. "But you did feel them? Once?"

She heard her mother open up the grinder and transfer the grounds into the top of the percolator. "Long ago, yes. When I was little more than a girl in Sicily, and your father was a young mafioso. All strut and big words." A smile saturated her voice. "In our hometown, there weren't so many opportunities as you have here. You either stole or were stolen from. You hit or were hit. The Mafia was sometimes the only protection we had. The government—" She made a scoffing, dismissive sound. "They were the worst criminals of all. But it was a small town. Not much to do, not much to make of yourself. So your father and Franco and Vanni all decided to come to America. They'd heard grand stories about the opportunities. I couldn't imagine a life without him, so we married, and I came too."

Sabina hummed out a sigh. "Very romantic."

"No." Mama's voice went stiff. "It was not, or not for long. For the first months, we lived in a shanty along the docks in New York. Twelve people stuffed in a small room, never enough food. Praying our numbers would be drawn in the lottery. Every penny we earned, the Black Hand would steal from us. Just like in Sicily, the authorities didn't care. 'Let the *dagos* kill one another,' they'd say. As if we were no more than animals."

The hatred in Mama's tone inspired Sabina to lift her head. She saw a matching bitterness in her mother's eyes. "It took a year before we got out of there, and we managed it only then because Manny and Franco made a deal with Lupo, offering to distribute some of his counterfeit money in Chicago if he would pay our way here. By that time, I was pregnant with Gianna, God rest her soul." She crossed herself, as she always did when mentioning either of the two children who had died before Sabina was born. "Once we were here, your papa got to work. Found ins anywhere he could, took them where they shouldn't be found, spilled blood when necessary."

Mama gave her head a sharp shake. "It was not pretty, Sabina, and not romantic. There were days I wanted to run away, but I had nowhere to go. Days I wanted to end it all, especially after my baby died in her cradle. Days I wanted to kill your father when he came home smelling like the cheap perfume of the women he had begun to sell."

Afraid she might be sick, Sabina squeezed her eyes shut and wrapped her arms around her stomach. "You've never told me any of this."

"Because I didn't want it to touch you." Her sharp tone belied her kind words. "By the time you were born, your father was in charge of three different bordellos, and he had used the money to buy this house. He wasn't a big enough threat to anyone to bring violence to our door like last night, but it was a steady income. It made it easy to turn a blind eye, to forget."

The sudden slam of coffee mugs on the countertop made Sabina start and tremble. Her eyes flew open to see that fury etched her mother's face. "And now he is competing with Torrio and the like. The government is bearing in on one side, other gangsters on the other. And you wonder why I have always pushed you toward Enzo."

Sabina's mind was too muddled to make sense of Mama's words. "What does he have to do with it?"

"Nothing." Mama spread her hands wide, her eyes wider. "Don't you see, Bina? That's the point. From the time he was a child, it was clear he'd be different. He thrived in school, he listened at church. He was never going to be a part of this world. The day he announced he wanted to go to college instead of join the priesthood was the happiest day of my life, because I knew it meant that one of us was getting out, and that he would take you with him. He will do anything to keep you safe—he proved that last night. He'll take you away from all this, he'll love you as no mafioso ever would. There will be no other women, cheap or otherwise. There will be no enemies to hunt you down. He will give you a *life*, Sabina, one untainted by fear."

In direct defiance of her mother's promises, terror skittered through her belly. Her voice came out as a scratchy whisper. "I don't know how to live any life but this one, Mama. Maybe that's why Enzo and I drifted apart. I don't know how to be anything but a mafioso's daughter."

Mama shocked her further by letting a few tears fall unchecked. Mama never cried—when something upset her, she just changed it. But right now, she didn't bother wiping the foreign droplets away. "Learn, *cara*. Please learn—otherwise you're going to make me regret every decision I ever made to stay here."

Feeling the weight of a far-reaching family on her shoulders, Sabina nodded. She would have to learn, if she intended to prove to Lorenzo that they could start over. She would have to figure out, somehow, how to let go of every connection he hated without losing the family she loved. But how? She couldn't see any paths through those brambles. Lorenzo didn't want to be beholden to Papa—but what was she supposed to do, refuse the gifts he gave out of love? Spurn him? He was her *father*, the one man in the world whose love she'd never questioned.

A man who ran bordellos and came home smelling of cheap perfume.

A man who had spilled blood—who, just yesterday, had walked out of jail after paying off people in high positions.

Her head was such a muddle she couldn't even see straight.

For a few minutes, the only sound was the happy, oblivious bubbling of the water in the percolator, then the sloshing of coffee into cups. Mama pushed one into her hands. "Tell me you'll try, Sabina Maria."

Her fingers curled around the hot cup. "I'll try."

❖

Lorenzo's key stuck in the lock. He jiggled it, tried to twist it, and succeeded only in making his head pound.

"Let me get it." Tony tried to elbow him aside—so gently that it was an insult—but Lorenzo slapped him away.

"I can open my own door." He had a headache—he wasn't an invalid. Though it had taken an embarrassing amount of time and two visits from the doctor to convince everyone to let him come home.

Mama's exaggerated groan sounded from behind them as she and Val finally reached his landing. "Those stairs! When we find you a house, Enzo, it will be one with a nice ground-floor parlor for receiving your poor mother."

In general, he loved "receiving his poor mother." Just now, he found himself wishing she hadn't insisted on seeing him home. "Mama, no one needs to find me a house. My apartment is fine." It would be years before he drew enough of a salary to warrant anything more.

Mama looked at him as though he'd suggested giving up pasta for the rest of his life. "Don't be absurd, Lorenzo. Parents always buy a house for their children when they wed—it is the way it's done."

In Palermo, maybe, when they could afford it. But it wasn't the way it was done *here*. "I don't want a house." He finally convinced the stupid key to turn and pushed open the door, standing aside to let Mama enter first.

"Of course you do." She turned the knob for the lights and bustled toward the small kitchen space. "And we have been keeping an eye out, Rosa and I. It is the bride's family's responsibility, of course, but as generous as Manny has always been with us, your father and I have set aside what we can too. You and Sabina will not have to knock around in this tiny place for long. It certainly won't do once the *bambinos* start coming."

Lorenzo blinked at his mother's back—she was already poking through his ice box and pulling out every single ingredient he had—and then turned to exchange glances with his brothers.

Val, of course, tried to cover a snigger. Tony, though, looked surprisingly serious. He closed the door behind him with a soft *click* and eased closer to Lorenzo. "Are you going to tell her you ended things?"

Lorenzo rubbed at his eyes. His head would never stop hurting. "I…"

"*Did* you end things?"

Leave it to Tony to see right through everything. He sighed. "I did. Before. Then…I may have agreed to give her a second chance."

Tony wasn't exactly frowning, but he certainly wasn't smiling. "*May* have? Do you *want* to or not? She played you wrong, bro. You don't deserve that."

"Don't I? I thought I was a *babbo*."

"Well, yeah. But you're the best *babbo* in town."

He breathed a laugh and gave in to the urge to sink onto his second-hand sofa. He darted another look toward the kitchen. Mama was singing in Sicilian, which meant she was cooking, though he had no idea what she had found to make. He didn't exactly have a fully stocked kitchen. Val dropped to the cushion beside him and propped his feet up. Lorenzo didn't even have the energy to chide him. He looked back to Tony. "I don't know what I want. But I guess—well, there's no reason to upset Mama with anything right now."

Tony just gave him a look. It required no words to interpret it—they all knew that if one didn't insist on something earnestly and repeatedly, their mother would simply steam ahead toward her own goals, chugging right over any minor objections. If he didn't announce now that the wedding was off, he didn't want to marry Sabina, he didn't want a house, there would be no *bambinos* to fill one, then the wedding plans would simply proceed. He'd find himself kneeling with Sabina at Holy Guardian Angel on August thirteenth with a new deed tucked in his lockbox and a list of approved names for their grandchildren mutually agreed upon by Capecce and Mancari parents.

He didn't have the energy for this. "I don't suppose you can pry her out of here so I can get some sleep?"

"Before she's spent an hour cooking?" Tony snorted a laugh and dropped into the chair. "Hilarious."

"Still can't believe you got shot." Val grinned at him and sent an admiring look to the bandage wrapping Lorenzo's head. *He* was the *babbo*. "And saving your girl. How could she *not* beg you for another chance after that?"

Lorenzo's frown deepened. Was that what it was? Not the fear of losing him, not genuine regret, but the tug of heroics? She'd compared his actions to O'Reilly's, after all. And hadn't Mama always said that every girl wanted a man who would be her hero?

That wouldn't get them far. She'd forget soon enough what he'd done and remember what he hadn't. Heroics couldn't bridge the gap of the last three years. It certainly couldn't undo her relationship with O'Reilly.

So why couldn't he make himself go interrupt Mama's song to tell her the wedding was off? Why had he nodded to Sabina's plea?

Val's elbow found his ribs. "You're doing it again, Enzo."

He flicked a glance at his little brother. "Doing what?"

"Thinking too much. I can practically see the gears turning inside that egghead of yours. You know what the problem is?"

Lorenzo quirked a brow.

"Tony and Joey didn't pound you enough when you were little. They shoulda punched you a few more times and knocked some of those extra thoughts loose."

Lorenzo snorted a laugh. "They tried."

Tony chuckled too. "He was too slippery. Always wiggling away and then running off to…"

To Sabina's house, just down the block. Lorenzo sighed. That was why he'd nodded, why he said nothing to Mama. He'd loved her too long.

A rap sounded on the door, bringing them all to attention. Lorenzo tried to tell himself to stand, but Tony was at the door before he could even brace his hands on the couch. It must not have been gun-toting rivals, because after a quick peek out the peephole, Tony threw open the door and held his arms wide. "Teo!"

Lorenzo was halfway up, but Val charged by and knocked him back to the cushion. He gave up and stayed there so his head could pound its way back down to a dull ache while his brothers greeted their cousin.

Mama danced her way out of the kitchen too, to greet her favorite cousin's son. She had a spoon still clutched in one hand, a thick white sauce clinging to it. "Teo, *caru*! It's been too long!"

Eventually, they parted enough for him to catch a glimpse of Brother Judah—not that his family ever remembered to call him by the name he'd taken when he took his vows. His cousin caught his gaze over Val's shoulder, winked—then his eyes went wide, and he pushed farther into the room. "Enzo—what happened?"

Enzo couldn't have answered if he tried. Val and Tony spilled the story, interrupting each other every few seconds. Mama had heard it all already, of course, but she still had to come press another kiss to his cheek and tell him he was a good boy before taking her cream-covered spoon back to the kitchen.

Lorenzo wondered how rude it would be to tell his brothers to scram so he could talk to Judah but decided he couldn't do it. Not today, anyway, when they were all here because they loved him and wanted to make sure he was okay.

Thankfully, Tony looked at his watch after not too many minutes had gone by and hissed out a breath. "We're gonna be late, Val. Better go. If you're okay, Enzo?"

"Go. Please."

Tony made as if to toss something at his head but then just waved. "*Ciao*, Mama! Going to work!"

"*Arrivederci*, Antonio," Mama called without leaving the kitchen. "Valente—behave yourself."

Blessed silence descended once Val shut the door behind them. Well, not silence—Mama was still singing in the kitchen. But close enough. Judah came forward with a wary shake of his head and took the seat Tony had vacated. "I thought I was coming over to talk to you about Sabina—I didn't know you'd been shot."

"Just grazed. It was the concrete step that really did damage." He lifted a hand toward the bandage but stopped himself before he could touch it. He'd already made that mistake enough times during his thirty-six hours at the Mancari house.

As always, Judah arrowed a glance straight into his soul. "That's not what's hurting you though. Did you want to talk now? Or…?" He nodded toward the kitchen.

Mama launched into a robust opera chorus, making Enzo's lips tug up. "I don't think we'll be overheard." He just didn't know where to start. The betrayal? The second chance?

No. He couldn't start with her. He had to start with himself. "Did I make a mistake, cos? Choosing marriage instead of the Church?"

Judah frowned, leaning forward to brace his elbows on his knees. "We had these conversations years ago—you were certain that you could serve

God with a wife, by raising a devout family. Absolutely certain. Why are you doubting now?"

Because he'd been so certain—and then made a mess of everything. It reeked of having put his own will above God's. "I thought I was respecting her, protecting her—but she thought I'd abandoned her. She…she turned to someone else, who turned out to be using her to get at her father."

"Enzo." Judah shook his head, and the lamplight glinted on the few gray hairs in his midnight hair. He was a decade older than Joey had been; he had actually been born in Italy. His family didn't immigrate until Manny, Franco, and Father had set up in Chicago and chiseled out enough of a life to offer security to all the cousins. Sometimes, in some of his vowels, Lorenzo could still hear Sicily in Judah's tones. It made him miss the place he'd never even seen. "I'm sorry. No wonder you're hurting."

Gingerly, Lorenzo leaned back until his head found the back of the sofa. "What am I supposed to do?"

"Forgive her." He delivered it evenly, with a lift to his brow that said, *You know this.*

"But does that mean giving her another chance?"

His cousin tilted his head to the side, the familiar light in his eyes. He liked a good debate as much as Lorenzo. "I suppose first we must ask if you're obligated to. You weren't married yet—but then, betrothals may not be the sacrament itself, but they're serious."

"Historically, they were considered marriage. Legal and binding." Lorenzo had always viewed it as such. Well, not legal—but binding, without a doubt. When he'd slid that ring onto Sabina's finger, he'd meant the forever that he promised.

"But there have always been valid reasons for ending things. Moses listed plenty—"

"'Because of the hardness of your hearts' though."

"Even Christ left room to leave when there was infidelity."

Lorenzo winced. "She wasn't—it didn't go that far." Did it? O'Reilly's bragging hadn't indicated anything quite that bad, and Sabina's shame hadn't seemed that severe. But did it matter, really? In her heart, she'd given to O'Reilly what should have been Lorenzo's. And either way, he had to forgive.

"Regardless, you could end it if you wanted. This is choice, not obligation. So as for your choice…" Judah chuckled and leaned back in his chair.

"I think it's pretty clear what you want to do. You're defending her even now."

"I can't help it. I'm a defense attorney."

Judah smirked. "That is *not* it. You love her."

Lorenzo sighed and listened for a moment to his mother's song. "What if I was wrong? What if I chose the easy way?"

"You think this is the easy way?" Judah gestured at Lorenzo's bandage.

A breath of laughter puffed through his lips. "Well…"

Judah tapped a finger to the arm of the chair as he studied him. "I think…I think there may be one way to the Father, Enzo, but there are many ways through our own lives. Many paths we could take. Is there a best way? Yes. And we should listen to the voice of the Holy Spirit so we can find that way whenever possible. But sometimes we misstep. And frankly, sometimes God remains silent. Sometimes, the path of trust and faith means making the best decision we can, stepping out, and trusting that God will take it and use it—continuing in the things we *know* are good and right. But also knowing that those things about which we doubt are often the ones God uses in the most profound way."

Continuing in the things we know are good and right. That meant things like caring for the poor, of course, but shouldn't it apply to his greater life decisions too? Perhaps he hadn't executed his decisions in the best way when it came to Sabina, but he'd been absolutely certain about his vocation as a lawyer and a husband instead of a priest. Judah was right about that. Lorenzo had good reason to question now—but to question his own wisdom or lack thereof, not God's direction.

He'd made mistakes on this road, without question. Missteps. Miscalculations. He'd hurt the woman he wanted to treasure above all. But he'd fasted and prayed for weeks before choosing this journey through life. He had spent countless hours in the quiet sanctuary, on his knees in adoration. He'd sought the council not just of Brother Judah but also Father Russo. He'd been so careful to make sure he could fully honor God, even as he loved Sabina.

He'd known true peace about his decision at the time, even though it hadn't been an easy path. A peace decidedly lacking now, when he considered breaking things off.

Ending things would not make him a better man. It would build a wall around his heart. Ending things without even trying to rebuild his relationship with Sabina when she'd asked him to would mean accepting no blame for his part of this fiasco. That wasn't who he wanted to be. "You know, Judah, you need to stop by more often."

His cousin flashed a grin. "If your mother were here cooking more often, maybe I would. Whatever she's making smells like heaven."

Come to mention it...it really did. Garlic, cream, parmesan—and she was even now cranking his little pasta machine in time with her song.

Maybe he wasn't so sorry she'd invited herself along after all.

◈

Sabina hesitated in the threshold to her father's study, her determination wavering. Papa sat behind his desk with a newspaper. The early morning sunshine slanted through the window, shifted through the rising steam on his coffee, and glinted off his full head of ever-black hair. From this distance, he could pass for a much younger man. His shoulders were broad, his arms thick, his silhouette one of power. It wasn't until one got close that the lines on his face became visible, chiseled out by hard decisions—and apparently hard living.

Sabina had questions for him—questions that had kept her up the past two nights, woven through her nightmares with flashes of Roman's smile and Lorenzo's oozing blood. She both needed and feared the answers. A minute ago, the need had been stronger, propelling her down here to catch Papa before he left for the day. But now that she was here, fear was quickly gaining ground.

Before she could spin away, Papa looked up, smiling when he spotted her. "Morning, princess. My, don't you look pretty today. Is that a new dress?"

She didn't even glance down at the blue-gray silk taffeta, though she had taken great pains in selecting it twenty minutes earlier. "I got it for my birthday but haven't worn it yet." She drew in a deep breath. "Do you have a few minutes, Papa?"

"For you? Always." He folded his paper with a rustle and set it aside. His smile was clear and easy, as if last week had completely faded from his mind. "Come on in."

His office was a work in wood and leather, all the highest quality. When the money started pouring in, this had been the second room he'd upgraded, right after Mama's favorite sitting room. The scent of cigar smoke always lingered, along with the musk of Papa's favorite cologne. She went over to his desk and perched on top of it in her usual place.

"Have big plans for the day? I can't imagine you got all dolled up for me and your mama," he said with a wink.

Sabina forced a smile. "I'm going to surprise Enzo later, meet him at his office and convince him to have dinner with me. I thought maybe we'd grab a pizza from Pompei's and take it to Arrigo Park."

Papa nodded. "That sounds good—it's a beautiful day for a walk and a picnic. It's been a while since you two have done anything together."

Though there was no condemnation in his tone, she still felt the censure. She flicked at the beading on her skirt.

Papa put a finger under her chin to raise it up. "What's bothering you, Bina? Something I can help with?"

Sabina drew her bottom lip between her teeth as she contemplated the best way to introduce the matters on her mind. "I don't know. Papa—do you want me to marry Enzo?"

His eyes widened. His brows lifted. "That's a silly question. You know I love Enzo like a son. If you love him, then nothing would make me happier. Why do you ask, *principessa*?"

She lifted a shoulder and ran her gaze over the shelf of books in front of her. Some of the titles were in Sicilian, some in Italian, others in English. They ranged from novels to philosophy to histories—and were mostly just for show. She could count on one hand the times she'd seen him reading anything but a newspaper. "It's just that I was talking to Mama the other day, and she explained why she's always pushed it so much. And when I was…seeing Roman. She always tried to talk me out of it. You never did."

Papa set his mouth for a moment, leaned back in his chair, and folded his arms over his chest. "I'm not sure what you're getting at. You know I didn't like the way you were treating Enzo. But at the same time, I want my *picciotta* to be happy. When I thought Roman might be better able to accomplish that than Enzo…" He held out his hands and shrugged. "The choice was yours."

"I guess I just wondered what you want for me. I mean, Enzo's made it pretty clear he wants a life apart from the one you and Vanni have. Roman, for all appearances, was trying to get into it."

"Ah, I think I see. Your mama wants you out—we've talked about it many times. But you were wondering if I shared her feelings, or if I'd prefer to see you with a mafioso."

She gave a short nod.

"There's no simple answer, Bina. When we're getting shot at, sure, I want you as far away from it as you can get. But you're still my daughter, so it's always going to be close to you—even if you're out. Just ask Enzo. And really, this life isn't so bad, not when you take precautions. We have a code. Even if you married a mafioso, you wouldn't be targeted. That's not the way we do things. Family is precious."

The remembered sound of bullets whizzing by her head screamed a contradiction, but Sabina bit her tongue.

Papa must have read her mind. His voice was a thrum, low and deadly. "Whoever dared to fire on me when you were so close breached that code. And he'll pay. Make no mistake about that."

"What about Roman?" she asked before she could stop herself. "While we're on the subject of payback, I mean."

Papa let out a long breath, steepled his fingers, and studied her. "He's got a free pass. This time."

The words were a relief, though she wasn't sure why. She could practically taste vengeance on her tongue and yet…her vengeance would never mean killing him. She was pretty sure her father's would. Which begged another question. "Why?"

The corners of Papa's mouth pulled up. "Enzo asked me to spare him."

Her spine went straight. Maybe she shouldn't have been surprised—but she was. "He did?"

"Mm. Didn't explain his reasons, though I can guess them. He tries to steer us away from anything illegal or immoral whenever he suspects it. And he'd be afraid it would hurt you more. That's why I agreed. And because I owe him—the fool wouldn't accept any payment above his standard legal fees." He shook his head with what looked like fond bafflement. "Actually—I should tell you now. I probably should have before. When you called him for me, he was furious. I'd promised him that if he pursued the law, we would never ask him to be a Mafia attorney."

Sabina's lips parted, but no words would come. *That* was why Papa had said, "not Enzo," that day? Not to spare her, but to keep a promise?

Was it anger that snapped inside her, or guilt? Or some simmering pot of both? "I didn't know." Why hadn't she? Why had no one *told* her of this agreement between her father and her fiancé?

She wasn't surprised that Lorenzo had secured the promise, now that she thought about it—now that she knew his strong convictions about staying away from the family business. Especially now that she had a better idea what those businesses were. But why, why had they kept her in the dark?

Papa patted her knee, chuckling like it was just some sweet little joke. "Of course you didn't know. He was angry with *me*, Bina, not you. He thought I'd made you call him. But we've straightened it out. After this is finished, we'll go back to our arrangement. I promised him that. If any troubles crop up in the future, I'll go to Darrow."

That pot of emotion inside her just kept simmering, despite his easy tone. Lorenzo would expect her to do this too—to separate the family from what the family did. But was he going to help her navigate how to do it, or leave her to bumble about on her own?

She scooted off the desk and turned to leave, though she got only a step before another ingredient in that pot bubbled to the surface. *What the family did.* She paused and turned again. "You really run bordellos, Papa?"

He answered with a quirk of his brow.

She shifted from one foot to another, fiddling with her beading again. "It's just…you raised me to believe in fidelity, so—so it seems strange you'd profit from…"

Papa reached for his coffee and took a careful sip. "Bina, things are different for men."

"Why?" When that eyebrow quirked again, she sighed with exasperation. "It doesn't make sense. I have a few dates with Roman while I'm engaged to Enzo, and no one questions his right to break it off because of that. And it's not like I—I mean…" She stammered to a halt, cheeks as hot as if she really were stirring a bubbling pot, but then she pushed on. "But what if *he* had been the one to have a few dinners with someone else—to kiss someone else? Would *I* have had the right to end it, or would everyone have told me I was being silly?"

The muscle in Papa's jaw flexed as he set his cup down again. "Bina, I know women are all about being equal with men these days, ever since you got the vote, but there are some things that will never change. Men and women are just made differently."

Tears threatened. Her hands fell limp at her sides. "So you wouldn't care if I married a man and then you caught him at one of your bordellos."

Papa's sigh said he was tired of this line of talk. "If it was Enzo? Yes, I'd be angry, because it would contradict everything he says he stands for. If it were Roman or someone like him, it wouldn't be a surprise. But there *is* a certain amount of discretion I expect. If he made a fool of you publicly, then yes, I would care. I would care very much. No one hurts my *bambina*."

No one? Then why was he doing it even now? A drop of brine spilled out of each eye, and she turned away again.

Papa's hands closed over her shoulders. He stepped in front of her and gathered her into his arms. "*Ti amu*, Sabina."

"I know, Papa." And she did. That had never, in all her life, been a question. Everything he did was for the family. When he said he'd do anything to protect her, he meant *anything*. She was just beginning to understand that. He would lie, cheat, bribe, steal. Kill.

It was love. But it was a love that suddenly weighed the world. Her shoulders sagged with it. "I love you, too." Her words emerged as a whisper, and she wondered if her love weighed just as much to him, to Lorenzo. A burden instead of wings.

A few more tears escaped her eyes on her way up to her room.

EIGHT

His step had a bounce as Roman made his way down from the elevated train platform and headed into the heart of the Loop. He had spent the early afternoon talking to Henry Jennings, and while the news wasn't as good as it could be, it was good enough. Which was why Roman had volunteered to take it to Capecce himself. A little gloating was called for.

A snarl in foot traffic forced him to slow down, and he drifted to a stop to avoid running into a woman badly in need of a corset. His eyes wandered to the storefront nearest him; his brow furrowed. Jewelry. Rarely did he notice the stuff before he and Sabina got involved, but she was always stopping to drool over some trinket or another when they were out together.

One time it had been a necklace much like the one in this window. Czech in design, a flower motif with some red stone making up the petals. She'd said something about how pretty it was, and he'd promised to buy it for her. As if he could afford to.

Temptation had flickered at the time. If he sold out, he'd be able to shower her with all the pretty baubles she wanted but never actually asked for—that was part of her charm. She had this way of appreciating a thing that made it clear she didn't need it or expect it. It was what had made him want to give it to her.

As always, he had chosen honesty. And as if to rub his nose in it, the next night he had seen some other well-dressed gangster's moll wearing an almost identical necklace.

Did Capecce feel the same tug to give her what he couldn't really afford? Was that why he'd sold out?

Which reminded him. He had a lawyer to torment.

Someone bumped into him from behind, a helpful nudge to get back to business. It was time to forget about Sabina—to tear his gaze from the diamond ring in the shop window that snagged his gaze and force her from his mind forever. The tune of "You Know You Belong to Somebody Else" spilled from his lips in a whistle as he started forward again.

The offices of Birdwell, Stein, & Associates stood in the heart of downtown, on prosperous North LaSalle Street. Gone were the dilapidated buildings of his own neighborhood, or even the hodgepodge of Little Italy, where the worn and tired were shoved up against the redone and rebuilt. Here, everything was scaled up and reaching for the sky, each building vying the next for height and style. His eyes traveled over graceful arches and intricate artwork in concrete and marble, contrasting colors and inlaid words declaring, "Money!" even more loudly than a building's name or number.

Roman's whistle turned to one of appreciation when he entered the proud brick building that matched the number he'd scrawled on a piece of paper. The sign proclaimed the law firm had existed since 1890. He knew for a fact that Stein, a German immigrant, hadn't been one of the title partners at the time, but still. Capecce must have been a heck of a law student to have found a position here straight out of school. If he worked his way up to partner in a place like this, he *would* bring in the dough, eventually. He'd bring it in faster, though, if he went crooked. He must have been impatient.

Well. Didn't matter how crooked he was, or how good a student he'd been. He wasn't good enough to get Manny out of this one.

Roman jogged up the stairs and flashed what his mother had always called his "killer smile" at the red-haired receptionist. She was pretty—very. The kind of pretty that should have made Sabina jealous, if she actually loved Capecce. The kind of pretty that would have made his own mother mutter in Sicilian and threaten to commit murder if she ever found a long red hair on Da's clothes. "Hello there, Miss..." He eyed her nameplate. "Gregory. Is Mr. Capecce in, by any chance?"

The young woman smiled demurely and glanced down at an appointment book. "He should be in his office. Can I have your name?"

"O'Reilly."

"Just a moment, Mr. O'Reilly. I'll go check." She rose, the sway in her walk bearing evidence of a figure curvier than her serge suit showed.

Roman shook his head. It was a crying shame that women were so bent on hiding their shapes these days. He was all for the slenderness that was in vogue, but *no* curves? Ridiculous.

The familiar scent of Murphy's Oil Soap teased his nose, matching well the tidy appearance of this outer office. On the walls hung a few framed newspaper clippings featuring verdicts that were presumably big wins for the firm. There was also a pretty decent painting of the Chicago skyline in the colors of sunset. He was still studying that when Miss Gregory re-emerged.

Her smile had gone taut. "Mr. Capecce's in the Point du Sable conference room. If you head back through the hall, it's the first door on your right. Can I get you some coffee or anything?"

"No thanks," he replied, not bothered by the cool tone of her voice. He didn't much care if Capecce had told her anything about him. He breezed right by her and turned into the conference room. Capecce was the only one present, though the number of files on the long table indicated that he was busier than one man ought to be.

The lawyer looked up only briefly as Roman entered. He wore a pair of spectacles, and his hair looked as though it had seen a few frustrated fingers jabbed through it. Roman smiled—then the glint of a white bandage at Capecce's temple caught his eye. "What happened to you?" Maybe he had somehow landed a punch the other night and it had just slipped his mind.

Capecce didn't answer but for a distracted, "Hm?" He kept writing on a pad of paper at a furious rate. After adding an enthusiastic period to the end of a long line of chicken scratch, he finally put down his pen and looked up.

Roman tapped his temple. "What happened to your head?"

"Oh." Capecce touched the bandage. He took off his glasses. "Nothing to worry about. Do you need something, O'Reilly, or are you just trying to give me another headache?"

Oh yes, he was going to enjoy this. Drawing in a contented breath, Roman hooked a toe around the leg of a chair opposite Capecce and pulled it out. He plopped down in it, then proceeded to pick up his feet so he could rest them on the immaculate tabletop. His mother would have boxed his ears and launched into a tirade about manners, but the lawyer didn't so much as scowl, which took some of the fun out of the position.

"I'm glad to give you a headache anytime, but as a matter of fact I do have a greater purpose for stopping by. It seems you weren't quite as successful on Friday as you thought. Charges of bootlegging are still being filed.

Granted, it'll only be a fine, but you're still going to have to appear before a judge."

Capecce sighed and pinched the bridge of his nose. "Well. Thanks for rushing over to tell me. Now if you'll excuse me, I'll go make a few calls before everyone heads home for the day. Did you bring the filing with you?"

Roman patted his pockets, pasting mock innocence on his face. "Oh, horsefeathers. Must've forgotten them. Guess you'll have to wait for Jennings to send them over in the morning."

Capecce muttered something Roman didn't quite catch, but the irritated tone brought a smile to his lips. He might have happily poked him a little more, but a new voice called Lorenzo from the doorway.

Capecce turned toward the door. "Did you need something, Mr. Stein?"

"Just saying goodbye. Heidi said to tell you she made your favorite cake, so feel free to come up this evening, son."

The young lawyer smiled. "Thanks, but I don't know when I'll have time. Apparently bootlegging charges are still being filed against Mancari, so I'll need to go tell him tonight."

Stein snorted. "Try not to get shot while you're there this time, will you?"

Roman's brows flew up, but since Capecce still didn't glance his way, he didn't say anything until the other man moved off again. He took the opportunity to examine the unease in his gut. Could be that he just didn't like someone else taking a shot at the man he had labeled *his* enemy, but it felt far too close to sympathy for that. He didn't like the kid—he didn't deserve Sabina, clearly didn't know how to love her right. Roman had spent more time than he probably should have over the weekend dreaming of landing a punch of his own on Capecce's nose. But he didn't wish him *dead*. Capecce was a hypocrite, not one of the Betsy-toting maniacs that destroyed lives.

"Shot?" Roman asked.

Capecce looked near exhaustion, which didn't delight Roman nearly as much as it would have a minute earlier. "Grazed. No big deal."

"Guess St. Lorenzo has more enemies than he thought." He had to work harder than he would have liked to achieve the scoffing tone that would keep clear boundaries between them.

"They weren't aiming at me. I just got in the way trying to get to Sabina, who was right beside Manny."

He wasn't going to ask. He wasn't. "Is she okay?"

Capecce's smile was small, sad. Roman cursed himself for revealing more than he wanted to. "Yeah. She's fine."

Before he could get himself in any more trouble, Roman pushed off and stood. "Well. I imagine I'll be seeing you in court after all, Capecce. Stay out of the way of stray bullets, eh? I want you in top form when I take you down."

"O'Reilly." Roman paused in the doorway and turned around. Capecce had stood, too. A few of his papers blew in a sudden breeze from the open window, but he paid them no heed. "Whatever's pushing you—this isn't going to help. Even if you had succeeded at putting Manny away, it wouldn't help."

Roman didn't so much as blink out of turn, even though a familiar face flashed before his mind's eye: laughing green eyes, Irish red hair, gleaming white teeth always ready to show off a smile. "I don't know what you're talking about."

Capecce sighed. "Play it that way, if you want, but you said something at the club the other night that made it pretty clear this fight is personal for you. Even if you win, it won't hurt any less. There's only one thing that can take that away."

Roman rolled his shoulders back. "Justice."

"No. Forgiveness."

He felt his lips pull into a snarl. As if he needed a homily from a hypocrite who'd socked him in the jaw in a gin bar. "Spare me." Roman strode back into the reception area and out the door without even pausing to flirt with Miss Gregory.

He jogged down the stairs, his mood spiraling with his altitude. He had a sudden yearning to turn back the clock, return to two weeks ago, when he had something to look forward to—the next time he could lure Sabina outside into the garden or convince her to join him for a meal. Or better still, if they joined Mary and Robert on the town.

No, if he was performing magic with time, he should go back a lot further than that. Take himself back to New York, when he'd worn a crisp blue uniform and a shining brass badge, when everything was right with the world. Back then, criminals were just criminals and good people were good people, and he didn't have to wonder who was who. It had all been clear.

Or maybe he'd just been naïve. Maybe the lines had never been where he'd thought them.

As he shoved out the door, the wind hit him in the face with what could only be termed homesickness. Not for the Big Apple, exactly, but for the way things used to be. For those green eyes that had shone with pride. For being the green kid who deserved that pride.

That had been a lifetime ago. No amount of anything would make returning possible—not wishing, not prayers, not answering the pile of letters ever growing in his miserable little apartment. No matter how guilty his mother made him feel for it, he couldn't go back. Not in time. And not to New York.

Too many ghosts haunted those streets for him.

He gained the sidewalk and turned to head back to the L, prepared to plow through any pedestrians in his way. He nearly collided with one after his first step.

"Roman!"

Instinctively, he reached to steady her; and once his hands were curled around her elbows, he couldn't convince them to let go. Sabina looked up at him with a strange mix of emotions rolling over her face—but she didn't pull away. "What are you doing here?" she asked.

"Business." The skin under his fingers was as smooth as the silk of the sleeve brushing the tops of them. "You?"

"Pleasure." She probably intended her smile to be haughty, but it was too wobbly around the edges. "I'm meeting Enzo. Let go of me, Roman."

Instead, he stroked his thumbs over her skin just so he could watch her pupils dilate in response. "Don't know if that's smart. Last time I obeyed that command, I got slapped."

She lifted her chin—her eyes flashed danger now instead of desire. "You deserved it." She focused her eyes on his jaw. "Though it looks like Enzo did a much better job than I did."

He dropped his hands and scowled. "He had an unfair advantage. He was sober."

A week ago, she would have laughed. Today she just folded her arms protectively across her stomach and prepared to step around him. "Good day, Mr. *O'Reilly*."

"Hey, wait." He took hold of her arm again, even though he wasn't sure what he wanted to say to her. He just knew it needed to be said, so he steered her out of the foot traffic and against the building. Then he realized what bothered him. "Why are you meeting Capecce, anyway? I thought you two broke up."

She lifted her perfectly sculpted brows. "Where would you get that idea?"

"I ran into Rob at the courthouse Saturday morning. He said Mary thought you were finally coming to your senses about him."

She rolled her sienna eyes. "Mary tends to project her own desires onto reality. No. Enzo's agreed to give me another chance." She held up her left hand in proof, though all he could see through her dainty little lace glove was the bulge where her engagement ring had always lived. "Not that it's any of your business. Now if you'll excuse me?"

He didn't move out of her path or even drop her arm. "Are you stupid, Sabina? You can't marry that guy."

"'That guy' is the best man I've ever known," she said with enough venom to turn it into an accusation. She tugged at her arm, but he refused to release it.

"No he's not. He's a blasted lawyer for the blasted *mob*." Something flashed in her eyes at that—a combination of guilt and anger that he couldn't begin to unravel on a busy Chicago street. Besides, there was an even stronger point to make. "You don't love him."

It was a mistake. He realized it the moment the words left his lips. She jerked her elbow free but didn't storm off. Rather, she poked him in the chest with an angry finger. "What do *you* know about love anyway? And who are *you* to judge me about who I decide to marry? I *do* love him!"

He glanced to either side to see how much attention they were drawing, but no one seemed to pay them any heed. Good. Still, he pitched his voice low. "Not like that. You're still in love with *me*, Sabina."

She spat a Sicilian phrase that painted a very colorful picture of her opinion of him. He grinned. His mother would love her—a thought he'd had way too many times. The Sicilian fire, the Sicilian dedication to family, the Sicilian obstinance. She'd have had one conversation with Sabina and started picking out names for grandchildren.

Sabina curled her hand into a fist, just like Ma did when she was barely hanging onto her temper. "I feel nothing for you but loathing."

She had to be lying—maybe she *wanted* to loathe him, but hearts didn't change that quickly, even when reason said they should. And her heart was his. He'd wooed it like her idiot fiancé hadn't bothered to do. He'd won it. He'd given her something she needed, and that didn't just go away. He lifted a hand to trace one of the waves of hair framing her face. "Well, I'm still in love with you."

She swatted his hand away, but that wasn't what surprised him. No, what really got him was the total disdain on her face. "Oh please. How stupid do you think I am, Roman? You pulled me into the middle of a gunfight."

"I acted without thinking." When that excuse did nothing to soften her expression, he tried again. "I knew they'd stop firing when they saw you."

"You threatened to kill me."

"Oh, like we didn't all know that was a bluff!"

She rolled her eyes and tried to push past him. He stopped her again, gazing into the wells of her eyes. He hadn't meant to fall for her—but how could he not? She was everything he'd tried not to want, everything sweet and stable. She was the kind of girl who cared more about a happy home than a night on the town. The kind of girl who deserved so much better than this world into which she'd been born. He let out a long breath. "Sabina…I'm sorry, okay? I know what I did to you was wrong, but you've got to believe me when I say that's not how I wanted things to end between us."

The apology achieved what excuses hadn't—her expression softened from disdain to exasperation. "Well how did you *think* it would end? Even if I hadn't been there on Thursday, it wouldn't have changed the outcome."

"I know, but…" At a loss, he stabbed his hand into his pocket. "I guess I hadn't thought about it ending at all. I was too caught up in it. Maybe I hoped I could take him down without you realizing it was me, that we could still run off together."

She stared at him as if he had taken leave of his senses. Maybe he had. "Roman—I'm not an idiot. I would have figured it out."

"Yeah, probably. But if I already had *my* ring on your finger by the time you did…" He reached absently to pick up her left hand, ran a thumb over that stupid diamond that had taunted him for months.

She shook her head and pulled her fingers free. "I'm not as forgiving as Enzo."

She prepared to move off again, which lit a burning panic inside him. "Sabina—you need to get away from this life."

She took a step to the side. "I will. By marrying Enzo."

"But he's *involved*!"

She took another step toward the building's doors. "No more than you. And only when it's to protect those he loves. *Addiu*, Roman."

"Sabina." He hated the plea in his voice, but he couldn't hold it back.

He couldn't let her walk away, even though he saw doom in every fancy bead on her expensive dress. "Please. I have to see you again."

Her spine turned to steel, her eyes to stone. "No," she said simply. And without another glance his way, she walked into the building. To *him*.

Roman could only stand there and curse.

❖

With a hand pressed to her fluttering stomach, Sabina paused just inside the door. That had gone better than she thought it would when she looked up into his familiar green eyes. She had handled herself well. Well enough, anyway. Now if she could just stop trembling, she'd push on with her plans and put him totally from her mind. Again.

"Oh, blast him," she muttered. Drawing in a deep breath, she smoothed her hair, her dress, and tried not to dwell on the absence of the hatred she'd been clinging to for days. She had truly expected to spit in his eye if ever she saw him again. But when he touched her, for a split second she'd forgotten all he'd done to her, to her family. She only remembered how he'd been the first one to really listen to her in years. The first one who seemed to understand how empty she felt after Serafina died. He had made her feel beautiful and wanted.

Well—she wasn't the first girl ever to have fallen for a snake. Lorenzo had inspired just as much passion once upon a time. They would find that spark again. "Enzo, Enzo, Enzo," she repeated to herself as she tapped up the stairs. "No Roman. Enzo."

She was familiar enough with his law office that it felt like a safe haven when she entered, breathed in that clean smell, and smiled at the receptionist. "Hello, Helen."

Helen Gregory looked up but did not return the smile. "Miss Mancari."

Her heart sank even as her brows lifted. "I thought we were on a first name basis." She had, in fact, never told Helen her last name.

Helen sniffed and turned back to the appointment book on her desk. "Is there something I can help you with?"

Her hands started shaking again, and her voice came out in a pathetic, meek little whisper. "Is Enzo still here?"

"Do you have an appointment?"

An *appointment*? Her throat went tight, and she had to fight the urge to just spin around and go home, back to the comfortable emptiness of her room and the ice in her veins. But then she saw Mama's face, heard Mama's plea.

She had to fight for Lorenzo, for a life with him. And if that started here with the firm's secretary, then…then she'd just mimic Mama's steel spine. Pretend to have strength until she felt it.

Sabina planted her fists on her hips and glared at the redhead. "I hardly need an appointment to visit my fiancé. Is he in his office?"

Helen picked up a metal file and went to work on her fingernails.

Sabina growled and decided she'd just answer her own question. At least Helen didn't try to stop her as she moved down the hall. She aimed for Lorenzo's small office in the back, but she paused when she saw an assortment of files on a table in the conference room, topped by a familiar pair of spectacles. She poked her head in and saw Lorenzo standing beside the open window, his hands in his pockets.

Her heart skipped a little when she saw him—joy? Nerves? "Hey there."

Lorenzo looked her way and smiled. "Hi."

Sabina motioned toward the door even as she advanced into the room. "Did you…tell Helen? What all's happened, I mean? She was treating me like an unwelcome stranger."

Lorenzo's eyes widened, and then he sighed. "I didn't. But she must have figured it out."

"How?"

He shrugged, his eyes sparkling with amusement. "I think she considers herself a Pinkerton investigator in training. Don't let her bother you."

Easier said than done. "Sure." She stopped beside him at the window. The warm breeze carried the scent of sausage from the vendor on the corner, which she breathed in with contentment—until she realized she could hear every word from the passersby below. She let out a long breath and looked up to see Lorenzo studying her. "You heard the whole thing, didn't you?"

His nod wasn't agitated, anyway. "I didn't mean to eavesdrop—I just came over to cool down after he left and—"

"You don't have to explain." Experimentally, she reached for his hand. His fingers gripped hers comfortably, so her shoulders relaxed. She grinned. "I probably would have eavesdropped quite deliberately had I been in your shoes. I just want you to know that—"

"Bean." He squeezed her fingers. "We don't have to talk about this. Really."

She almost relented, until she looked in his eyes and saw the unease hiding in the hazel depths. "I think we do, Enzo. If we're really going to start over, we can't have him between us."

He shifted his weight from one foot to another. "Look, I know we're supposed to be friends, open and honest, but—but, well, we *never* talked about the guys you were interested in, and—"

"Sure we did!" She grinned and moved so she could bump her shoulder into his companionably. "Don't you remember Benny Gustoff? I had the most terrible crush on him."

Lorenzo chuckled. "And you were all of ten at the time."

"Still. I was heartbroken when he gave a note to Mary on St. Valentine's Day instead of me."

He grinned, leaning into the wall by the window. "You cried buckets."

"And you held me and let me blubber for an hour. Then you handed me your handkerchief and said, 'The guy obviously has no sense if he had a chance with you and let you go.'"

"Mm." He looked down at their joined hands. "That applies here, too. O'Reilly obviously has no sense."

"So long as you do."

Their gazes locked, and Sabina knew well he was reading her heart. He hadn't bothered lately—or maybe she had stopped letting him. Maybe she'd felt so empty for so long that she'd just shut him out. But now she forced herself to stay open, to let him see her as clearly as he once had, even if it meant glimpsing those feelings she wished away. The flicker in his eyes told her when he'd found what he was looking for—that there was still something inside her with Roman's stamp on it. Something that *he* had brought to life again, when it should have been Lorenzo to do so.

It did no good to blame either of them for that. It was a fact, and they had to deal with it. Had to heal from it.

She forced a smile. "I'm trying, Enzo."

"I know." Surprising her, he raised her hand to his lips and pressed a kiss to her knuckles. "You did good out there, *bedduzza*."

The approval felt like rain in her parched spirit, and she soaked it in. "So, are you done for the day? I thought maybe we could go for a drive and then take a pizza to the park."

His face fell. "That sounds great, but I really have to talk to your father as soon as possible."

A month ago, she would have left it at that, and let the door close on her heart. Papa, not her. Always something above her. But she wasn't going to hide from him anymore, or let him hide from her. Maybe he never told her things because she never asked. "About what? Something to do with Roman's visit?"

Lorenzo nodded and ran his thumb over her knuckles. "The bootlegging charges apparently weren't dropped with the others, after all."

It was bad news, but the ease with which he shared it—that was a victory. "Those aren't that serious, though, right? Just a fine if he's found guilty?"

"Yeah, since this would be a first violation. But the catch is that he only gets one pass. If he's convicted again, it's guaranteed prison time."

She rocked back on her heels. Papa in jail for a night had been bad enough. Papa in prison? She couldn't imagine what that would do to the family. "Do you think you'll be able to get them dropped? Or get him off?"

He lifted a shoulder. "I'll try."

And he *would* try, she knew, even though he'd never wanted to be put in this position. Her heart skittered again. She loved him for wanting something different for them—but she also loved him for doing everything he could, now that he'd committed to helping. "Enzo—Papa just told me today that you'd made him promise not to turn to you. I'm so sorry I got you involved in all this. If I'd known, I never would have called you, except to ask you to recommend someone else."

He squeezed her fingers, and his eyes went soft. "I should have told you. It's my fault I didn't. *I'm* sorry I didn't see that protecting you didn't mean keeping you in the dark. I guess I'm more like our parents than I thought, in that way."

They were probably both more like their parents than they wanted to be. But there were good parts, too, of what they came from—like the way they always put family above all when it came down to it. "Still, the fact that you're helping Papa—I appreciate that. And I'm so proud of you for all this." She waved her free fingers at the conference room. "You're doing so well, Enzo, and even though I realize now that this isn't the kind of defense you want to be part of—thank you. I know he's done things he shouldn't, but I don't want my papa to go to prison."

He obviously understood that—he surely felt the same about his own father. And, praise God, he grinned, instantly lightening the mood. "If I can't get him off, he'll just have to consider a change in profession."

Sabina snorted a laugh and let herself relax. "Right. Well, Papa wasn't home when I left anyway. I don't think he's going to be back until about seven, so we could still take that drive. You could talk to him when you drop me off."

"In that case," he said, releasing her hand so he could drape his arm over her shoulder, "let's go." He grinned again and gave her a friendly squeeze. "Pompei's, right?"

"Where else? It's our place." Maybe reclaiming it would help them reclaim the ease they'd enjoyed running up Taylor Street together as children, their thoughts only on pizza.

If only things were still that simple.

NINE

The air was ripe with memory as Lorenzo strolled with Sabina through the park. Their woven fingers called to mind another day much like this one, a little over five years ago. It was her sixteenth birthday, and he had taken her for a walk during an unseasonably warm May afternoon. It was the first time he had mustered up the courage to reach for her hand, and when she gripped his in return, giddiness had all but lifted him off the ground.

Maybe, had he done it more often over the years—had he not been so afraid of how his body responded to the touch of her—time would have tempered that reaction. But he'd been so careful, measuring out each touch, weighing the risk of each embrace. Wisdom? Failure? Some odd mix of the two? Regardless, the result was the same.

Heat still filled him at having her fingers in his. And his heart still warmed when she tilted a smile his way. His pulse still tripped when they claimed a bench and took the first bites of their pizza, and she leaned into his side.

At some point since their engagement, she'd given up such gestures of affection. Only now, when she dared to lean into him again—when there was so much between them she was trying to lean across—did he realize it. Only now did he see how much she needed that physical comfort. How much he did too.

Once the pizza was gone, they took to the familiar path again. It wound out before them, the sky blue overhead, pink and purple toward the horizon. Too many people walked with them—and not just the neighbors strolling through the park, the parents chasing their children, the little ones squealing and laughing. No, they walked with the invisible specters of their parents, and of Roman O'Reilly. But most of all, they walked with the ghosts of the Lorenzo and Sabina of yesteryear, who had forgotten how to laugh together, who had let the world steal their joy.

"That's a serious face."

Lorenzo grinned to shake himself from his pensive mood. "I was just remembering your sixteenth birthday. We came here for a walk, and you let me hold your hand."

Sabina squeezed his fingers. "I remember. I thought you were just trying to make me feel better after Tony insulted my new dress."

"Oh, you give me *way* too much credit. My motives were purely self-ish." He glanced down at her perfect face. He knew it so well, had studied it so long, but still she left him in awe. It wasn't just the features she'd inherited from her mother, the dark eyes that went on forever, the rosebud shape of her lips. It was the fact that those deep eyes were always looking for how to help someone else. Those lips were always encouraging someone. It was the fact that she loved her mother's face, called her so beautiful, knew she resembled her but never seemed to realize it made her beautiful too. She took care of her appearance not for herself, but to please her family. Always, always that was what drove her. Family. Little G and Serafina—God rest her soul. Mama Rosa and Manny. She loved fully and deeply, from the inside out.

How could he not want to be one of the people she loved? To be *the* one that she loved?

She smiled up at him now, making him realize how little she'd done so in recent years. How had he not noticed? "Doesn't matter," she said. "It still made me feel better. You always had that effect on me. And it didn't hurt that Bianca Esposito, who had just moved to the neighborhood and thought she was the prettiest thing in the world, saw me strolling along with a college man."

Chuckling, Lorenzo tried momentarily to put a face to the name but gave it up. "I don't remember her. So she obviously wasn't as pretty as you." No one ever was.

"Sweet and blind, Enzo. You never noticed the other pretty girls."

"What was to notice? None of them had anything on you." They were quickly closing in on their usual exit from the park, so he slowed them down just a touch. He looked around, just because it was so true: no one else was as beautiful as Sabina. Not the trio of girls under the tree, not the mother pushing a pram, not the graceful woman there by the statue of Columbus.

Though his gaze moved on, it flew back to the statue. The woman under it. The two muscle-bound men lingering not far behind her. She was familiar. So were they.

Client? No. The vague image he had of her didn't involve either a courtroom or a conference room. What then?

"*Bona sira*," Sabina called, waving at the woman.

He relaxed, though not entirely, given the goons who came to attention at her greeting. They moved a few inches closer to the woman. "You know her?"

The woman's face lit up, and she lifted a hand too. "Good evening, Sabina!" Her voice, unlike most of the neighbors of her age, bore no trace at all of an Italian accent. For that matter, she didn't look particularly Italian—not that all of Little Italy really *was* Italian, of course...just most of it.

Sabina gave his fingers a squeeze. "Only to say hello. I see her around the park, occasionally at church—not at Sunday mass, that I recall, but if I go with Mama to light a candle or for daily mass, sometimes she's there. Why?"

"Just trying to figure out why she looked familiar—but that's probably it."

It wasn't though. He tried to catalogue her features without staring—she was probably in her forties, had auburn hair with a single streak of gray at the right temple, wore nice clothes, jewels around her neck.

He looked her way again—he shouldn't have. The two goons took a menacing step toward them, one of them putting a hand on his hip.

Sabina must have craned her neck around too because she gasped. "Is he pulling a *gun*?"

"Hush. They're not going to hurt you." He dropped her hand, but only so that he could slip an arm around her and pull her tight to his side. *That* was why they'd all looked familiar. Strange what made it click—but he'd definitely seen them before, and the taller one had made that same move the first time.

They hadn't been in Little Italy, though. He wondered if Manny knew the woman came here, spoke to his daughter. Went into his church.

Of course Manny knew. How would Manny *not* know what his own mistress did? He was the one paying for the goons, after all—no doubt they reported to him.

Still. Something didn't add up. Manny's goons shouldn't be fingering guns around his daughter. He was missing something.

And Sabina was clearly on the verge of panic. Her breath came too fast. She shook against him. Of course she did—she'd been involved in two gun fights in the last week. How would she *not* be ready to fly to pieces at the thought of someone pulling a pistol on her in the park?

He could only think of one thing to say to calm her. "They're your father's men."

"They're—what?" Her gaze flew to his face. He could feel it boring into him. "How do you know that?"

"I've seen them before. Once or twice. When I was with Tony and Joey."

There, her shoulders eased a bit against him. "You're sure?"

"Completely." No doubt if he looked over his shoulder again, the woman would be chiding them, reminding them who Sabina was. They'd beat a hasty retreat, not stick around to try to intimidate them away.

Sabina sucked in a long breath and expelled it slowly. "All right. Though if they're Papa's men, I don't know why they'd act like that." She sent a teasing look up at him, or a weak version of one. But he gave her credit for trying. "You must look really threatening today, Enzo. That bandage, I suppose."

"Must be." He flashed her a grin and steered her toward the park entrance. "And I don't think that crew is usually in this part of town, to know who we are."

If she gave it more thought, she'd probably realize the men were with the woman, and that would make her wonder who the woman really was—questions he didn't feel equipped to answer. He didn't want to fall into the old trap of protecting her too much, but he also didn't want to have to be the one to tell her this particular detail.

He'd slip into church on his way home later and pray for guidance on that one.

For now, he would try anything to bring the light back to her eyes. "I've always been the intimidating brother, you know. That's really why I had to bow out of the business—I just lit *too* much fear in everyone."

She laughed, and it tied a pleasant knot in his stomach to hear it. It had been too long since he had. "That's my Enzo—the brute of the Capecce family."

He grinned and led her to the exit onto Loomis street, content to let the familiar sounds of the city put distance between them and the scene behind them. And he left his arm around her shoulders—something he hadn't dared to do before. There came the awareness, yes, but far stronger was the desire to help, to give comfort. It wasn't, he realized with both relief and joy, about him at all—it was about her.

"If Joey had lived," Sabina said quietly as they were turning onto Taylor Street, "do you think he would have stayed in the business? Or gotten out?"

Thoughts of his oldest brother always made Enzo sigh. "I don't know. Isadora wanted him out, so he was looking for honest jobs before he signed up. But it was for her, not for him. You know? I'm not sure it would have stuck when things got tough."

"Mm. I feel so bad for her. Losing him, then her mother's illness— she hasn't caught a break in years. But she's always so...peaceful." Her brows knit. "I envy that about her. I say all the same prayers, I do the same things—but I...I've been so *empty*, Enzo. Since Serafina died."

"I'm so sorry, Bean. I should have been there for you. Talked to you about it all. I know talking through it with Judah helped when Joey died."

She tilted her face up toward his and looked deep into his eyes. "Did you struggle like this? With feeling empty?"

"For a while, yes." But he hadn't told *her* about that—that's no doubt what she was thinking. He'd turned to his cousin but not to the woman he loved, who had suffered so similar a loss of her own. His breath gusted out now. "It helped to realize that the words of the prayers, and even more the sacraments...they can do their work in us even when we're too numb to realize it. Because those words are meant to remind us of how we should be inclining our hearts. And those actions—they are *God* working, not us. Whether we feel it or not, whether we are aware of it or not, He's there. He's present. He's pouring out His grace on us."

Contemplation settled on her face, drawing a sweet little pucker into her lips, but before she could say anything more, someone shouted, "Bina!"

It was Little G, though Enzo had to crane his head around before he could be absolutely sure—his voice was deepening to match his height. He still looked like the little boy Lorenzo expected him to be, though, when he came barreling toward them, waving a book in the air. "Bina, look what I did today! Max let me do the whole thing—set up the press, run the pages, and even do the binding on this one."

He reached them, his chest puffed more with pride than running. "Look, look! It's not perfect, but I'll get better."

"G, it's beautiful!" Sabina took the book in her hands, running her fingers over the crooked spine and the gold-stamped letters that weren't quite square. "And the foil stamping? You did that too?"

"Yep." He grinned, turning it to Lorenzo too. "Pretty neat, huh? Max says I'm a natural at setting the type. This is just the proof, see—we have to check it over, make sure all the plates are right before we run the whole order. I told him I'd check it tonight. I have to go through every page."

"Cousin Max must trust you implicitly." She smoothed his hair back from his forehead and smacked a loud kiss onto his cheek. "I'm so proud of you, G. To think my baby brother has made a whole book!"

G's cheeks went pink, but pure pleasure shone in his eyes. "Shucks, Bina. It's not like I wrote the thing."

"And without printers like you, an author's work would never get into anyone's hands. Who is to say which is the more crucial? They depend on each other."

Little G accepted the book back from her hands. "Printers like me. You think I could keep doing it? I mean—you think Papa...?"

Sabina's face went soft. "I think Papa will be very proud of you, whatever you choose to do. Just look at how proud he and Vanni are of Enzo! And Mama—Mama would be over the moon."

G kept his gaze on the book, ran his fingers over the cover. "I'm his only son, though. If I don't follow him into the business..."

Sabina settled her fingers over his, on the cover. "You were born to create things, Giorgio. Ever since you were little, that's what brought you joy. Papa would never begrudge you that." She straightened, lifted her chin. "I wouldn't let him, even if he tried."

G laughed and ducked away when she tried to reach for his hair again. "Good—he can never tell you no like he can me." He pivoted toward the house. "I have to show Mama."

Sabina pressed her hand to her heart. "He's almost a man. How did it happen? My Little G."

Lorenzo was tempted to rub a hand over his own chest too. His sweet Sabina. "You really think he'll stick with it? The printing?"

Doubt flickered through her eyes as they started walking again, and he could have punched himself. But then it settled into determination as she reached for his hand. "I'll pray for it, for him, every day. Maybe God will grant that petition. For his sake."

Something in that statement needed to be dissected, perhaps cross-examined, but before he could give it the attention it deserved, Manny stepped through the front door and greeted them with arms stretched wide. "Bina, Enzo! It does an old man's heart good to see you looking so happy."

"You're far from an old man, Papa." She gave Lorenzo's fingers a squeeze before releasing them, and then moved over to kiss Manny's cheek. "I'm going to go get some coffee while you two talk. Enzo, do you want any dessert? I think Cook made tiramisu."

"Of course he does," Manny said, slapping a hand to Lorenzo's back and ushering him into the foyer. "We haven't had ours yet, either, so just tell your mother we'll all take it together in the parlor in a few minutes." As soon as she left, Manny turned back to him with raised brows and closed the front door on the beautiful evening. "What do we have to talk about?"

Lorenzo saw no point in wasting time. "O'Reilly paid me a visit this afternoon. The bootlegging charges are still going through."

Manny muttered a Sicilian curse and led the way into the parlor. "All right. What are our choices?"

"They'll probably offer to settle out of court if you plead guilty. You'll get a fine, that'll be that. Until the next time, when a conviction would carry guaranteed prison time."

Manny grunted and paced to the unlit fireplace.

Lorenzo took his favorite chair. "We can take it to court and hope you're acquitted. Based on what you told me the other day, you've got a pretty secure safety net set up. We could probably force the evidence to point away from you, but until I see what they've got, I can't know for sure."

"No good." Manny tapped his fingers on the mantel in a nervous tattoo. "There's still the chance we'd lose." He cursed again and rolled his shoulders, his face hardening into a mask that Lorenzo knew he rarely donned within these walls. This wasn't Giorgio, doting papa and husband. This was Mancari, Mafia boss. "What do I pay these people for if not to avoid these situations? Prison time, even in the future, is not acceptable."

"Then perhaps you shouldn't make a living through crime." He didn't *mean* to say it—it just slipped out.

Manny angled him a look more amused than annoyed. "We've never tried to change your inclination toward the straight and narrow, Lorenzo. Don't waste your time trying to persuade us away from the wide and lucrative."

Lorenzo hooked one ankle over the opposite knee and gusted out a sigh. "If this goes to trial, you might want to keep in mind that I have absolutely no experience in heading up a defense. I've been second counsel with Mr. Stein a few times, but those were all *his* cases. I'd hate to think that my incompetence could play a role here. Maybe you should consider hiring Darrow or—"

"Enzo. If you want me to take this elsewhere, just say so. I have not forgotten my promise to you."

Lorenzo sighed again. Maybe he *should* just let him take it to Darrow. It would be easier all round. But O'Reilly had made it personal. This wasn't just about defending a criminal. It was about reclaiming his girl. "I'll finish what I started. The agreement can be reinstated after this mess with O'Reilly is cleared up."

"All right then." Manny pursed his lips for a moment and then gave a decisive nod. "Well, there's no help for it. We'll just have to call the senator."

"Senator?"

"These are federal charges, aren't they? Then our best bet of getting them dismissed is to go to the federal level. As soon as you know the details of the charges, we'll give a call to our good friend in Washington. I helped get him elected, and if he wants my help again next time, he'd better return the favor."

"Right." Lorenzo pinched the bridge of his nose, wondering who he'd be calling next. He suddenly wouldn't have put it past Manny to be owed a favor by the president, too.

⬥

Sabina switched on a lamp that bathed her in a soft glow as she entered her room, humming. Over coffee and dessert, she had let her mind wander back in time, trying to remember what had really gone through her head in those first days when Lorenzo's intentions became known. In the beginning, she had been excited that Lorenzo, the smartest person she knew, the fortress in all her tempests, was interested in *her*. The thrill of being seen on the arm of a college man and the steady comfort of knowing that by his side, she'd be cared for every day of her life.

It had indeed all started on her sixteenth birthday, when his simple move of taking her hand made the day shine. Smiling, she moved over to her small secretary and picked up one of the few books she kept there. *Wessex Poems and Other Verses* by Gerard Manley Hopkins. Lorenzo's gift to her that day.

She ran her fingers along the cloth cover, smiling again at the joy that had been on Little G's face. Maybe someday he'd be printing copies of this book, or others like it. Maybe her table would be filled not only with books given as gifts, but ones pieced together by her own brother. It was a dream she hadn't known to dream for him, a prayer she hadn't known to pray. But she knew now. She'd light a candle every day if she had to—maybe this time it would make a difference.

Lorenzo had said God was there, at work, whether she felt it or not. But was He? For *her*? For him, yes, she could see the Lord at work. But maybe God just didn't regard her as highly as He did Enzo. *Jacob have I loved and Esau have I hated*, right? How was she to know who she was in the Lord's eyes?

Flipping open the cloth cover, Sabina sat at the desk chair and read the careful inscription on the end leaf.

> *To Bean, on your 16th birthday. They say that poetry is the language of the soul; Hopkins has always spoken deeply to mine. My prayer is that as you read these words, a chord is struck in your heart and you come to see, as I have, the glory of the Lord through the eloquence of man. Enzo. P.S. Read them out loud—trust me, it helps.*

She had sat down that very night to delve into these lauded verses—and had fallen asleep less than halfway through the fourth poem, the daunting "The Wreck of the Deutschland." Either out of intimidation or forgetfulness, she had never delved into it again, even if she had given it a place of honor by her stationery and her favorite fountain pen.

Maybe it was time to read the words he so esteemed. Maybe she'd find the meaning in them that he obviously had. This time, she decided to forego the beginning and that too-long "Deutschland." She opened the book to the middle, surprised to see a piece of paper stuck in the page written in Lorenzo's script. How had she not noticed this when she first opened it five years ago?

There were two poems on the page, the first called "The Leaden Echo" and the second "The Golden Echo." Before reading them, she scanned Enzo's note.

> *When I look at you, I see a young woman whose beauty surpasses any other. So you may find it strange that I think of you when I read these two, at least if you were to stop after the*

*first, which tells about how mortal beauty fades into nothing-
ness, even encouraging you to despair. But I think you'll understand once you read the second and see how it echoes every
cause for despair in the first with hope—hope in the Lord,
who offers an "everlastingness" of youth. Your true beauty is in
your heart, Bean, and it will be eternal so long as you entrust
that heart fully to the God who grants us peace in our days and
holds eternity in His hand.*

How had he...? He couldn't have known, of course, that she would
wait so many years to read this. That they would have had a conversation about beauty and peace on the very night she decided to open it. He
couldn't have known—but there it was. Proof of...what? Something bigger
than her, bigger than him. Sabina's hand shook as she put the note aside
and read. Her voice echoed softly into the room; and long after it faded on
the last word, she sat there wondering who this man really was that she had
determined to marry. A man who could praise her beauty and see beyond
it—a man who spoke of Almighty God as easily as she spoke of her father.

She read the poems again, becoming increasingly certain that she was
not what Lorenzo hoped her to be. In the five years since he wrote this,
what had she become? An empty husk. A woman so desperate for affection
that she'd turned to another man. A sap who believed every lie he spoke.
A daughter who nearly brought down her own father. A fiancée who had
broken the heart she should have been working all these years to know.

She slid the book onto her bedside table and reached for her rosary,
but even the words she'd learned as a child wouldn't come to her lips. He'd
wanted her to be that golden echo, full of light and truth and virtue. But
she'd proven herself leaden indeed.

* * *

"This place gives me the creeps."

Roman smiled at Cliff's observation as they sidestepped a street cleaner.
They were otherwise the only people out and about so early in the morning
in this part of town. Which was the whole point—maybe if they showed
up at Ava's Place early enough, the staff would still be hung over from the
night before and too groggy to see through his cover story.

He glanced around as they walked. The Levee had always struck Roman as a strange part of town. Traditionally, it was filled with the cheapest

housing and the filthiest businesses—the underworld at its worst. Upstanding folks would take care never to be seen here, though as home to most of the city's bordellos, many of the men made their way to its dubious charms after nightfall. But then a few mafiosi had decided to bring some class to their operations, and the result was a confused neighborhood that had dilapidated shanties on the same street as Colosimo's, a bordello, restaurant, and gaming house known nationwide for its solid gold chandeliers, gold and silver paneling, and velvet drapes.

Trying to operate on the paltry salary given him by the Prohibition Bureau, an apartment on the Levee's fringes was the best Roman could afford. And when he was working undercover with the Mancari operation, he had gone often into the heart of it with one young mafioso or another, out to prove himself. He had never succeeded at reconciling the ostentatious with the shoddy. But he had gotten pretty good at ignoring it.

His partner, on the other hand, who had not been undercover here for the past six months, had no such blind eye.

Roman elbowed his friend playfully in the ribs. "Aw, come on, Clifford. You're a man of the world."

"Not *this* world," Cliff muttered. "I can't believe you're dragging me down here. Why can't you be content with the bootleg charges, anyway?"

"Because," Roman said slowly, "Mancari is a snake. If he can slither out of them, he will. I want to be ready with more ammunition. Right now all we have solid evidence of is one speakeasy. I want to pin him down on the cabaret house we all know he owns, the brewery that is more than likely his, the other gin bars, and anything else he's tied to."

Cliff released a blustery sigh and looked up into the clear June sky. "Roman, we've spent six months trying to get all that information. When are you going to face that he just covers his tracks too well? When are you going to let it go and be content with what we've got?"

Roman clenched his teeth for a long moment before responding. "When we get called off, that's when. As long as they keep us in Chicago, I'm going to be hunting this guy down. If the bosses in Washington don't like it, they can send me somewhere else."

"You've let this get way too personal, O'Reilly."

Roman snapped his head in his so-called friend's direction. "Excuse me?"

"You heard me." The other agent lifted his brows in a challenge, his blue eyes glinting like a stormy sea. "This isn't about justice for you anymore, if ever it was. It's about bringing down the people that bested you and proving to Sabina that you're the better man."

Roman pivoted and poked a hard finger into Cliff's shoulder, halting his forward movement. "Hey, this has *nothing* to do with her."

"Yeah, right." Cliff brushed off his jacket as if it had been soiled by Roman's anger. "That's why you're so set on bringing down Lorenzo Capecce, who you were always willing to admit had nothing to do with anything?"

Roman shook his head and started walking again. "He has something to do with it now. He's defending the man, isn't he? And his father and brothers are even more involved. Bet we can get quite a few citations on them."

"He's a defense attorney!" When Roman didn't reply, Cliff mumbled a mild curse and rolled his eyes. "You're obsessed. You know that, right? Obsessed and spiteful. There's no reason in the world to go after his brothers except spite—we all know they're of no interest to the Bureau. They want the guys in charge, not the barkeeps or bouncers."

"Val's a runner, too."

"You've got no proof of that."

Irritation pulled Roman's fingers into fists. "He went out to the brewery, didn't he?"

"Yeah, so did you. And according to your report, all he did was hand over an envelope, the contents of which you hadn't seen, and then leave. You didn't see him ever transport liquor—heck, you didn't even see that there was any contraband in the place. For all we know, they could really be making that non-alcoholic swill they say they are, *and* it could really be owned by the ninety-year-old German whose name's on the deed."

The failure burned him up, but he'd sooner pull his own fingernails off than admit it. "You know, Cliff, you're starting to sound like you're turning. Giving up on the mission. Where are your priorities?"

Cliff stopped him with a merciless grip on his shoulder and spun him around. His aristocratic features were schooled into a granite mask of pure fury. "You wanna talk priorities, pal? I'm not the one carrying a torch for the old man's daughter."

"I'm not—"

"Oh, just shut up! You think I don't know you that well? We've been working together for two years, I *know* you. You're in too deep, you've lost your perspective. You're in love with the daughter of a mafioso, and you don't know whether you want to spite her or win her back. And until you figure it out, maybe you oughta just sit back and cool off instead of dragging me into the stinkin' Levee at nine in the morning to interrogate a prostitute."

Roman's mouth cracked into a grin. "You do look a little out of place, I gotta say."

Mumbling something incoherent, Cliff shoved his shoulder and started moving again. It didn't take much longer for them to reach their destination. Ava's Place was one of the better-looking buildings in the neighborhood, a pristine white against the red and brown crumbling bricks around it. It was one of those joints that offered it all: singers, dancers, food, and alcohol on the main floor, gaming in the back, entertainment of a more intimate sort upstairs. Roman had wandered in once a few months back, not realizing it was Manny's. Had he known, he would have paid far more attention to the details and far less to the high-caliber celebrities socializing in the restaurant.

"How are we going to get in?"

Roman's answer was to push open the door and hold out a hand to usher Cliff in first. He shut the door behind him once he had followed. The interior was dim, the scent of tobacco clinging to the brocade drapes and oriental rugs. Roman looked around for signs of life, finally spotting movement back the hall. "Excuse me."

A spindly man poked his head out the door of what was presumably an office, his long face pulled into a frown. "Yes? I assume you know we're not open right now."

"That's why I'm here. Manny said this would be the best time to copy down a few things from the books he wants for his personal records." Roman was careful to keep his face neutral, casual.

The man's face didn't relax. "I'm sorry, I—"

"Tom?" came a female voice from the staircase just past Long Face. "Were you talking to me?"

"Oh. No, Ava, I was talking to…I'm sorry, who are you?"

Roman opened his mouth to answer, but his vocal chords froze when Ava stepped into view. Her hair was a rich auburn with a single streak of gray, her figure full and unabashedly displayed by a tight-cinched dressing gown. But that wasn't what stopped him. It was her face—not the features or the grace or the beauty, but the familiarity.

He knew her. And it took only a second to figure out where he knew her *from*. With a quick spin away, he grabbed Cliff's arm and dragged him the five feet back to the door. Still he heard her shout from behind him, proving she had recognized him, too. He ignored her command to wait and chugged out the door, onto the street, and down the first alley that came to hand.

Cliff cursed as he jogged beside him, obviously agitated. "What? What in the world just happened? Where are we going?"

A savage grin bloomed on Roman's lips. "To pay a visit to the local cops. I think we just nailed Manny for murder."

TEN

Wert thou my enemy, O thou my friend,
How wouldst thou worse, I wonder, than thou dost
Defeat, thwart me?

-Gerard Manley Hopkins,
from "Thou art indeed just, Lord, if I contend"

For a long moment, Sabina stood before the closed door and debated. What were the chances that Isadora would be home and Mary out? Guilt washed over her for wanting to avoid her friend, but what could she say? She needed some advice, and Isadora was far more likely to have the sound kind. With a sigh, she shifted the basket she held and knocked on the door to apartment 2B.

Mary opened it with her usual bright smile and dashed all such hopes. "Bina! Thank heavens, a distraction. Come on in. Say, is something wrong?"

Their apartment smelled like cleaner and medicine—a sharp contrast to Mary's smile. A low moan came from behind the closed door to the right of the small living area, which Sabina knew was Mr. and Mrs. Bennato's bedroom. Her eyes tracked that way before flicking back to Mary. "How's your mother?"

Mary didn't answer. Just held her gaze for a moment, long enough for Sabina to see the war going on somewhere deep inside her. Then a switch flipped, and the smile reemerged. "Ask Izzy. What's that?"

"Oh." Sabina held out the basket. "I sweet talked Cook into letting me into the kitchen so I could practice my pastry crust. I thought maybe you all would enjoy the results."

What she'd actually thought was that it wasn't fair that they had a cook and a maid and wasted enough food to feed an army, while her friends had a mother wasting away, a father who never bothered coming home, and, as far as she knew, no money to spare on anything beyond the necessities. When she'd explained to Cook that she wanted to make something for the Bennatos, the terrifying little woman had actually patted her cheek and said—in Sicilian, of course—that she was welcome in the kitchen any time.

Mary lifted the napkin covering the food, let out a squeal, and snatched up one of the warm *genovesi*. Sabina had to press her lips against the smile as Mary took a huge bite. Powdered sugar clung to her lipstick, the custard filling oozed out, and for one blissful moment, they were kids again and everything was right with the world.

Mary laughed and licked the custard from the corner of her mouth, then the sugar from her fingers. "I don't have to share these, right?"

Right on cue, the door to her mother's bedroom eased open, and Isadora slipped out. Given the expression on her face, she was probably ready to chide Mary for her squeal—Sabina had witnessed the tension between the sisters many times—but when she spotted Sabina, she smiled instead. And eyed the pastry in Mary's hands. "Is that *genovesi*?"

Mary made a show of holding the basket to her chest. "Mine. All mine."

In days gone by, Isadora would have gone along with the joke, argued for her share, perhaps even pretended to wrestle her sister for the treat. But those were the days when she didn't have shadows under her eyes as dark as the ones Mary smudged on with kohl, when her face wasn't as pale as the plaster behind her. She padded closer but didn't reach for a pastry. She just offered Sabina a tired smile. "That was thoughtful of you. Thank you."

Poor Izzy. And Mary. They reacted so differently, but both were just *reacting*. That's all life could be for them right now. How well Sabina knew the feeling. She smiled back. "I made way too many—I didn't realize Cook's recipe was meant to feed the whole village. What to do but share?"

"Here." Mary shoved one at her sister and then spun into their tiny kitchen. When she opened the icebox, Sabina tried to see what else was inside without making it obvious that she was looking.

The shelves were empty. *Empty*. Her heart clenched. They needed more than pastries, and she'd have to see what she could do about that. It would be too obvious if she showed up with a whole meal, but it would only take a few whispered words to a few busybodies, and all of Taylor Street would soon be dropping by.

That's what a village did, after all. Once they knew it needed doing.

She refreshed her smile and moved her gaze from Mary to Isadora. "Do you have a few minutes to visit, or…?" She glanced at the closed bedroom door.

Isadora nibbled at the treat and looked over her shoulder. "She's resting for now. I shouldn't leave her for long, but she'll be all right for a few minutes."

Mary hurried back out, taking Sabina by the wrist and tugging her toward the other bedroom. "I was just about to do my eyebrows. We can do yours at the same time."

Sabina let herself be pulled toward the room Mary and Isadora shared, but not without objection. "Touch my eyebrows and I'll be forced to break every one of your fingers, Mary."

Laughter filled the hall. "Oh, come on. It's all the rage. If you pluck them out, you can draw them on however you like. Don't you want a higher arch?"

Even Isadora's chuckle sounded exhausted. "Stand firm, Sabina. Your arch is beautiful."

"Oh, what do you know, Izzy? You won't even bob your hair."

"I like my hair long."

"And I like my eyebrows, thank you very much." Sabina pulled free of Mary's grip and sat down on her bed.

Mary slid onto the rickety stool of her vanity and picked up her tweezers. "I'll get you both fashionable one of these days, you just wait and see." Leaning close to the mirror, she met Sabina's reflected gaze. "Izzy told me about the ambush the other night. Is Enzo okay?"

"Still getting headaches, but otherwise he's fine."

"Good. I'd hate to think of him starting his new single life with an injury."

Sabina sucked in a breath and looked to Isadora for support. "About that. I'd appreciate it if you wouldn't go around telling people that we broke up."

"Why not?" Had she had eyebrows, Mary would have lifted them. "It's true, isn't it? Izzy said he came over to break up with you."

Isadora sighed and leaned back against the wall at the head of her bed, closing her eyes. She looked as though she might fall asleep just like that, if given half a chance. "I also said he took a bullet for her, so I didn't know where things stood now."

When Mary turned around, expectation covering her face, Sabina had to force herself to look into her eyes. "It's not fully settled, but he agreed to give me another chance."

"Bina!" Mary tossed her tweezers back on the vanity. "Why in the world would you *want* one? He's boring, he's self-righteous, he's—"

"A good man. I was terrified when I thought I lost him, Mary, can't you understand that? I had a lot of time to think while I was sitting up with him that night, and it made me realize what a huge mistake I'd made. How much I wanted to make things work with him. How...how ashamed I was of what I'd become. Sneaking out, going to gin bars, carrying on with Roman like I'd done." She shook her head, heat stinging her cheeks again at the thought.

A thunderhead clouded Mary's eyes. Sabina hadn't meant it as an indictment of her—but it probably sounded that way. "It was just a little fun, Bina. And after the way he's ignored you all these years, you *deserved* a little fun."

Isadora stiffened. Sabina had the feeling this wasn't just a conversation about her, but one the sisters had been having for who-knew-how-long about their own choices. She'd have to tread very carefully. "That's what I wanted to believe. But the cost—it was just too high. My bad judgment nearly got my father put away for life. If any of these charges stick, that's on me." She splayed a hand over her heavy heart. "I have to live with that."

Mary moved to sit beside her on the bed, took her hands. "I get that. I do. But I saw the way Roman looked at you, and it wasn't for show, pussycat. I swear it wasn't. There's something there—and the way you lit up with him! You came to life again. Can't you see? If you go back to Enzo, you'll just fade away again, and I can't let that happen."

"It won't." She looked deep into Mary's eyes, begging her to see the truth. "I promise it won't. We've talked through it, we know where we misstepped before. It'll be different this time."

"No. He'll be just like he always is, and you'll just *let* him, like you always do." Mary shook her head, something a bit wild in her eyes, and pushed to her feet. "Why didn't he just become a priest, like everyone thought he would? That's where he belongs—taking vows like his cousin Teo, engaging in all that stuffy talk all the time. Why'd he have to drag *you* into all his nonsense?"

Sabina tried to swallow, but her throat felt swollen.

"He loves her." Isadora's words were quiet but sure. "He's always loved her. Joey said that was why he wanted to go to college instead. So he could marry her someday. It was all for her, always for her."

Sabina felt a flush steal through her—and then overheat her. It was heady, to think he'd loved her so much, for so long...but it was heavy too. Lorenzo had always taken matters of faith so much more seriously than anyone else in their families. It was no great thing for their mothers to go to daily mass and confession every first Friday like clockwork, but she remembered the way his brothers had mocked him for doing the same when he was no older than G.

The faith, the call to serve—that had been everything to him. Had he really given it up for her?

She hadn't ever thought about it in quite those terms. She'd only been fifteen when he announced he was going to college. Sixteen when she realized he was courting her. Eighteen when he slid that diamond onto her finger and promised her a lifetime together.

She twirled it around her finger, watching the spots of light dance over the walls of Mary's side of the room, with her posters and theater programs tacked up. Isadora's side had nothing on the wall but the cheap tin crucifix that had been there forever.

Did Enzo regret choosing her? Was that why he'd hesitated when she asked for another chance? Was it about far more than her bad choices with Roman?

Maybe *that* was why her prayers all these years had gone unanswered. Maybe God dealt harshly with *puttanas* who lured His chosen priests away from their vocations. Maybe God was so real and present to him because he was chosen for something special, called to sainthood—and maybe He would never extend the same to Sabina.

Mary huffed. "He doesn't love her. He wants to change her."

"No." Isadora's proclamation was soft, but it resonated deep inside Sabina's heart. "He may want her to change—for her own sake, for the good of her soul. He may want her to leave behind the behavior that got her into this. But that doesn't mean changing who she *is*."

Didn't it? When she read that poem last night, she hadn't been so sure. Lorenzo talked about the inclination of the heart; those poems talked about a beauty that stretched into eternity. She was only a woman—not a saint. A woman whose heart had been cold as ice for so long. What if she could never stretch beyond who she was now? What if she could never figure out how to walk the line between Enzo and Papa, God and the Family?

What if she spent the rest of her life disappointing all the people who mattered most?

❖

The old clock on the cabinet of the police station ticked into the silence, effectively measuring the disbelief of the homicide detective before whom Roman and Cliff sat. Detective Bannigan eyed Roman with a gaze shared by all good cops—measuring, probing, wary, and more than a little cynical. Roman didn't blame the guy for the doubt that oozed from his posture—he would have shared it had he been on the other side of the desk.

He'd used that look himself whenever some joker waltzed in with a cockamamie story and wild accusations. A few years ago, he'd have been the one tapping a finger to his stained blotter, trying to weigh information against gut instinct and reason. He'd have been the one looking from the tired old clock on the cabinet to the busy bullpen full of friends and strangers, cops and criminals. He'd have been the one debating whether this case would make or break his career—see him promoted or send him into a gutter with a gangster's bullet in his head.

"So let me get this straight." Bannigan waved a finger in a circle, glancing from Cliff to Roman. "Two months ago you were out at an illegal bar with a known gangster. When you were there, you saw a prostitute come in on the arm of another known gangster who ended up dead later that night. So you assume that the gangster *you* were with is responsible because you just realized the other one's moll is really his?" The detective leaned forward, his eyes bright with mockery. "Son, you've got imagination, I'll give you that, but you're sorely lacking in common sense if you think we can make an arrest based on evidence as flimsy as that."

Cliff sent him an I-told-you-so look, which Roman ignored. He leaned back in his uncomfortable chair, projecting an air of supreme ease. "You left out a few key details that make it slightly *less* flimsy, but I'm well aware that it's a stretch right now. Let's call it a gut instinct."

Bannigan snorted and shuffled some papers on his desk, as if Roman's theories weren't even worth his full attention. "No offense, but you Prohibition boys aren't notorious for your killer instincts."

Roman shrugged off the too-accurate insult. "Maybe not, but I come from a family of good, old-fashioned Irish cops in New York. I was on the fast-track to detective before I decided to join the Bureau instead. Maybe you can give me a little credit for the badge I wore before this one, the one my father and grandfather wore too."

The bid for camaraderie earned him only a sigh. Perhaps there was a slight softening in Bannigan's rock-hard eyes, but that could have been wishful thinking. "Listen, O'Reilly. The political climate right now doesn't much lean toward pinching the guys who bring liquor into the city. I'd think you'd have learned that after last week's fiasco that had your name splashed in the papers. If you're not careful, the Mafia will run you out of town, and you'll be lucky if you're alive when they do it."

Roman hid his clenched fist under the edge of the desk. "I'm not talking about bathtub gin or cheap hooch, Bannigan. I'm talking about murder. Think about it, will you? This dame isn't one of your run-of-the-mill hookers anymore. She's got her own place, which means she can afford to be picky about her clientele. As Manny's moll, she's *not* going to be out on the town with his rival, not unless he tells her to be. And she certainly wouldn't show up with him at the very bar where Manny's sitting in the shadows."

Bannigan ran his tongue over his top teeth. "Not if she knew Manny was there."

"She knew. As soon as she came in, she looked right at him, even though we were practically hidden at a back table. Looked at him and smiled, nodded a little. I thought at the time it was just someone who knew him, maybe even someone who usually worked the joint. Now that I know who she is, I think it was planned. Maybe she was pumping the guy for information or something, I don't know. What I *do* know is that later that night, Manny sent me on a useless errand. That was about the time Eddie was killed. And it didn't take Manny too long to start making runs out to Eddie's brewery, probably taking over his operations, which sure lends a suspicious light to it if you ask me."

"Even if you're right, and I'm *not* saying you are…" Bannigan frowned and tapped that contemplative finger on his stained blotter. "It's still not enough, and I don't think we can get any more. When we heard the rumor of Manny taking over Eddie's brewery, we obviously started looking at him for the murder. We already checked all the leads we could find, and they got us nowhere. Knowing this prostitute was with the guy might back up a theory, but let's be realistic. She ain't gonna talk. And unless she talks, she's no help."

Not good enough. Roman sat up straight again in his chair and tapped his own finger to the desk. "She knows something, though. The way she reacted when she recognized me—"

"Could have been outrage at realizing that a mole was standing in her hallway."

Roman scowled at Bannigan. It was time to play his trump card. "According to the papers, one of the only pieces of evidence found with Eddie's body was a necklace of undisclosed design, is that right?"

Looking for all the world as though he were thoroughly bored, Bannigan leaned back in his squeaky chair and nodded.

Roman held the other man's steady gaze. "I bet I can tell you what that necklace looked like. Czech in design, or a good imitation. Red stones—could be garnets, could be rubies, couldn't tell from the distance. Heavy gold chain. Three connected pendants shaped like flowers. Pretty large, rather bold. Hit the lady about here," he said, drawing a line a few inches below his clavicle, "whatever length that would translate to."

Bannigan didn't move for a long moment, other than the pulsing muscle in his jaw. "I assume you saw this necklace on the prostitute." At Roman's nod, he continued. "I gotta ask. Why in the world would you remember something like that two months after the fact?"

Roman had a feeling the detective wouldn't allow him to chalk it up to amazing investigative skills, so he opted for the truth. "My girl had been eyeing something similar the day before, so it struck me when I saw it on Ava."

For the first time since they entered the bull's office, Bannigan's mouth cracked into a grin. "That's the one thing you've said that makes sense, O'Reilly. Unfortunately, it also proves a different point—that design is pretty common for Czech jewelry. Trust me, we already looked into it."

"But put together with—"

"All the other circumstantial evidence you've got? If that was the caliber of your evidence for the charges you shot at Manny last week, it's no wonder he's walking the streets again."

Roman forced himself to hold his temper in check, though it was a challenge. "He's on the streets again because of the politicians in his pocket. Look, just give me a chance to prove my theory. Now that I know who was with Eddie, I think I can put some other pieces together for you. I'm not asking you to expend any manpower on this, I'm just asking for your go ahead, since it's your jurisdiction."

"And what about your bosses? They wouldn't mind you chasing a few wild geese on their dime?"

Roman gave him a crooked smile. "Come on, Bannigan. The Bureau isn't exactly famous for the tight rein it keeps on its agents."

Bannigan snorted a laugh and leaned forward again. "Okay. You wanna look into this, go ahead. Just be careful not to interfere with my guys—and bring anything you find straight to me. Politicians aren't the only ones in Manny's pocket, if you get my drift."

Roman nodded, stood, and held out a hand. "I'll check in again in a week."

Bannigan gave Roman's hand a squeeze hard enough to serve as a warning. "Fine. Just be careful out there, O'Reilly. I don't want to have to be investigating your homicide next."

Cliff grunted his agreement as he sidestepped his chair. "Or mine. Don't worry, detective, I'll keep him from doing anything too stupid."

Bannigan's chuckle followed them away from his desk.

Outside, Cliff drew in a long breath. "So. Do you think *he's* on the up and up? Or is he one of the ones on the graft?"

Roman lifted a disinterested shoulder. "He strikes me as honest, though who ever knows when it comes to this sort of thing? When I find what I'm looking for, you can bet I'll make sure of whomever I'm passing it along to. At this point, it's enough that he didn't get in my way."

Cliff nodded. "Well if we're going to do this, we need a plan. Let's sit down and hash it out. Your place or mine?"

"My walls are better for tacking things up if we need to." Which was to say, they were blank plaster. Lousy plaster, but that hardly mattered. As soon as they reached his rooms, he surveyed the empty walls with a pleased nod.

His mother would have been horrified at each empty place where an icon should have been. She'd been the one to pack them up from his place in New York, wrap them carefully in newspaper, place them just so in the box, muttering prayers over each one. If she realized he'd shoved the whole box into a corner, she'd have something to say about it.

But as far as he'd seen in life, none of it really mattered anyway—not the religion itself and not these stupid *things* meant to remind him of it. How was he supposed to respect a Church filled with mafiosi, whose priests accepted their dirty money in exchange for absolution? How was he supposed to put any stock in a God who let criminals get rich while good, honest men bled to death in a sewer?

No. The only justice in this world was what they enforced for themselves, and the only righteousness was what put murderers behind bars. God, if He existed, clearly didn't care enough to do a blasted thing for humanity, and no tin crucifix hanging on his wall was going to convince him otherwise. Maybe Jesus suffered—but it hadn't stopped anyone else from suffering since.

Roman had had enough suffering. It was time for the bad guys to take a turn at it, for once.

Cliff tossed a few pens and blank notebooks onto his ancient table and pulled out one of the two chairs. "Well. I guess this answers my question about what you plan to do about Sabina. You *do* realize that if you go above and beyond to get him for murder, she's going to go above and beyond to hate you, right?"

Roman pulled out the second chair, wishing that his partner wouldn't insist on reminding him of why even making the bad guys pay had become so blasted complicated. "I'm not an idiot, Cliff." But Sabina's sculpted face filled his mind's eye. His fingers ached for the touch of her so-soft skin. He could hear her musical laughter trilling in his ear and even smell the light, flowery fragrance she favored.

Cliff shook his head without moving his gaze from Roman's face. "I don't get you, man. You're seriously smitten with this girl. Yet here you are, doing everything you can to tear apart her family. You're inviting a broken heart, and I'm not looking forward to picking up the pieces."

Roman stood and paced to the ill-equipped galley kitchen for a drink of water. "Don't worry about me. I'm just going to do my job and forget about her."

"Right." Cliff's voice dripped with sarcasm. "You know who you need to talk some sense into you? A certain little Sicilian lady I know."

Roman spun around to glower at his friend. "You wouldn't."

Cliff lifted his fair brows, looking far too pleased with the idea. "I can just see it now. She'd tug on your ear, wag that finger in your face, and launch into a lecture that could send an army running for cover. You'd either be over Sabina in a minute or else convinced you'd better marry her and let this whole investigation drop."

Roman held out a finger of his own to wag. "You call my mother and I'll tell *yours* about your determination to steer clear of all the debs and their high-society demands for the rest of your life. If she realizes this working-class life isn't just a phase for you…"

Cliff winced. "All right, all right. Truce. We leave our mothers out of it. The last thing Chicago needs is those two terrors descending on the city. So. Let's get back to work. What crazy scheme are you cooking up to get the information you need?"

They spent the next couple of hours hashing out the rudiments of a plan and then hit the town to follow up on the first steps. Not surprisingly,

Roman's leads had long since gone cold. They went their separate ways at dusk with nothing to show for their efforts but added frustrations. Cliff declared himself ready for a good dinner and maybe a book, but Roman paused on the corner once his friend was gone and stuck a hand in his pocket.

Indecision kept his feet planted. He should get back to his apartment, go over his notes again, or else get a bite to eat. But neither idea appealed. Already thoughts of Sabina were encroaching on his mind, and he knew they'd only grow stronger when he was alone on his couch. He turned and headed back into the Levee. He knew of only one way to drive away the images of a girl.

Sally answered her door on the second knock and gave him a sultry smile as she leaned into the frame. "Well, well. I gotta say, champ, you look a far sight better than you did last time you were here. You're real handsome without those circles under your eyes. Though the chin's turning some interesting colors."

Roman flashed his most charming smile. "Glad you approve, doll. Mind if I come in?"

She pushed the door wide and stepped back inside, her eyes never leaving his. "I've got an hour or two. Why? Got something else to prove?"

"Nah." He followed her in, toeing the door shut behind him. Sadly, it was no worse a room than his own. Maybe even a little nicer, given the curtains at the windows and the vase of flowers on the table—homey touches that women seemed able to put on a place with two pennies and an hour of time. Every time they'd moved into a new apartment when he was a kid, Ma'd have it looking like *theirs* in minutes.

He wouldn't have expected it of a dame like Sally, though. He'd seen plenty of rooms of girls like her in his work with the Mancari operation—collecting payments, checking out complaints. Most of them didn't bother with things like curtains and flowers. Most of them didn't care enough—or they spent whatever cash their pimps let them keep on something to dull the pain, not to brighten the room.

In spite of the temperate day outside, it was a few degrees above comfortable in here. Maybe she'd been cooking. He shrugged out of his jacket. "Paid a visit to Ava today."

"Yeah?" She reached out to take his coat, draping it with precision over the back of a chair, lining up the seams. "Why do I get the feeling she was less than helpful for you?"

Roman chuckled and sidled over to her, lifting a hand to trace the line of her low-cut dress. "Didn't even get to talk to her, actually. We took one look at each other and realized we'd seen each other on another occasion. By now, she'll know who I am."

"Hm." Sally trailed a finger down the line of buttons on his shirt. "And who, exactly, is that?"

He saw no reason to lie. "Prohibition cop."

Recognition lit her eyes, but her arms still encircled his waist. "That O'Reilly character the papers mentioned?" At his nod, her lips tugged into a half smile. "My, my. A veritable celebrity. I can certainly see why Ava would steer clear of you if she realized you were trying to pinch her man."

"Exactly." He leaned over so he could run his lips over her jaw. "Sally? How loyal are you to Ava?"

She pulled back enough to look at his face while she pursed her lips in consideration. "Well. She *was* nice to me when I hit the city. Although not nice *enough*," she tacked on, glancing around the closet she called home. "Why? Whataya got in mind, champ?"

"Just a little undercover work. Compensated, of course."

Sally's golden brows lifted. "You boys don't have the highest budgets. I don't see how you can afford *that* if you still intend to spend money on *this*." Her hands drifted down his back in illustration of what she meant.

"I can find it. I've got a little put away from my past career." Not exactly from the career, but he didn't need to mention that. It wasn't money he'd ever planned to touch—but this would be fitting, wouldn't it? If he could use dirty money to cut off at least one head of the mob, that would have a certain poetic justice. "Or."

"Or?"

He tilted his head, studying the truly beautiful lines of her face. "You can do better than this life, Sally."

Her arms fell away, and her face went hard. She even retreated a step. "Don't make promises you can't keep, O'Reilly."

"I never do. If you want out, I'll arrange it."

Her nostrils flared, but he couldn't tell what emotion fueled the physical response. She spun to the kitchen, the small porcelain sink, and turned on the tap. Wet a washcloth and proceeded to wipe down the table that had not a speck on it to begin with. "You think it's that easy? That I can just walk away with no consequences? I got *debts* to Al, and if I don't pay up on 'em, I get *dead*."

Roman held out his hands, palms up. "Hey. I'm just making an offer. I've got enough connections that I could make it happen, but if you're too scared or too stuck, fine. I can find another way to pay you, either with something you can put toward those debts or something you can keep Al from knowing about. It's up to you, doll. I'm just offering."

The ice left her eyes and the rigidity left her posture, though whether by force or honest relaxation was anyone's guess. In any case, she tossed the cloth back into the sink, dried her hands on a pristine white towel, and moved closer again. "I'm sure we'll think of something. Are you gonna tell me what you want me to do now, or would you rather wait until later?"

He drew her flush against him with hands on her hips. "Later sounds good."

Even her laugh was sensual. "I thought it might."

ELEVEN

Lorenzo slid the letter for Brother Judah into the mailbox in his building's lobby and let a ragtime ditty spill from his lips in a whistle as he turned to the door. He needed to run over to the Mancari house to let Manny know what the senator had said, and if he timed it right, there might just be a plate of home-cooked dinner in it for him. Mama's get-well alfredo was long gone. He turned to the door, though he hung back when it swung open—then grinned when he saw Tony stride in, looking over his shoulder.

"Tony. And Val?" Yeah, Val rushed in behind his brother, all but shoving him out of the way and letting the door fall shut behind him.

Val shot him a grin. "Hey, Enzo. Thought you could use some company. Didn't we, Tony?"

Tony sent the baby of the family a scowl. Hard to say why, but he always found a reason to scowl at Val.

Lorenzo chuckled. "Thoughtful. But I was just heading over to Bean's." He needed to let Manny know he'd spoken to the senator—but more, he wanted to see Sabina.

"That'll do too. We'll ride with you. Won't we, Tony?"

Tony gave Val the wide-eyed look that meant *Shut up, babbo.*

Lorenzo narrowed his eyes and leaned toward Val. Sniffed.

"Hey!" His brother shoved him away. "What are you doing? Do I look like a loaf of bread?"

"No, but I expected you to smell like a bathtub full of gin. Why are you so...?" He couldn't think of a word to capture Val's jumpiness, bright eyes, or constant glances at Tony, so he just waved a hand to encompass his whole self.

Tony snorted a laugh and hooked an arm around Lorenzo's neck so he could pull his head down and rub his knuckles into his scalp. "If we knew *that*, am I right?"

The only way for Enzo to escape one of Tony's headlocks was to dig his fingers just under his ribs. Always worked like a charm. Tony yelped and jumped away, laughing. "All right, already. We're driving, right? Looks like it could rain."

Did it? Clouds must have moved in while he was finishing his letter to Judah. Which was fine, he'd been ready to drive anyway, since it could be late when he came home. "Sure."

Val pushed open the door again, and they all stepped out into the balmy June evening. The sun dipped low, bathing the buildings in gold. A beautiful evening, perfect for a stroll.

And there wasn't a cloud in sight.

A hand-cranked siren wailed by on the next street over, whistles shrilling out along with it. Lorenzo crossed himself and muttered a quick prayer for whoever was in need as he led the way to his Nash.

Tony shook his head. "Come on, Enzo. Do you have to do that in public, where anyone can see?"

He rolled his eyes. "So sorry if my concern for whatever life is in danger embarrasses you."

"Apology accepted." Tony yanked open the passenger door and slid inside. Val snickered again and jumped in behind him.

Lorenzo shook his head. Something was definitely off with those two—but he didn't really have time to sort it out now. He slid behind the wheel and soon had them on their way.

His brothers jabbered on while he drove, though Val's laughter was too bright, and Tony kept looking out the window like he expected to see Charlie Chaplin strolling down the street. It made Lorenzo's shoulders go a little tighter, and he was glad to finally pull up in front of the Mancari house so his brothers could tumble out of his car.

Val emerged with a hoot and a clap, then charged toward the door.

"What is *wrong* with him tonight?" he asked Tony.

But Tony, instead of laughing with him, wouldn't meet his eyes. "Crazy kid. Who knows?"

Tony did. Obviously. They'd arrived together, worked together most days. Whatever was going on, Tony knew. And didn't want to tell Lorenzo.

Blast it all. Now he couldn't help but try to piece together the puzzle, when this was *not* what he needed to be thinking about tonight.

He trailed his brothers into the house, following the sound of Val's laughter into Manny's study. Their godfather shifted his frustrated gaze from Val to Tony. "What are you doing back here? You were supposed to take it to the millinery, and—Enzo?" Manny's spine snapped straight, and his brows slammed down.

Lorenzo looked from Manny to Tony to Val. His fingers curled into his palms, and he could feel the blood rushing into his face. "Tony. What *exactly* were you doing at my building?" He saw again his brothers rushing in the door, looking over their shoulders while a siren wailed by.

Tony ignored him and faced Manny. "Thought we shook the tail within a couple of blocks of the brewery, but they found us again. We had to ditch the car, but they didn't see it, don't worry. We'll go back for it soon."

Brewery? Ditch the car? Lorenzo had to brace a hand on the back of one of the leather chairs to keep from lunging at his brother. "You used me as a *getaway*?"

Tony spun back to him, hands up in a placating gesture. "Now calm down, Enzo. We just went for a ride with our brother, that's all. Someplace you were already planning to go."

He clenched his teeth so tightly he could feel his pulse in his jaw. Still, it wasn't enough to keep the words from spilling out. "So your original plan was simply to hide in my apartment until the cops stopped circling the block. *My* block. Where you'd come with your contraband."

"Now, Enzo—"

"Don't you 'now Enzo' me." He sliced a hand through the air. "You're all idiots. You know that, right? You *know* O'Reilly's still gunning for you. You *know* he's filing bootlegging charges and will have made sure every suspected venue is covered. So what do you do? Make a run to the brewery that you took him to a month ago! Did you think you *wouldn't* get chased by the cops?"

Manny's face went blank and hard, his gaze calculating as he leaned back on his desk and turned his attention from one brother to the other.

Val shifted from one foot to the other. "Ah, come on, Enzo. It was an emergency. The bars were almost out of beer."

"Oh, well then. I can see the earth would have stopped spinning had you not gone and risked your lives."

"Now Enzo."

He spun toward Tony again. "Say that one more time, Antonio. I dare you."

Tony shifted too—out of arm's reach. "The risk was controlled. But don't you see that the reasons you named are the very ones that meant we *had* to go? We couldn't trust this run to anyone else. But it had to be done. No booze means no customers, no customers means no money—and worse, people talking about how Manny's places aren't dependable. People start going elsewhere, and it's perceived as weakness. Other gangsters start moving in our territory. Is that what you want? More of Torrio's men here, in our neighborhood? Shooting at our families? We do this to protect you—to protect *everyone*."

Fury pulsed through Lorenzo's veins with every beat of his heart. With them. For them. He couldn't even tell the difference anymore. "Right. Every time you break the law, it's for *me*."

Manny pushed off from his desk, coming to drape an arm over Lorenzo's shoulders. "For you—yes. So you could go to college, to law school. For Sabina, so she can walk these streets in safety. We make these hard choices so you can live the life you want."

The old, familiar guilt sliced through him. He'd tried to find a way to achieve his dreams without relying on Mafia money, but in the end, he'd accepted Manny's help with school. Just as he'd accepted the food his father put on the table all his life. He'd told himself that at least it would enable him to cut those ties, and it had. Finally. But those chains, the reminders, were still there.

And worse still, his brothers were now in the thick of it. He looked over at Tony and saw the insolent way he perched there, arms crossed. He looked like Father. Like Franco. Like Manny. Like nothing Lorenzo could ever say would make a difference.

It wasn't calm that banked his anger. It was defeat. "The moral of the story being, once again, that I shouldn't ask you to make different choices, to live a different life, as I've chosen to do."

Manny gave his shoulder a friendly shake and left his side, heading for his chair. "I knew a smart young man like you would understand. Now, I assume you didn't come here just to yell at your brothers. Did you speak with the senator today? Or are you just here to visit with Sabina?"

Lorenzo looked again from Tony to Val. Most young mafiosi proved themselves by spilling an enemy's blood—had they? He hoped not, prayed not.

But even if they hadn't yet, how long would that last? How long would they *want* it to? How long before the two brothers he had left, his best friends, abandoned the last of the morals their mother had tried to instill in them and embarked fully on the path of their father?

How long before those hands that had teased and shoved him all his life were red with an enemy's blood?

One of these days, Manny would either retire or be unable to avoid a bullet. Franco or Father might take over, but they were both reaching that point in their lives when they might wish for a slower pace. And with Little G, the heir apparent, wanting a different life…who did that leave?

Tony. Val.

He squeezed his eyes shut, wishing he could believe that it wasn't true. They'd never get that deep or go that far. But he knew it was only wishful thinking.

He'd spent his life in a Mafia family too—he'd seen it all. He understood what drove them. The desire to protect their families, their neighbors…no matter what it took. The satisfaction that came with accruing more and more power, more and more territory. Expanding the Family, growing the neighborhood. Doing what the government wouldn't, restoring what other gangs had taken. The thrill that came from crooking a finger and having desperate girls do whatever they were told, of having underlings grovel and obey.

And the money. One couldn't forget the money.

Yes, Lorenzo understood it. He'd seen it, watched it change the face of his neighborhood, his family. He had prayed that they would turn away from those temptations. He prayed it every day, with every candle, at every mass since he was thirteen years old and first tasted the communion wafer, since he first felt that surge of something beyond the natural come over him. He prayed that they would see the destruction they wrought.

Ten years of prayers hadn't been enough, apparently. He drew in a long breath and turned to Manny. He'd follow the example of St. Monica and pray for another sixteen, or another sixty. However long it took. "The senator said not to worry. He'll take care of it. I expect him to call back in a day or two."

"Excellent. I knew he'd come through. *Grazii*, Enzo."

Lorenzo jerked his head in a nod and spun back toward the door. Let his brothers find their own way back to wherever they'd stashed their beer-laden car.

"Enzo?" At Manny's soft word, Lorenzo turned back around. Worry lined the elder's face—worry that he reserved for family. "Be sure to speak with Sabina before you go, will you? She's seemed down these last two days. She won't talk to me or her mother, so we don't know what's wrong. She seemed happy enough when you left the other night, so we know you didn't fight again but…"

Lorenzo nodded as his stomach clenched. Figuring she'd be in the parlor with her mother, he headed that direction. When he poked his head in, though, he saw only Mama Rosa. "Hi. Is Sabina around?"

Mama Rosa looked up with a strained smile. "Oh, Enzo. Good. Maybe you can drag her out of that kitchen."

Lorenzo's brows stretched upward. "Kitchen? Since when does Cook let anyone in the kitchen?"

Rosa sighed. "They reached a truce, somehow. She's been in there almost nonstop since yesterday. Said something about practicing for when you get married and taking a few meals to the Bennatos, but it's getting ridiculous. She's hiding in there, but she won't tell me why." Rosa sighed, her face weary. "See if you can get her out of the house, will you? Go for a walk, a drive, something. The girl hasn't tasted fresh air since she got back from Mary and Isadora's yesterday."

Lorenzo nodded again, pushing his hand into his pocket and jingling his change as he tried to think of what might be bothering her. When he realized he had borrowed his boss's habit, he quickly drew his hand out again with a crooked smile. He soon stood in the kitchen doorway, watching silently for a long moment as Sabina drew a perfect loaf of bread from the oven and then turned to a bowl filled with flour. "Bean?"

She jumped, spraying fine white powder all over the table and floor as she spun around. She pressed a floured hand to her already dusty navy housedress. "Enzo! Don't scare me like that!"

He looked around the room and noted the considerable pile of bread, pastries, and a few items he couldn't readily identify. "Bean, what are you doing?"

She waved him off and turned back to her bowl. "Just practicing some of the recipes I hadn't perfected. I have to be able to feed us, you know."

"Us or all of Little Italy?"

Rather than laughing or even smiling at his joke, she ignored him and carefully measured a spoonful of salt into her bowl. Lorenzo allowed the silence and studied her. Her dress was smeared with flour and dough, her feet were encased in slippers rather than her usual heeled pumps. Her hair, though neat, was unwaved and even had a few streaks of flour turning it gray. He moved over to the table, mainly so that he could lean around it to look at her face. As he had suspected, dark shadows circled her eyes, and her usual golden skin was pale.

"Bean? Are you okay?"

She flicked an irritated glance his way. "Do you mind? You're in my way."

"Good. I intend to stay in it until you answer me."

Sighing, Sabina rested her palms on the table. "Did Mama and Papa tell you to talk to me? Because there's nothing wrong. Really. I'm fine."

"Then you won't mind taking a walk with me." He tilted his head to measure her reaction, pleased at the self-awareness that flashed in her eyes.

"Are you out of your mind? I can't go out in public like this!"

He let himself smile as he reached up to rub a smear of crusted dough off her cheek. "So go change. But make it snappy—we've only got so much daylight left out there."

She opened her mouth, eyes aglint at the command, but then pressed her lips together and nodded. "Give me five minutes."

While she was gone, Lorenzo poked through the mountain of baked goods, helping himself to a calzone that he found cooling by the oven. And a *cassatelle*, when he spotted the plate of them—his favorite.

He was licking ricotta and chocolate from his fingers when Sabina came back into the kitchen with lifted brows. "Helped yourself, I see."

He grinned. "I think you've perfected those, Bean."

Her lips twitched up into an indulgent smile, but her eyes remained flat and dark. "Good to know I can cook to your liking, anyway."

The words could have been light, jesting. Or they could have hinted at someone else's disregard, had she emphasized the "your." But her tone instead implied that cooking might be the only thing she had to her advantage, which made a frown crease his brow. After wiping his fingers on a napkin, he held out his hand and nodded toward the back door. "Come on. You're going to have to explain that one once we're outside."

Her fingers laced through his, and she drew in a long breath. Once they gained the back stoop and the fragrant June evening, she let it out again, and it seemed like her whole being sagged on the exhale. "Enzo, why do you love me?"

He halted with one foot on the stoop and the other on the ground, equalizing their heights. It made looking her in the eye easier physically, though the uncertainty and insecurity he saw there squeezed at his heart. "You're not pulling any punches these days, are you?"

She lifted one corner of her mouth into a lopsided smile. "It shouldn't be that hard a question. I can tell you why I love you—because you're fair, dedicated, loyal, faithful, selfless, and dependable. You're honest. Sweet. Considerate."

"All very nice adjectives." Not caring to have this conversation on the street where any passer-by could listen in, he tugged her over to the bench placed beside her mother's small garden plot. Vegetables rioted in various stages of growth: arugula and rapini, Melrose peppers and tomatoes, onions and zucchini and eggplant. Most wouldn't be ripe until later in the summer. Would their relationship ripen again with them? "Yet by your own admission, you fell in love with someone else."

Sabina sank to the bench with a sigh. "I thought you didn't want me. That you were just too good to break it off. I thought—why did you choose me, Enzo? Over the Church?"

He took the hard seat next to her, keeping his eyes on her face. "I didn't choose you over the Church. I chose both. I chose to serve God through loving you, raising a family with you." Yet her hand felt unfamiliar in his, and disbelief shadowed her eyes. "I haven't done a very good job of that. Yet. But I will, Bean. I promise you. I love you."

She stared at the ground for a moment before regaining herself and sending him a smile that fell a few degrees shy of sincere. "You didn't answer me about that."

Lorenzo emptied his lungs and rubbed his thumb over the smooth skin of her hand. "Why do I love you?" She nodded. He looked long and deep into her depthless eyes, trying to find words for what had always just been. "I love you because you give until you have nothing left, and then you find more. I love you because you see the good in people who have only a sliver of it. I love you because...because you're air to me. Necessary for every basic function. Because without you I feel like I'm going to suffocate."

"And yet you barely saw me the last three years."

"Because I was afraid. Sabina." He stretched his hand out under hers, until their fingers aligned, until the frisson of desire ran through him. "I'm not so unlike all the other men in our families. The other mafiosi. You're so beautiful. *So* beautiful. When I kissed you, I…" He had to squeeze his eyes shut. "I didn't know how strong I could be, if I did it more often."

Silence pulsed for a long moment. Then she whispered, "You mean it wasn't because you didn't want me—it was because you wanted me too much?"

He nodded, wishing from his very soul that he'd been stronger. Wiser. That he'd just suggested they marry right away, never mind how difficult it would have been to support themselves while he was still in school. Wishing, because then he would have spared her so much pain he hadn't realized he was causing. He wouldn't have made her think that if she wanted love, she had to find it in the arms of another man. "Can you forgive me? For making you ever doubt your own worth? For…for practically forcing you to him?"

Her fingers shifted over his palm, curling into the spaces between his, right where they belonged. "I forgive you." Yet the pain still underscored the words.

Of course it did. It still underscored his too, when he said, "And I forgive you."

Another beat of silence, another deep breath drawn into his lungs. Another low whisper from her rosebud lips. "That doesn't erase it, does it? For either of us."

He shook his head and scooted just a little closer, until their arms were pressed together. "Brother Judah said once—I don't remember when, but it stuck with me—that forgiveness isn't a ticket you buy, a one-time thing bought and paid for. Forgiveness is the train you choose to ride through life's journey. You have to stay on it, even though sometimes you don't know where it's taking you. You have to trust it to protect you from the elements that rage outside—and inside."

Her eyes slid shut. Behind her, the sun dipped below the top of a building. Shadows sprang to life, one seeming to hunch over her, curling its fingers over her shoulders.

Lorenzo fought back a shudder. For a few months when he was twelve, before he realized that a life with Sabina was all he really wanted, he had indeed planned to join the Church and thought that he would be called to something truly spectacular—like exorcism. He'd read all he could find about angels and demons, on how the godly battled forces they couldn't see.

Then he decided that he didn't need to be spectacular. But it had opened his eyes. He started looking at his world in a new way. He had begun to see that his father, his godfather—they didn't just deal in violence and sin. They dealt in darkness they didn't fully understand. He didn't fully understand it either. But he knew enough to fear it—what it could do to a man's heart, his soul, his family.

How many times had he seen his mother go to the kitchen and sing at the top of her lungs to keep from crying when Father came home injured or drunk or smelling of a bordello? How many times had he seen spatters of red on the cuff of a relative and known it meant someone out there was tortured or dead? How many times had he clung to his rosary or fallen to his knees in the empty sanctuary of Holy Guardian Angel and prayed for new warriors to fight in the battle for his family's souls?

Somehow, he'd never thought it would touch Sabina, though. Val, Tony, Joey, G, even Mama and Rosa—he'd known to pray for them. But he'd assumed that since he would get out, he would take her with him, and she would be safe.

What a fool he'd been. The Mafia wasn't the only thing that preyed on people. Satan had a gang of his own, always prowling the world, ready to devour. Sabina, with her gentle heart, would be a prime target. And he'd just left her there, alone inside a house where the devil already held sway, to fight off the ravenous jowls of despair and doubt by herself.

He transferred her hand to his other one so he could slide his near arm around her shoulders and tuck her against his side. He pressed a kiss to the top of her Brilliantine-scented hair. "We're on this journey together, Bean. We are. Every day, we'll forgive each other again. Every day, we'll pray for each other. Every day, we'll fight for this. For us."

She nodded, turned her face into his shoulder, and seemed content to rest there, against him. But she didn't say anything.

Had he lost too much ground already? What would he do if she didn't actually get on that train with him, if she didn't find her way back to joy and faith? What would he do if she realized in another week or month or year that his arms just didn't make her feel like O'Reilly's had?

What would he do if their paths didn't lead to each other?

TWELVE

—And when Peace here does house
He comes with work to do, he does not come to coo,
He comes to brood and sit.

-Gerard Manley Hopkins,
from "Peace"

At long last, Sabina put away the *biscottu* she'd been starting when Lorenzo showed up and trudged up to her room. Exhaustion dogged her steps, but what right did she have to even feel it? All she'd done today was whisper a few well-placed words to a few women in the markets about the Bennatos and then bake a few more batches of cookies and calzones for dinner. She hadn't sat up all day, all night with a dying mother. She hadn't worried all day, all night about a father who never came home anymore.

But guilt was tiring, and she'd felt it with every measure, every stir. Guilt for what she'd done to Lorenzo—first in taking him from the life he was surely called to, then for betraying him, when he'd given up so much for her.

She switched on the lamp on her bedside table and sank to a seat on the mattress, too tired even to untie the ribbons on her pumps and toe them off. What had she hoped when she asked him tonight why he loved her? That he would admit he didn't, that he regretted everything? No. That wasn't what she'd wanted to hear. She'd wanted to hear exactly what he'd said—that she was his everything. But surely that, too, was sinful, for her to *want* him to desire her above the priesthood. Especially when she'd been so blind to his life, when she'd turned to another man.

"Yet by your own admission, you fell in love with someone else."

She could still hear the heartbreak in his voice. He said he forgave her, would keep on forgiving her, but it would always be a specter between them.

Why? Why had she done it? She tried to remember when she'd made a decision, when she'd walked through the doorway...but she couldn't. At first, they had just started talking, completely innocent. But then he'd *seen* her, and she'd started looking forward to those moments. Had that been the first step into sin? It must have been. And the path was so slick, so steep that she'd just slid down like a child on a slide, too exhilarated at the rush to think about what waited at the bottom.

It had only been a couple of weeks ago that she'd thought, with that giddy, lightheaded certainty lent to her by cheap gin and loud music, that finally she'd found *real* love. She'd thought this excitement, this fire in her veins was what life felt like, and she could grab it. She could forget everything else—grief and mourning and promises that felt as useless as Lorenzo's diamond on her finger—and take hold of something new with both hands. Roman Oliveri was the path to everything she wanted, worth any rocks in the road, any disapproval.

She'd thought Lorenzo would be relieved when he realized she was gone.

She'd called it love. And the other day outside Lorenzo's office, Roman had called it that too. Her father hadn't corrected her, but Mama had tried. Mama had known the difference between the rush of excitement and what could actually stand the test of time. Mama had known who would bring heartache and who would walk beside her through every trial life tossed at her.

Mama loved her too much, though, to see that she didn't deserve Lorenzo.

Sabina reached for the book of poetry and turned the pages until she found the one with his note tucked in. It was a short poem, entitled "Peace," but her eyes sought his handwritten words on the marker before the printed ones on the page.

> *With the news of Joey's death in Europe still so fresh, this poem is especially striking. How true that Peace is elusive and, even when present, brooding. It is our nature, I think, to fight one another. Perhaps because all around us is raging a spiritual war we cannot see. But it is my prayer that you and I, at least, might convince Peace to "coo" for us. You're my dearest friend, Bean. I never want to fight with you.*

"Oh, Enzo," Sabina sighed, resting her head on her hand. "It's as if you already saw what was coming and wrote this to prick my heart."

She read the poem aloud twice and then just sat there as the rhythm echoed through her room. *Peace*. It was something she hadn't felt since Serafina was still alive to laugh and dance. It was something she'd given up chasing because it had seemed as fruitless as running after the pigeons that always fluttered away when you got too close. It was something she craved like water or salt or the *collorelle* they only ever made at Christmas.

Her eyes drifted to the cross on her wall—not cheap tin like the one Isadora clearly treasured, but sterling silver, with a gold Savior hanging on it to remind her of what He'd done to prove His love. Yet even looking at it every day, she hadn't really seen. Every prayer had felt like nothing more than chasing a pigeon. Hope, faith, peace always fluttered away, just out of reach. So how could she make it coo for her and settle at her feet?

Were it really a pigeon, she'd have to be still. She'd have to sacrifice a bit of her bread or cookie or crust for it, scatter it before her. And wait.

She sprang to her feet, let the poetry book rest on her bed, snatched up her favorite cloche without any thought to whether it matched her dress, and hurried back down the stairs, through the foyer, out the front door.

"Sabina Maria! Where are you going?"

Papa's voice slowed her, but it didn't stop her. She just tossed over her shoulder, "To church!" and jammed the hat over her wave-less hair.

She heard him bark a command, though it wasn't at her. The words, in fact, didn't even process until she saw two men take shape from the mounting shadows and fall into step behind her. Her heart pinched. This was the life her father had built for them, a life where she couldn't even dash down the block to church without needing bodyguards to flank her.

It was no wonder peace had proven so elusive.

She didn't slow for her new shadows, tried not to think about them back there—at least until the stone façade of Holy Guardian Angel loomed ahead of her…and a whistle pierced the twilight.

She froze, her breath balling up in her chest. There was nowhere to take cover, nowhere to run. Her gaze flicked every direction in search of the lookout who'd just announced her presence, for the gunman who'd be raising his Betsy and mowing her down.

She saw only a little old man tottering down the sidewalk after a dog who was dragging a dropped leash. He whistled again, and the dog barked and returned to him.

Her shoulders sagged. Her heart calmed—or perhaps started thumping again. And her two shadows drew so close to her that she could smell the garlic from their dinner.

"You goin inside, Miss Mancari?" one of them asked.

The other jerked his chin toward the door.

No, not toward the door. It was a greeting to another shadow who lounged by the entrance, who jerked his chin back.

Her brows knit. Wasn't that one of the goons from the park the other day? The one who had reached for his belt when she and Lorenzo looked his way? One of Papa's men, Lorenzo had said, and those chin-juts seemed to confirm it. But why was he stationed here now?

Something brushed her elbow, and she jumped a step forward.

The first guard, the one who had spoken, didn't apologize for startling her. He just held out an arm, inviting her to go up the steps and, no doubt, stop standing on the sidewalk like an imbecile.

Every sound rang too loud in her ears as she obeyed. The scuff of her shoes against the stone steps, the squeak of the massive wooden door, the boom of its closing.

Only one of the guards came inside with her, and he took up position in the narthex rather than trailing her any farther. Good.

She turned toward the confession booth but made it only two steps before she halted again. Father Russo wasn't in there; the curtain was pulled back to reveal his empty seat.

Of course he wasn't there. He was never there at eight o'clock at night. What had she been thinking? A sigh leaked from her lips. She could come back tomorrow for the overdue confession, but that wouldn't help her find her missing peace now.

The beauty of the sanctuary beckoned, the flicker of the candles by the altar promising that prayer was a light through the darkness, doing its work even after her whispered words fell silent. She aimed her feet up the long center aisle.

There were only a few other people in the pews, all of them women, most of them of her mother's generation. Mothers themselves, she'd bet, praying for wayward sons and prodigal daughters. Sons and daughters likely led into the tares by men like her father.

Her steps dragged. It seemed like it took a century before she made it to the front, and she wondered if there was any purpose to this. Could her prayers undo her father's work? Could the coins she dropped in the offering box to pay for the candles even matter when they were earned by violence and gambling and prostitution? Would God even hear the words of a mafioso's daughter?

As she approached, another woman kneeling at the front crossed herself, stood, and turned to exit. She glanced up as she passed Sabina and paused, a smile wreathing her face. It was the woman from the park the other night, the one whose name Sabina didn't know but whose face was familiar here.

The woman leaned closer, her voice barely a whisper. "I heard about the attack last week. Is your family all right? Your brother?"

Sabina nodded, her own questions easing back to make room for this near-stranger's touching concern.

The woman rested a hand on Sabina's forearm and gave it a friendly squeeze. "I can imagine how it's haunted you. I said a prayer for you and your mother. I lit a candle for you."

She had? Eyes stinging in gratitude, Sabina could only mouth a thank you and blink.

The woman withdrew her hand, smiled again, and continued down the aisle.

Sabina felt ten pounds lighter. This, perhaps, was how God assured her that He saw her. She dug a few coins from the pocket of her dress to drop into the offering box and reached to pull one of the wooden tapers from the vase of sand. She touched the end to one of the candles already burning and transferred the light to an unlit votive—a simple task she'd done hundreds of times over the years. But tonight, the light seemed to glow brighter against the gathering night. *He is the Light of the world*, they seemed to sing with their golden flickers. *And the light shineth in darkness, and the darkness did not comprehend it.*

She sank to her knees on the padded altar rail and crossed herself. She had always not comprehended Him, truth be told. But she wanted to understand Him. She needed to know Him like Lorenzo did, like Isadora. She could understand why Mary ran headlong into the darkness instead; Sabina had tried that path, but it wasn't the one she wanted. That wasn't the life that would ever let peace flutter down to coo at her.

She whispered a Hail Mary to ground her, to open her heart. And then she held that heart open. She pushed aside the old familiar thoughts that whispered, *He won't hear you, you don't matter* into her ear. She tried to believe. Christ was her bridegroom, even more than Lorenzo.

Lorenzo. His face flooded her mind's eye. His name pressed itself into her heart with such force that her breath caught. Lorenzo—the boy she'd always loved best in the world. The man she'd come to think was so far above her, so far beyond her that he couldn't possibly love her. The fiancé whose heart she'd broken, the betrayed who had sworn he would give her another chance and begged for *her* forgiveness.

Lorenzo, the man who was just a man, with a man's weaknesses. *"Not so unlike the other men in our families,"* he'd said an hour ago—a confession of his own. He was afraid of his own nature because it was as frail as her own.

Her thoughts flew briefly to the woman who'd just left, who'd prayed for her and Mama, who'd lit a candle for them.

It mattered. It made a difference. Maybe her prayers would too.

Lord Jesus, You were a man with a nature like ours, like Lorenzo's. Make his nature more like yours, as I know he wants it to be. Strengthen him. Strengthen me. Strengthen us.

Help us, somehow, to be a light instead of part of the darkness.

Lorenzo parked behind his apartment building as the last colors of dusk faded into the gray of night. The streetlamps were already on, as were lights in most of the windows of the building. He could see Heidi Stein standing in front of her top-floor window, looking out into the twilight, the electric light behind her making her white hair glow. When she spotted him, she gave an enthusiastic wave.

Lorenzo lifted a hand in reply and smiled up at his boss's wife. His brothers had thought him a *babbo* for renting an apartment in the Steins' building, but he'd just been glad of the good price. He didn't mind calling his boss his landlord, at least not when it was Mr. Stein. He was a good man to learn from, a good man to have watching over him. And his wife liked to show her fondness in crisp German butter cookies and well-seasoned sausage, which he wasn't going to complain about either.

A few minutes later Lorenzo had climbed the four flights of stairs, fitted his key in the lock, and turned the knob. He stepped inside, stretching to turn on a lamp as he closed the door behind him. He spotted the figure only when the familiar but out of place voice reached his ears. "It's about time you got home."

Shoulders stiff, Lorenzo narrowed his eyes at the redhead who unfolded herself from his couch. She had put aside her jacket to reveal a silk and lace waist whose femininity belied the severe cut of her suit—and whose presence in his locked apartment belied her supposed role in his life. "Miss Gregory? How did you get in here?"

The secretary rolled her eyes. "Your lock's a simple pin and tumbler—no trouble at all."

His mouth fell open. "You *picked* my *lock*?" That just didn't fit with his image of the thorough, professional woman who ran the office, even if she *did* have that amateur-sleuth mentality. Or not so amateur, perhaps.

Miss Gregory chuckled and slid around his couch, trailing a hand over the back of it as she moved toward him. "How else was I supposed to get in? You weren't home yet, and I know Mr. Stein wouldn't have used his master key to let me wait for you."

"Because an unmarried woman has no business waiting in the apartment of an unmarried male acquaintance," he felt the need to point out. "Which begs the question of why you were so determined to do so that you'd break in."

She kept advancing, and, not knowing what her intentions could possibly be, he moved into the kitchen, partially to avoid her and partially to tuck the food Sabina had sent home with him into the icebox and cupboards. He turned back around to discover she had followed him, which shouldn't have surprised him, but it did. She stood only a foot away, her slender arms crossed over her chest.

"Well, I'll tell you, Enzo. That is what everyone calls you, right? I like it. It suits you better than Lorenzo, and certainly better than Mr. Capecce."

He had never, in the eight months since he had made her acquaintance, heard her beat around the bush even that much. Curiosity seeped through his unease, but he folded his arms over his chest to keep it at bay. "Miss Gregory. Your point."

"Helen." She smiled the same bright smile she always gave him, but it looked different in his kitchen—warmer, more personal.

Dangerous.

"Fine. Helen. What are you doing here?"

Her smile faded. "Helping, I hope. I don't want to see you get hurt again, Enzo."

Confusion knitted his brows. "When have you seen me hurt to begin with?"

Her answer was to reach out and brush the bandage still protecting the wound on his temple. He drew back from her fingers, arms falling to his sides, but then she just settled her hand over his heart. Had he not just backed himself into the table, he would have fled. As it was, he almost leapt onto it to get away from the unfamiliar touch.

"She broke your heart." Voice low and vibrating with emotion, Helen raised her chin. "And your association with her almost got you killed. Can't you see that she's bad news? I mean, you're a man of faith, not to mention a lawyer, but you're associating with *criminals!*"

Her concern, though too pronounced to be appropriate, was nevertheless sweet. He covered her hand with his so he could pull it away from his chest. Of course, then she just held onto his fingers. "Helen, I appreciate that you're worried about me. But you really shouldn't be here."

"When else am I ever going to get the chance to talk to you? You're buried in work all day at the office, and it seems like every time you leave, you're running to the Mancaris' house to see *her* or her father."

"Sabina." He untangled his fingers. "*Her* name is Sabina."

Helen tossed her arms into the air and spun around, stalking away. "As if I don't know her name! You talk about nothing but *Sabina* every chance you get."

"So what?" He pulled out a chair but didn't sit. She was pacing his way again, and he didn't really want her to corner him in a chair. "She's my fiancée, it's—"

"No." Too near for comfort again, she poked a delicate but steely finger into his chest. "She *was* your fiancée. I think she forfeited the honor of that title when she let another man touch her the way she did."

Lorenzo's shoulders stiffened, his eyes narrowed. "You don't know—"

"*Yes.* I *do* know. I made it a point to find out, and it wasn't too hard to track down someone who saw them at one of her father's speakeasies. Said that man's hands were places no decent woman would have allowed them to be."

Had the spark in her eyes been victorious, he would have physically forced her from the apartment, but it was concern that lit them, and an anger that he didn't understand. She must have counted him as more of a friend than he had ever thought, to be so offended on his behalf. For that reason, he made his tone gentle. "I realize she did wrong, but I've made mistakes too. We've agreed to give each other another chance."

Distress flooded into her face and tears into her eyes. "But *why*? She's not good enough for you. She doesn't know how to love you. Don't do this to yourself again—give *me* a chance instead."

He gripped the back of the chair for support, sure he had misheard. "*Scusi?*"

Tears streamed unchecked down her ivory cheeks, and she was shaking, proving her words cost her. "I love you, Enzo. The moment you walked into the office last year as an intern, I fell for you—but you were engaged. And I knew you loved her. So I tried to forget about it, and I kept my distance. I figured, if she made you happy, I could stay quiet. But not now. This is my only chance, and I deserve it far more than she does. I know how to love you. I could—" She started to say something more, but her tears increased to sobs, choking off her words.

Lorenzo just stared at her, at a complete loss. When Mama cried, he gave her a hug. When they were children and it was Sabina in tears, he'd pat her back and snatch her a sweet from the kitchen. Neither of those options seemed appropriate right now.

Suddenly aware of the chair he still gripped, he moved it slightly and urged her into it with a hand on her arm. Once she was sitting, her shoulders slumped and quaking with her tears, he crouched beside her. "Miss Gregory…you've taken me off guard here. I don't know what to say."

She shook her head and swept furiously at her cheeks. "Nothing. Please. I know—I've made—a fool—of myself."

He patted his pockets until he found the clean handkerchief he'd shoved in that morning. It felt like a paltry offering, but she took it readily and wiped at her eyes and nose. "If you have, then you're in good company. I've never felt a fool as many times as I have this past week."

Helen laughed around her tears and, still smiling, drew in a long breath that was a clear attempt to regain control. Her emerald eyes only darted his way once. She focused on the handkerchief she twisted around her fingers, and her smile faded. "I'm sorry, Enzo. I know you love her, that you've never even looked at me that way. I shouldn't have come here. But—" She sat up straighter, raised her chin, and met his gaze. Under the bravado, uncertainty still skittered. "I knew if I didn't say something now, I never would. And then I'd always wonder. Worse, if she hurts you again, I'd feel like if I had just warned you—maybe you can't see it, but I can. She doesn't love you like you deserve to be loved. She couldn't, if she'd go out with another man like that. She doesn't love you like I do."

Her earnest, intense expression forced him to look away. "Helen, you and I barely know each other."

She huffed out a frustrated breath. "Why do you say that—because we met less than a year ago? So what? You've known her all your life, and how well did you really know *her*?"

Better than I know myself—that would have been the answer three years ago. But now? So much had changed since Serafina died, and he hadn't been around to see it. "Point taken." He tilted his head and dared to look at her face again, incredulous that he was really having this conversation. "But it's not only her fault. I'm to blame too. It isn't as simple as just laying it all at her feet and washing my hands of her."

Challenge glinted in Helen's eyes as she leaned forward. "That's the problem with you lawyers. You complicate everything. It could be simple, if you wanted it to be—just tell her you want to see other people before you make a commitment."

"Helen." He wasn't sure what he wanted to say, and he didn't have the chance to figure it out. She scooted to the edge of her chair and leaned forward a little more to press her mouth to his. Her lips were soft but insistent, bidding him to respond. His first instinct was to obey, but then good sense took over with such force that he jerked back. He'd been balanced on the balls of his feet, and the action sent him reeling. His arms flew out to grab at something to steady him. Unfortunately, the something that they landed on was Helen's arms.

She was unprepared for the weight of his backward fall. Not only did he thump his back against a cabinet, he pulled her down with him. She sprawled gracelessly across his legs, holding herself up with one knee and one elbow.

Laughter struck them both at the same instant. Far from what Helen must have intended to be a moment of romantic revelation, Lorenzo knew they must be a picture of ridiculousness. And he thanked the Lord for it— there was nothing like levity to diffuse a tense situation.

Giggling, Helen crawled over his legs and plopped down beside him, facing him. Lorenzo chuckled one last time and rubbed a hand over his eyes. Maybe now she'd get up, brush herself off, and go. Surely she wouldn't stick around after this. As for how they could possibly pretend it had never happened in the office tomorrow—

Without warning, her mouth was on his again, one arm snaking around his neck and the other resting on his chest. Retreating was impossible, so he gripped her shoulder with the intention of peeling her off and gently pushing her away.

He wasn't sure how it backfired so thoroughly. In one second he was preparing to disengage, and in the next the kiss had deepened and his arms had forgotten their mission. Her soft curves pressed against him. Her hair fell forward to frame his face, caressing his cheek with its silk.

The race of pleasure. The allure of the forbidden. What a heady realization, that a beautiful woman actually wanted *him*—not Joey, not Tony, not Roman O'Reilly. Him.

No. No, he couldn't. He couldn't be like them, the sort of men who sat beside their wives at mass on Sunday morning after spending Saturday night with their mistresses. He couldn't be the kind of man who promised one woman he'd love her forever and then kissed another just because he could.

He pushed her away, pushed himself to his feet, and shoved a hand through his hair. "I'm sorry," he whispered. "That shouldn't have happened."

To his utter surprise, Helen's smile was serene. "You wouldn't be you if you'd let me get away with it." She shrugged and pushed herself to her feet. "I guess I'm just hoping it'll give you something to think about. Show you what you're missing." Her grin turned cheeky as she sauntered over to the couch and picked up her discarded suit jacket.

Lorenzo sucked in a steadying breath, prepared to see her out. He decided to ignore her statement and took a step toward the door. "I'll show you out… Helen, what are you doing?"

Instead of heading to the door, she was striding toward the window. She unlocked it and pushed it up, turning her head around to flash him another grin. "Going down the fire escape. I can't very well go out the door and risk the Steins seeing me. I was lucky to avoid him and the missus when I came in, but I'm not risking it again."

By the time he arrived at the window, she had already shimmied out of it. She stuck her head back in. "See you in the morning, Enzo. Sweet dreams," she added with a wink.

Lorenzo watched to make sure she got down okay, shaking his head as he closed the window again. Then he stalked into his bedroom, picked up his rosary, and dropped to his knees.

THIRTEEN

What hinders? Are you beam-blind, yet to a fault
In a neighbour deft-handed? Are you that liar
And, cast by conscience out, spendsavour salt?

-Gerard Manley Hopkins,
from "The Candle Indoors"

The morning was bright, warm, and leaning toward afternoon by the time Sally stepped out into it. As she turned the key in the lock, she went through her mental checklist one more time. New sheets on the bed, old ones soaking in the tub. Yesterday's clothes scrubbed, dried, pressed. Table, wiped down. Dishes, washed and dried and put away. Floor swept. Rubbish bins emptied.

She took a step away, but then stopped. Her chest itched, and rubbing a hand over it wouldn't help anything. Ignoring it would just mean that the thoughts would plague her through her whole outing. *Dirty. Filthy. Rotten.*

She spun back to the door, let herself in, and charged for the sink. She wiped it down one more time, then the table. She washed her hands until they were pink from hot water and Ivory soap.

The voice still tried to echo, but she twisted the tap back off and snatched up the clean towel. "Take that, Dad."

Speed was the answer now. Get outside, away from it all, before she could think about it again. A minute later she was back on the crumbling sidewalk and, shielding her eyes from the sun, she surveyed the sky. Not a cloud marred the blue expanse. Good. She didn't want to be caught out in the rain in one of her two good dresses.

She set off down the street, humming a little ditty that had been played in the dance hall the night before to drown out the last echoes of her father's voice. Her nerves jumped to the ragtime beat, but she told herself the excess energy was excitement.

Maybe things would finally turn around. She hadn't suspected it when those Italian fellas dropped Roman at her feet, but he might just be her ticket out of this hell.

Daddy Dearest roared in her head again, and this time she could see his mottled face too as he thundered after her, out onto the pristine white porch of their pristine white house. *"You leave here,"* he'd bellowed after her, *"and you'll go straight to hell!"*

She paused at an empty intersection, dragged in a breath, blinked until she saw the familiar buildings of the Levee instead of the multicolored patchwork of autumn in the Appalachians. She rubbed that never-ending itch in her chest. Turned out Dad was right. Hell reigned freely in Chicago's Levee, and she was pretty sure the devil himself answered to the name Al Capone.

She crossed the street and hurried onward, then around the corner at the next intersection. A few cars motored by, but otherwise there wasn't much action in the Levee this time of day. That made it easier to pretend, on those days when she cared to, that she was back in Cumberland, strolling through downtown, ready to duck into McMurphy's for a soda at the fountain before she did the week's shopping.

Today the pretense brought her way too close to the memories of Dad. Besides, it was time to stop looking back and think about the future. If she played it right, this particular hell might not be quite as eternal as she'd begun to fear.

A car motored through the intersection where she needed to cross, so she paused and toyed with the neckline of her dress. She had grown unaccustomed to the modest cut, and whenever she put it on, it felt almost suffocating. But it wouldn't do to go to a fashionable boutique looking like what she was—not if she actually wanted help in spending the bills tucked safely in the little beaded bag Grandma had given her for her last birthday at home. Roman had handed over the dough reluctantly, so she figured she'd better spend it wisely.

Her lips, which she'd carefully painted a stylish scarlet, curved up into a smile as she gained the street where Ava's Place made its home. She'd never been gladder that she'd kept up her acquaintance with the older moll. If she hadn't made a habit of stopping by once a month or so, it would look mighty strange to do so now. As it was, when she let herself in and Tom poked his long face out of his office, he greeted her with a smile.

"Sally. I figured you were due for a visit soon. Ava and the girls are all upstairs. Go on up."

"Thanks, Tom." She sashayed down the hall, stopping at his office so she could lean in and smack a kiss onto his lips. Never hurt to keep on the good side of men like him, even if they weren't the ones with real power. "How's the missus treating you?"

"No complaints," he said with a grin.

Sally stepped back into the hall and winked. "Too bad. Don't work too hard, now. It's a beautiful day out there."

He made a noncommittal hum as she turned to the stairs. She knew her way around here well enough to head up and search out Ava. She found her, as she expected, in her cozy sitting room with a needle, beads, and silk dress in hand.

Sally waltzed in, no need to pause and prepare herself for the coming encounter. Roman had said something about learning her role, acting the part. But this wasn't acting. Acting was the smiles she'd had to don every day at home when people talked about what a wonderful man her father was. So good. So generous. Such a pillar of the community. Acting was saying, "Yes, Daddy," every time he finally decided she was bloody enough and asked if she'd learned her lesson. Acting was telling him every night that she loved him, no matter what new bruises or broken bones he'd given her that day—to make her holy, he said. To whip the sin out of her.

No, this wasn't acting. This was just being exactly what he'd made her: a girl who did whatever she had to do to survive.

Ava looked up as she entered, a smile blooming on the older woman's elegant face. "Sally," she said with obvious pleasure. "I was hoping you'd be by soon. And aren't you looking lovely today."

Sally leaned over to kiss Ava's cheek as she usually did, giving her a grin. "I'm going shopping and was hoping I could convince you to come. I'm gonna need some advice."

Putting aside the dress, Ava lifted her brows. "A shopping trip sounds fun. What's the occasion?"

Sally laughed and sat beside her. "You're going to get a kick out of this one. So I met this john, right? Good-looking guy, and he really knows what he's doing, if you get my drift. But his mind's obviously on other things— asks me if I know any of Manny's girls."

Ava drew in a deep breath that straightened her spine. Her face went hard, blank. "Let me guess: this man answers to the name Roman O'Reilly."

"Yep." Sally made a show of rolling her eyes. "I play it up, right? He already knows this is one of Manny's places, so I point out how close we are, and he bites. Says he'll pay me for any information I can get from you to put your man away. Actually believed me, and didn't bat an eye when I said

I'd need a cover story for visiting you. So he agreed to take me to Colosimo's and gave me some money to buy a new dress, as an excuse to get you to go shopping with me."

Ava looked caught between caution and amusement. "So you need my advice on…"

"Clothes. I don't know what to wear to Colosimo's, I've never been to the joint. And I figure while we're out, you can give me the line you want me to feed him. I gotta have *something* to report, or he won't keep peeling off the bills."

Ava smiled again and relaxed a little. "Sure, Sally. Let me grab my things, and we'll head out. Did he mention what it is he's looking for information *on*?"

Sally followed Ava out of the sitting room and into her bedroom, the largest on the hall. She waved off the question. "He was pretty vague. I tried to get him to spill, but I don't think he trusts me *that* much. Just said to try to confirm some rumors, like whether or not Manny had taken over Eddie's brewery. That sort of thing."

"Ah." Ava picked up a purse and looked around, presumably to see if there was anything else she needed. She favored Sally with a warm smile. "I'm sure we'll come up with something for you to tell him."

"I'm sure we will." Which was hardly her concern. As they left Ava's Place and headed for the shopping district, Sally concentrated on getting Ava to relax even more, never so much as bringing up Roman again except as the john she needed to look good for that night. Predictably, Ava was laughing with her by the end of their first hour, fully engrossed in the process of selecting the perfect gown within her budget.

"This one's divine," the elder declared, holding up a rose silk with intricate beading.

Sally looked at the price and smiled. "It is. But I was hoping to have enough left to buy a string of beads to go with it. Maybe crystal ones, like yours."

Ava frowned and shook her head. "You'd have to settle for a far simpler dress if you wanted crystal. Why don't you just borrow mine?"

Sweet, predictable Ava. For a second, Sally's conscience wiggled to life. But she had long practice at shoving it aside. Ava couldn't get her out of the Levee—how could she, when she'd made it her home? So she couldn't afford to give Ava her loyalty. Sally pasted hesitation onto her face. "Are you sure?"

Ava smiled and pressed the dress into Sally's arms. "Of course. You know I don't mind if you borrow my things. Come on, we'll buy this and head back to my place. You can look through my necklaces to find the perfect one and help me pick out what I want to wear tonight while you're there. Manny's taking me out, too."

This was going far better than Sally had hoped. She gladly forked over Roman's money to the salesclerk and headed back into the Levee with Ava, their arms locked together and their laughter bright. The conversation stayed on easy subjects until they were once again at the bordello, closed in the safety of Ava's elegant bedroom.

"Here." Ava urged Sally onto a padded stool before her vanity, which had sides that opened out into an armoire. She pulled out both little doors, revealing her full collection of necklaces, some expensive and others just pretty. "You can borrow any of the beads. I need something special, though. I'll go try on my dress so we can see what would work best."

This was so easy that Sally wasn't even sure she could trust it—nothing in life came easily. Nothing worth having, anyway. Still, she flashed her friend a smile and poked through the jewelry while Ava disappeared behind a dressing screen. Finding a string of beads that would look good with the pink dress was simple. Trying to verify the absence of the Czech piece was by nature more difficult. She poked through all the gold, all the silver, setting a silver-and pearl filigree pendant swaying with a finger. She didn't see any red-stoned flowers. But how could she be sure Ava hadn't just lent it to some other girl?

Then Ava emerged in a burgundy gown with a low V of a neckline, solving that problem for her—if ever a dress demanded a red necklace, it was this one. Sally let out an appreciative whistle. "Your man sure keeps you in style, Ava."

Though Ava laughed, sadness lit her eyes. "I've earned it. Trust me."

She didn't know Ava's story—none of the girls did. Sally had asked, when she first found herself in the Levee, but Ava kept her own council. Still, it didn't take a genius to figure her tale had been an ugly one. A dame like her didn't end up running a bordello and wearing a mob boss's jewels without making some compromises over the years.

"I've no doubt." Sally tapped a thoughtful finger to her mouth. "Do you have anything red? I don't see anything."

"I'm afraid not."

Not anymore, she meant. "Well then, let's see how this double strand of pearls looks."

Ava stepped closer so that Sally could stand up and secure the strand around her neck. They looked at the reflection in the mirror, both smiling at how well the dress and necklace complemented.

"You have a good eye." Ava touched a finger to one of the smooth, iridescent pearls. Then she met Sally's reflected gaze. "Don't get too involved with this cop, Sally. It'll only be bad news if you do."

It was a warning, but it wasn't a threat. No, the look on Ava's face was the same one Mother had worn that last day she'd sent her off to school, when she'd said, *"Be a good girl, honey. Don't make Daddy angry."* The day Sally'd gotten home and found no Mother.

She couldn't blame her for getting out. But that last directive haunted her—as if she had any more control over her father than she had over Al Capone. Sally swallowed hard. "Why?"

"Because the more questions he asks, the more enemies he makes. Enemies that you don't need to share. Trust me on this one. That young man is only alive right now because Manny's daughter's fiancé asked for him to be spared. If he doesn't let this go, Manny's mercy may run out. And even if it doesn't, O'Reilly's stirring a pot that has more gangsters in it than he probably thinks. Others will be happy enough to do what Manny won't if he keeps digging."

Ava turned to face her and gripped her fingers. "Tell him I wouldn't open up to you so that he keeps you out of this. The risk of having anything to do with him isn't worth what little he can pay you."

Cynicism crept in, tugging Sally's mouth up in one corner. "With all due respect, Ava, that's easy for you to say with your gold and jewels and nice clothes. I need every dime I can get if I ever want to pay off Capone and Torrio."

Ava pressed her lips together and shook her head. "Sweetheart, you're never going to pay them off. You think they don't make sure of that? Your only hope is finding some rich john who wants you enough to give them however much they ask for you."

Sally breathed a humorless laugh. "Like that ever happens."

"Not often, no. More likely is that you catch the eye of another mafioso who convinces Torrio to move you to another brothel, maybe even pays your debt—but then you just owe *him.*"

A sigh leaked out of Sally's painted lips.

Ava gave her fingers a comforting squeeze. "Do you know how much you owe?"

In actual debt? Down to the penny. But once Al tacked on this fee and that interest and decided she owed him for the very air she breathed, too? "Not exactly."

"Find out. If it's reasonable, I'll talk to Manny about getting you out from under them and bringing you in here. Daisy's retiring after her birthday in September, and we'll need to fill her room. You're my first choice."

Wariness came as easily as breathing. "And why would Manny pay to bring me in when he could pick up a new girl without my debts?"

Ava smiled. "Because I want you here. And because if you help get this O'Reilly character off his back, he'll consider himself in *your* debt."

"I guess that's something to consider, isn't it?" It would be, honestly, if Roman weren't dangling actual freedom in front of her. Any pimp had to be better than Al. And Ava's Place had class, at least. She wouldn't have to stand on the corner. Wouldn't have to scrub her hands until they were raw just to feel clean.

No—that wouldn't change. Gold-plated filth was still filth—another something Dad had gotten right. She freed her fingers from Ava's and reached for the crystal necklace that would go best with her new dress. "I'll tell O'Reilly you were close-mouthed and bring this back in a few days. Thanks, Ava."

As soon as she was back on the street, the smile she had given Tom on her way out faded into nothingness. Funny how quickly loyalties could get hazy. She liked Ava. She really did. She considered her a friend, maybe the only one she had in Chicago.

The thing was, Sally couldn't afford to have friends. They cost too much. And she already had more debt than she did years to pay it off.

⚬⚬⚬

The long table in the conference room was all but covered with paper. They had even tacked up a large sheet on the wall to use as a chart, where Helen Gregory dutifully cataloged the evidence. This would be the first time Lorenzo assisted against charges of homicide, and he had to admit that the complexity of the case was overwhelming, especially when Stein stood up with a frantic exclamation. "I'm going to be late for court!" Shaking his head at himself, the older man made haste around the table. "You two keep at it, will you? I'll be back as soon as I can."

Lorenzo got out no more than an affirmative before Stein disappeared into the hall. The moment he was gone, unease pounced. He sent a covert glance to where Helen sat at the other end of the table. He had tried to convince his boss that they didn't need her help with this. His argument might have been more successful had she not proven herself a huge help in past cases. He ran his hands through his hair.

From behind the files he heard her say, "Relax, Enzo. I don't have time to flirt."

"Good." He was careful to keep his mutter low enough that she wouldn't hear. After the greeting she had given him that morning—leaning over his shoulder to put his coffee on his desk and all but falling into his lap, then having the audacity to touch her nose to his neck and comment on his cologne—he fully expected her to use this opportunity to get under his skin.

His focus returned to the deposition in his hands. His job was to find something in it that would substantiate their client's claims of innocence, and thus far he was coming up empty. He got through one more paragraph before Helen interrupted him.

"Going to the Mancari house tonight to pass on the news from the senator?"

He looked up, fully prepared to relate his impatience with a glare. All he saw was the top of her red head over the file she had open. "Obviously. He'll want to know the charges are dropped."

"Mm. And did you have a nice lunch with Miss Mancari?"

"Very nice. Now I really need to concentrate on—"

"Guess you didn't tell her then."

Because his gaze was boring into that folder, he saw her peep up over the top, though she retreated again quickly.

"About the senator?" he answered. "I didn't hear back from him until after lunch, if you recall."

She dropped the file and pursed her lips in obvious exasperation. "That's not what I'm talking about, and you know it. Are you going to tell her about last night?"

Lorenzo sighed and removed his glasses so he could pinch the bridge of his nose. Truth be told, he had felt guilty all through lunch because he *hadn't* mentioned it to Sabina. It would only upset her, and she had enough to work through. Why add the worry that her idiot *fidanzata* might give into temptation and betray her like she had him? She'd probably think she had it coming. She'd probably remind herself that their mothers had to deal with this all the time, bite her tongue, and paste on that smile that every mafioso's wife had learned.

He didn't want to do that to her. He didn't want her to have to worry about him. But a fist clenched up in his chest, because maybe she needed to. Maybe he'd been right to fear his own blood.

"I love it when you do that." Helen rested her elbow on the table and propped her head on her hand, her eyes dreamy and her grin lethal. He lifted a brow in question. "When you pinch your nose. It's so…scholarly. Makes you look like you're thinking deep thoughts."

His indignant snort turned to a laugh. He couldn't help it. "You're an odd bird, Helen."

"Maybe. But you just used my first name at the office, so I think my approach is working." She winked and sat up straight. Her expression moved swiftly to sobriety. "So are you? Going to tell her, I mean."

He stared blindly at the page before him, unsure what to make of the thoughts ricocheting around his head. He didn't want to. But maybe if they could be honest and open even about this, they could tiptoe around the pitfalls together.

"Enzo?"

He sighed again. "Yes. I plan to, when we have more than my thirty-minute lunch break at our disposal."

"Good." His eyes flew to hers. She offered that cheeky grin again. "It's only through testing that love is proven—or disproven. I'm anxious to see what her reaction is when she realizes she has competition. I'll bet you a dinner date it won't be what you want it to be."

"I'm afraid I'm not a betting man." Which was a good thing, because that was a bet he wouldn't have wanted to take.

Obviously reading his mind, Helen chuckled. She offered nothing more, so Lorenzo tried to focus on the papers in front of him again. He got through another paragraph before a knock sounded on the open door.

His breath eased out in a near-moan when he looked up. "O'Reilly. What do you want now?"

The agent's expression had been sour, but at the testiness in Lorenzo's tone, he grinned. Blast it.

Helen put down a file and stood up, and O'Reilly directed his grin toward her. "Afternoon, Miss Gregory. You're looking lovely today."

Helen glowered at him. "Save the charm for your next conquest. Or—oh, wait. You don't much need it with your current girl, do you? Not much of a conquest when you can rent her company by the hour." Chin high and eyes sparking, she strode to the door, pausing beside him and smiling up into his slack-jawed face. "Have a nice day, Mr. O'Reilly."

O'Reilly pivoted to let his eyes follow her out the door. "How did she—?"

Unfazed by both the fact of her knowledge and its implications, Lorenzo smiled. "Miss Gregory is a fount of information about other people's business. I've given up wondering how she comes by it."

"Hm." O'Reilly leaned back out into the hall and called after her, "If you want a job where you can use those investigative skills, just let me know."

Helen replied with a short, rude recommendation of what he could do with his offer.

O'Reilly chuckled and stepped into the conference room, shaking his head. "Spitfire, isn't she? Well, what's all this?" He craned his head around to take in the mountain of paperwork.

Lorenzo closed the folder in his hands. "Nothing to do with you. And as a matter of fact, it looks as though none of my work will have to do with you anymore. I trust you got the message that the bootlegging charges have waved goodbye as well?"

"Actually, I got the message that you'd be hearing back this afternoon and figured I'd stop by to find out the news. Somehow," he said with a hard smile, "I'm not surprised. And that's okay. There are always more allegations to look into."

The arrogance didn't just annoy Lorenzo—it alarmed him. "O'Reilly, what are you doing now?" Not waiting for an answer, he pushed himself to his feet. "Don't you realize you're playing with fire every day you don't let this drop? Keep asking questions about things you're not supposed to, and no one's going to care what they promised me—they're going to take you for a ride."

O'Reilly pulled out a chair and plopped into it. "So you admit to the illegal tendencies of certain parties? Can I get that in writing?"

Lorenzo stared at the man across from him for a long moment. "Six months undercover, and you apparently learned nothing. Mess with the Mafia, O'Reilly, and you'll make more enemies than you bargained for. The gangsters may be more than happy to take out each other, but they're not going to stand for letting *you* do it."

O'Reilly splayed a hand across his heart. "I'm touched by your concern.

Really. And while I'm *sure* you're right, I think I'll take my chances. I haven't run into any danger thus far." He dropped his hand and narrowed his eyes. "What promises, out of curiosity?"

Lorenzo braced his hands on the edge of the table and kept his gaze on O'Reilly's. "I told you last week I'd do all I could to see you got out of Chicago alive. That would be much easier if you'd leave before you get yourself in more trouble."

The idiot shook his head, perhaps in incredulity or perhaps in denial. "You really are righteous, aren't you?"

"You make that sound like an insult."

"Maybe because I can see how little good it does. It sure didn't keep your girl from falling for *me*." Lorenzo clenched his jaw, but O'Reilly just grinned. "Face it, Capecce. It's that holier-than-thou attitude of yours that lost you Sabina. She wanted a little excitement. If you're looking for a girl who'll praise you for all those pious thoughts, maybe you should have gone for Prudence instead."

Though he had opened his mouth to retort to the first part, Lorenzo had to stop and try to process the last. "Who is Prudence?"

O'Reilly made a distasteful face and waved a hand. "You know— what's-her-name. Mary's sister."

In spite of himself, Lorenzo's lips quirked up. "That would be Isadora."

"Right. Perfect woman for you."

He rolled the smile off his mouth. "Maybe, if she hadn't been the perfect woman for my brother first."

O'Reilly was visibly putting the pieces together. "Didn't realize her Joey was your Joey. He was in the war?"

"Mm. Marine, in the Fifth Regiment attached to the Second Division. Died in the Battle of the Somme."

The agent sat forward, his face relaxing into an expression of interest. "No kidding. I was in the Second, Army side, but my regiment left that part of France before Somme. Worked with the Fifth for a while in '17, though. Say, did your brother ever mention a Sergeant Brentwood?"

Lorenzo shook his head, almost wishing he could nod instead. That they could find some common ground other than Sabina, something to make this man see that Lorenzo wasn't his enemy—ultimately, the two of them were on the same side. "Sorry. Plenty of sergeants made their way into his stories, but none of them were Brentwood."

Roman's gaze went distant and his posture relaxed a few degrees, like even thinking about Brentwood—whoever he was— made him look at the world a little differently. "He was a good man. When I first met you, at that birthday party for your cousin Max—you reminded me of him. I thought…I thought maybe there was one good egg in the bunch."

Lorenzo didn't even remember Max's birthday. He certainly didn't remember meeting O'Reilly there. Still, the information settled on him like a coarse blanket—warming, perhaps, but uncomfortable nonetheless. "Your opinion of me seems to have changed. Because of Sabina?"

Roman's eyes flashed flinty again. He tapped a finger onto the table. "Because of *this*. Because you're helping him wiggle out of charges for crimes we all know he committed. That *you* know he committed. It's men like you that help keep power in the hands of men like him. And it's men like him that make the streets unsafe for everyone."

It was on the tip of his tongue to say he'd never wanted to, that he never would again. With this case, these particular charges officially dropped, his duty to Manny was finished. His career as a Mafia lawyer was over. But what did it really matter what Roman O'Reilly thought of him? His greater point still stood. The Mafia was a monster with many heads, many hands, many feet. Try as he might to separate himself from it, he'd never fully succeed—not as long as he ate at Manny's table and called his family *famigghia*.

He heard Helen Gregory's voice down the hall, reminding him again of his own weaknesses. Mafia blood didn't just stain his streets and his family's hands; it flowed in his veins.

He could claim all he wanted that he wasn't one of them. But the hard glint in Roman O'Reilly's eyes said he still had a long way to go to prove it, and the memory of Helen Gregory's kiss agreed.

FOURTEEN

We hear our hearts grate on themselves: it kills
To bruise them dearer. Yet the rebellious wills
Of us we do bid God bend to him even so.

-Gerard Manley Hopkins,
from "Patience, hard thing! the hard thing but to pray!"

Sally was leaning against his door when Roman got back to his apartment. Her stance was provocative, her dress becoming, her eyes inviting—and her lip busted and swollen. Roman frowned as he unlocked his door. "What happened to you?"

She shrugged, following him inside. "Ran into a door."

"Yeah?" He dropped his keys onto a small table. "This door got a name?"

Sally snorted. "Sure. Al Capone." She shut the door behind her and looked around his apartment. "Champ, you need to either learn to pick up after yourself or put up the dough for a cleaning service."

Roman didn't spare his untidy living space a glance. "Marking up his own merchandise? Seems like bad business to me." At her wince, he sighed. "Sorry. Didn't mean—"

"Yeah. You did. But you're right, so who am I to argue?" Shaking her head at the room, she reached out and picked up an old newspaper, folding it back into a neat rectangle. "And this time, that was his point. He was waiting for me when I got back from my shopping trip this morning and didn't much care for me spending all of your money without giving him his cut. Said he wanted to make sure you knew how stupid I was before you invested any more in me."

"Sounds like a real nice guy."

"Oh sure, he's the cat's pajamas." She shuffled a few other newspapers into a neat stack as she rolled her eyes, then moved on to gathering the dirty dishes strewn around the apartment. "But the trip was a success. Ava and I had a good time, and she invited me to look through her jewelry once we got back. No Czech necklace."

Roman pumped a fist in the air in victory. "I knew it. And you managed to look without raising her suspicions?"

Sally laughed and carried an armload of plates to his minuscule kitchen. "Are you kidding? I came right out and told her you were paying me to pump her—made her think I just wanted to get what I could out of you and that I'd only tell you what she wanted you to know."

That dampened his joy considerably. "That's not how we agreed—"

"She trusts me now." Dishes in sink, she headed back to the living room and began rearranging pillows. "And this way if someone sees us together, she won't think anything of it. Trust me, champ. I know how to work Ava. By the time I was through, she was offering me a room at her place as soon as one of her older girls retires this fall."

"Hm. Of course, by this fall her place will be under new management."

Her tight-lipped grin disappeared behind the blanket she snapped open and began to fold. "A development I'll certainly take into consideration before accepting her offer."

He surrendered the point. "Fine, do it your way. As long as it gets me what I need. So what else did she say?"

"That I should steer clear of you because you're going to be collecting enemies like Aunt Nellie does porcelain dolls—and that if Manny doesn't bump you off for your questions, someone else probably will." She offered him a sunny smile and picked up the sack of laundry he had never gotten around to putting away. "Bedroom back here?" Not waiting for an answer, she spun toward the corner and the only place a bedroom could possibly be.

Roman trailed behind. "That's a familiar refrain today."

"Yeah?"

"Mm." He leaned his shoulder into the doorframe as she stopped inside his bedroom and made a disapproving noise at the mess. He followed her progress as she abandoned his clothes for now, heading instead to his bed and its rumpled covers. "Manny's lawyer said the same thing. Of course, Mr. Capecce isn't all that fond of me, given that I stole his girl. You make that look so easy."

Sally chuckled as she adeptly tucked the sheet around the mattress. "Ain't hard, champ, just takes a little practice." She smoothed out a wrinkle and reached for the bedspread. "Stole his girl—as in, Manny's daughter?"

"That'd be the one."

Sally shook her head and plumped his pillow. "Ava mentioned him, too, I think. Said the only reason you were alive was because his daughter's fiancé asked him to spare you. Must be a heck of a guy—no offense, but I wouldn't be so merciful to someone who went behind my back with the person I intended to marry."

His bed was a picture of neatness now, so she picked up the laundry again and began emptying the contents onto the mattress, sorting it by type. Studying her seemed a far better idea than dwelling on thoughts of Lorenzo Capecce. He had spent the entire trip back from the Loop drawing comparisons between the lawyer and his buddy from the war. Thinking about Brent, though, just made him aware that his friend would disapprove of him now. Cliff had nothing on Brent's high standards, and those standards had gotten him through the war. Brent's teaching had made him stand tall and straight before Ma and Da when he got home and let him put his crisp blue uniform on again, knowing he'd lived up to the promise on the brass badge. What would Brent say if he saw him now?

Nothing good.

Watching Sally refold his trousers, on the other hand, was almost entertaining. She lined up the creases as if war might break out in Europe again if they bore an extra wrinkle. "Want me to introduce you to Capecce?" he offered. "You can help him see what a lousy match he and Sabina are."

Sally laughed and picked up the stack of shirts, headed for the chest of drawers against the wall. She opened several drawers, her eyes arching up another degree with each one. "Good grief, what have you been wearing? They're all empty."

Suppressing a smile, Roman motioned to the single chair, where a few clean clothes lay stacked from the last sack of laundry. "Why put them away? I'll just have to get them back out again."

She mumbled an observation about men and inserted the shirts into the top drawer. "Hey, wait. Not quite empty."

It took him a second to recognize the object she pulled out—the framed photo of Sabina she had given him a month ago. "This her?" At his nod, she tilted the portrait so that it better caught the light. "She's beautiful. Easy to see why you'd fall for her. So do you love her or what?"

"Yeah." He shocked himself at the ease with which he admitted it.

Sally put the photo carefully on the bedside table and turned to face him again. "Then why are you so set on bringing down her father? Just because you can't have her?"

He lifted a shoulder and finally stepped into the small room. "It's my job."

"No, champ. Enforcing the Volstead Act is your job. Not solving murders."

"It used to be." Until he realized that solving them didn't accomplish anything. The criminals just walked free, and it didn't bring the dead back to life. He had to stop them before they could do the killing. He had to stop the bosses that paid the thugs.

He picked up two more stacks of clothes and shoved them in the dresser. Sally put the pants away, but somehow even her silence accused him.

Her words were worse. "Getting him pinched won't make it better, you know."

He spun around to face her. The afternoon sunlight made her golden hair glow and lit a fire in her eyes. "What are you talking about?"

"I don't know," she said with a half-smile. "But you do. You're a man with ghosts if ever I saw one."

His mind flooded with the image of that last corpse he'd processed, the last murder he'd helped to solve. The last widow who had wept onto his shoulder.

His hand closed over the St. Michael medallion he always wore. It clearly did nothing to keep good men safe. He yanked it off and dropped it into the drawer, slid Sabina's photo back in, and slammed it closed. "What, are you a philosopher now?"

"Always have been." She grinned. "It just doesn't pay very well."

Determined to change the subject, Roman returned the grin and tackled her playfully onto the bed.

The complex series of jumps Little G executed left one lonely red checker on the board. Sabina groaned. Either her head wasn't in the game or her brother had been practicing in secret because usually she did the trouncing—she'd never been on the receiving end before, and frankly, she didn't like the experience.

From behind her came the unmistakable sound of Lorenzo's suppressed laughter. "You know, Bean, you should have moved—"

"Aa." She held up a hand, then snapped it closed to show him what his mouth should do. "The day I need advice from you on checkers…"

"Would be today, it seems." He leaned over her shoulder, and she shoved him away.

"This is all your fault, Enzo. Hovering and distracting me. Go bother

Mama. Or visit Cook—she made some *arancinu* earlier. With cheese, just like you like. Go get one."

Instead, he put his hands on the table on either side of her, caging her with his arms. He winked at Little G, whose grin was broad and victorious. The imps. "My hovering has never distracted you in a game before. You usually just ignore me."

He had a point, but rather than think about that, she studied the hopeless board before her. One piece left, and it wasn't even a king. Well, there wasn't much strategizing she could do. She only had one move that wouldn't result in instant elimination and was about to make it when Lorenzo's breath tickled her neck. Turning her face to glare at him, she found his nose nearly touching hers.

It took all her willpower to keep from laughing at the glint in his eye. Oh, how she'd missed him. "Go away, *me amuri*. You're going to make me lose, and you *know* how I hate losing."

"You do?" He widened his eyes in feigned innocence. "But it happens so rarely, how can you be sure?" Chuckling at her narrowed gaze, he drew away by a whole inch. "If it'll make you feel better, you can play me next, *me tisoru*."

She hadn't lost a game to him in eight years—which was why he usually refrained from playing her. She grinned and seized the offer before he could retract it. "You're on."

Little G leaned over to snap a finger in front of them. "Hey, remember me? I'm about to win here. Stop procrastinating and let me taste the sweet flavor of victory before you move on to destroying Enzo."

"Yeah, yeah, yeah." Not much caring about the loss in light of what was sure to be a win in another few minutes, she moved her red piece to the only possible black square. It took two more moves before her brother whooped with joy, leaping out of his chair and running out of the room with arms held high. Silly boy. Maybe she should have let him win a time or two before, just to watch his antics.

Nah.

Lorenzo took G's vacated seat and grinned at her. "If that was any indication of your form today, I'll be dancing soon, too."

Sabina stuck out her tongue and began setting up the board for the next round. "How was your day, *caru*? I thought I'd see you last night."

"I would have come over, but when I got out of the office your father was waiting for me to see what the senator said, and then Tony and Val showed up to inform me that Mama issued a command for all to be present for dinner."

"Oh?" She arranged the last of her pieces and waited for him to do the same. "Any particular reason?"

Lorenzo smiled anew. "Yeah. Said she hadn't had all her boys together on a weekday in seven months."

"Ah. Well, I'm glad you stopped over tonight. I missed you."

He lifted a brow, pausing with his fingers on the last black piece. "New strategy, Bean? Telling me you miss me, using endearments? If you think that'll distract me from the game…"

She smiled, even though his words stung. "I don't need to distract you to win. And I *did* miss you."

Given the tic in his jaw, it looked like her words stung him too, though that hadn't been her goal. Would they ever get this right?

He drew in a breath and slid a black piece into a new position. "I should have made time last night. *Mi dispiaci.* It's been a long couple of days."

She slid one of her reds out of line. "That murder case you're assisting with?"

"Among other things."

She could have let it go at that, but they couldn't fall back into those old patterns of silence—not if they wanted to build something stronger than they'd had before. "Anything you want to talk about?"

Lorenzo snorted a dry laugh and moved another black. "Want to? No. But it's something you need to know."

"Okay," she said around the lump in her throat. Her hand shook slightly as she reached out to make her next move.

"The other night when I got home, Helen Gregory was waiting for me."

"What?" Her gaze snapped back up to his. "At your apartment? *Why?*"

His expression was blank. It was the same careful look he wore when he was trying not to rise to his brothers' bait, the one he had perfected when they were kids and Joey and Tony used to taunt him, calling him *Saint Lorenzo*. He always wore that look when something affected him more than he wanted it to. He mumbled, "To try to convince me to give her a chance instead of you."

Sabina's mouth fell open. She felt like she had in that second between the whistle and the bullets' barrage—like her life hadn't been destroyed yet, but it would be. "*Scusi?* Helen Gregory has a crush on you?"

"According to her, she's in love with me." If anything, his eyes got even blanker. "You look shocked. Is it so unthinkable that another woman would be interested in me?"

"Of course not. It isn't that kind of shock, it's…" Dread. Fear. The same old emptiness yawning before her. She could feel herself tumbling into it. "You work with her. Every day. And she's pretty and smart, an independent woman who hasn't already hurt you, and…"

"And you're the one I love. The one I chose, then and now." He smiled, but it didn't look exactly worry-free. "It's your turn, Sabina."

She glanced down at the game but was unable to focus on the colored squares. She hadn't even noticed him move and couldn't have said which piece he had selected. At the moment, she didn't much care. She looked back up into his hazel eyes, searching for some warmth to accompany those assuring words. "What did you *want* to tell her? Do you…" She had to pause to wet her lips. "Do you want to start seeing her?"

His gaze shifted to the window. When he spoke, his voice was low and unfamiliar. "No, it's not that. But when she kissed me—"

"She *kissed* you?" She pushed herself to her feet, toppling the chair behind her. Her hands were shaking. Outrage? Fear? She didn't know. "And you *let* her?"

Lorenzo didn't point out how hypocritical that accusation was—but then, he didn't have to. As soon as she spoke the words, she felt the weight of her mistakes again. Never mind that she'd found Father Russo and made her confession, never mind that she'd done her penance. Forgiveness didn't change the past. Reminding herself that their relationship was a journey, that this was just another of the stops along the road, didn't make her hate herself any less. He had every right to hate her too—to pay her back in kind.

Yet Lorenzo wasn't the type to do that, she knew. So then why did he look so torn? Did he care for Helen in return? "She took me by surprise. But the point is that it made me aware again of all I am. All I'm not." He turned pleading eyes toward her. "What if I'm no better than them, Bean? What if we end up just like our parents?"

A month ago, she would have argued that such a fate wasn't so bad. They were still together, weren't they? Their mothers still laughed and planned weddings and talked about future grandchildren. Their fathers adored their wives and their children and made no qualms about saying so. They all sat together at every Sunday mass, every holiday. They had a good life—but all of it was a lie.

She sank back into her chair and reached across the board to grip his hand, not caring if she knocked the pieces out of place. "We won't. We *won't*. You're not like them, Enzo. You never will be."

"How do you know?"

She'd never had to be the one to reassure him before, not when it came to his own convictions. But then, the one thing she'd never had to doubt was his goodness. "Because I know you, Lorenzo Capecce. You are a man of honor."

His larynx bobbed as he swallowed, but he held tight to her hand. "I never want to hurt you again. Definitely not like that. But I need to know you'll hold me to that honor. You won't turn a blind eye like our mothers."

"It's different for men, principessa," Papa had said. "I promise." She glanced back down at the board, though she didn't really see the pieces.

Then she realized—Helen had been waiting for him after he'd left here the other night. "Wait. That night, after you left, I went to the church. I lit a candle, I was praying for you. At that very time." She could feel those candles burning inside her even now. Her prayers—*her prayers* had made a difference. She had lifted him up before the Father even as he faced temptation.

God had heard her. Her fiancé had stood strong.

There was hope for them yet—and the proof of it was in Lorenzo's slow-blooming smile.

FIFTEEN

What do then? how meet beauty? | Merely meet it; own,
Home at heart, heaven's sweet gift; | then leave, let that alone.
Yea, wish that though, wish all, | God's better beauty, grace.

-Gerard Manley Hopkins,
from "To What Serves Mortal Beauty?"

I can't believe you're dragging me here." Cliff's words barely reached Roman's ears above the loud jazz spiraling through the room. "We should be shutting this place down, not stopping in for a drink."

Roman punched his friend lightly in the shoulder. "Relax. Think of it as research. We're getting a feel for the place—maybe we'll run into someone who knew Eddie."

Cliff snorted. "Do you always make excuses for yourself like that? 'Cause I for one am not going to buy it."

Elbowing a tanked patron out of the way, Roman stepped up to the bar. "One gin, one beer."

"Coke," Cliff corrected, scowling at Roman. "One gin, one *Coke*."

Roman rolled his eyes. "Puritan."

"Traceable to the *Mayflower*." Cliff took a seat and sent a superior snarl across the room. "This joint stinks. Literally."

"You know, Brewster, you're sucking all the fun out of the evening." Roman smiled at the barkeep and handed off the bottle of Coca-Cola to Cliff, then accepted his gin. "Thanks, pal."

Because he didn't feel like dealing with his friend's irritation, Roman took a stool closer to the bandstand and focused his attention on the wailing brass. A second later, recognition struck—it was the same group that had been performing that night Sabina snuck out to meet him, playing the same set. As a matter of fact, this was the song they'd been playing when he took her outside for a kiss—a kiss that had turned into more and still haunted his dreams.

Cliff scooted his stool closer and leaned in to be heard over the music. "Why didn't you bring that new girl you're seeing, anyway?"

Roman arched his brows at him. "What girl?"

"You know—the blond I saw leaving your apartment the other day." Obvious pride sparked in his blue eyes, as if he thought he'd uncovered a secret.

Roman's mouth twitched. "That wasn't my girlfriend, Cliff. That was just Sally—you know, the hooker helping with the case."

Suspicion replaced the gleam of pride. "You let her in your apartment?"

"What's she going to do, steal half a loaf of bread? Please. She's dropped by twice now with updates on her conversations with Ava. And cleans up the place while she's there," he added with a grin. "Not a bad arrangement if you ask me."

Cliff stared at him, unblinking. "Please tell me you're not sleeping with her." When Roman just looked back at the band, Cliff let out a vehement expletive. "You are such a hypocrite, O'Reilly! You claim to be an honest agent, but you frequent bars and—"

"It's the Mafia—"

"You hate. I know. So stop spending money on booze and women that'll put it straight into their pockets!" Cliff stood, smacking his Coke bottle onto the bar. His face was a mask of stony anger. "I'm your friend, Roman, probably the only one you've got left. It's my job to tell you what I'm seeing, so I'll say it again. You're obsessed and blind. I don't know if it was the stint undercover or losing Sabina or a festering of old wounds, but you'd better straighten yourself back out before it gets you fired or killed."

Sermon delivered, Cliff spun on his heel and stalked toward the exit, shouldering aside anyone stupid enough to get in his way. Roman raised his glass to his retreating back. So much for company.

"You've got a lot of nerve showing your face around here."

With a sigh, Roman turned to the girl he'd gotten to know pretty well over the last six months. "Hi, Mary."

The flapper put a hand on her hip and pursed her red lips. "I'm surprised you're still in town. Thought Manny and his boys woulda run you out by now."

"Guess I'm not so easy to shake loose." He looked over her shoulder, where her boyfriend stood with a crooked grin. "Nice to see you again, Rob."

Mary spoke again before Rob could open his mouth. "You're a real sap, you know that? Doing what you did to Bina. You coulda had yourself a girl who's the berries, and you threw it all away on a bust too weak to stick."

His mood plummeted still more. "Thanks for leveling with me there, Mary. Just in case I hadn't figured that out for myself."

"Well if you knew it, why didn't you do something about it? You could have had her up the middle aisle before you made a move for her old man."

Roman blinked, sure he had heard incorrectly. "You're kidding, right? Shouldn't you be saying it's a good thing I showed my true colors before Sabina got involved with me any deeper?"

Mary rolled her eyes, took Cliff's vacated seat, pulled out a cigarette, and lit up. "Look, I'm not a pushover, okay? Maybe you fooled us all about who you really were, but you couldn't have faked your feelings for her. Marrying you might not have been great for the rest of her family, but at least you make her feel something. If she goes through with this engagement to Lorenzo, she's going to shrivel up and fade away before she hits thirty."

His vision blurred at the thought of her marrying Capecce, going to his bed, having his children. Mary was right, it was a fate far worse than a life with him would have been. They might have had to leave Chicago to avoid her father's wrath when he figured out the truth, but at least they would have had fun together. "Maybe it's not too late."

Mary blew out a ring of smoke. "Says you. The way I see it, you've made your bed and will be lying in it alone. She's determined to marry Enzo now."

His knuckles whitened around his glass. "Can't you talk her out of it?"

She snorted around her cigarette. "She won't listen to a thing I say. What about you? Have you tried to talk to her?"

"Not since the Monday after." Roman sighed and made an effort to loosen his grip on his gin. "She wasn't very receptive, though I could tell she still has feelings for me."

"Well, that much is good. Maybe you should try again."

"When?" Frustration leaked into his tone. "She's always either at home with Mama and Papa, who would never let her out of the house if they saw me, or with her precious Enzo."

"No." Mary drew the word out thoughtfully and leaned back against the bar. "She's come to our place by herself a few times—Papa Manny doesn't always even assign a guard. Not that you could meet her there, what with Izzy always around and—" She cut herself off, covering it with a cough that didn't sound real.

Roman frowned. Someone was sick, right? A mother or grandmother or something. Sabina had mentioned it.

Mary apparently didn't care to. She took another drag. "Maybe I could get her to the park or something though, and you could be there."

Hope began to burn in his chest. "You'd do that?"

"Maybe." She crushed out her half-smoked cigarette in an ashtray on the bar. "If the opportunity presents itself and it still feels like a good idea in the morning. Tell you what—we've been coming here every Saturday. Check in with me next week and we'll see where we stand." Scooting off the stool, Mary hooked her arm through Rob's and aimed her body back toward the dance floor. She halted and turned again with a hard glint in her dark eyes. "But Roman? You mess up again, and I'll help Manny's boys run you out. Got me?"

He saluted her with his drink. For the first time in weeks, his heart was light. This time he'd do things more carefully. Make Sabina his—*then* bring down her father.

Sabina felt lighter than she had in years as she hurried with the wind, her mind tripping from one memory to the next. Some old ones that she and Lorenzo had been laughing over from their childhood, some new ones they'd made the last few days as they took walks on his lunch breaks or chased younger cousins through Arrigo Park after he got off work.

Every noon, she met him at Birdwell, Stein, & Associates. Every evening, he took her hand in his and led her out for a stroll through Little Italy. He smiled at her, and she talked to him, and for the first time since he'd slid the ring onto her finger, she actually felt like a bride-to-be.

Even if Helen Gregory still sent her probing looks every time she came through the office doors. Even if Papa was always there in the evenings with one underling or another. Even if two guards still followed them wherever they went.

Her life wasn't without shadows—but it was *real*.

Sabina turned at the corner…and stopped as she saw the street in front of Papa's building. When she'd offered to bring over the attaché case he'd forgotten that morning, she hadn't paused to think that she hadn't been here since *that day*. The day Bureau cars had strewn the pavement and guns had pointed at all the exits. The day Roman had propelled her right into the fight. The day all her sins had crashed down on her.

Her breath shook as she drew it in. No cops today, no Roman—just an old jalopy chattering along. Still, it took a solid minute for her to convince her feet to move again. Why hadn't she just let Mama send Papa's case with one of the guards?

"Bina, *ciao*."

She spun around, digging up a smile for her future father-in-law as he came up behind her, a paper bag in hand that smelled of onions and garlic. "Hi, Vanni. I was just heading up to see Papa. Is he available?"

Vanni, who was usually stationed inside the front doors, smiled warmly. "He's just reading the papers until I get back with lunch. I'll walk you to the door." He turned back around and offered his arm. She tucked her hand into it. "Fran really enjoyed having you over to dinner the other night, *cara*. You'll have to come by more often—she likes talking of all those female things the boys never want to discuss."

She smiled, made herself say something about appreciating Fran's decorating tips, but she couldn't help seeing him, this street, everything through a new lens today. Vanni, a man she'd always loved like an uncle, had killed before. He, like her own father, ran bordellos. He welcomed his sons into the Mafia's ranks. His sins dogged Lorenzo, made him question his own judgment. Yet still he grinned down at her with a twinkle in his eyes, like any future father-in-law would.

They passed by the place where Roman had held her, right across from the door, and she stumbled.

Vanni covered her hand with his free one and pulled her onward. Quietly, he said, "I'm very glad you and Enzo have worked things out, Bina. I have too long counted you as a daughter to deal with the thought of losing you. Seeing you enjoying each other so much the other day was a balm to my soul."

She moved a little closer. "Me too, Papa Vanni. You've raised a wonderful man."

"Mm." He turned his eyes to the distance, his smile small and a little sad. "He is that. Though very little of it is to my credit. Had he turned out as I raised him, he would be working with Tony and Val, preparing to take over your father's operations."

"Take over?" She stopped a few steps away from the door. Keeping the frown from furrowing her brow took monumental effort. "Since when are they taking over?"

Vanni cleared his throat. "Well, your father and uncle and I are all getting old, Bina. And Little G told your father last week that he wants to pursue printing with your cousin instead. Of course, if he were to change his mind—"

"I didn't mean to imply you're muscling out my brother. I'm the one who encouraged him to talk to Papa." She had stood outside the study door through the whole conversation, her ear pressed to the wood, ready to charge in and defend his right to choose if needed. But G had held his own, presenting his desires calmly and clearly. Her heart had swollen with pride as he made his case. And she'd nearly sagged in relief as their father gave G his blessing to pursue whatever brought him joy.

She hadn't paused to think about what that meant for the Family. "I just didn't realize Tony and Val...knowing how Enzo feels, I mean, I always thought..."

"They love and respect his choices. But his choices aren't theirs." Vanni drew his arm away, though he still smiled. "They either step up, or we bring in someone new to groom. No one wanted that."

"Does Enzo know?"

Vanni shrugged. His discomfort shone in his hazel eyes. "He's a smart boy. I'm sure he's picked up on it."

He hadn't said anything to her...but maybe he was still piecing it together. Gathering the evidence, saying nothing until he could convince both judge and jury. Or maybe it just hurt too much for him to know how to put it into words. Sabina sighed and, when Vanni opened the door for her, walked inside. She lifted a hand in farewell before turning to the stairs, wondering how to get Enzo to talk about this. She didn't want to ruin the fun they'd been having—but he shouldn't have to carry that burden alone.

She walked slowly and silently down the hall to Papa's office. As she neared his partially opened door, she shifted the case to her other hand so she could better reach for the knob.

She froze a step away when she heard a feminine voice. Peering in, she saw a woman pacing before Papa's window. At first, with the glare of the midday sun behind her, Sabina could see nothing but the outline of an expensive dress and the curvy form it accentuated. Then she saw the hair—auburn with a single streak of gray—and caught a glimpse of a familiar face.

The woman from the park, from church. What was she doing here?

Sabina eased back a step. It was a dangerous question. People from all over Little Italy sought out Papa—he was their protection, the one who provided jobs for their sons. He was the one who loaned them money...

and who then came to collect. Did she really want to hear this woman begging for a favor or an extension?

Before she could decide, the woman came to a halt and sagged to a perch on the corner of Papa's desk. The pose looked so comfortable and familiar, it made Sabina's brows knit. "I don't know what else she should tell him, Manny," the woman said. "He won't back off. Sally says he's still digging elsewhere and apparently finding enough to keep him going."

Her father sighed, the sound coming from the area of his desk, though he wasn't within her line of vision. "Perhaps you shouldn't have trusted this Sally. She's one of Torrio's girls, after all, and he'll benefit greatly if I get put away."

The woman craned her head back to look at the ceiling, her frustration obvious. "She's a good girl."

"She's a whore."

The woman's head snapped back down, and she glared in Papa's direction with more fire than most acquaintances would ever dare send his way.

Suspicion crept up Sabina's spine, twisted around her heart.

Not a woman asking for a favor for her son. Not a woman come to beg for a little more time on her loan. This woman *knew* him.

Sabina heard the squeak of Papa's chair, signifying that he was getting up. "Well I'm sorry, Ava, but you know as well as I that most of them can't be trusted."

"Torrio's got her in a hole in the wall. I promised her Daisy's room if she helps us out, which will be a big step up for her. If being my friend isn't enough to make you willing to trust her, you can at least trust her because it's in her best interest to be truthful with me."

Torrio. Rooms. Whores.

Sabina's stomach turned. This woman—this kind woman who always smiled at her, always greeted her, always asked after Mama and Little G and lit candles for them at Holy Guardian Angel—she was a...a...what? A *madame* at a bordello? One of *Papa's* bordellos?

Papa stepped into view, moving over to Ava and cupping her shoulders with gentle hands. "All right, *cara*." His voice took on the placating tones that Sabina knew well. Though she tried to dismiss the endearment as perfunctory, she didn't quite succeed. Not given the way his fingers rubbed over her shoulder, or the way she leaned into his touch. "We'll assume Sally can be trusted, and that she's telling the truth. But you still don't need to worry."

Ava breathed a laugh and crossed her arms over her chest. "He saw me with Eddie the night he was killed, Manny. What if he's spoken to the police and knows that it was my necklace found with the body?"

"The man was twice your size and killed by a broken neck. No one is going to blame you for that, even if you *were* there."

"No." She slid back to her feet, pulling away from his touch, but then reached out and grabbed his hands, her eyes imploring. "They'll blame *you*. We both know it. That's why we have to stop this investigation, *me amari*. If they charge you with his murder, it will be because they have a lot of evidence, and you might not be able to get out of it. And then where will we be?"

Papa lifted her hands and kissed each of them in turn. "You know you'll be taken care of, *cara*, no matter what happens to me. I've made provisions."

"That's not my only concern!" Ava blinked back tears that were nevertheless audible in her words. "What about Rosa? Giorgio Jr.? Sabina? None of us just need your money, Manny, your *provision*. We need *you*!"

Papa's face looked exactly like it did when Mama was crying for him to fix something—placating, loving, just a bit impatient. "No one's losing me."

Ava shook her head. "We could *all* lose you. I know the children and Rosa don't want to face life without you any more than I do, which is why you have to take me seriously. This isn't about bootlegging or bookmaking. This is murder."

"All right. Okay. Hush now." He pulled her to him, wrapping his thick arms around her as she cried against him. "I'll take care of it. I'll see that any trails lead nowhere, and I'll talk to Enzo about whether I should hire Darrow."

Sniffing, Ava raised her face. "You need to cut it off quickly, Manny. You can't let this get in the way of the wedding. Rosa will never forgive you if it interrupts things, and poor Sabina—she's been through the wringer already, these last couple weeks."

"I know. I do. Nothing will ruin my princess's day." Papa leaned down and kissed her lightly.

The tender touch was more devastating to watch than a passionate embrace would have been. Sabina knew well how passions could lead one into trouble, but this kiss spoke of habit, affection, a longstanding relationship. She glanced down to see that her knuckles had gone white around his case's handle.

"Try not to worry, *bedduzza*. I'll take care of this."

"I'm a worrier, Manny, you know that. It's all I've been able to think about since Sally told me what was going on. I'd hoped to handle it without involving you—"

"There is no need for that." He kissed her again, presumably to stop her words. He wore an indulgent smile. "What you *do* need is a night out, a distraction. I would take you tonight, but I already promised Rosa I'd be home for dinner. Tomorrow, though, we'll go out. Okay?"

"You're so good to me." She stretched up to kiss him more fully.

Every pulse pounded like a drum in Sabina's ears. It was one thing for her mother or Lorenzo to vaguely mention other women, brothels, and spilling blood. It was quite another to see her father's arms around a woman who apparently lived in such a place, discussing a murder he had presumably committed.

And *this* woman—this woman! How dare she speak of her and G and Mama as if she knew them, as if she cared? How dare she walk in their park and sit in their church and light candles for them, as if she weren't... weren't...

"I love you, Manny."

Papa didn't even hesitate. "*Ti amu, me tisoru.*"

Fury rocketed through her. She acted before she could think better of it. One hand pushed open the door, her feet propelled her in, and she sent the briefcase flying at the desk so that she could hear the satisfying crash as it hit the surface and sent pens and papers and who knew what else scattering. "How *dare* you!"

He at least had the decency to jerk away from his mistress. "Sabina! What are you doing here?"

"Learning the truth about you, apparently. How *dare* you dishonor Mama this way? Not just keeping a woman like *that* as a mistress, but flaunting it to the world? And giving her the exact same words you give your *wife*!"

Papa's face went hard, muscle by muscle. "You've a right to be angry. But you will show some respect."

"How can I show what I don't have anymore?" Seething, she turned her hard gaze on the woman her father apparently found so irresistible.

Ava didn't look like some temptress, a home-wrecker. Her eyes shone with regret as she said what Papa should have. "I'm sorry, Sabina. I never meant to hurt you."

The apology brought tears dangerously close to the surface. Sabina wanted to blame the older woman, claim that Papa had been beguiled, that Ava had deliberately inserted herself into their family with the purpose of ripping it apart. She wanted to bring her to her knees with accusations.

But she was the woman who watched them from a distance in the park, who always asked after those who were absent, who always had a smile. She was the woman who worried about gunfights and lit candles for them in church.

Papa. Papa was the one to blame. The illustrious Giorgio Mancari, who took whatever he wanted and proudly bent the world to his will. In all likelihood, Ava had just been one of his many prostitutes until he chose to raise her up to the office of mistress. One could hardly blame her for accepting the promotion.

Sabina spun to glare at her father. "How could you do this to Mama? Don't you love her?"

"Of course I do!" Genuine fervor colored the words, which had slipped into Sicilian. "Your mother stood beside me through everything, gave me my children. She is the love of my youth, the best wife I could ever ask for. My relationship with Ava has nothing to do with her."

He believed it, clearly, even if she had no idea how. She replied in English. "I don't think Mama would agree with you about that."

"She understands these things, *principessa*."

"No, she *suffers* these things. And you—you're the one who makes her suffer. You're the one who makes us *all* suffer. You're a *monster*!"

"Princess." Papa strode over to her, reached for her, but she ducked away. "You have been through a lot lately, so I will overlook these bursts of disrespect. But I expect better from you in the future."

Sabina took another step away. "Or what? You'll cut off my allowance? Kick me out? It hardly matters—I'll be married in a month."

Her father's temper flared too, sparking in his eyes. "You think Lorenzo will want a vindictive wife who sees fault in everything?"

"Well, if he doesn't want me, I can always take to the streets. You obviously have no problem with other men's daughters doing that."

The arrow hit its mark. Papa let out a string of Sicilian curses as he strode away, only to spin back around and point a finger at her. "You are being deliberately crude and ridiculous. Think what you will of my methods, but everything I have done has been for your mother, you, and your brother and sister. I have built a kingdom for you, *principessa*, so that you might have anything you want."

"I don't want this *kingdom*." Her voice broke on a sob, and she wished she had something left to throw. "I hate everything about it. I hate *you*."

His nostrils flared; he dropped his finger only to curl the hand into a fist. "You do not mean that."

"Yes I do!" Chest heaving, she stumbled back, tripping over the rug, reaching for the door. She had to get out of here.

Papa shook his head. "You love me, and you know I love you. I love all of you."

He said it like it should mean something—as if love made any difference when you used it as an excuse to tear the world apart. "*Sì*. But you love the Mafia more. And I'm through trying to compete with that." She spun around and fled before he could reply.

SIXTEEN

━━━━◆·◆·◆━━━━

Elected Silence, sing to me
And beat upon my whorlèd ear,
Pipe me to pastures still and be
The music that I care to hear.

-Gerard Manley Hopkins,
from "The Habit of Perfection"

"Come out with us tonight, pussycat. That'll wipe that frown off your face."

Sabina just stared at Mary, too numb to even think up a refusal. She had walked until her feet hurt, not even noticing until she'd been wandering Chicago for an hour that she had somehow managed to escape her guards when she left Papa's office. She had walked, and she had seethed, and she had prayed every prayer she knew and a few she made up on the spot. She had wrestled and cursed and then, as the sun sank low in the sky, finally headed back to Taylor Street.

But she still couldn't go home. So she had come here instead, hoping Isadora would have something to say to make it all right. But Mary had opened the door and dragged her into her room. Mary had chattered about drop-waists and hemlines and whatever was the cat's meow today while Sabina stood there in the center of the room, her hands hanging at her sides and her gaze not quite able to focus on her friend.

She looked at her now and barely even recognized her. What happened to the Mary who wore her hair in two braids and was the best hop-scotcher in Little Italy? What happened to the girl whose biggest rebellion was eating a *gelato* an hour before dinner? What happened to the innocence they'd once shared?

Mary heaved a sigh and shook her head. "Enzo's the one doing this to you. You need to shake free of him. Get back to *living*. You look like a walking corpse."

She winced at the word. *Murder. Murderer.*

Papa.

She forced a swallow. "It isn't Enzo."

"Yeah. It is." Standing on one foot, Mary pulled a high heel onto the other, hopping to keep her balance. "You know what, Bina? I'll prove it to you eventually. In the meantime, let Izzy bore you to sleep and help yourself to a calzone, if you're hungry. Every nosy neighbor in Little Italy has been coming by with food this week for some reason."

It almost, almost made her smile. On any other day, it would have. Today, all she could manage was to trail Mary out into the main room and stand there like a mannequin as she let herself out without so much as a goodbye for her sister.

The door to the other bedroom was open. Isadora sat in the chair by the bed, jerking to attention when the door slammed.

She spotted Sabina, smiled, and wandered out. "I didn't hear you come in."

She looked a little better today, the shadows under her eyes not so dark. Sabina mustered a smile. "How's your mother?"

Isadora wrapped her arms around herself like it was winter instead of the first of July. "I don't know. She barely wakes up anymore. But the neighbors have arranged a rotation for sitting with her. A few hours in the morning, a few hours in the afternoon. I never dare to go far, but at least I can sleep a little, here and there."

Not knowing what else to do, Sabina reached out and squeezed her elbow.

Izzy sighed. "I know you're the one who gave them that idea, let everyone know how bad Mama had gotten. Thank you. I just…couldn't."

"I know. And you don't have to thank me." She glanced at the door behind her. "Has Mary even gone in there?"

Her friend shook her head. "Not in weeks. She won't even talk about her. If I say anything, she just…leaves." Her shoulders sagged, but then she blinked and pulled them up again. "You look out of sorts. Are you all right? Did something else happen with Enzo?"

Sabina opened her mouth, but then she just smiled and shook her head. "No. Everything's fine with Enzo." How could she burden poor Izzy with her drama with Papa? She had too much on her plate with her own parents, with Mary, with *everything*. "I just wanted to check on you." She suspected Father Russo wouldn't even make her say an extra Hail Mary for that lie.

Isadora leaned over to wrap her in a tight hug. "You're a good friend, Bina. Thank you. For everything."

"Of course." When she pulled away, she took a step toward the door. "If you need anything—anything at all—please let me know. Okay?"

Isadora nodded, wrapped her arms around herself again, and turned back to her mother's room. "Just…would you pray she goes quietly? She's suffered so long."

Sabina nodded too and let herself out of the apartment before she gave in to tears in front of her friend. *Suffered.* The word echoed in her head, her own voice shooting it at her father like a projectile.

Everything she had said to him was true, but she wasn't sure yet if she regretted saying it. All she knew was that if she didn't go home now, she'd add to Mama's suffering, so she set her feet on the familiar course to her own back door.

The two blocks home passed quickly. All the thoughts that had kept her walking that afternoon were gone, still, mum. *Numb.* Ice? No. A different kind of numbness, one more like a charred patch where a fire had burned itself out.

Once she gained their small yard, she breathed a grateful sigh to see no family members out enjoying the last of the day. With any luck, she'd be able to sneak through the kitchen and up to her room without garnering any attention.

Luck was not with her that day. "Sabina Maria Mancari! What were you thinking? I have called Enzo's office, I have sent your brother all over Little Italy—where have you been all day?"

Sabina halted in the middle of the kitchen, the room rife with the heavy scent of *saracena*, the Sicilian olive oil that Cook used in abundance. Her mother blocked the exit. Papa loomed behind her. His face lacked the consternation on Mama's but nevertheless showed concern.

How touching.

A few of the embers stirred to life in those charred remains, and a wind blew across them, fanning them. She focused only on her mother. "*Mi dispiaci*, Mama."

"You're sorry?" Mama glowered and planted her hands on her hips. "That's all you have to say for yourself after worrying me sick? I think I deserve an explanation as to *why* you disappeared for over six hours!"

The flames licked up again. Sabina moved forward, slipping past both parents and gripping the banister. "Then ask your husband. He always has all the answers." She started up the stairs.

"Giorgio?"

Papa was apparently not ready to answer Mama's questions, either. "Sabina. You will not treat your mother this way."

As if *he* got to talk about how one should treat Mama. She charged into her room and slammed the door. From below she heard her parents' voices, though she couldn't make out the words. Not surprisingly, her mother's footfalls soon sounded on the stairs, and the door opened as Sabina flopped onto her bed.

Mama closed the door softly behind her, her expression now one of caution. "Your father said only that you're angry with him. Talk to me, *cara*."

Sabina pulled a pillow onto her lap and wrapped her arms around it. "Let's just say I won't be running any errands to Papa's office anymore."

Mama let out a long breath and perched on the edge of her bed. "What did you see, Sabina?"

She averted her face, latching her gaze onto the purple glass of her old oil lamp, kept handy for power failures.

"It will be more painful for both of us if I have to start guessing."

That was probably true. Still, she couldn't talk about this, not with Mama. She couldn't look into her beautiful face and say she'd seen Papa's other woman.

Mama laced their fingers together. "Well, I imagine if it were anything else, you'd tell me, so it must have been Ava."

Sabina's head snapped back around, her fingers tightened. "You know—?"

"Of course I know, *cara*. How could I miss something that's been going on for twenty years?" Mama used her free hand to brush a waved lock away from Sabina's face. "I've accepted it. That doesn't mean I like it."

Did she know that the woman haunted their neighborhood? Was that something she *should* know? Sabina averted her gaze, studying the familiar print of her bedspread instead. "He told her he loves her. Called her his treasure, just like he calls you."

Mama's lips tightened, but her posture remained unchanged. "I imagine he *does* love her, after all this time. He would say that doesn't detract from his love for us."

"He did say that, when I burst in and called him on it." She shook her head, exhaustion weighing down on her. "It doesn't matter to him—but it matters to me."

Mama leaned over and pressed a warm kiss to her forehead. "Mafiosi live by their own rules, *picciridda*. A mafioso's wife has little choice but to follow. But his daughter—his daughter is free to choose her own way. I told you before I wanted to keep all this from you, but perhaps this is the better way. You can see it for yourself and understand why I want better for you."

She squeezed her eyes shut and made no objection when Mama slowly caressed her hair. "It hurts, Mama. To realize that the Papa I thought I knew isn't the same man when he walks out of here. To think that he raised me to be a God-fearing lady, but then he goes out and makes his living from sin."

"I know. But you should be glad your own children will never know that pain. Enzo is the same everywhere he goes."

He was—because he knew he had to fight to be, every day. She peeked her eyes open again, watched the pain flicker over Mama's beautiful face. "You know about her—do you *know* her? Have you…met?" Did she realize that the woman she greeted easily in the aisles of Holy Guardian Angel was the same woman who entertained her husband on nights when he wasn't home?

Mama's face went hard. "There are some lines even your father knows not to cross. He is hers in the Levee. He is mine in Little Italy. There is no meeting of those worlds."

Sabina let out a slow, quiet breath. Perhaps Papa knew that line—but it seemed Ava didn't. Still, she couldn't bring herself to tell her mother that. "It's just…she talked about us like she knew us. About how the wedding was soon and…"

Mama pursed her lips, but then she shrugged and stood. "Your father undoubtedly tells her about his family. After so many years of hearing stories, she probably feels as though she knows everyone."

Maybe that explained it, at least in part. Maybe that was why she seemed to…care. But clearly it wasn't something Mama wanted to think about. She moved to Sabina's door. "I will bring up your dinner tonight. But you can't avoid your father forever, *cara*. For all his sins, for all his faults, he loves you more than life itself."

Sabina just hugged her pillow to her chest and tried not to wonder what "life itself" really meant to a man who would snuff it out so easily.

It didn't take but a New York minute for Sally to determine that the man called Topsy Nosotti was about as far from the top as a man could get and still be walking. She ran a hand up his arm and gave him the smile that always made men go stupid, but mentally she was calculating how many bars of Ivory it would take to feel clean again.

More than she had the coin to buy, that was for sure. And the count went up every time he ran his eyes down her figure.

She hoped he was as broke as his outdated hat promised, that he wouldn't fork over the fiver for more than a look. "No kiddin." She said it in the drawl that half the folks back home used to stretch their vowels. "Baltimore? I'm a Maryland girl myself, but from the western side."

He gave her an ugly little smile that revealed three missing teeth. "Yeah? I thought they was all hicks in that part of the state, but you sure don't look like no redneck."

She laughed and trailed the tips of her fingers over his shoulder. It seemed smarter than using them to paint a couple of claw marks down his face, which was what she'd have preferred. "Won't say there aren't some of those, sure. But my family—we come from good German stock. My opa came over...gosh, back in the fifties, I guess. He and Papi ran a little brewery there in the hills until Prohibition shut 'em down."

She made her face fall, even though the idea of her high and mighty father ever making a living from "the devil's drink" made her want to giggle instead. "I think I tasted beer before my own mother's milk—or so the joke in the family goes."

He laughed like it was real funny—and slid an arm around her waist. "German, huh? I was over there in the War, you know. I bet you'd look real cute in one of those—whatda-ya-call-ems." He dropped his gaze to her décolletage.

She bet she would too, but *he'd* never see it. And she wasn't here to talk about costumes. "Did I hear the bartender there say you were a brewer too, before the sauce stopped flowing?"

"Before? Sure." He reached for the shot of bathtub gin sitting by his elbow on the bar and tossed it back. It dimmed a bit of the caution in his eyes. "Master brewer. Eddie Weisenheimer brought me out here from Baltimore special. No one knew hops or wheat like me."

Yes. On the right track, finally. She put a little extra appreciation in the hand she moved to the back of his neck. "Oh, Papi would *love* to talk to you. He can go on about it all forever. Not that he ever worked for an operation as big as Weisenheimer's, of course. That stuff was popular even in Cumberland and he always—say!" She pulled back a little, trying not feel every single particle of filth she'd picked up from him. "Guess that was your brew we were drinking. Ain't that something?"

His eyes went bright. Brighter still when he tossed back another shot. "Yeah. Really something. You know, doll." He leaned closer, pulled her tight again. "I could get you some, if you wanted to reminisce. The good old stuff, not this swill they're brewing now."

She held the smile tacked in place. Ivory might not cut it. She might need some old-fashioned lye. She made a show of looking around, leaning closer. "I heard they're still brewing. And that it's under new management. But didn't they keep you on? A master brewer like you?"

He hiccupped right into her face, and she nearly lost her measly dinner. His face contorted into three different expressions before finally settling on something he no doubt hoped looked like pride. "Course he did. Eddie—I was his right-hand guy, you know. Heard him…the night Manny came. Made him promish me a…a place. And ol' Manny, he knew my repertu… my repatate…my reputation, see? He wanted me on board. But me—I'm loyal to Eddie. I heard things get heated, and when he turned up dead, I walked away. Loyalty, see." He pounded a fist onto his chest.

"Wow." She toyed with the hair at the nape of his neck. It was greasy, and she could only hope he didn't have lice that were leaping even now onto her hand and marching their way up her arm. Her shudder wasn't put-on. "You heard them that night? When Mr. Weisenheimer was killed? If I were you, I'd a high-tailed it out of Chicago after that. Wouldn't want that gangster coming after me next."

Topsy patted her hip, as if that would provide her with some comfort. "I ain't no coward."

"Obviously. Still." She shook her head, making sure a blond wave touched her face just so. "Seems like if that Manny fella knew you'd heard them out there right before Weisenheimer got himself dead…"

"Manny don't know nothing. I didn't broadcast I was there listening."

"Oh good." She pressed a hand to her chest, widened her eyes, and then leaned over to press a kiss to his cheek. "That makes me feel better." She was going to need a new tin of tooth powder too, if she had to do that again.

But he was grinning like a gap-toothed fool. "Say, doll, wanna get that beer? I got a whole stash back at my place."

She just bet he did—or the empties, anyway. "That sounds great, Tops. Just give me a minute to freshen up, will ya?" She nodded toward the hall that led to the water closets and, the very second his arm loosened around her, beat a hasty path through the early crowd. She kept half an eye peeled behind her, so when he turned back to the bar—either for one more gin or to settle his tab, she didn't much care which—she darted toward the exit and didn't stop hoofing it until she was ducking into an alley a block away.

Shoulda gone to the water closet first though, to wash her hands. She wiped them on her dress, but that didn't help a bit.

"Well?"

She jumped, then cursed herself for it. She wondered if Roman would take it personally if she tried to spit the taste of Topsy's cheek from her mouth. Better not risk it. She didn't trust him to buy her freedom if she wasn't both useful *and* attractive. So she smiled and put some extra sway in her sashay as she moved to where he waited in the shadows. "He was there that night. Heard Eddie and Manny talking over the purchase. He says they didn't know he was there. Also tried to convince me that Manny offered him a job, and that he refused out of loyalty to Eddie."

Roman snorted. "Manny doesn't hire drunks to work at breweries. But he was there. He heard them."

"He heard them."

With a low laugh in his throat, he picked her up, squeezed her, spun her in a circle. Maybe it would have sent her head spinning in laughter if the squeeze didn't make her hiss in pain first.

He put her back on her feet, hands gentle on her hips, and turned her into the streetlight. "What? Did I hurt you?" Then his face went hard. "Let me guess—the door caught you in the ribs this time."

She shrugged and tried to give him the cheeky smile he seemed to appreciate. "Wily things, those doors." Then she sighed. "I asked him how much it would take to buy out, and he immediately assumed I was squirreling away money that should have gone to him. He was somewhat appeased when I told him another mafioso was interested in moving me to his bordello. Figured he'd buy that before the idea of a john helping me."

Roman's fingers dug into her hips. "And? Did he tell you how much?"

"Fifteen hundred." She delivered it as evenly as she could. As if it were just any old number—not a number so high she didn't have a hope of making it back in this lifetime or the next.

Roman muttered a curse, and his hands fell away. "That's over half my annual salary. You know that, right?"

Sally turned toward the opposite exit from the alley—the quickest route back to her territory. If Al didn't see her on her street within the hour, that price would only tick up. "I warned you it'd be high. That's not actually what I owe, but he tacked on some extra to cover the rent until he can replace me, or so he said."

Roman fell into step beside her, silent for a few clicks of her shoes on the pavement. "I can swing it if that's the way you want to go. I have some money…put aside."

He'd been a cop before he was an agent—she'd gleaned that from poking through his things as she straightened them up. It didn't pay a whole lot better. If he had money, it couldn't be much—not if he was honest.

"We'll see. Haven't quite made up my mind." If the price went up again, if Roman couldn't swing it, she'd be worse off than she was now. Al didn't take kindly to girls who weren't loyal. "That would still leave me with the problem I had before I hit the streets—no way to make a living honestly. But if Capone catches me job hunting…"

"From where I sit, there's not much of a choice, Sally. Your only other offer is Ava's Place, and after Manny gets put away—"

"One of his lieutenants will take over, and they'll honor any promises Ava made. They're not a street gang, champ. Cut off the head, and this snake will grow another one." She picked up her pace. "Surely you know that."

"Maybe."

She shook her head and looked both ways when she hit the end of the alley, just to make sure neither Capone nor Topsy were in sight.

Roman, on the other hand, charged out into the lamplight like it didn't matter who saw him. Then he stopped. "I'm going south here."

Fine by her. She'd just as soon not let Al see her with him. Though she narrowed her eyes when she turned to say goodbye and saw that he was wearing a sharp black suit with white pinstriping. Not his usual choice. "You're all dolled up. Hitting the town?"

"Meeting one of Sabina's friends. She said she might try to help get us back together." He sounded so…hopeful. Like any guy pining for any dame. Like he wasn't trying to put away her old man—and keeping company in the meantime with a dame like *her*.

She couldn't quite stop the shake of her head.

Roman scowled. "What? Maybe it's a pipe dream, but I've gotta try."

"Well, good luck, then." She angled her face up and flashed him another saucy grin. "And if she passes you up, it's her loss."

Roman chuckled and caught her with a hand on her neck, spinning her around and dropping a kiss onto her lips. "Be careful out there, Sally. Okay?"

He'd kissed her. Kissed her, like any guy would kiss any dame he liked. Not like a john who's just passed her a bill and decided he could. For that matter, not like he ever had, when he was just a john.

Sally couldn't quite summon a flippant response, so she just nodded, hoped her smile was cheeky enough, and sauntered on by. She hoped so hard it was nearly a prayer that Roman didn't get himself dead before this was over—and that Sabina Mancari slapped him down so hard he'd come spinning back to her for a little comfort.

He wasn't perfect. But she could do a whole lot worse.

◈

Roman headed for the same speakeasy he'd gone to a week earlier and arrived as darkness fell and life kicked up inside. Through the smoky haze and swinging jazz, he searched for Mary and Rob. After locating them on the dance floor, he headed for the bar.

He was halfway through his gin when Mary sidled up. She leaned close to his ear but still had to shout to be heard over the music. "Arrigo Park, next Saturday, seven o'clock. It's the best I can do."

He grinned as she spun away again. One more week, and he'd have another shot with his girl. If he played his cards right, he could marry her before her family ever knew he'd come back into the picture. Then he'd turn all his evidence over to Bannigan and be able to hold her while she cried about her poor papa being locked away for life, making sure she thought it was Bannigan who had done the investigating, not Roman.

It would work. All he had to do was convince her, and he knew a sure-fire way to do that. One kiss, and she always melted.

SEVENTEEN

I walk, I lift up, I lift up heart, eyes,
Down all that glory in the heavens to glean our Savior;
And éyes, héart, what looks, what lips yet gave you a
Rapturous love's greeting of realer, of rounder replies?

-Gerard Manley Hopkins,
from "Hurrahing in Harvest"

The sun glinted off the small white ball that arced through the air, landed with a thud, and rolled to a rest in the grass. Lorenzo picked up his two green bocce balls and gauged the distance to the pallino. The park didn't have a backboard or sand court, so they were playing by Manny's rules—throw the pallino anywhere they wanted and see which team could get closest with their bocce balls.

"Prepare to be humiliated, old men," Tony taunted with a grin, stepping up beside Lorenzo with his similar green balls.

Their father scoffed. "You hear him, Manny? As if we have not been playing bocce since before they were born!"

"Insolent pups," Manny said with a grin.

Familiar refrains, both of them. For as long as he could remember, Lorenzo and his brother had been playing the two older men on Independence Day. It was as much a part of the celebration as the Italian sausages roasting on the grill, the firecrackers kids kept setting off, and the multi-lingual shouts of greeting from the entire neighborhood as picnics were unloaded and shared.

Today, however, his attention wasn't focused on the game. He kept glancing over to where the women were setting up their food, his eyes on Sabina.

She looked cool and gorgeous in her white dress, but distant. Hollow. Like she'd looked last year, the year before, rather than how she'd been looking for the past month. Something had happened. What, though? He'd tried to find time to come over for the last few evenings, but the murder case he was assisting would be heard in court tomorrow, and his choice was either to work late in the evenings or to come in today. He'd voted for having the holiday off.

Maybe he'd made the wrong call.

"Focus, Enzo." Tony punched him lightly in the shoulder, his face wreathed in grins. "We have to prove that last year wasn't a fluke."

Sabina chose that moment to look up and catch his gaze. Her lips curled up into a soft smile that did wonders to ease his worry, and life glinted through that haze of emptiness. Whatever had her upset, it must not be his fault. She even headed his way, settling onto a blanket beside Val and Little G to watch the game.

Lorenzo grinned and turned to his older brother. "I'm focused."

"Yeah, *now*." Tony tried for a disgusted look but lost the battle to a grin. "Just think, little bro. At next year's picnic, she might be sitting there with your *bambino* in her arms."

Manny threw the first ball, which rolled to a stop mere inches from the pallino. Lorenzo smiled anyway. "A happy thought indeed. You taking the lead, Tony?"

His brother replied by taking up position and swinging his green ball through the air. It landed with a thud practically on top of Manny's, pushing the elder's red one out of the way. Their young audience erupted into wild cheers.

Manny narrowed his eyes and shook a playful finger. "Antonio, you are asking for it. Show your upstart sons how it's done, Vanni." He stepped up beside Lorenzo while Father took careful aim. "Will your landlady be at home tomorrow, Enzo?"

Lorenzo moved into position behind his father, determined not to let the off-the-wall question throw him. "Should be." He gauged the weight of the ball and the distance it needed to travel, then let it loose, smiling when it rolled right up to the white ball and gently tapped it. "She usually is. Why?"

Manny took his next turn, cursing mildly when his ball landed a few feet away from the cluster. "I'm having a phone installed in your apartment."

"What?" Lorenzo stepped out of Tony's way without taking his eyes from Manny's face. "Why?"

Manny grinned. "What if I need to reach you quickly, but it isn't during business hours? Especially once you and Sabina marry. Although I have heard that there may be a house on Claremont Avenue for sale soon too—if you'd prefer we wait to install your line there, I suppose we could."

Lorenzo forced himself to swallow. He didn't mind having a telephone. What he minded was Manny not asking him if he wanted one, and then only giving him two choices—tomorrow or when he bought them a house. Which he also didn't want, or at least, not with Manny's money. "Manny..." For all his years of law school, Lorenzo still didn't know how to say such things. He sighed. "You know I appreciate all you do for us. But Sabina and I will choose our own house when we're ready for one."

Manny weighed the ball in his hand, though it was Father's turn now. "It's how it's done, Lorenzo."

"No, it's how it used to be done in Sicily." He sighed again and waved a hand at the banners of red, white, and blue that fluttered at intervals. "We're not *in* Sicily anymore."

From his other side, Tony sing-songed, "Wasting your breath."

Manny shot Tony an amused look, though it went a bit stiff when it landed on Lorenzo again. "What would you have us do, hmm? Never make another calzone? Forget our mother tongue? Play baseball today instead of bocce?"

"It isn't about bocce or calzones or what language you greet someone in, as you well know." He turned, looked his godfather straight in the eye. "You came here for opportunities. That's what America was supposed to be about, right? Dreams of equality and freedom. But you brought with you all the things you wanted to escape. The broken systems, the preying on each other. You took the worst of Italy and planted it here."

Manny glanced over at his daughter. "It is easy for you to judge. You never faced the things we did. It is our choices that gave you the luxury of making your own. Never forget that, Lorenzo."

Father sidled up to them, then crouched down to examine the lay of the grass. "You two look far too serious. Let's leave the philosophy until another time, eh? It's a holiday."

It seemed like the perfect holiday to discuss this particular philosophy, but Lorenzo folded his arms over his chest, the final green ball still clutched in his hand, and buttoned his lips.

Father's shot went wide, which meant that Lorenzo and Tony would sweep the points for this round unless Lorenzo did something stupid like knock the pallino away from their balls and closer to their elders'. He opted for safety and deliberately bowled away from the white ball. From the blanket, Val and G and Sabina all whooped their approval.

Father stepped closer to Manny. "Has Sabina started talking to you again yet, Manny?"

Manny grunted and folded his arms across his chest. "Not so much as a '*bon giornu.*'"

"What? What happened with Bean?" Tony asked from behind him.

Manny didn't answer. Their father, on the other hand, had no such qualms. "She saw him with Ava. I had just left for lunch and didn't see Ava go up, or I would have kept Sabina down..."

What? When was that? Lorenzo pivoted to stare at the older men, looking from one drawn face to the other. What had she seen—or heard?

"It isn't your fault, Vanni." Manny shook his head and paced over to the collection of balls.

Tony arched a brow at Lorenzo. "She's that upset about her father's mistress? Guess it's a good thing you're a straight arrow."

Lorenzo pressed his lips together and turned to the blanket where their fans resided. "Hey, Val. You wanna take my place?"

His younger brother jumped up as if he'd been waiting his whole life for such an offer, leaving Lorenzo free to abandon the field in favor of the blanket. He ignored Tony's call of, "Aw, come on, Enzo! You know Val's aim is no good!" He did, however, smile when he heard Val punch Tony in the arm for the insult.

Sabina tilted her face up when he approached, the brim of her hat casting her features in shade. She smiled, but it didn't chase all the shadows from her eyes. "Surely you didn't need a break already."

Lorenzo held out his hand. "I just need a walk with my girl."

She opened her mouth, looking poised to protest, but then just let out a breath and put her hand in his. He pulled her to her feet and tucked her fingers into the crook of his arm, aiming them toward the edge of the park. Once they were removed from the crowds of family and neighbors, she asked, "What happened? What did he say now?"

He wanted to wrap her in his arms and say they didn't have to talk about it. He settled for brushing his arm against hers and getting straight to the point. "Papa just told us what happened on Friday at your father's office. That Ava was there."

She stiffened and glared straight ahead. "You know about her? Did you—did you recognize her that day by the statue? And you didn't *say* anything?"

He cleared his throat. "Well…it isn't a topic one discusses with a young lady. I knew it would upset you. Frankly, it makes me uncomfortable, too. I debated but—I'm sorry if I made the wrong choice. I wasn't even sure who she was, not until I saw the guards. I've only seen her once or twice over the years, in passing."

"Then why…?" She bit her lip and came to a halt, tugging on his arm so that he turned to face her. Her eyes were hard yet underscored with vulnerability. "They were talking for a while when I was outside the door. She was talking about us all like she knew us. And she was *here*, and in our church. She told me she prays for us and—I don't know what to do with that, Enzo. What am I supposed to think about that?"

He could only shake his head. "I thought it seemed strange too, when I realized who it was. Did you ask your father?"

Her face went hard. "I'm not asking him anything. Ever again." She spun on her heel and took off again, leaving him little choice but to move with her.

"Bean," he started, but then he sighed to a stop. What could he really say? He couldn't defend Manny—didn't *want* to defend Manny. But for Sabina's sake, he had to try something. "You can't let this send you back into that empty place you were in after Serafina's death. Please."

She came to a halt again and managed to surprise him by turning into his chest. His arms came around her of their own volition, and he was glad of it when a shudder rippled through her. "It's *like* a death. Like the papa I always loved, always thought I knew is gone. Or…or never *was*, I guess. He only existed in my mind. But now I don't have that illusion anymore."

"I know." He'd never had quite the same revelation—they hadn't kept the sons in the dark like they had the daughters. But even so, there was always that moment when you first saw a beam of light and realized you stood in shadow. And then, after you finally fought your way into that light, came the moment when you looked back and saw clearly for the first time how dark those shadows really were. "I could tell you he's still there, still alive, that he loves you—and it's true. But it doesn't change it, I know that. He isn't the man you want him to be, and he never was. But you don't have to face that alone."

He didn't know if it would make a difference. But she lifted her face from where she'd buried it in his shoulder so that he could see the beautiful, stormy depths of her eyes.

"I don't know what to do with all this new information. It's just so much, Enzo, all at once. The arrest and the attack and—and then I hear my father discussing murder with his mistress, who's obviously a lady of the night, but who I knew as a kind woman from church, and—"

"Wait." He ran a hand down her back. Frowned. "What murder?"

She lifted her brows, uncertainty flickering in her eyes. "He hasn't talked to you about it? He said he was going to, to see if he needed to hire Darrow. They were talking about someone named Eddie, and how Ava had been seen with him the night he was killed. About the evidence pointing to him. I'm assuming it's Roman looking into it."

Lorenzo let out a gusty breath and looked around as he tried to gather his thoughts. His gaze snagged on a head of red hair, and he blinked to try to convince himself he was imagining things. He wasn't. Of all the times for Helen Gregory to show up, did it really have to be now? He glanced quickly away, praying she didn't even see them in the crowds of other dark-haired neighbors flocking the park.

Apparently that was too much to ask. "Enzo!" rang through the air, and when he followed Sabina's lead and looked up again, Helen was waving with far too much enthusiasm and hurrying toward them. "I was wondering if you were around here somewhere."

She was walking at the side of a vaguely familiar woman, dressed far more casually than he was used to and grinning as if thrilled to be interrupting an obviously intense conversation.

Sabina spoke before he could open his mouth. "Hello, Miss Gregory. I didn't realize you knew Bianca." She edged a little closer to his side. A proprietary move that he'd have to be blind to miss...and which made his lips want to grin, despite the lingering echoes of the word "murder." "You remember Bianca Esposito, don't you, *caru*?"

The name rang a distant bell. It took him a moment to remember that Sabina had mentioned her recently—the girl who had moved into the neighborhood a few years ago and thought herself the prettiest thing in the world. A title she certainly didn't deserve, especially compared to his Bean. Lorenzo forced a smile. "I remember you mentioning her, but I don't believe we've met. It's a pleasure, Miss Esposito. You and Miss Gregory must be friends."

Bianca's face improved only slightly with her smile. "The best. We were in correspondence school together. She works in your office, right? She's mentioned you too."

"I'm sure," Sabina muttered under her breath.

He gave her side a warning squeeze, though her ill humor lit something far more positive in him, and he had to tamp down a grin. "Indeed. Miss Gregory is a fantastic secretary—Mr. Stein would be lost without her."

Helen scowled at him. She hadn't been happy when he reported, at her insistence, that Sabina's reaction to the news of her interest proved her feelings, and that he had no intention of pursuing any other relationship. At work she alternated between brisk efficiency, cold temper, and what struck him as a desperate flirtation. He had prayed nightly that she would call a retreat before she got hurt any more, and before dealing with her every day got any more difficult.

Bianca cleared her throat. "I, uh, invited Helen to picnic with us today—told her she hadn't experienced the Fourth until she'd seen it Little Italy style."

Helen flashed a feline smile, a fair warning for Lorenzo to brace himself for a verbal pounce. "And she was right, of course. Though I confess I didn't expect to see you out and about, Miss Mancari. As reclusive as you've been this week, I feared you and Enzo must have had another fight."

"*Tu antipaticu spia!*"

Though Lorenzo had to agree that she was acting the part of vindictive spy, he gave Sabina another warning squeeze. "Not at all," he said to Helen, making his voice deliberately placating. "Your sources have apparently dropped the ball this time."

"Doubtful. I said that was my *fear*. I'm well aware it's her father she actually argued with. And I certainly can't blame you for that, Miss Mancari. I'm only surprised you haven't found cause to disagree with him before now."

He could see Sabina's hackles rise and almost expected claws to flash. Her voice, however, remained low and cool. "Watch yourself, Miss Gregory. It's my right to argue with my father, but he's still my father."

Helen's smile bordered on a snarl. "And you're his daughter. Does that mean I should fear for my life if I offend you?"

Sabina coiled onto the balls of her feet as if ready to leap onto the redhead and tear her to shreds. Lorenzo tightened his arm around her to restrain her. "Calm down, *cara*," he murmured in Sicilian. "She's trying to rile you."

Bianca's mouth had fallen open, and her face had gone pale. If he wasn't mistaken, there was actual fear in her eyes as she said, "Helen!"

"Miss Esposito's stupefaction is well placed." Lorenzo narrowed his eyes at his secretary. "This face doesn't suit you, Helen."

"So what?" She tossed her head back, chin raised. "I've got nothing to lose at this point, do I? Come on, B. I'm not so sure I care for Little Italy's offerings after all."

The two walked off—Bianca darting a wary glance over her shoulder—leaving Lorenzo confounded and Sabina still vibrating with rage. Helen had seemed so reasonable about things when she showed up at his apartment. What had happened?

Sabina was apparently wondering the same thing. "It's been a while since I've read Shakespeare, but I seem to recall him making a sage observation about a woman scorned."

Enzo sighed. "I've been praying for her—maybe you could too? Light a candle next time you're there?"

Was it asking too much? Sabina had plenty of other things to pray about. But she nodded, and they headed back to the bocce ball game.

He'd never realized how aggravating it could be to have a woman in love with him.

=====◆=====

Sabina pulled her cloche hat into place, adjusting it until it sat just where she wanted it to and then fussing with the waves of hair underneath. In the mirror, her reflection pursed its lips. It was far too nice a hat to wear to the park with Mary—one of the ones Mama had bought for her trousseau—but Lorenzo was going to meet her there and take her to a movie afterward, so she wanted to look her best. She tilted her face first to one side and then the other, satisfied at last that her hair was in place.

She adjusted the angle of the mirror and stepped back to see how the rest of her looked. Waistlines were dropping, and she'd never worn anything with one quite as low as this. It felt strange, but she liked it. The otherwise simple bodice provided the perfect canvas for the long bead necklace she'd looped twice around her neck.

She drew her lip between her teeth. What would Lorenzo think of the fashion-forward styles? Would he like them, or would he wish his bride-to-be had chosen something a little safer?

A glance at the clock told her she didn't have time to change even if she wanted to, so she set the question aside and hurried down the stairs. She paused when she saw G in the dining room, an odd assortment of books and tools spread out before him. She stepped inside and ran a hand over his cowlick. "What are you up to, G?"

He was so intent upon whatever it was that he didn't even duck away from her hand. "Book repair. I've been watching old Mario at work, and Max said I could practice on this—it's not a valuable book or anything, but it sure was falling apart."

Her chest went happily tight to see her brother, sitting there with a stout needle and thick thread, folded signatures of paper, glue and cardboard and cloth. Making something. Fixing something.

She leaned down and pressed a kiss to the top of his head. "You maybe should have set up somewhere else. You'll just have to move it in an hour."

"Nah, not today. Papa's going out, you'll be with Enzo—Mama said I could. We're going to eat outside."

"Ah." She fought to keep her tone bright...and not to wonder where Papa was going. "Well then, have fun. Proud of you, G."

He waved her away, but his eyes sparkled when he grinned up at her.

Her own smile tensed when she stepped into view of the parlor door. Papa might be going out, but he hadn't yet. He sat in there with Mama, a newspaper folded open and resting on his knee. She cleared her throat and decided to look between them, rather than only at Mama. It was the best she could offer right now. "I'm heading out to meet Mary, and Enzo'll pick me up there. I should be back about ten."

Papa's smile was sad, which cooled the fire of anger inside her a little more every day. She didn't like seeing the hurt in his eyes every time he looked at her. "Don't leave the park until Enzo shows up, *principessa*. I had to assign the guards elsewhere today. You should be all right in Arrigo, but no farther."

No guards? That made a strange sense of freedom sweep through her, chased by a moment's panic. What if Torrio's men came at them again? What if...but no. She had to get used to this. When she married Lorenzo next month, the protection would stop. They'd already discussed it. She nodded.

"Let me know if the movie's any good." Mama grinned over the top of her book. "Not that it's ever a hardship to watch Valentino."

Sabina smiled, careful to flash it at her father too. The brightening in his eyes made it worth the cost to her pride. "*Arrivederci*."

The walk to the park didn't take long, but when she got there she didn't see Mary. She must be running late too. A turn around the six acres proved she wasn't waiting in any of their usual places, so Sabina selected her favorite bench under the trees and settled in.

Five minutes lazed by, her mind wandering ahead to her evening with Lorenzo. She was looking forward to the film—even more, she was looking forward to spending the time with him. He would hold her hand, maybe even slip an arm around her shoulder. And maybe, just maybe he'd decide to risk a kiss. She respected his reasons for not wanting to toy with that danger—now that he'd explained it to her, anyway. But just a little kiss in a darkened theater wouldn't be too bad, would it?

"Sabina."

Hands landed on her shoulders—hands far larger than Mary's, the voice far deeper. Panic surged through her, freezing her muscles and making it impossible to obey her brain's command to flee. She squeezed her eyes shut and prayed that it wasn't really him.

One of his hands lifted, the other running over her neck onto the opposite shoulder as he came around the end of the bench and sat beside her. "I know you want to leave, but please, just give me a minute. Hear me out."

Though she had to clasp her hands together in her lap to keep them from trembling, her voice, at least, came out evenly. "What are you doing here, Roman?"

EIGHTEEN

Mannerly-hearted! more than handsome face-
Beauty's bearing or muse of mounting vein,
All, in this case, bathed in high hallowing grace...

-Gerard Manley Hopkins,
from "The Handsome Heart"

He was too close. A few weeks ago Sabina had enjoyed the frisson of sensation his proximity caused, but now his presence made her feel trapped. The memory of attraction was stifling instead of sizzling, the sight of his smile colored by the truth of his betrayal. Something still jumped to life in the pit of her stomach when he ran a thumb over the nape of her neck, but wariness now overcame it.

His voice thrummed across her nerves. "I had to see you again. To talk to you. So Mary—"

"*Mary* set this up?" Fury gave her limbs the impetus to move, and she jerked to her feet.

Roman jumped up to block her from taking off in the direction of her so-called friend's apartment. As he held out his arms to fence her in, his green eyes flashed and his lips curved up into the same charming smile that had fooled her before. "Don't be mad at her, Bina. She just wants you to be happy, and she knows good ol' Enzo can't do it."

"No, what she knows is that *she* wouldn't be happy with him. She doesn't get to speak for me, especially when she hasn't listened to a word I've said in weeks."

His hands landed on her upper arms. She jumped at the touch, which made his smile grow. "Man, I've missed you. Seeing that fire in your eyes. The way you respond to me. I love you, Sabina. So much. I can't get you out of my head. I can't think of anything but you."

"Ha." She attempted to shrug away from his touch, but he wouldn't be shaken. Trying anything more forceful would mean more contact—which she had the common sense to avoid. "You've obviously had no problem filling your time, trying to pin a murder on my father."

His face didn't change, didn't shift, didn't give anything away. But his hands tensed slightly on her arms. "I don't know what you're talking about. Murder isn't even my jurisdiction, baby. I'm a federal cop, and it's a state crime."

She lifted her brow much as Mama always did whenever she caught one of them in a lie. "That's not what Ava told Papa while I was standing in the hall unobserved."

His curse told her that her supposition about the identity of the investigator was correct. He dropped his hands, raked one through his hair, but then grabbed hers before she could make a dash for it. "Okay. I've been looking into some things for the local boys. But I'll stop, I'll even lie to them about what I've found if you'll just give me another chance."

"Are you trying to blackmail me?"

"What?" His genuine shock might have been amusing had the situation not been so serious. "No! Come on, Bina, that's not what I meant, and you know it."

"Do I? I don't know how low you'd stoop, Roman. I don't know you at all." She tugged at her hands, but he gripped them all the tighter.

"That's not true." He sidled closer, and she had no room to retreat. "I may not have told you my last name, my job, but everything else was real. All the stories, all the memories I shared. That's *me*, Bina. You know me." He raised her hands to his mouth and kissed each of them. "You love me."

The trembling returned, born from anxiety mixed with anger. "Maybe I did, before. Or maybe I was just caught up in attraction, because it certainly didn't last once I learned the truth. It doesn't matter, because I don't love you now."

"Okay." Danger glinted in his eyes, proving the agreement was anything but surrender. "So let's talk about that attraction. About how I made you feel then, and how I still make you feel now. I can see it in your eyes, baby, the heat, the passion. It's there."

She squeezed her eyes shut and wondered if God would accept the frantic beating of her heart as a prayer. It was the best cry for help she could make. "Not for you."

"No?" One of his hands released hers and cupped her cheek a second later. "But it's already mine, remember? I lit it, I stoked it. You were afraid of it, afraid to give in. Isn't that what you said that night outside the speakeasy? Afraid I'd take what I wanted and walk away. That's when I promised

I'd marry you, that we'd run away together. A promise I intend to keep. You're already mine, Sabina. I claimed you that night."

The weight of her sin, of her promises, pressed her down until she felt like she must be in the bowels of the earth. She should have trusted her fear that night and held fast to the principles that had meant so little in the heat of the moment. She should have pushed his hands away and fought back her desire. She should have drawn the line long before she did. But she hadn't.

She opened her eyes and look directly into his, the green depths issuing an invitation that still tried to tug her away from what she knew was right. "I think that must be the exact look that was in the serpent's eyes as he held out the apple to Eve."

Roman chuckled. "Eve bit."

"And lost everything." She shook her head and raised her arm to keep him from putting back the hand she'd shaken loose from her face. "I'm not going to bite. Not this time."

His gaze dropped to her mouth. "But you've already tasted the apple, Sabina. You've already got the knowledge it brings, and now you're just hiding behind fig leaves and pretending it didn't happen." He leaned down, but to the side, so that he could whisper in her ear. "Eve couldn't fool God. Do you think you can fool Enzo? Convince him you love him when we all know you don't? Pretend you feel passion where you're cold? For that matter, would he even want you if he knew the truth about us? You might not have come home with me that night, but we both know he's as bluenosed as they come. He may have forgiven the kisses, but what about the rest?"

Tears rushed her eyes, but she blinked them back. "This is how you convince me you love me? By reminding me of all I've done wrong?"

"*I* don't judge you, sweetheart. *He's* the one who will."

"No." She needed to get away and pushed at him until he backed up a step. She sucked in a deep breath and edged off to the side. "No, that's not right. *You're* not right. You don't know him, and you're not going to guilt me into coming back to you."

"Bina—"

"Don't!" She batted away the hands he lifted and took another step away. "I'm not doing this again, I don't want anything to do with you. I want to marry Enzo. It's him I love."

"You're lying to yourself. And I can prove it." He gripped her arms again and, before she could wrangle herself free, aimed his mouth for hers.

Lorenzo sped around the corner, breathing a prayer of thanks when there was little traffic in his way to slow him down. He glanced again at his watch, wondering how he had gotten so caught up in work that he lost track of time so badly. He had thought for sure he'd be able to head home to change his clothes before picking up Sabina from the park. But when he'd checked his watch a little while ago, it was an hour later than he'd thought.

He must have gotten thrown off when the timepiece stopped. He had forgotten to wind it that morning and realized it only when the hands halted mid-afternoon. Helen, still apologetic about her outburst on Wednesday, had wound it for him. It would have been easy to say she'd set it wrong, had it not agreed with the clock in the conference room that he'd been going by all day.

Regardless, he was here now. A few minutes late, but here. He parked on the street, near the entrance closest to Sabina's favorite bench. She always used that as her starting and stopping points for a walk, so it would be the best place to find her.

Hopping out of the Nash, he set off in a half-jog. He barely got into the park before he halted again, his heart leaping up into his throat and choking him. Finding Sabina at the bench was expected. But finding her in O'Reilly's arms?

Fear and fury propelled him closer, close enough to hear the snake say he'd prove Sabina was lying to herself. The fury throbbed, overcoming the fear, when O'Reilly leaned down to kiss her. He gave Sabina credit—she tried to push him away. At least, for a few moments. But when her shoulders sagged and her head tilted, allowing the already intense kiss to deepen still more, fear galloped up and overtook its companion.

If O'Reilly could really subdue her objections that easily, then Lorenzo was fooling himself to think they'd ever have a future together. He needed a wife he could trust, who could resist temptation until it fled. How could he possibly give his faith and promise to someone whose resistance lasted only a second?

A spark of light flared up in his mind, revealing the truth in stark clarity. He couldn't judge her for this—hadn't he lapsed for a moment too with Helen? But Sabina had been praying for him, and he had found the strength to pull away. "Lord, strengthen her," he whispered. "Fortify her. Speak to her heart and mind."

The instant he spoke the words, Sabina jerked her mouth away from O'Reilly's and pushed against his chest to try to break free of his arms. Lorenzo felt his lips creep upward. "Atta girl."

She managed to put a few inches between her and O'Reilly. "Let go, Roman. That's not going to work this time. I'm not as stupid as I was a few months ago."

"Bina." O'Reilly sounded frustrated, if determined. "Come on. You're obviously still attracted to me—"

"I believe," Lorenzo said from between clenched teeth as he stepped closer, "she told you to let go."

"Enzo!" Sabina turned her face his way, and the relief in her eyes soothed a few of the edges inside him.

O'Reilly hissed out a breath but made no move to drop his arms. "Impeccable timing, Capecce, I'll give you that. Now how about stepping away so Bina and I can resolve this between ourselves."

Incredulity lifted Lorenzo's brows. Did O'Reilly *really* think he'd go for that? "Take. Your hands. Off her."

O'Reilly obeyed, but the stubborn lift to his chin matched the sneer on his mouth. He stepped around Sabina, chest puffed out like Val when he was ready to brawl. "You wanna settle this now, Capecce, once and for all? You're no match for me when I'm sober."

Lorenzo's only move was to cross his arms over his chest. "Don't tempt me, O'Reilly. I grew up with three brothers. I may not choose to fight often, but don't think I can't handle myself."

"Oh, stop it." Sabina scowled as she shouldered her way between them, but when she turned to face Lorenzo, her mouth hinted at a grin. She took her place at his side and wiped the humor off her face as she looked back at O'Reilly. "Picking a fight's only going to convince me you're a bully. You're not getting another chance, Roman, so just go away."

"Fine." There was no acquiescence in his tone. He smirked as he pulled a piece of folded paper out of his pocket. "Here." He slipped it into her beaded bag. "My address, so you know where to find me when you change your mind. You'll want that when Enzo dumps you again. Ask her about the sordid details of our dates, Capecce. I think you'd like to know just how fiery our little bearcat is."

With a parting chuckle, he spun around and whistled his way down the path, hands jammed in his pockets.

Lorenzo unfolded his arms so he could slip one around Sabina's quaking shoulders and pull her close. He wasn't going to so much as acknowledge that parting shot. If O'Reilly wanted her to tell him something, it didn't take a genius to realize it wasn't something he wanted to know.

"*Mi dispiaci*," he said as he rubbed her arm and led her toward his car. "If I'd been on time…"

Sabina looked up at him with drawn brows. "What are you talking about? You're almost an hour early."

"I'm—what?" He flipped his wrist up to look at his watch. "No, look."

She shook her head and held up her own timepiece. It was set an hour earlier than his. Which, now that he thought about it, far better matched the angle of the sun. He frowned and ran his tongue over his teeth, flabbergasted as to how this had happened. The conference room clock hadn't been wrong all day, because they'd used it for their court appearances, and that's what Helen had…

"Oh." He breathed a laugh and shook his head. "Guess that's what she meant when she said she'd make it up to me."

"Huh?"

He gave Sabina a closed-lipped grin. "My watch needed to be reset, and Helen did it for me while I ran an errand. She must have reset the office clock, too. Then she pointed out the time to me and said I'd better hurry. Our little detective must have figured out O'Reilly would be here."

"*How* does she—oh, never mind." Sabina adjusted her hat so that it blocked the sun from her eyes. "So, what, she figured out he was coming instead of Mary and thought you'd see it and break up with me?"

He gave her a squeeze. "No, Bean, I think she must have thought you'd need a little help getting away from him." When she made no response to that interpretation of events, he sighed. "She apologized for the way she acted on the Fourth. She had apparently just gotten a letter the day before and learned that her father's seriously ill."

Sabina harrumphed out a breath. "Well, if that's true, I guess it excuses her. A little." They cleared the line of trees around the perimeter of the park and stopped at the Nash. He opened her door for her, but she just turned to face him, clutching her bag in front of her. "Aren't you going to ask me what he was talking about?"

His fingers tensed on the door. If he'd had any question of what she meant, the anxiety in her eyes would have answered it. "No."

No relief softened her features. "Why not?"

He forced himself to swallow. "Because it doesn't matter, Bean. I already know it went too far, and I forgive you. I don't need details."

"Even if I had...?"

Neither the pained expression on her face nor the wariness in her voice told him whether the question was hypothetical. He swallowed past a sudden lump in his throat and forced back the instinct that demanded to know so it might judge. With a silent, urgent prayer, love filled the recesses in its stead. "Even if you had."

Her eyes flooded with affection instead of relief. She reached for his hand. "I didn't. But if you could have forgiven that, I'm willing to believe you forgive this. I...I know how serious this sort of thing is to you. Given what we come from and..."

Lorenzo sighed and leaned into the side of his car. Her fingers were still in his, and the warmth that coursed through him was only partly from residual adrenaline. He took a moment to study her, to see her as O'Reilly did, or as any stranger in the park would: the sculpted hair, the expensive clothes, the gorgeous face, the figure that would make any man take note. He still didn't regret his decision to respect her—he'd known their engagement would be long, and he'd known how hard it would be to remember that decision if he could hold her, kiss her whenever he pleased. But they only had a few weeks until the wedding. He wasn't going to forget himself in that amount of time, at least not when they'd been so open about the risk.

More than that, he didn't want Roman O'Reilly's kiss to be the thing that bullied its way into her mind at night when she was drifting off to sleep. He tugged her closer, slid an arm around her waist. *"Me tisoru."*

His pulse pounded like someone trapped behind a locked door in a burning building. It would have been easy to crush her to him and show her what fire, what kisses he had held back for years. But her hands shook, and vulnerability shone out from behind the heat in her eyes.

He lifted her hand and pressed his lips to her palm. "I love you. No matter what has come before, no matter what comes after this. I love you, and I will spend a lifetime proving it to you."

She rested a hand on his cheek, her fingers warm and soft. Her gaze was just as much a caress. "My Enzo. You're unlike any other man in the world. Please believe that there's no one else who could ever hold my heart like you always have. I forgot that for a while—but I love you. I've always loved you."

His answer was to lean down and brush her lips with his once and then again. When she kissed him a third time more insistently, he accepted the invitation. She probably heard the blood humming in his veins. Certainly she would have felt the harmonic resonance of his nerves through the hand on her waist. Perhaps it struck to life the matching chord in her, or perhaps she was just in tune with him, because her response was quick and consuming.

The hand on his cheek moved to press against the back of his neck, pulling him in even more. The hum in the back of her throat spoke of desire. He'd have been willing to bet her heart raced to keep up with his. Love for her sang through every cell of his body and into his soul, drowning out the birds in the trees and the noise of passing cars.

It couldn't, however, block out the humored voice that intruded a minute later. "You know, if it were anyone but you two, I might be offended at coming across such a scene in a public park. Luckily, I'm so happy to see you guys lost in each other that I'll overlook the impropriety."

Sabina barely pulled away and didn't bother looking over at the newcomer. "Go away, Izzy. We're busy."

Isadora's chuckle sounded so tired that Enzo nearly peeled his eyes away from Sabina's face to look at her. "I see that. Where did Mary run off to?"

"Got me." Sabina narrowed her eyes at Lorenzo's mouth and wiped at his lip with her thumb. Seeing the color that came off, he scowled. If they kept this up, they'd have to have a little chat about lipstick. "She never showed—sent Roman in her place."

"Roman?" Isadora muttered something Lorenzo didn't catch and then pronounced, "I'm going to smack that girl. Are you okay?"

Sabina chuckled. "How do I look?"

Isadora sighed. "If you see her, will you ask her to *please* come home?"

That finally made Lorenzo look her way, and what he saw made his gut churn for this girl who had nearly been his sister. "Your mother?"

Isadora pressed her lips together, but tears still pooled in her eyes no matter how fast she blinked. "I don't think she's going to last through the night. Mrs. Zumpano is sitting with her while I look for Mary, but… She needs to come home. She needs to say goodbye."

Sabina stepped away from him, hand held out for her friend. "I know her usual places. We'll go look for her, okay? We'll find her."

"And I'll drag her home kicking and screaming if I have to." Dredging up a sad smile, he added, "Joey would want me to."

Isadora nodded, mouthing a thank-you even though no sound came out. She turned and hurried back toward her family's building.

Lorenzo opened the Nash's door for Sabina. "Well, doll. Looks like you and I are hitting the speakeasies tonight."

Despite the sobriety in her eyes, the corners of Sabina's lips twitched. "Who'da thunk it?"

He chuckled and helped her in, closed the door behind her. Then he shoved a hand into his pocket, let his fingers tangle with his rosary, and prayed the Holy Spirit would lead them straight to Mary, wherever she was.

NINETEEN

Each be other's comfort kind:
Deep, deeper than divined,
Divine charity, dear charity,
Fast you ever, fast bind.

-Gerard Manley Hopkins,
from "At the Wedding March"

The edges of Sabina's mind were fuzzy when she made it home hat night, like when Mary had insisted she try a gin. Except that her senses were unimpaired, heightened even, and her throat was absent that tickling burn. Her fingers remained linked with Lorenzo's as they sauntered up the walk to her stoop. The evening had proven far more fun than they'd dared to hope. They'd found Mary at the first place they stopped, and she had actually listened. Tears smudging her kohl, she'd told Robert to take her home.

Sabina and Lorenzo had made their movie after all, and after checking on the Bennatos—their friends' mother was still hanging on—they'd taken a moonlight stroll through the park before aiming for Taylor Street again. Sabina didn't bother asking if he would come inside with her for a minute. She just opened the door and pulled him in. It was her best bet for getting another kiss.

He closed the door, and the moment it clicked, Sabina locked her arms around his neck and grinned at him. "Ha. Gotcha right where I want ya."

Lorenzo chuckled and slid his arms around her waist. His hazel eyes sparkled with every shade of color between green and brown, alight with love and passion. It made her feel like the most important woman in the world. The *only* woman. "And why, Miss Mancari, would you possibly want me right here?"

Her smile felt flirtatious on her lips, but he didn't seem to mind. His eyes sparkled a little more, and a smile curved that too-serious mouth of his. She took off her hat, tossed it onto the marble topped table nearby, and pulled his head down to hers.

It was so funny. A few short weeks ago she had dreaded his company, and now…now she would be happy to stay right here forever. His arms fit so perfectly around her. The scent of his soap teased her nose in a way at once familiar and heady. And his kiss—oh, his kiss.

Yes, Roman had been exciting. But it was beautifully different with Lorenzo. She knew she was the only one he had ever loved, ever wanted. He didn't make her feel like a prize to be won, but like a treasure to be cherished. *So tisoru.* His treasure.

"Oh, come on! I do *not* need to see that!" Little G's exclamation startled her enough that she jumped a few inches away. She looked over to see her brother making a face as he watched them from the entrance to the dining room, his book repair project still scattered on the table. "Papa! Bina and Enzo are necking in the foyer!"

Papa was home again already?

The low, rumbling laugh from the parlor said he was. "Good. Leave them alone, G."

With a roll of his eyes, her brother turned back to his book. Sabina returned her gaze to Lorenzo and found him biting back a grin. She didn't bother containing hers. "Nothing like a brother to ruin the moment."

"We'll have plenty more. Of course, there are plenty more brothers to ruin them." He ran the tips of his fingers down her cheek. "Well, Bean, much as I hate to say so, I guess I should get home. It'll be time for mass before we know it."

"I know." Not that she pulled away quite yet. In fact, she held him a little tighter and gazed long into his love-filled eyes. "I'd apologize for the way the evening began, but it's hard to be sorry for something that ended so well."

Lorenzo's chuckle danced over her. "Yeah, I have a feeling it didn't go quite the way O'Reilly envisioned. Not that you need to apologize on any count—it was *his* doing, not yours."

She granted that with a tilt of her head, but still it bothered her. "I don't know why he's trying to win me back. Or why, if he honestly wanted to, he keeps pursuing Papa."

Lorenzo sighed. "Sadly, that's something I can understand. He loves you, Bean. But he still has a job to do, and pride to assuage."

Warm fingers constricted around her heart, making a strange sensation surge up her throat. "Do you think it's okay if I pray for him?"

"Okay?" He rested his forehead on hers. "Sweet Sabina, I think that's the wisest idea I've heard in a while." He kissed the tip of her nose, which lit a warm glow in her chest. "We both will."

She let her eyes slide shut, kept her hand pressed to his chest, and just focused on the beat of his heart under her fingers. Three years she had doubted him, doubted his love, doubted whether she was really meant to be his wife. Part of her still wondered if he could really be hers, if God really would share him. But she hoped so. How she hoped so! She wanted to be Lorenzo's wife. She wanted to build a life with him. She wanted to learn with him how to love these people around them who gave so generously, loved so fiercely, yet exacted such a price for it all.

She blinked her eyes open again and looked up into his face. It was still tilted down toward her, but his eyes were focused on nothing, his head turned just a bit as if he were listening to something she couldn't hear. Then he smiled down at her and picked up her left hand. "Can I see this for a minute?" He wiggled the diamond ring.

She frowned. "Why? I mean, sure, but…"

"Just bear with me." He slid off the ring he'd slid on three years ago. She flexed her fingers, amazed at how bereft they felt. In spite of all her second thoughts, mixed desires, and betrayal, she had never once taken off the diamond. Somehow its absence amplified her hope to keep that ring on her finger forever.

"Okay." Lorenzo let out a quick breath, dropped to one knee, and held their hands between them.

Her jaw dropped along with him. "Enzo, what are you doing?"

"Hush. I was hoping this would be easier the second time around, but for some reason I'm even more nervous than I was three years ago." An adorable vulnerability shone out of his eyes. He cleared his throat. "I love you, Sabina. More than anyone but the Lord. I want you to be my wife."

Unexpected tears stung her eyes, and she had the strangest sensation that it wasn't just Enzo declaring himself. It was God, declaring this *good*. She wasn't pulling Enzo away from his vocation. She was leading him toward it. "Oh, Enzo. I want that too."

Little G's voice intruded again. "*Now* what are you doing?"

Lorenzo's lips turned up in a grin. He looked past her to where her brother undoubtedly stood in the dining room doorway. "Proposing."

"Uh, Enzo…I know you've taken a bullet to the head recently, so maybe this slipped your mind, but you already did that. A couple years ago."

Sabina sighed and craned her head around. As expected, Little G stood there with a paintbrush in his hand and the particular shade of disgust on his face that only a thirteen-year-old boy could ever muster. She grinned. "Scram, kid. We're in the middle of something here."

G held his arms wide. "In front of the door. In plain sight of every room in the house. Excuse me for living here."

"I will," she said, jerking her head to the side, "if you *scram*. Fully. To your room, now."

He took a moment to return his brush first, muttering all the way up the stairs. She shook her head and turned back to Lorenzo, who still knelt before her, grinning.

"I suppose I'd better get to the point before we're interrupted again." Lorenzo poised the ring at the tip of her finger. "Will you marry me, Sabina?"

"Yes." It came out breathless, but she didn't care. As soon as he slid the ring back into place, she tugged him to his feet so she could wrap her arms around him. She reveled in the joy that surged through her, marveled at the wave of feeling that overwhelmed her. "I love you, Enzo."

The kiss he gave her seared her lips, locking in the promise with a touch of fire. When he drew away, his eyes were bright and intense. "Things are going to be different this time, *bedduzza*. We're going to be honest with each other. When we have problems, we work through them together. Walking away is never going to be an option again. Okay? This is forever."

"Okay." Another kiss was called for, so she leaned up to seal the deal. "Forever. Honesty. No outs. Got it, and I fully approve."

"Good." One more lingering kiss, and then he backed away, grinning. "I'm going this time. Really. *Bona notti, me tisoru.*"

"*Bona notti, me amari.*" She pressed her fingers to her lips and blew him one last kiss as he opened the door and stepped out. The air she drew in tasted sweet, and her lips were yet again stuck in their smile. For a night that started out a horror, this was an ending worthy of a fairy tale. "*Grazii,* Lord," she whispered, crossing herself.

As soon as the door clicked shut, a rustle of newspaper sounded from the parlor. Papa appeared in the doorway a moment later, his smile soft. "Sounds like the last of your wrinkles have been ironed out, eh?"

At the moment, she couldn't even be mad at her father. She floated across the floor until she could stretch up to kiss his cheek. "*Sì,* Papa." Her ring shimmered in the light of the chandelier, and she gazed at it as if she hadn't seen it every day for three years.

"Good. You had me worried. I was afraid I'd hurt you so badly you wouldn't even trust Enzo. That was never what I wanted, *principessa*. Your happiness, it's everything to me."

"I know." She turned her gaze to his face. This past month had aged him, deepened the wrinkles around his eyes. A few of the shadows were no doubt her fault. But then, he had put a few in her eyes as well. "You *did* hurt me, Papa. But I'm not going to judge Enzo for your sins."

Papa's lips pressed together. "You've always known who I am."

Hadn't they already had this argument? Weary of it, she shook her head. She walked past him into the room and sat down on the sofa, knowing they had better finish it this time. She didn't know where Mama had gone or why Papa hadn't left, but she'd make use of the time. "Papa, I knew you were a mafioso. Yes. But I could tell myself you weren't like the others. You raised us in the church. You taught us right from wrong. Then I hear you talking to a prostitute you've made your mistress about murder—"

"That's enough." He stood tall and rigid, the line of his shoulders defensive. "There are lines, Bina, that I can't let you cross again. Don't ask me about my business. Don't make me choose where to lie and what truths to give you—you won't be able to sort between them anyway and will resent me all the more. Just stop asking."

Sabina dropped her gaze to the rug. "Even when they're accusing you of murder?"

"You *know* I've spilled blood!" He paced, cursing mildly in Sicilian, and ran a hand over his hair. "You want me to assure you I didn't do it this time? I can tell you that. I can tell a fine story about what really happened, too. But would you believe me?"

Exhaustion bore down on her and made her shoulders sag. Would she? No. She would want to, *need* to, but he'd just said it—he'd killed before. He would kill again. And he spoke lies as easily as the truth. "Papa, I don't want to see you arrested again. I don't want to see you killed. But if you keep this up—"

"Trust me to be what I am, Bina. You just worry about your wedding, about Enzo."

Speaking of whom…she cleared her throat. "Did you talk to him yet? About this?"

"Mm, I stopped by this afternoon. His boss made an introduction to Darrow for me. Looks like I'm going to be keeping a lawyer on retainer,

Sabina, but it won't be Enzo. I promised him that again, and I'll keep it this time."

She rose, moved over to where he stood by the unlit fireplace, and wrapped him in a hug for the first time in over a week. He had more faults than she cared to count, but he *did* love them. She would just have to learn to accept that much and keep beseeching God about the rest. She would light candle after candle in prayer until the light of faith dispelled a few of the shadows of the underworld. "*Ti amu*, Papa."

"Oh, princess." He held on tight for many long moments. "I just want you two to be happy. Whatever it takes."

As she headed for bed a minute later, she decided not to let that last promise scare her.

Sally swirled the spoon lazily through the sauce simmering on Roman's stove without taking her eyes from him. Ever since he had gotten back from his meeting with Bannigan, he had been pacing the confines of his living room and spewing a steady stream of curses. The English ones she understood, but then he'd toss in a few in what sounded like Italian. Even more interesting were the ones she assumed to be Gaelic.

"Oo. What's that mean? Sounds vicious."

He sent her an evil eye that would have done her daddy proud. "Shut up, Sally."

If he meant to slap her down, he'd have to try harder than that. He was a kitten compared to Al or Dad. "Hm…no, I think I've heard that in every language under the sun, and that's not how you say it in Gaelic."

"Cute." He tossed himself onto his faded couch and hooked an arm over his face.

Sally tapped the wooden spoon on the side of the pot, wiped up the spatters of red that she'd made, and put the lid back on the sauce. Then she washed her hands—more quickly than she'd have liked—and headed to the sofa. Taking up position on its threadbare arm, she slid a hand behind his head and massaged the tense muscles of his neck. "You need to relax, champ. I told you it wouldn't be enough. For a man with fewer connections, maybe, but your Bannigan's not going to file charges against Manny until we can bring him a witness that saw the actual crime."

He grunted.

Sally rolled her eyes, an indulgence she allowed herself because he wouldn't be able to see her do it. In some ways, men were all the same. When their pride got wrapped up in a thing, they just didn't want to listen to facts. But it was time he got over himself. She'd been spending every minute she could steal from Al pumping potential witnesses, and before long all the lowlifes would know to keep an eye out for her and go mum. "Everyone we've talked to has agreed that if anyone saw it, it was Timothy Baker. So we wait for him to get back from his trip down south, and we talk to him."

"I'm tired of waiting. I've been waiting for weeks."

And had been in a sour mood for most of them. Ever since that fiasco of a meeting with Sabina three weeks ago, he'd alternated between grizzly and teddy bear—either turning into her arms and holding on tight or snarling at her if she opened her mouth. If anyone ever bothered to ask her, she couldn't have said why she found the dichotomy so endearing. Maybe she was just a sucker for an aching heart.

Or maybe it was because even a testy, growling Roman never raised a hand to her.

"Two more weeks. That's all." When he dropped his arm, she took the opportunity to lean over and trail a line of kisses down his face. It was the best way to gauge his mood. If he turned his mouth to hers, it meant he'd be receptive to whatever she had to say. If he turned away, she might as well hold her silence.

He just sat there this time. Well, she could work with that. She kneaded a particularly stubborn knot in his neck with her thumb. "You'll never guess who dropped in to see me today."

"Hm. The Queen of England."

"Well sure, but I meant *after* lunch." That earned her a chuckle and relaxed his neck a little more. Perfect. "This particular guest is a lovely redhead, secretary to a certain lawyer you're none too fond of."

He sat up so quickly that he nearly knocked her off her perch. "Helen Gregory came to see you? Why?"

She'd known that would get his attention. She decided not to take it personally that he got so excited about anyone with a link to Sabina Mancari. After all, she wasn't after his heart—just that grand-and-a-half he was offering her. She tried not to think too hard about the fact that he was the only john who didn't make her feel like she had to scrub her skin clean off after he left her side.

But back to the ginger. "Couple reasons. First off, she says she's in love with Enzo Capecce."

Schemes lit up his eyes and drew his lips into a smirk. "Yeah? What's she willing to do to get him, I wonder? I bet she could help me break them up. If she—"

"Hey." She snapped her fingers in front of his nose to get his attention. "You wanna know what she actually said, or are you just gonna go off on your own tangent here?"

His smirk turned into a grin. "Sorry. Go on."

"That's better. Anyway. She apparently started with that same idea— break 'em up. Says she even considered coming to you to work together on it. But after your disastrous attempt at that a few weeks ago—"

"Hey!"

"Her words, not mine." She bit back a grin. "Says she's the one who sent him to the park early to catch you together. Figured it would be a spark to a powder keg one way or another. They'd either break up or decide they never would. After watching them together these last few weeks, she figures nothing's going to come between them now. Says Enzo's more crazy about Sabina than ever and that Sabina's definitely in love with him too."

"Not possible." He levered up and took to pacing again. "He's probably just doing this to spite me. He's a self-righteous hypocrite, there's no way he'd actually want her after learning how involved she was with me. He'll either keep it official until he thinks I'm gone and then end it, or marry her just so he can lord it over her. As if I'd let *that* happen."

Sally folded her arms over her chest as she regarded him. He was convinced of his own reasoning, that was obvious. The question was whether or not he was right. "You sure about that? I mean, I'll be the first to admit there are self-righteous bigots out there"—one of them in her own life answered to Dad—"and they're capable of ruining lives, I'm testament to that. But there are also people who are genuinely good. Capable of forgiving." There had to be. She didn't know any of them herself, but there *had* to be. The whole world wasn't the Levee or, for that matter, Washington Street in Cumberland. So why, when she ran away from the one, had she ended up smack dab in the middle of the other?

"Sally, I'm not exactly interested in your life story right now, okay? I need to think about this."

She bit her tongue—literally—to keep from labeling him with a few choice names. It wouldn't pierce her. She wouldn't let it. It couldn't, because he was nothing to her. Just a john. Just a grand-and-a-half.

She stalked back into his postage stamp of a kitchen and turned on his tap. She'd already washed his dishes, but she'd wash them again.

He sighed and followed her. "That wasn't what I meant."

"Yeah, champ. It was." She took a Brillo pad to the stain on the old skillet that she'd failed to get off every other time she tried. The scrubbing helped—not the pan, but her heart. Just enough to paint her lips with a smile as false as their bright red color. "But hey, what's it to me, right? You're not paying me for my life story."

He leaned into the wall and studied her. "What else did she say?"

Predictable. Sally scrubbed a little harder. "She says Enzo's happier than she's ever seen him, and Sabina too. She's convinced they'll be happy to-gether—moreover, that they'll *only* be happy together—so she's taken up their side. Asked me to warn you away from any other stupid attempts—again, her words—to win Sabina back. Says it'll only make Manny mad, and he's about reached the end of his rope when it comes to you."

Roman snorted his opinion of that.

Sally ran her tongue along the edge of her teeth. If he didn't like *that*, he definitely wasn't going to like the next part. "She also said that the day of the infamous park scene, Manny stopped by the law office to talk to Enzo about Eddie's murder."

Frozen in his tracks, he gave her his undivided attention. "Yeah? Boy am I going to have fun looking at Capecce in court and shooting his faith in Manny to pieces."

"That's not gonna happen, champ. Apparently he was only there to get an introduction to another firm. It's Clarence Darrow you'd be seeing in court." Seeing his shoulders sag, hearing his curse—English this time—Sally had to shake her head. "You've got an awful lot of emotion pinned on this. What if Ava's right? What if Manny didn't do it, and talking to this Baker character proves it? What'll you do then?"

His shrug was unconcerned. "Take down the gangster who is, I guess. And then convince Sabina I made sure her father didn't take the rap for it for her sake. Might buy me a few points, huh?"

Sally lifted her brows and rinsed the pan, holding it up to the single bare bulb dangling from the ceiling to see if she'd made any progress on the stain. It hadn't budged. "You really want my opinion? I think you need to face that she's made her choice. It's time to move on."

"Why the devil would I do that? I love her. I can't just give up."

Oh, Roman. He was all stubborn Irish and passionate Italian, and in this particular case, the combination equaled heartache for him. She knew he didn't want her take on it. But someone had to give it to him straight, and who else was going to do it? "If you loved her, you'd want her to be happy. She is. So step aside. *That's* what love does."

He snorted and strode down the hall to his bedroom. "Like *you* know anything about it."

If there had been anything breakable at hand, she would have smashed it into a wall just for the pleasure of hearing the crack and the catharsis of picking up every little sliver afterward. Given the Spartan nature of his apartment, she had to settle for spewing a few volcanic phrases.

The front door thumped with the heavy rap of a fist, but the cursing from the bedroom didn't let up. Sally rolled her eyes and sauntered over to the door with a sarcastic, "Don't worry, Roman darling, *I'll* get it. My pleasure. Really. You just put your feet up."

She wrenched the door open, not exactly surprised to see Roman's fair-complexioned partner standing on the other side. She was equally un-surprised to see the derision in his eyes upon spotting *her.* Maybe it was that ramrod spine of his, or maybe it was the way he dismissed in a glance anyone who didn't measure up to whatever ideals he had in that blond head, but he reminded her way too much of Daddy Dearest.

She leaned into the doorframe and gave him her most provocative smile. And boy did it provoke him. He looked like he'd take great pleasure in tossing her out with all the other trash. "Well, well, well," she said in the throaty tone she had perfected after a few months on the street. "If it isn't the illustrious Clifford Brewster. We finally meet face to face."

"Hm." His glance barely touched her before dismissing her. "Where's Roman?"

"Sulking. Come on in." She stepped aside so he could enter, thoroughly enjoying playing hostess simply because it would annoy him. "I was just fixing some spaghetti for dinner. You're welcome to stay."

Cliff crossed through the door, shut it behind him, and glared at her. "Cooking for him, now? Don't think you're going to get away with this. I see right through you."

"Oh yeah?" She put an extra swing in her hips as she sashayed into the kitchen. "Well, you *look* right through me, but I have my doubts that you see much."

"Wanna bet?" He swept a hand out to encompass the clean apartment. "You're ingratiating yourself. Trying to get him to see you as something more than a whore, so that when he practically goes bankrupt to pay off your debts, he'll keep you around. Well, it isn't gonna happen that way."

Okay, maybe she hadn't given him enough credit. Still. She stirred the sauce again, tasting it to see if it needed anything more. The flavor was perfect—it just needed to thicken. "Probably not. But that's okay. I enjoy cooking and making a place livable. And believe it or not, I like Roman."

He laughed. Actually laughed. "Sure, sweetheart. Your kind's notorious for falling for your johns."

"Just like johns are notorious for going bankrupt to save a girl." After wiping up a drop of sauce that had splattered on the stove, she turned to meet his gaze, hip cocked and hand resting on it. "This ain't your usual situation, *sweetheart*. I'm far from naive, so I know I'm nothing but convenient for him. He's in love with Sabina. But you know what? I'm fine with coming in second, if I can rank at all."

He stepped closer, probably just so he could look down his nose at her. "Do us all a favor. When he gets you out, go find yourself some rich dope that can set you up somewhere far away from him. He's got enough problems without adding you to the list."

A huge crash came from the bedroom, followed by some enthusiastic cursing. Sally couldn't contain a chuckle. "You're right about those problems, anyway. The Italian seems to come out when he's at his angriest."

"Sicilian."

"Hm?"

He motioned toward the hall. "It's not Italian, it's Sicilian. They're pretty touchy about that."

Thoughts raced through her mind in an attempt to piece together the puzzle that was Roman O'Reilly. "So is that why he's got this vendetta against the Mafia? Did people judge him guilty because of his Sicilian blood?"

"It's far deeper than that." Cliff shifted uncomfortably, his eyes darting down the hall. When they rested on her again, they were assessing.

She didn't expect him to tell her what that deeper thing was. At some point in the eighteen months since she'd woken up on a street corner in the Levee, bruised and bloodied and so hungry she couldn't see the trap in Al "Brown's" eyes when he offered her "a place to stay," she'd gotten used to people judging her. She was used to people who thought that anyone who sold her body must not have a soul or a heart or a mind. She'd gotten used to being garbage, just like Dad had always said she was. And Cliff Brewster was cut from the same cloth.

Then he rolled back his shoulders and sighed. "The Mafia killed his father."

TWENTY

ROSLYNN M. WHITE

sold her body, must not have a soul or a heart or a mind. She'd potion used
to being garbage, just like Dad had always said she was. And Cliff. He were
was cut from the same cloth.

Then he talked about how his—how the force had—. The Mafia killed his
father.

But quench her bonniest, dearest ǀ to her, her clearest-selvèd spark
Man, how fast his fi redint, ǀ his mark on mind, is gone!

-Gerard Manley Hopkins,
from "That Nature is a Heraclitean Fire
and of the comfort of the Resurrection"

Surely he hadn't heard what he thought he had. Roman stepped out of
his bedroom, certain that Cliff, who never had a constructive word to
say about him working with Sally, would not have told her *that*. Cliff
knew that talking about his father's death was off-limits.

Once again, Da's face flashed in his mind. The laughing green eyes,
always ready to tease his family but which could turn as hard as stone when
he was working. The deceptive freckles across his nose that made him look
young and innocent, even after years as a cop. Those pristine white teeth
flashing out as he smiled—or snarled at a lowlife. All framed by deep red
hair that branded him as Irish before he ever introduced himself.

He'd been so proud when Roman joined the force. So proud as he'd
slipped that St. Michael medallion over his neck as Ma pinned on his badge
for the first time.

But Da's matching medallion hadn't kept him safe, nor had all those
prayers Ma said every morning, every noon, every night. He'd still ended
up in a gutter with a Mafia bullet in his head. And the two thousand dollars
that had shown up the next day—hush money? Some convoluted apology
to his Sicilian mother?—had spurred Roman to turn in his badge and sign
up for the Prohibition Bureau.

The Mafia had to pay. They had to be stopped before they could take
any more husbands from any more wives, destroy any more good men.

Roman stomped out to the kitchen loudly enough to warn the two
gossips standing there that he was none too pleased. "Brewster. What do
you think you're doing?"

Cliff didn't even have the grace to look chagrined at being caught. He
just leaned into the wall and crossed his arms over his chest. "You have her

risking her life for this obsession of yours. She deserves to know what drives you."

A flicker of something hot and guilty flashed through him when he glanced at the blond stirring dried noodles into a pot of boiling water on his stove. "What would that help? And since when do you even care if she's risking her life?"

Sally's back went rigid, and it was on the tip of his tongue to assure her that *he* cared—and he did. He didn't want her hurt, certainly not killed. But this was so much bigger than either of them. He would make sure to tell her that later, when his partner wasn't glaring at him.

Cliff folded his arms over his chest. "I don't want you to have anything to do with her. That doesn't mean I want her dead."

"I knew we'd find something to agree on," Sally said as she dropped a handful of noodles into the pot.

Cliff didn't even glance her way. "I understand why you hate them— you know I do. I commiserate. I hate them for you. But it's gone beyond coloring what you do. It's become your only reason for doing anything. You're acting like bringing down Manny will bring back your father, which is just stupid."

Roman clenched his teeth until it hurt. He knew nothing would bring Da back. Nothing would make the ache any less for Ma. Nothing could ever, ever undo the damage those gangsters had done in that Brooklyn street. But he had to do *something* to stop the same thing from happening to someone else.

Sally turned her inquisitive eyes on Cliff. "Was it Manny who—?"

"No." Cliff's eyes shot familiar reproof at him. "Which is *why* it's so stupid. It's not even direct vengeance, it's some convoluted form that isn't going to make him feel any better. Because he *knows* that the Mafia isn't one single entity, that striking off one head wouldn't hurt another. Chances are, the gangster who killed his father doesn't even know Manny."

Maybe not. But cut off enough heads, and eventually the beast would writhe its way to Hell where it belonged. Plunge enough daggers into its heart, and it would bleed out. He had to believe that. Or what was the point of anything?

"Hm." Sally cocked her head to one side so that golden waves touched her shoulder and studied Roman like he was a newly discovered species of insect. "You know, this makes it supremely ironic that you fell for a mafioso's daughter."

"You think I don't know that?" Roman rolled his eyes and stormed over to his grimy window. He hadn't meant to fall for Sabina—but she deserved to be redeemed from this lousy underworld, and Capecce had already proven he couldn't do it. "Butt out, both of you."

"Not a chance, buddy." Cliff strode his way, stopping only when he was close enough to poke a finger into his shoulder. "I don't want to see you end up like your father just because you don't know when to call it quits. Pack it in and tell your little light-skirt over there to take a hike."

"Maybe he's right. About the packing it in part, I mean." Her disembodied voice came from the kitchen and created far too homey a sensation. How many times had his parents carried on conversations in two different rooms like this? A parallel so insane that it could only have been inspired by the talk of his father. "Miss Gregory is undoubtedly right about Manny losing patience. I don't want you to get hurt over this."

Cliff snorted. "Yeah, you might lose your ticket out then, right? She wants to be your mistress, Roman. Hopes you'll set her up."

She...what? They'd been having a good time when they weren't out risking their necks pumping gangsters for information, sure, but he knew well he'd been taking his foul temper out on her. Why the devil would she want to stick around? "As if I could afford it."

Her blond head poked out of the kitchen, sunny smile in place. "You haven't seen elasticity until you've seen me stretch a dollar, champ."

In spite of himself, a bubble of amusement floated through his system. Under the lipstick and that devil-may-care attitude of hers, she had real gumption. "I have no doubt of that, Sally. But it's not going to happen."

"Thank heavens," Cliff muttered.

Roman ignored him. "On my salary, I can support myself, but even adding a wife is going to push it. No way I can take a mistress after I marry Sabina."

Cliff sputtered. "Are you kidding? That train has chugged out of the depot, my friend."

"It's not too late until she walks down the aisle, and I have no intention of letting *that* happen. I've got a plan."

"Roman..." Cliff stretched his name out to four syllables.

"Relax. Some time with me, and she'll forget all about Capecce. I just need to remove her from the situation for a while. And don't get any ideas." He leveled an accusing finger at Sally's far-too-peaceful face. "You sabotage my chances with her, and I'll leave you with Capone."

Sally held up her hands, one still gripping the spoon. Something glinted in her eyes, but he couldn't put a name to it. "Hey, I'm on your side here. Especially since you've done a peach of a job of sabotaging yourself."

His meddling friend chuckled, convincing Roman that he'd have no peace from either of these two until he had a band on Sabina's finger.

<hr />

Lorenzo mounted the few steps up to the Mancari stoop, smiling at Manny when he looked over the top of his newspaper in greeting. The evening was beautiful—cooler than usual for early August, with a rose-scented breeze blowing by—and as Lorenzo had walked the blocks from his apartment, he had seen many a neighbor outside enjoying it.

"*Bona sira*, Enzo," Manny greeted with a grin. "You'll want to stay out here. It's a madhouse in there, what with wedding favors and gowns and the gifts that have begun to arrive. The President sends his apologies for missing the festivities but sent a lovely crystal vase."

Unsure whether his soon-to-be father-in-law was serious about that last part, Lorenzo smiled. "It's crazy at my parents' too. Mama's trying to help Rosa as much as possible, and she's got all this—stuff—covering every table."

Manny chuckled. "Just steer clear. The women love this nonsense, so leave it to them. For my part, I just hand over the money and head outside. Only way to keep from going mad. But rest assured that with Rosa at the helm, this will be the talk of Chicago for a decade. Sounds like every person of any import will be there."

"Mm." Lorenzo plopped down on the top step and glanced at Manny's paper, not caring to think about what celebrities might soon be watching him. "Anything interesting in the news today? I haven't even had time to open mine."

"Alexander Graham Bell passed away. Funeral's tomorrow."

He said it as though it were of personal relevance, eliciting a grin from Lorenzo. "Going?"

Manny shot him a humored glare. "It's in Nova Scotia."

He chuckled. "Could be tough, then."

Manny grinned and turned a rustling page. "There's going to be a minute of silence tomorrow on every phone line and switchboard on the continent to honor his memory. They haven't announced at what time, yet."

Sabina stepped outside before he could reply, book clutched in one hand and a smile lighting up her face. His heart tightened, leaving Enzo pleasantly breathless. It was good to see her looking happy—too many of the times he'd stopped by over the last few weeks, there had been a pall over the house, over the neighborhood.

Mrs. Bennato had finally passed away. Mr. Bennato hadn't shown up since. Isadora had had to shoulder the entire responsibility of the funeral, the wake, the bills, and Mary…Mary had been nearly as absent as her father. Lorenzo knew Sabina had been doing everything she could for her friends, but it had been wearing on her, especially because he knew she felt guilty to have the joy of their wedding coming so soon on the heels of grief.

But through all the trials, her heart had shone through—proving her mettle, reminding him why he'd always loved this girl who loved others so well. "There's my bride," he said in greeting.

Her smile turned into an excited grin. "Ten more days. I still can't believe it. Mama and I got the beading on my dress done this morning. It's so gorgeous, Enzo."

Manny folded his paper and stood up from his chair. "As if it could be anything else, when it's on you, *principessa*." He stepped over to her, pressed a kiss to her temple, and turned to the door. "You two enjoy your evening. There will be no peace to be had once your grandmothers arrive from Palermo on Monday."

They laughed at his exaggerated shudder, and then Sabina sat down beside Enzo as Manny disappeared inside. Her smile faded. "Mary came by this morning."

He sucked in a breath. "How was she?"

"I don't know." She rubbed a hand over her eyes and sighed. "She eloped with Robert a few days ago, apparently. Wanted my help in breaking it to Isadora. She didn't say a thing about the funeral, about the fact that she'd just left her sister to deal with everything on her own, she just…" She rolled a hand through the air as if ushering in more words and then dropped it to the book she held in her lap along with her gaze. "They're leaving Chicago—Mary and Robert, I mean. He got a job in Kansas City. They leave in two days. She won't even be here for the wedding."

"Bean." He reached over, covered her hand with his. "I'm so sorry. Wasn't she one of your bridesmaids?"

"Yeah. That part's okay—Isadora's just taking her place, which feels right." A soft smile curved her mouth again. "You should have seen her when she tried on the dress we'd been making for Mary. Joey would have declared her the most beautiful woman in the world."

A shaft of longing for the brother he'd never joke with again sliced through Lorenzo. Joey should have been here now to tease, to guide, to assure him that he'd be a good husband and father. He bumped his shoulder into Sabina's. "I'd have fought him over that. I believe that honor *always* goes to the bride—especially when the bride is you."

She grinned and bumped him back. Then they just rested there, their arms pressed together. "Tell me Mary will be all right. That they'll settle down, that they'll be happy. That the next time I see her, she'll be laughing over how wild she used to be and apologizing to her sister for all the worry she caused."

He gave her fingers a squeeze. "I hope so. We can pray so. I know you wish there was more you could do, but you've been a good friend. You have to leave her in the hands of God now."

"Yeah."

She didn't sound any more at peace, and he knew why—because of the *other* shadow that had been plaguing her. Her father, and the accusations of murder. "Has he said anything more? Papa Manny, I mean, about O'Reilly's investigation?"

Eyes glued to the pavement, Sabina shook her head. "It's like the whole situation doesn't even exist within the walls of our house. I tried broaching the subject a few times, just to see if there have been any developments, but he cuts me off. Says we aren't to worry Mama with such nonsense."

As if murder charges were nonsense. Lorenzo sighed. He'd have loved to have been able to offer her reassurances, but the truth was that Manny hadn't told *him* anything about it either, even when he'd come to the office for official counsel. But then, that counsel had simply been a recommendation to Darrow. He'd been otherwise tightlipped, saying he wanted to keep Lorenzo out of it.

Suddenly he didn't know whether to be grateful for that or not.

"I don't know what else we can really do, Bean. Other than pray he didn't do it, pray the law sees that, pray the investigation doesn't interfere with the wedding."

Her lips turned up just a bit. "And pray that I can stop feeling so guilty for focusing on the joy of that when there's so much to be sorrowful and anxious about."

"We're meant to cling to the joys, though, whenever we can. There's no need to feel guilty over it." Wind danced up the street. Laughter rang out from somewhere nearby, and a dog yipped a friendly hello. Proving his point for him—that no matter what might befall them, life marched on. He let it speak its reassurance for a minute and then looked down at the book in her lap. "What's that? G's latest project?"

She grinned but shook her head and showed him the spine. It was the book of poetry he'd given her all those years ago. He didn't know whether to smile or wince at all the "wisdom" he vaguely recalled tucking into the pages. "Ah. My annotated gift. Still working through that?"

"Yep." She grinned and nestled closer. "Well, I have one left. You had a note on this one to read it with you, so I saved it for last. 'That Nature is a Heraclitean Fire and of the comfort of the Resurrection.'"

"My favorite. Not that I've read it in years, so we'll see what insight I thought I could offer you. Have you been reading them out loud?"

"As directed." She opened the book to where a piece of paper stuck out, covered in his scrawl. "Would you do the honors for this one?"

"Sure." He positioned the book between them, then cleared his throat and found the first line. HHHe paused to pull his glasses out of his pocket and position them on his nose. "Much better. Okay. 'Cloud-puffballs, torn tufts, tossed pillows | flaunt forth, then chevy on an air- / Built thorough- fare: heaven-roysterers, in gay-gangs | they throng; they glitter in march- es....'"

He read the lines slowly, careful to observe the odd syntax of the phras- es; no sentence ever seemed to behave normally, nouns turning into verbs and verbs to nouns, the breaks in the middle of each line usually also in the middle of a clause, sometimes even in a word. But despite that oddity, or perhaps because of it, the verses had always captured for him the glory of a vast nature. Ever changing, as Heraclitus always said. Man but one small, easily extinguished part.

"Man, how fast his firedint, | his mark on mind, is gone! / Both are in an unfathomable, all is in an enormous dark / Drowned....'"

Each time he read this poem, he remembered studying it in school and realizing how true the words were. How quickly the flames of men—na- ture's dearest, as Hopkins called them—were quenched by the seas of time.

In the world of Little Italy, it had seemed especially true, and all the more so now, with Isadora and Mary mourning the death of their mother and the abandonment of their father. With Joey lost to war. With all the pain they'd endured this summer thanks to their fathers' world.

Father. Manny. He could see their faces, their smiles, the love in their eyes—but also the shadows there, always there. They were always looking around, over their shoulders, waiting for the next strike. All their lives, their fathers had striven to build something from the wobbling blocks of men's vices, to profit from their darkest passions and purposes. But how often had Lorenzo seen mafiosi just like them snuffed out with a bullet, a blade, a rope, an angry hand? They knew it—it was a risk they accepted. But it wasn't a risk Lorenzo ever wanted to take. He knew that anyone who lived that life also died an eternal death. Despair always waited around the corner, threatening to consume anyone who looked up and saw the infinite universe crashing over his speck of existence.

He had chosen life instead—to partake of something greater that would buoy him over those vicious seas. He, like Hopkins, clung to the comfort of the Savior who had the power to calm treacherous waves with a single word.

"…Enough! the Resurrection, / A heart's-clarion! Away grief's gasping, | joyless days, dejection. / Across my floundering deck shone / A beacon, an eternal beam…."

Sabina's fingers laced through his and gripped them tight. He thought she was even holding her breath. The sounds of the neighborhood faded, and he felt again what he had the first time he'd tasted the Body of Christ, the Presence that was usually only clear to him when he sat in a quiet church in adoration. He became aware of the settling of the Holy Spirit on this mafioso's front stoop in Little Italy—the Breath of Heaven, here in the bowels of the earth. Light in the darkness.

"In a flash, at a trumpet crash, / I am all at once what Christ is, | since he was what I am, and / This Jack, joke, poor potsherd, | patch, match-wood, immortal diamond…"

Sabina's voice joined him for the last words. "'Is immortal diamond.'"

Silence beat its wings for several heavy seconds, the outside world held at bay by the intensity surrounding them. Sabina drew in a long breath. When she spoke, her whisper somehow compounded the quiet. "Wow. I get it."

Lorenzo traced her finger with his thumb. "The poem?"

"The truth." Her eyes slid shut, rapture written upon her face. "That was how I felt all those years, Enzo—all those dark things. Like I was noth-ing worth loving, nothing worth saving, nothing worth hearing." Her fingers held tight to his. "I felt so alone. But I never was. Because Christ made himself nothing too. And that because of that…"

He could feel his pulse in every limb. "Because of that, we become what He is."

"Mm." She rested her head on his shoulder, her eyes still closed, her lips turned up in a beatific half-smile. "'Away grief's gasping, joyless days, dejection.' I didn't think, before all this, that they'd ever go away. I didn't think they *could*. I thought…then I thought if ever they would, it would be because I made them. All my efforts just made the ship toss on the waves, but He was there still. Shining that beacon."

"And because of Him, we get to be part of that Light too. The matchwood—lit by His fire, touched to the candle's wick. We're how His light is carried on. We're what pierced the darkness."

They were the immortal diamond.

As morning light filtered through her window, Sabina rose with a smile on her face. She had fallen asleep with her rosary still clutched in her fingers, not exactly praying, just…basking in the peace that had enveloped her on the stoop with Lorenzo. Sweet images had filled her dreams that she couldn't have put to words. Everything looked different now. She was more aware than ever of how small her spark of life was in the darkness of the world. But she was also more aware that it only took one spark to dispel the darkness. Somehow, she and Enzo could make a difference in their families. They didn't have to fight them. They could just hold the light.

The peace buoyed her as she dressed, combed the night's rag curls into waves, and tied her shoes. She practically floated down the stairs, into the kitchen. She exchanged a Sicilian greeting with Cook and poured herself some coffee.

Then Mama snapped into the kitchen like a live wire. "There you are. What have you been doing up there when you know we have so much to get done?"

Sabina nearly choked on her sip of coffee. She hadn't seen that look on Mama's face in ages. "Just getting ready. I thought I would help Cook today." She motioned to the counters overflowing with pastries for breakfast, pastas in varying stages of readiness for upcoming meals, sauces both completed and their composite ingredients waiting to be blended, meats and cheeses ready to be combined into a feast.

The sad thing was, none of it was for the wedding itself—it was still too early to cook for that—but just to feed the steady river of family that had been pouring in every day. The cousins and aunts all claimed to be coming to help, but more often than not they just got in the way and offered advice that no one had any intention of taking.

Mama glared at her. "You will not be in the kitchen today. Cook can handle everything. That's what we pay her for, isn't it? We have to go to the florist's to discuss your bouquet, you need to get your hair trimmed, your veil and headdress still need to be made, and I need you to try your gown on again so we can decide what jewelry you're going to wear. Fran wants you to wear her pearls, but they would need to be restrung. Maybe we can substitute the ones your father gave me last year and she wouldn't notice."

Sabina sipped her coffee, fighting for calm. "Okay. The florist and barber then. I'll be ready to go in just a minute." She picked up a *cornettu* and sank her teeth into it, closing her eyes in delectation as the jam and chocolate inside the croissant mixed on her tongue.

When she opened her eyes again, Mama was frowning. "You've been eating too many sweets. I don't want to have to get you a new corset just to fit into your gown."

Was it too late to retreat back into the peaceful sanctuary of her room? She sighed and considered her croissant. "I can't just waste it—but I won't have any more sweets today, I promise." Her corset fit just fine, but it wasn't worth the argument.

Mama grunted. "Bring it with you, then. Let's go. I need to pick up some more *saracena* for Cook, too."

Forfeiting her coffee with a sigh, Sabina followed her mother out to where the Pierce-Arrow sat waiting. Twenty minutes later, they were settled in at the flower shop, one of their bodyguards on his way home with the olive oil for Cook. They spent an hour poring over sketches and photographs, settling on a bouquet that cost as much as the silk for her dress. And that wasn't including the blooms for her headpiece and bridesmaids.

Mama tapped a fingertip to her lip. "I suppose Cat and Izzy both need a bouquet, too. Although why you insisted on two witnesses—we only ever had one in Sicily."

Sabina sighed, repeating the refrain she and Lorenzo had been doling out left and right, it seemed. "We're not *in* Sicily, Mama."

Mama ignored her, just as she always did. "Well, there's no help for it. We'll make them match, I suppose. Keep them simple."

Since agreeing seemed the easiest course of action, that's what Sabina did. They finally left the florist's and headed for the barbershop, where Mama elbowed her way through the line of long-tressed girls awaiting a bob, insisting they had an appointment.

Sabina knew well that in this case her "appointment" was little more than name recognition. When Mama said, "Miss *Mancari* is here," no one dared to object.

She couldn't wait until she was Mrs. Capecce instead. No more people starting in fear whenever they heard her name, no bodyguards shadowing them… Sabina offered an apologetic smile to the young ladies waiting in line. "Mama, let's wait our turn."

Mama scoffed. "We haven't got all day! Besides, you're getting married in a week. I'm sure all these girls understand how busy you are. Isn't that right, girls?"

A chorus of affirmatives rang out, though whether out of sincerity or intimidation was anyone's guess. Sabina sighed and took a seat in the barber's chair, looking at the older gentleman who draped a cape over her. "Just a trim," she said.

"A very small trim." Mama took up her general's stance by the mirror, scowl in place. "No shorter than necessary to look well groomed. Your grandmother will have a fit as it is. You know how she liked it long."

Pressing her lips together seemed like the best response. Yet another argument that wasn't worth having.

Within minutes the barber had shaped up her hair and had a handsome tip in hand, and they left again. The car had barely made it a block when Mama ordered it to stop. Sabina looked around, wondering what they had to do now. Her confusion didn't lessen as Mama pulled her into a furniture store to a display of buffets.

"Which do you like? The mahogany? The cherry?"

Another sigh swelled up, and she barely repressed it. "Mama, they're both lovely, but we don't have room in the apartment for something like that."

"Of course not." Mama waved a hand at her. "But the house will be practically bare. Enzo has so little."

Sabina trailed behind as Mama headed for a section with tables. "House?"

"The Horowitz family just moved from that lovely stone townhouse down the street, so your father snatched it up. He wants it to be a surprise, but I knew you'd want to choose your own furnishings."

So he'd just bought it? Without even letting them see it first? What if they didn't *want* the Horowitzes' house? What if they wanted something closer to Birdwell, Stein & Associates? What if she'd been looking forward to sharing that cozy little apartment with her groom for a while first, putting all the old connections behind them? "Mama, we don't need a house right now."

"It's done, *cara*." Mama pursed her lips. "I think we'll go with cherry all round. Make it all match. It'll complement your china perfectly."

Sabina lifted her arms and let them fall in defeat. Her opinion was obviously not needed.

She tried to remind herself of how lovely she'd felt that morning, but holding onto it proved impossible as the weight of her family settled on her shoulders again. When Mama positioned her in front of the full-length mirror in the master bedroom at home an hour later, her wedding gown felt far heavier than it had the last time she tried it on.

Still, the image brought a smile to her lips. The silk had been imported from Italy, trimmed with Spanish lace, and beaded with pearls. Cut in the latest fashion, the waist was low, nearly to the hip, and made her look even more slender. The skirt almost reached her ankle—longer than she would have liked, but necessary to appease the older generation. Lorenzo would love it. She could imagine the look on his face when Papa walked her down the aisle, the way his eyes would light up, maybe even go misty. He would take her hand, kiss it, and murmur something soft and sweet about how much he loved her.

Mama drew Fran's pearls out of a box and fiddled with the clasp. A second later, the sound of beads hitting the floor mixed with an exasperated exclamation. "Worthless things! They weren't even knotted between the beads. I *told* her they needed to be restrung. The thread just frayed and snapped! Here."

Sabina accepted the new string of pearls Papa had bought and watched while Mama collected those from the broken one. She held the necklace up to her throat but lowered it again. Much as she didn't want to point out the obvious, Mama would see it for herself in another moment. "The whites don't match, Mama. Why can't I just wear the pendant Enzo gave me for my birthday?"

"Because it's *gold*. You know you can't wear gold on your wedding day until he puts the band on your finger."

"That's just a superstition. I—"

"Sabina." Mama raised herself up and huffed out a breath. "Humor me. You are the first ones in our families to get married in America, which means we are all used to the Sicilian customs. They're what we know, what we love, what we're looking forward to. We've humored you with your insistence that it be in August, with your desire for two bridesmaids, with countless other things. Grant us the rest of our traditions."

It felt like she'd done nothing *but* grant them their traditions. She bit her tongue—but she also held up Mama's pearls to show her how they looked against the silk.

Mama's wince said it all. "We'll find something else, then. I don't know what, but if we need to go shopping again, we will. Take off the gown, *cara*."

She obeyed, folding it carefully back around the tissue paper and into its box, since all the beading made it far too heavy to hang. She smiled as she closed the lid and her ring caught the light from the window, flashing a dozen rainbows over the wall. *Immortal diamond*.

She glanced at her mother. "Do you mind if I run over to the church for a little while? I can light a candle for Nonna's safe journey." And try to reclaim a bit of last night's peace.

Mama looked about to object, but then her face cleared. She drew in a deep breath. She nodded, even managing a smile. "Say a prayer for your mother's patience while you're at it too, would you?"

Sabina grinned and moved to kiss Mama on the cheek. "The wedding is going to be beautiful. You're a wonder, Mama. I'm so grateful to have you."

Mama's eyes went as misty as she'd imagined Lorenzo's, and she reached over to pat Sabina's cheek. "I'm so proud of you, Sabina Maria. The way you raised your brother and sister when I could not—the way you held this family together. I know you will be a good wife. A good mother to your own children. And I am so proud. *So* proud of the heart I see inside you."

If she tried to say anything to that she'd probably start crying, so Sabina just gave her mother a hug and then dashed down the stairs, out the door, down the street. She didn't slow until she was climbing the church stairs and slipping into the cool, shaded interior, out of August's sticky heat.

"Sabina. I prayed you would come."

She froze at the feminine voice, her eyes blinking against the sudden blindness after being in the sun.

Ava stood just inside the sanctuary, in the last pew. She wore a modest black dress, clutched a handbag in front of her. She looked for all the world like any other woman seeking solace in the quiet church.

Sabina very nearly spun back to the door and ran home again. But she felt the encouragement of the diamond on her finger. If God listened to a mafioso's daughter, if He heard her, saw her, answered her prayers, who was she to say He didn't also hear the prayer of a mafioso's mistress?

She forced a swallow, drew in a breath, and took one step at a time until she was looking Ava straight in the eye. No one else was in the pews or praying at the altar, and though she could see Father Russo's feet in the confessional, he wouldn't hear them from here unless they shouted.

She didn't intend to shout. Mostly she intended to listen. But first she had to ask the question that had been niggling at her since she saw Ava in Papa's office and realized who she was. She asked it softly, in a whisper that she hoped didn't sound like an accusation. "Does Papa know you come here?"

Ava shook her head, her gaze darting past Sabina, to the corner where she'd noticed the guards before. Sabina hadn't even seen them this time, but there they were. "The boys just tell him I go to church. They don't tell him where. Will you...will you sit with me? Just for a minute?"

Though it still took a heartbeat to gather the courage, Sabina nodded and slid around the end of the pew. Ava slid over to make room for her, and they both sat on the polished wood. The kneeler was out, lending credence to Ava's claim to have been praying. About what, she had to wonder. Them? Papa? That they'd somehow be able to wiggle out of the murder charges?

Sabina smoothed a hand over her skirt. She didn't know what to say now, so she just sat there, looking from the familiar, graceful arches of the building to the not as familiar, graceful face of the woman beside her.

Ava's smile wobbled. "I'm so sorry you heard what you did at your father's office. I'm so sorry I...I've stayed away from here since then. I didn't want to hurt you any more. But—you're getting married so soon, and I..." She trembled to a halt.

Sabina still had no words. But she had patience. She offered a small smile and stayed still.

Ava dashed a tear away from the corner of her eye. "I was twelve. When my father sold me. My first pimp, he—he made sure I could never have children. And I didn't want to, didn't want to bring any innocent lives into this ugly world. But then…" She looked forward, toward the crucifix at the front of the church, then over to Sabina. "I know you hate what your father's done, what he's put your mother through. But he saved me, Sabina. Maybe he shouldn't have. I know the pain I've caused you and your mother. But he saved me, he gave me safety. He gave me a better life than anyone else ever would have. And when I cried to him about my empty arms, he… he told me about you. Little G. Serafina, God rest her soul." She crossed herself.

Sabina did too.

Ava's eyes slid closed. "You won't remember it, but there was a time—your mother was with child, between you and Little G. Something went wrong, wrong enough that Vanni and Fran rushed her to the hospital. Franco came to find your father, and he didn't have time to take me home first, so…I don't even know how it happened, but I ended up at your house, staying with you while you slept." She squeezed her eyes tight. "If your mother ever found out that I'd stepped foot in her house, watched over her daughter, I can't imagine how upset she would be."

Sabina couldn't imagine it either, and she had no intention of being the one to tell her. She shook her head.

Ava opened her eyes again, though they focused on the bag in her hands. "For hours, I just sat there in the nursery with you, watching you sleep. Wishing I had some part of this side of Manny's life, that I had some claim to *family*, real family. That I had someone bright and innocent to love."

Her gaze lifted, tangled with Sabina's, and tears glistened there in her eyes. "I know I didn't—that I don't. I know I'm just the other woman. But to *me*, Sabina—his family is all I have. You, your brother. Even your mother. She may hate me, but the way he talks about her, the love in his voice… the heaviness of it when she was sick." She shook her head. "I prayed for her then, the first I'd prayed since I was twelve years old. I didn't know where to go to church for it, so I came here. I thought, if this is where Manny prays, where Rosa prays, then this is a place where God will hear my prayers for them. For you."

That must have been when she started seeing her here, back when Mama was in the sanatorium. She couldn't really remember when her face started appearing in the park or these pews. She certainly never would have thought that it appeared because of them. *For* them.

A few weeks ago, she had found it strange, even frightening, to think of this woman encroaching on her family. Today, it made her blink back more tears of her own. She couldn't hate a woman who loved them. She couldn't hate a woman who had prayed for them in their darkest hours. "He did hear you. He always hears you, wherever you pray."

They sounded like Enzo's words, or Isadora's. But they felt like candlelight on Sabina's lips.

Ava smiled a little. "I watched you grow, from a distance. Watched how you cared for your brother and sister. You made your father so proud—he was always talking about you, telling me what a good girl you were. The light of his life. His *principessa*."

It was Sabina's turn to squeeze her eyes shut. She'd always known he loved her. She'd never doubted that. Even so.

Even so.

Ava sniffed, and the soft click of a metal clasp made Sabina open her eyes again to see her opening her little handbag and pulling out a handkerchief. She didn't touch it to her face, though. She unfolded it, revealing something nestled inside that shone silver and white in the church's dim lights.

"And now here you are. Grown, ready to start a family of your own. I know I have no part in that. I know that. But..." She paused, drew in a long breath, rolled back her shoulders before she raised her eyes to Sabina's again. "You're the closest thing I will ever have to a daughter."

She reached into the cup of her palm and pulled up the delicate length of silver and pearls and crystals, a backward stream, until the only part touching her hand was the large pearl drop of the pendant. "This was my mother's. My father pawned it, of course, but I knew it the moment I saw it, years later. Her father had made it for her himself. Her name was Pearl, you see. She..."

Ava paused, shook her head. "I had a bit of cash by then, thanks to your father. I bought it. I reclaimed that much, at least, of who I'd once been." She offered a shaky smile. "It would mean the world to me if you would take it. You don't have to wear it," she rushed to add. "But if you just take it, then I can pretend you're wearing it on your wedding day. Or carrying it somewhere, or—I don't need to know the truth. It's selfish of me to even hope you'll accept it. But if you would, if you'd let me give you this one thing..."

Where she expected a tumult inside her, Sabina found only that strange peace of the night before. Where she expected outrage, there was only love. Where she expected resentment, there was only the light of a dozen candles shining like prayer onto silver and pearl.

She cupped her hand under the necklace and let Ava drip it into her palm. She didn't know how to say that she forgave her. That she didn't hate her. That, a little at least, she understood. All she could figure out how to say was a "Thank you" so quiet it barely moved the air. But from the way Ava's eyes filled with grateful tears, it was as if Sabina had said all those other things too.

The door at the back opened again, and a few old ladies came whispering their way inside. That was Sabina's cue to leave. She still hadn't lit a candle or prayed, but…she felt like she had. She found the courage to press a hand to Ava's shoulder as she stood, to nod to the guard as she exited. And to march straight home to Mama's house, to Mama's bedroom, where Mama still sat fussing with Fran's broken string of pearls.

She let the necklace dangle, the alternating crystals and pearls on the chain, the larger single pearl with its pretty fitting, twirling in the light. "How about this, Mama?"

Her mother looked from the necklace to her. "Pretty. And I think it will match the dress perfectly. But where did you find it?"

Sabina moved to the mirror, fastened it around her neck, and smiled. "It was a gift from a friend."

The deep gold sunlight of early evening slanted through the windows by the time Sabina finished helping Mama with her veil and made her way back downstairs. She heard Fran and Aunt Luccia in the kitchen, bickering with Cook about something, so she did an about-face at the bottom of the stairs and aimed herself toward the other side of the house instead. She bypassed the mounds of packages that had arrived that day—wedding gifts, she was sure, but she'd wait until Enzo came over to open them. Besides, she'd had enough wedding preparation for one day. Her big plan for the evening was to walk out the front door, sit on the stoop, and hope Enzo found the time to stop by.

Papa's voice drew her to a halt, though the name he spoke wasn't hers. Still, it froze her in her tracks beside the small, rarely used drawing room adjoining the preferred parlor.

"O'Reilly again?"

"Yeah." The second voice was unfamiliar, male, and uncultured. "Stopped by the precinct again today. Still doesn't have so much that Bannigan's willing to make an arrest, but he thinks he will after he talks to Tim Baker."

Papa spat out a harsh Sicilian expletive. "Baker! He's a slimy swine, he'll say anything to anyone if he thinks it'll profit him. No honor, and certainly no loyalty to anyone with Sicilian blood. He would say anything to see me put away."

Squeaking sounded within, the kind the stately, uncomfortable couch made whenever someone dared to sit on it. "There's more. I've had Kelly trailing him, like you asked, and he says O'Reilly's getting real agitated as the wedding date approaches. He's started planning something stupid to try to stop it."

Sabina's blood ran cold with dread. Papa cursed again. "How stupid?"

"Try to steal away the bride stupid."

She heard the drumming of Papa's fingers on something wooden. "She wouldn't go with him."

No. No she definitely would *not*. And why would Roman think she would? Hadn't she made herself clear that day in the park?

"Manny...I don't think he really cares what she wants at this point. Sounded to Kelly like he planned to snatch her away whether she wanted to go or not."

Glass shattered against the wall at her side, making her jump. "He'll do no such thing. Call the boys. Tell them our suspicions were right, and the plan's a go. If he's still breathing in the morning, I'll have *their* heads."

Fear eclipsed her heart: fear for Papa, for herself, and even for that stupid man who wouldn't take no for an answer. She didn't want him dead.

More, she didn't want her father guilty of his murder. Forget that it was Roman—he was a *cop*. She had been taught all her life how to avoid them, how to sniff them out, because crossing a cop was dangerous business. Hadn't Papa been the one to teach her that?

Had she thought she could convince him to relent, she would have stormed into the drawing room and demanded he take it back. But after her last episode of storming a room after eavesdropping, she didn't think he'd be willing to listen. But there had to be someone...

Lorenzo. If anyone had a hope of setting things right, it was Lorenzo.

Her stomach churned and her pulse skittered as she took off at a run for

Papa's office and the phone. Time was of the essence. She'd call him, arrange to meet somewhere, and they could plan out what to do.

Papa's desk was orderly and clean, nothing on it to show the decisions he made there. Not the top of it, anyway. But in that locked drawer she'd been ordered to empty if they ever had to leave town, there was probably plenty.

This would not make its way into that drawer. She'd find a way to stop Papa before those orders could be executed, before Roman's death could ever be noted as an innocuous-looking payment in one of his ledgers.

She forced down the bile that stung her throat and reached for the gleaming black receiver. Her hand shook as she held it to her ear. "Hello? Operator?"

Nothing.

She juggled the handle, trying to disconnect and reconnect.

Nothing.

She tried dialing Lorenzo's number directly. Still nothing.

Sabina slammed the receiver back onto its hook, nearly letting loose a choice word. There was no time for this nonsense. She'd just have to go to his apartment. It was inappropriate to go without a chaperone, but at the moment she didn't care.

The hall sped by as she ran and slammed into the kitchen. She did *not* look at her mother when she demanded to know why she was in such a hurry. She just flew out the door and called over her shoulder, "I have to talk to Enzo." Then she tore through the garden and onto the street before Mama could stop her.

The blocks between her home and his had never seemed so long. Every building stretched endlessly between them, and the faster her feet moved, the farther it seemed they had to go. It felt like an hour later that she paused to catch her breath outside the building Mr. Stein owned. Once she'd sucked in a deep lungful of air, she opened the main door and headed up the stairs.

The vigorous knocking reached her ears before she could see who was pounding on what door, but her heart suspected the worst. Seeing Helen in the hall outside Lorenzo's apartment only confirmed it.

"Helen?"

The redhead looked up with hope instead of guilt, which allayed one suspicion anyway. "Sabina, thank heavens. Do you know where Enzo is?" Helen's nose was red and her voice had been hoarse.

Sabina shook her head and closed the distance between them. "I was hoping he was home. I tried to call, but there was no service."

Helen gave a short laugh. "You must have tried when the phones were down to honor Bell. Five twenty-five?"

"I don't know. I guess it could have been. I didn't wait to try again, just ran over here." If he weren't here, she didn't know what to do now, either. Panic leapt onto her shoulders and sank in its teeth. "Could he still be at the office?"

Helen shook her head and sniffled. "I didn't go in today, I was sick— but they had court this afternoon. They weren't planning on being in the office at all after lunch. Are you okay, Sabina?"

Her knees buckled, and Sabina sank down against the wall. Tears welled up, then multiplied, and she could only manage a shake of her head.

Helen crouched down beside her. "I have a feeling we're here for the same reason. I was at one of your father's joints last night and heard something I shouldn't have. The one time I wasn't trying to learn something, and I overheard a doozy."

"He's going to bump off Roman." Her voice came out as the barest of whispers.

Helen's fingers found hers and squeezed. "It's worse than that, Sabina. It's Enzo's brothers he wants to do it."

"No." Fierce denial propelled her back to her feet, shut off the tears. She pulled Helen up with her. "We have to stop this, Helen. If my father sanctions the murder of a cop—and if it's Tony and Val doing it..."

"You don't have to tell me. It'll tear Enzo to pieces. But what do we do?"

She shook her head again and wiped at her eyes. *Ice.* But not numb. No, *resolved.* She would find them. Somehow. She would stop this. She would not let his brothers break Lorenzo's heart, would not let their hands be stained with the blood of Roman O'Reilly, federal agent.

Opening her bag, she reached for a handkerchief to mop off her face. A piece of paper came out too, fluttering to the ground like a tiny pigeon's wing. She bent over to retrieve it and unfolded it as she rose again.

Her fingers fisted around it. Roman's address. She could go warn him. If he got out of town before Tony and Val could intercept him...but if that faceless voice in the drawing room was right, he might try to take her with him against her will.

She squeezed her eyes shut, not sure if she was thinking or praying or just begging for an answer to jump out and scream at her.

"Go."

Sabina opened her eyes. It was Helen's voice, not the Lord's, but filled with strange intensity. "Go where?"

Helen shrugged. "I assumed you'd know. I just heard the word 'go' and knew it was for you."

Heard it? Well, maybe the Lord answered a desperate cry with a word in the ear of a rival. Who was she to argue? She balled her fist a little tighter. "Okay. You stay here, wait for Enzo. Tell him everything you heard last night, and tell him that someone came to see Papa just a little bit ago. Papa authorized the kill, said it had better be done tonight. Lorenzo will probably know better than anyone where to find his brothers so he can stop them."

Helen nodded but didn't release her hand. "What about you?"

She swallowed. "I'm going to convince Roman to skip town before they can get to him."

"Sabina…" Helen's hesitation pinched her features. "Enzo's not going to like that. Let *me* talk to Roman, you stay here and wait for him."

She shook her head before Helen ever finished. "You'd never convince him. I'm the only one who can do that."

Capitulation and determination battled in Helen's eyes, joining together a moment before her eyelids closed. "All right. Go. I'll stay here and pray that you'll be safe—and that Enzo will understand."

"Amen to that." After crossing herself in punctuation, she reached to give Helen's hand a squeeze and then spun around and headed back down the stairs.

She prayed with every step that she wasn't going alone.

TWENTY-ONE

What life half lifts the latch of,
What hell stalks towards the snatch of,
Your offering, with despatch, of!

-Gerard Manley Hopkins,
from "Morning Midday and Evening Sacrifice"

Insistent knocking at the door interrupted Roman's calculating daydreams. With time running out, he had been focusing much of his energy on figuring out how to get Sabina away from Capecce. Part of him still hoped that if he could get Baker's deposition by August thirteenth, they could arrest Manny and halt the wedding as a side-effect, but he wasn't going to bet on that. Baker was still out of town, and though due back soon, "soon" wasn't good enough. He needed a backup plan.

All he had to do was get her away from Capecce for a while. A day or two with him, instead, and she'd break free of the sense of obligation that tied her to Capecce. He understood that she felt bad for hurting her old friend, that both their families expected them to get married, that expectation could be a strong motivation. He came from two families who could lay the guilt on as thick as Irish cream. But she couldn't let that dictate her life. She couldn't marry a Mafia lawyer and go on living in Little Italy forever, until that life snuffed out her own. He couldn't let that happen to her.

"Coming!" he barked at whoever thumped on his door. Probably Cliff or Sally. One or the other of them was always pestering him these days.

For two people who snarled and spat at each other every time they ended up in the same room, they were in surprising agreement about Roman—especially his need to let go of both Sabina and his vendetta against the Mafia. *They* said that was good reason to listen to them. *He* said it was good reason to avoid them. And if they were here again just to annoy him...

He wrenched open the door, but his accusing words dried up in his throat. He could only get out a low, "Sabina."

He'd looked at the picture of her every day, dreamed about her every night. But seeing her here, framed in his doorway—her beauty was a punch straight to the gut.

She stepped inside but held up a hand, palm facing him, to keep him a step away. Her face was cool and determined. "I'm not here because I changed my mind, so don't get any ideas. I just came to warn you."

His hands itched to reach for her, but that look in her eyes made him shove them into his pockets instead. He couldn't screw this up like he had the meeting in the park. "This oughta be good."

Folding her arms over her chest, she turned her head to take in his apartment. He was glad Sally had been by yesterday and had tidied up, even if she *had* kept up a steady stream of nagging the whole time. "Papa found out you intend to talk to Tim Baker, whom he says would say anything to have him arrested. Moreover, he was told you plan on stealing me away before the wedding."

Her eyes came back to his, still cool and determined. His fingers curled up into his palm. Where was the fire he loved? Had Capecce snuffed it out entirely? "You have to get away from him, Bina. He's no good for you."

"I already said I haven't changed my mind. I'm just here to tell you to get out of town, fast. I overheard Papa give the order to kill you. Tonight. You have to leave now."

His shoulder muscles tensed at the suggestion. "No way. I don't run away from a fight, especially when it's exactly what I need to—"

"Put my father away?" Her lips parted in incredulity, and she shook her head. "Stop thinking like a cop for one blasted minute and consider what's at stake. You really have a mother waiting for you in New York? And is your father really dead?"

Who knew her words could be a punch too? His mouth went so dry that he couldn't reply with anything but a nod.

Her face softened into a plea. "Then think about her, will you? You stick around to play hero and you'll be leaving Chicago under a sheet. That's not how you want to go home to her."

He blinked—just a blink, one moment when his eyes shuttered out the world, but that was all it took. Ma's face was before him, that pleading look she'd worn when he told her goodbye. She'd tried to talk him out of joining the Bureau, chasing the Mafia. She'd tried begging, pleading, commanding—and when all those things failed, she had ordered him to come home alive.

He folded his arms over his chest, too. "Fine. If you come with me."

"Roman, listen." She held out a hand. He took it without hesitation, loving as always how perfect her elegant fingers felt in his. "I care about you. You woke me up from a stupor and made me realize that I didn't have to settle for emptiness anymore. But I don't want to be the person I was with you."

His throat constricted. "Sabina…"

"It wasn't love. You were exciting. I was a challenge. It was all heightened because it was forbidden. But if I had really loved you, it wouldn't have turned to ice so fast when you made your move two months ago. And if you really loved me, you wouldn't be plotting to steal me away from my own wedding. You just want me to be another nail in Papa's coffin. Putting him away isn't enough, you want to take something more from him."

"That's not it!" It couldn't be. He tugged on her arm to pull her closer, raised her hand to his mouth. "I love you. You don't get to tell me I don't."

She sighed. Her eyes turned sorrowful. "Maybe not. But I *do* get to tell you how *I* feel. I love Enzo, Roman. I know you can't believe it, but I do. He's…everything."

He shook his head, hoping he didn't look as wild as he felt. "He can't protect you! He won't get you out of that world."

"And you will?" Her breath of laughter sounded harsh in his ears. "*You're* the one with gangsters on your tail, Roman! You're the one so set on fighting the leviathan that you can't see its tentacles are all around you, can't see that you've already let it win!"

He shook his head, reached to frame her face. She let him, but there was no flicker of joy or desire. "You want me to quit? I'll quit. I'll pack it in, go back to Washington or New York or wherever you want to go. If you just come with me, I'll—"

"No you won't." Her words were soft, but all the firmer for it. She gripped his wrists, but not to cling to him—only to pull his hands away. "You're just like them. My father's love for me will never be stronger than his devotion to the Mafia—and *your* love for me will never be stronger than your hatred for it. What girl would ever want to compete with that?"

His hands fell back to his sides, useless. He didn't want to grant that she loved Capecce, but he couldn't exactly argue with her. But now she was saying it wasn't just Capecce—it was *him*. She wanted to get away from everything that drove him, everything that shaped him, everything that made him who he was. He was the good guy, fighting the bad guys. Wasn't he?

The knight in blasted shining armor. But the princess only saw his battle scars—and the dragon reflected in his visor.

His hands balled into fists. "Fine. Go then. Marry your Mafia lawyer and have a dozen little Mafia babies. Keep the Family growing."

She shook her head, stared at him for a long moment, and then reached for the door. She paused with her hand on the knob. "Please get out of Chicago, Roman. If you ever loved me, then do this for me. Leave now. Pack your bag and *go*."

He jerked his head in what he hoped looked like a nod. He hoped too that she couldn't see the truth in his eyes.

His last reason to consider walking away from all this closed the door behind her. And he had no idea what to do in her wake.

When Lorenzo saw Helen sitting on the floor, he and Mr. Stein both came to a quick halt at the top of the stairs. Her eyes were closed, her face pale—except for her red nose—and she looked exhausted. So why was she camping out in their hallway instead of at home resting?

"Miss Gregory?" Mr. Stein left Lorenzo's side to move to Helen's.

At the sound of her name, she blinked her eyes open and struggled to rise, accepting the hand her boss held out. "Oh, thank heavens. I've been waiting an hour, and we're running out of time. Enzo, you have to stop your brothers. They're going for Roman."

"What?" The breath stopped up in his lungs. "What do you mean?" He knew what she meant—some part of him knew. But the words hung suspended in his mind, nonsensical, too horrible to be believed.

She darted a glance to Stein but apparently decided his presence was less important than her news. "I was at the speakeasy at the dry goods store last night, and someone came in to talk to them. Told them it might be necessary to take him for a ride, and that the boss wanted them to handle it. I tried to tell myself that it was nothing, but I couldn't rest for worrying about it, so I decided to come over to tell you. And then Sabina showed up—"

"Sabina?" His stomach tied into knots.

"She was real upset—she'd just overheard her father giving the go-ahead. Came to get your help, but we didn't have time to sit around, so she went to warn Roman, and I said I'd stay to tell you, so you could get to your brothers."

No. His eyes slammed shut, willing this all to be a dream, a nightmare, not real. This couldn't be happening. He'd known his brothers were being groomed, that they had probably already done more than bootlegging and running rum. But this was murder—of a federal officer.

He opened his eyes again, but he still saw Tony, hands red with blood. Val, a smoking Betsy in his hand. He saw two matching caskets at the front of Holy Guardian Angel instead of white runners and wedding flowers.

Sabina. Sweet, foolish Sabina, so determined to save others that she'd just run straight into the dragon's teeth herself. How was he supposed to both chase after her and stop his brothers?

He had to try. He turned, ready to sprint down the stairs and to his Nash when Mr. Stein's hand landed on his shoulder. "Just a minute, son. We're going to pray before you go running off to save the day."

He forced himself to relax and nodded. Drew the sign of the cross as Mr. Stein began a brief, poignant prayer for safety, wisdom, and speed. At its close, Lorenzo looked straight into his boss's eyes, his question silent but clear.

Stein smiled and patted his shoulder. "Don't worry about me, Lorenzo. The only action I'm going to take is to see Miss Gregory home and then keep praying. Go, stop your brothers. I'd just as soon not have to defend them."

Lorenzo gave both him and Helen a tight-lipped smile, and then sped back outside. But where to go? Whom should he chase?

Sabina—his heart always moved first to Sabina. But he didn't even know where Roman O'Reilly lived, so how was he supposed to follow?

He shut his eyes, tried to breathe past the invisible hand around his throat. But it squeezed. He couldn't go after Sabina—he'd just be running without direction, chasing the wind. He had to entrust her to the hand of God. The only good he could hope to do was to follow her instruction: stop his brothers.

He flew into his Nash and squealed away from the curb, praying he could reach them before it was too late.

Sabina stepped back onto the sidewalk of crumbling bricks and looked around for a long moment. The street was empty. She spun in a frantic circle, willing the taxi to appear, as if it were just hiding behind the next streetlight. She'd paid the driver more than enough to wait for her, and he had promised he would. Now what was she supposed to do? She had no idea where she was or how to get home. Maybe she'd have been able to figure it out during the day, but night's shadows stretched over the skyline, distorting distances and positions.

Clenching her teeth didn't stop her jaw from quivering, and blinking rapidly didn't make her eyes stop burning. In one direction lay the most dangerous part of Chicago, in the other the safety of home. And she had no idea which was which.

She just had to get an L platform. That was all. If she could find the nearest station, she'd be fine. Or she could just walk until another taxi drove by, hail it, climb in, and tell the driver to take her to Taylor Street.

She spun around once more, just to make sure she hadn't missed anything, and then heaved out a breath. Much as it would grate against her pride, she'd better go knock on Roman's door again and ask him to see her to the L, or at least to point the way. He might be angry with her, but he'd never want to see her harmed. He would help her.

Probably.

But first he had to answer his door. She knocked, called out, even tried to explain the problem through the slab of wood, but he didn't answer.

A neighbor hung her head out the window to yell, "He ain't home, sweetheart! Went out the back way like his tail was on fire."

Rats. She opened her mouth to ask the neighbor if *she* knew how to get to the L, but the window slammed closed again.

Fine. Okay. She could figure this out. Crossing herself and muttering a few disjointed prayers, she stumbled back to the sidewalk.

The cabby had dropped her off right here. They had come in from the left, so she'd head that way. Not that she remembered how long they'd been on this street, and it looked different walking. The previous turn had been a left, right? So she should go right at the corner. The buildings down that street didn't look any nicer than the ones on Roman's, but that didn't mean anything. She couldn't recall how long they'd been on the border of poverty during the drive, but it had been a minute or two. Which translated into quite a while of walking, didn't it?

Half an hour later, her feet hurt from her impractical shoes and her hands shook like autumn leaves. Nothing looked familiar—and everything looked *bad*. When she saw the women standing on the street in their scanty dresses, calling out to men who perused their wares with wolfish interest, she knew she was in trouble. She'd gone into the heart of the Levee, and nowhere did she see a taxi eager to take her home.

God, she cried silently into the night. *Where am I? And where are you?*

"Mm, you look like a fresh one. How much, baby?"

She jumped as a hand gripped her arm, tried to pull away but only bumped into a foul-smelling chest. Fear poisoned the air as she looked first at the rough, feral face of the speaker and then the matching one of his leering friend. "No, you don't understand. I'm not—"

"You don't want to charge us?" The second man chuckled. "Fine by us, sweetheart."

"Fine indeed."

She fought back a sob. "Please, gentlemen. I'm lost. If you could just help me home—"

"Hear that, Topsy? 'Gentlemen.'" The first man laughed, spewing liquor-laden breath into her face. "That's rich, sweetheart. But men we certainly are, and if you behave yourself, maybe we'll try for the gentle."

"Oh, God." It was all the prayer she could manage. In that moment, she wasn't sure it would be enough.

TWENTY-TWO

S ally slipped one of her working dresses over her head, barely refraining from rubbing the fresh bruise on her arm. She cast a sideways glance at Capone, who was whistling as he used her mirror to knot his tie. With her money tucked in his pocket, he'd be heading out for a night of carousing.

She'd be hitting the streets to replace what he just took.

A few more weeks. As soon as Baker came back to town and she got what Roman wanted from him, she'd be out. She didn't know where she'd go or how she'd survive when she got there—all she knew was that she had to get gone.

She'd had the same thought eighteen months ago, back in the mountains of Maryland, when she couldn't take one more belting, couldn't stand to hear one more time that she was the very Eve who had destroyed all of mankind. *Anything*, she'd thought, *anything would be better than this.*

She'd been wrong then. But she surely wasn't now.

She couldn't scrub away the filth from the constant stream of men anymore. She couldn't keep things tidy enough to offset the discoloration of the bruises. She couldn't keep painting a smile on her face for the likes of Capone.

It didn't matter where she went. She could make it work. She was a whole lot smarter now than she had been upon arriving in Chicago. Smart enough not to make the same mistakes again, anyway.

"Say, Sally." Capone tightened his tie and turned to face her. His smile stopped a few degrees shy of warm. "I'm thinking of moving you to the Four Deuces. With your looks, we can make a lot more from you than we're doing here."

A few months ago he had made a similar announcement, moving her up from one of the hovels with its cots and cubicles and bare bulbs. She had jumped at the lure of a room to herself, a real bed. He obviously assumed she'd be jumping again now.

Sally reached for a shoe. "Is this required, or are you asking my opinion?"

"Why?" Capone's black brows pulled down. "You really wanna stay here?"

"No, but..." She didn't pause to wonder why she was about to steer the conversation this direction. Doing so had just become second nature lately. "Well, Ava offered me a room at her place, said Manny would pay off my debt to you."

Capone snorted and shook his head, smirk in place. "Sure, baby. Of course, it's also going to go down fast when the old man's pinched."

This was getting too easy. "You think he will be?"

"You oughta know. You're the one playing spy for the Prohibition cop."

His tone was dull, flat. Not accusing per se, but only because he'd already judged and condemned. She silently cursed herself for not considering that he'd have her followed, especially after that dress incident. He thought he had to have to control over everything.

Of course, reacting at all would be tantamount to admitting subservience, and she wasn't about to do that. She pasted indifference on her face and shrugged. "A buck's a buck, right? But he don't tell me nothin. And heaven knows Manny's gotten himself out of everything else they've thrown at him."

"Not this time." A low chuckle rumbled out of his throat. "Not as long as he sticks to that stupid, dated code they brought with them from Sicily."

Sally lifted one inquisitive brow, turning her mouth up at the corners. She had practiced that expression in the mirror and knew it made her look amused, impressed, but also cynical. The weapons she carried on these streets. "Code?"

"*Omerta*. You know, the thing that says it's fine to kill another mafioso, but you better never turn him in to the cops. In this particular case, it means that all the evidence is pointing at Manny, thanks to Eddie getting a bit too fresh with the old man's moll and ripping her necklace off, and he's too old-fashioned to point somewhere else."

She cocked her head to the side and made a show of studying him.

Not that he was making any attempt to cover up his point, but she was still surprised. "You saying you framed him, Al?"

His grin was positively mean. "I'm usually for a more direct means of getting my way, but once in a while it's expedient to let the bulls take a guy down. If I put a bullet in him, his lieutenants would step up and then come after us. Manny and Torrio have been rivals long enough that they'd know it was us. But let the cops take him down, and it'll result in a nice, long trial. Turmoil. Perfect set-up for us to step in and start muscling them out." He shook his head, eyes glinting. "Wasn't so sure it was going to work, there for a while. But that boyfriend of yours stepped up when the local boys didn't."

"Yeah, good ol' Roman." She moved over to him, straightening his tie even though it didn't really need it.

He gripped her wrist and glowered at her. "Let's get something straight, doll face. I don't trust you. I've let you play your little game with O'Reilly because it was convenient for me—the sooner these old-world bosses get taken out, the better. But once Manny's out of the way, that means your cop's gonna start looking around for another target, and it ain't gonna be me. So when this thing's over, you better sever your ties with him, or I'll have your neck snapped as easily as I did Eddie's."

She lengthened that neck with a lift of her chin. She knew well that showing any fear would get her trampled. "If you don't trust me, why risk telling me that Manny didn't kill him?"

His fingers tightened around her wrist, guaranteeing new bruises, and he chuckled. "You think anyone's going to take the word of a whore above that of an honest businessman like Tim Baker? Think again."

Roman would. Maybe. But Capone didn't need to know that, so she shrugged again and tossed in a self-deprecating smile. "Touché. And whatever. You're the boss, Al. You want me to ditch a particular john, he's gone. At least we've made some decent scratch off him, though."

He grunted and dropped her wrist. "You wanna go to another brothel, be my guest, so long as I get my money. Just don't try to play me, Sally. It won't work. Keep your nose clean, you unnerstand?"

"Sure thing, boss," she muttered to his back as he strode to the door. Once he was gone, safely removed from sight, she ran to the sink and turned on the water as hot as it would go. She got out a new bar of Ivory and scrubbed.

She scrubbed long enough to give him time to get well ahead of her. After she dried her hands, Sally coated her lips in red and left her apartment.

The street was pretty active for a Friday night and would undoubtedly be busier still tomorrow. Even thinking about it made her want a bath. With a sigh, she glanced up and down the sidewalk to scope out a good place to take up position.

A scuffle in front of the building next door drew her attention. Jimmy—one of her usual johns—and...was that Topsy? Oh, boy. And both of them drunk. She could only catch glimpses of the figure between them, but those were enough to pull her closer. Expensive shoes and conservative silk dresses had no place on a street like this. Neither, really, did the pleas she heard as she got closer.

No one else paid them any heed—not surprising. Sally might have turned away, too, if freedom weren't sparkling on the horizon and washing away some of the hopelessness. Instead she edged a little nearer.

Topsy moved behind the girl, gripping her arms, and Jimmy stayed in front. The sound of ripping cloth brought Sally another step closer, in a direction that would reveal the girl's face. Her brow furrowed.

Dark chocolate hair. Deep brown eyes swollen with tears. Olive skin, enviable bone structure...gorgeous, but no one she knew. Yet so familiar...

Recollection hit her with a crack, propelling her right into the fray without so much as blinking. Sabina. Roman's Sabina.

"Just what do you two think you're doing?" Sally elbowed Jimmy away and jerked her head at Topsy. They had obviously not expected to be called out for their behavior—shock made them obedient, exactly as she had hoped. "I oughta take a frying pan to your heads, accosting my cousin like this. Look! You ripped her dress."

As soon as her arms were free, Sabina folded them over her chest to hold the gaping fabric closed. Her hands shook, and tears coursed down her cheeks. Her gaze moved from the ground to Sally and back again.

Jimmy rubbed his ribs where she had dug in her elbow. "Now, Sally, how was we to know she was your cousin? She don't look nothing like you. And what's she doing here, anyway, if she don't want some attention?"

"Now *that's* a good question." Sally put a gentle hand on Sabina's shoulder and drew her a step away from the goons. "Sabina, I told you never to visit me here, especially at night. What were you thinking?"

"I..."

Not giving her time to say something that would give lie to the impromptu story, Sally plunged ahead. "We'll go fix your dress, then I'll see you home. *After* these idiots apologize."

Topsy puffed his chest out. "Apologize? When a girl's in this part of town—"

"Does she *look* like she belongs here?" Sally shook her head, not having to feign disgust. "Any man with a shred of decency would have offered to help her home, not tried to have his way with her. I bet her daddy would love to have a little chat with you about that. What do you say, Sabina, wanna go introduce them to Uncle Manny? Bet they'd love to meet a celebrity like him."

Were they a little more sober they'd probably have realized that no niece of Manny's would be on these streets either, but the name did its work thanks to the haze of alcohol. They all but tripped over each other as they backed away.

"So sorry, miss." Topsy doffed his dirty hat.

"Didn't mean you no harm," Jimmy added.

Sally couldn't resist issuing the famed warning of another gangster. "Remember the *Maine*, boys!" She still wasn't sure exactly why the mention of the ship from the Spanish-American War elicited such fear, but hey...it worked. They turned and scurried away.

She slipped her arm around the still-shivering Sabina and aimed them at the door of her building. "Come on. We'll take care of that ripped seam and then get you home."

"Thank you." Sabina's voice shook. She cleared her throat and turned to face Sally. "How do you know who I am?"

Sally pulled open the door, glancing inside warily. Good—none of her neighbors were in the hall with their men of the hour. She had a feeling such a sight would have panicked the poor girl beside her. Ushering her unexpected guest inside, Sally offered a small smile. "I recognized you from the picture Roman has."

"Roman...? Oh." A world of realization echoed in that single syllable.

Sally felt almost guilty for shattering any illusions Sabina still had about him. She searched her mind for a plausible lie. Or better still, a half-truth. "I've been cleaning his place once a week or so. Trying to earn an honest buck, you know?"

Sabina's dubiousness saturated her tone. "And how did you meet him, for him to offer you such a job?"

"Uh..." Giving up the game, Sally shrugged, smiled, and opened the door to her apartment. "Okay, you caught me. But I don't want you to judge him—I mean, he's a far sight better than most men. And he sure loves you."

Her guest stopped a step inside the apartment, looked around, and snorted her opinion of that last statement. "It doesn't matter. I'm getting married in just a few days."

"I know." Though she couldn't imagine that either her fiancé or Roman would be too thrilled to see her in this part of town. Where were they, anyway? Shouldn't one or the other be rushing to her rescue? A girl like her—she was the sort men clamored to protect. Wasn't that what Roman kept going on about? How he needed to get her away from this world, keep her safe?

Some knight he was turning out to be.

Well. Sally put on a cheeky smile and urged Sabina into the light. When the guys failed—which they did plenty—the dames would just have to step up. "Hm, I don't think we'll be able to fix the dress while you're wearing it. I have a kimono in the bathroom. Why don't you go on in and change? I'll get you a nice cup of tea ready, and you can get yourself calmed down while I stitch that up."

Sabina nodded and even took a step toward the bathroom. Then she stopped and spun back around. Actually looked her in the eye, no judgment in her own. Just…gratitude. "What did they say your name was?"

It took Sally a moment to get her throat working. In the face of that look, she very nearly answered honestly. Caught herself just in time. "Sally."

"Well, thanks, Sally. I don't know why you're helping me, but…I thank God you are."

Sally shifted from one foot to the other. "It was nothing. Worse, it was probably selfish. Roman offered to pay off my debts so I can get out of this life, but he wouldn't if I'd let anything happen to you."

Sabina smiled as if she knew that thought hadn't entered Sally's mind until that very moment. "Sure. Well, thanks all the same."

Grateful when she closed herself into the small bathroom, Sally headed for the kitchen to make some tea. She wasn't exactly sure how she was going to get Sabina Mancari out of the Levee without getting herself into trouble with Al, but she'd think of something. She was nothing if not resourceful—even Dad had always had to grant her that.

Sabina's hands shook so badly she could barely grip her dress to pull it over her head. Every time she blinked, those two ugly faces raced to fill her mind's eye, and she could still feel their hands tugging at her. She shuddered. A few more minutes, and things would have ended differently. She could have screamed at the top of her lungs, and no one on that street would have cared.

Except Sally. Sabina selected a clean washcloth from the neat pile of them on the shelf, wet it, and pressed it to her face. Her thoughts were a muddled mess. She didn't know what to think of the woman in the other room, with her pretty young face and old, cynical eyes. A year ago, a month ago—heck, maybe even a day ago—she would have labeled Sally for exactly what she was and washed her hands of her. But she still had Ava's necklace around her neck, the memory of her sorrowful eyes in her mind. People were never just what they did, or just where they found themselves. People were never just their sins.

She held the warm cloth against her face for a long moment and breathed in the clean, fresh scent of laundry soap—a reminder that even in the filth of the Levee, there could be something good. A single prayer made all the difference, even when it was more cry than words. God had seen her. God had heard her. God had sent her the unlikeliest of saviors.

Shrugging into the borrowed kimono, Sabina stepped back out, torn dress in hand. Sally stood in a corner of the small apartment outfitted as a kitchen, pouring steaming water into a heavy mug. If one discounted the cheap, revealing dress and glaring red lipstick, she would have looked like any other young beauty with the world at her feet. It just went to show how deceiving were appearances and the stigmas that came with them. Sally hadn't acted the part of a mercenary out there—she'd acted the part of a friend.

"Here we go." The blond sashayed over with a bright smile and held out the fragrant tea. "This should chase away the shakes."

"Thanks." Sabina traded her dress for the cup. "Mind if I sit? My knees are still a little wobbly."

"Go right ahead." Sally waved her toward a chair as she studied the rip. "This isn't too bad, right along the seam. I'll only be a minute on it."

Sabina sank down into the old chair and set her cup on the small table beside it. She heard Sally move into the bathroom, humming some little ragtime ditty. Exhaustion weighed her down. The shadows surged again. She leaned her elbow onto the arm of the chair and rested her head on it, tempted to close her eyes.

Then a book on the table caught her eye, its binding facing her so that the gold-etched letters caught the light from the bathroom. *Holy Bible*. She reached for it, surprised and not sure why. She'd just seen Ava in her own church, after all. Why should she be surprised that Sally kept a Bible on her table? Those the world said deserved Him least…well, weren't they the ones who needed Him most?

The pages fell open to where a few dollar bills were stuck in. The heading on the left page said Zephaniah, but Haggai began on the right. Two books Sabina couldn't ever remember reading. She let her gaze glide lazily over the text until a few words caught her eye on the Zephaniah side of the book, at the fifteenth verse of the third and final chapter.

The Lord hath taken away thy judgments, he hath cast out thine enemy: the king of Israel, even the Lord, is in the midst of thee: thou shalt not see evil any more.

A silent cry wracked her, forced her head down. If only that were true. If only her past, her family's past, had been blotted out and her future lay pure and white ahead of her. If only there weren't always the threat of more evil. If only all her enemies were vanquished and the Lord stood beside her. If only…

She jerked up her head. The Lord *was* beside her. Hadn't He proven that already? He was there—here. No matter who her family was, He was her Father. No matter how dark the world they created, He was the light.

She couldn't control what others did. She couldn't make them change. But she could do what Mama did. What Ava did. What Fran and Aunt Luccia and Nonna did.

She could pray. She crossed herself and closed her eyes. She bowed her head and breathed an Our Father. *Lord, I don't know how to fight this darkness. I don't know how to keep the men I love away from it. But I know you who made all the heavens and all the earth are bigger than any underworld they can create. You can work here, even here. You can light up this darkness. You can make a way through this night.*

"Sabina? Are you all right?"

She drew in a long breath before she opened her eyes, letting the silent prayer linger on her lips. Sally stood in front of her, concern etched onto her face and mended dress in hand. Sabina smiled. "I've never been better."

Sally didn't ask why. She just glanced down at the Bible and made a sound that was half laugh and half grunt. "Well, glad it's doing someone some good. Here." She held out the dress. "All better."

"Thanks. Again. I owe you big time, Sally."

Golden hair swayed as Sally shook her head. "No, you don't. Really."

"I'm not going to argue about it." Sabina reached for her cup and took a careful sip of the tea. It nearly burned her tongue, but the flavor was full and aromatic. "I won't forget how you helped me. So if you ever need anything…"

Sally's nostrils flared, and her hands landed on her hips. "Look, Sabina. First off, I work for Torrio, who's out to bring your father down at any cost. I've been helping Roman gather evidence that he's guilty of a murder which I've come to realize he didn't commit. And to top it all off, I've been sleeping with the man who was supposed to be pining after you. You owe me nothing."

Sabina leapt to her feet so fast she nearly sent her mug to its side. "Wait—what? What do you mean, that he didn't commit the murder Roman's trying to pin on him?"

Sally frowned. "Just something my pimp said right before I went out and saw you. Made it pretty clear it was one of Torrio's guys."

The bare bulb above them seemed to glow extra bright. *A light in the darkness. A way through the night.* "So you haven't had a chance to tell Roman yet. Do you think he'll believe you?"

"Don't know why he wouldn't. I've got no reason to care who did it. Why?"

Sabina let her hostess go and turned back to the bathroom. Her mind raced as she went. "Maybe that'll be enough to convince him to leave."

"Leave?" Sally trailed her across the living area. "Leave Chicago?"

"Mm. Papa found out what he's been doing and ran out of patience. I heard him tell someone he'd better be dead by morning, so I went to Roman's to try to convince him to leave. He said he'd think about it, but…" But somehow she knew his rush out the back door hadn't been to save his own skin.

Sally seemed to know it too, given her sigh. "But he's not going to walk away from what he'd think of as an opportunity to get his man." She muttered a mild curse and then snapped her fingers. "It's worth a shot. Get a wiggle on, girl. I might as well go double or nothing and play hero a second time tonight, and you're going to have to come with me. I'm not letting you walk these streets by yourself."

Sabina jumped into motion. As she dressed, she kept up a silent litany of prayers. She couldn't help but grin as she exited the bathroom a minute later.

Sally was obviously thinking the same thing. "He's going to be surprised to see us together, isn't he? Maybe that'll be enough to convince him to listen."

Sabina grabbed her bag and followed Sally to the door. "It better be."

TWENTY-THREE

Í say móre: the just man justices;
Kéeps gráce: thát keeps all his goings graces;
Acts in God's eye what in God's eye he is-
Christ

-Gerard Manley Hopkins,
from "As kingfi shers catch fi re, dragon fl ies dráw fl áme"

Roman had walked around the block a time or two, but despite what Da had always claimed, it hadn't improved his mood, nor made any brilliant solutions jump into his mind. By the time he slammed back into his apartment, he could still only see two choices.

Run like a coward for the sake of Ma and still likely end up in a ditch, in some other city, at some other gang's hands. Or make his stand here, now, and take a few mafiosi down with him.

He strode back through the dingy little hall to his dingy little room and pulled open the drawer that actually had his clothes tucked neatly away. For once, he bypassed the picture of Sabina and reached instead for the silver chain, the cool medallion that should have been warm against his chest.

St. Michael soared in the center of the oval, his wings outstretched, the sword of justice raised in one hand and scales in the other. Roman had always clung to that image—that justice wasn't just balance, but also a sword. It was a vengeful angel, smiting the wicked. Even when the wicked smote back. That wasn't when the good guys ran—it was when they fought their hardest.

He slipped the necklace back over his head, pausing to kiss it like Da had always done, and then tucked it under his shirt.

He had done a lot of things Ma wouldn't like, a lot of things that would make Da shake his head. But he wasn't a coward. He wasn't on the graft. He wasn't going to give up on justice just because he fell for the wrong girl.

If the Mafia was going to mow him down, at least he'd go out fighting.

A fist pounded on his door just as he was switching off the light. Maybe it would be Cliff. If so, he'd tell *him* to get out of town, go report back to

Washington. Let them know he'd fought till the last and deliver whatever was left of him tomorrow to Ma.

He should write her a note. Send her a wire. Something. Something to let her know he loved her, that he was sorry he'd let her down. And Sally. He looked around at the order she'd brought, could see her red-lipped smile all through the place. That blood money still sitting in his account in New York needed to be withdrawn, for Sally's sake. Maybe someone, at least, could escape from this place.

The knocking grew louder, more insistent. Well, at least that proved it wasn't the Mafia. They weren't big on drawing attention to themselves before an assault. "Coming!" He turned back to the door and tugged it open. But it wasn't his partner standing outside.

The man was of average height, ruddy complexion, and mediocre looks. It took Roman all of three seconds to place him. "You're one of Bannigan's detectives. Norton, isn't it?"

The detective smiled. "Good memory. Yeah, that's me. Bannigan sent me over. We got wind of a plan of Manny's that might be of interest to you."

Roman snorted. "Yeah, you think? Maybe that he's planning on killing me?"

"How'd you guess?" Norton sighed and shook his head. "From what we could gather, he's fed up with your investigation. Plans on sending a group over tonight to take you out."

He swung the door a little wider and stepped aside so Norton could come in. "So you're what? Backup? Or are you just warning me so I can leave?"

"Neither. The boss thinks this is our chance to bring down some of Manny's top guys. Our tip says they're meeting up at Ava's Place any time now. If we go over there..."

For a second, Roman could only stare at him. Help. Actual help. No one in law enforcement had offered him any since the first disastrous arrest, and the sudden outstretched hand sent a surge of hope through him.

Maybe he'd make it home to Ma after all.

Roman lunged for his holster and stepped outside. "Let's go."

Sabina ran up the street as the car pulled away from Roman's building, heading in the other direction, Sally a step behind her. Sabina hadn't recognized the driver, but her instincts screamed, *"Cop!"*

"Okay, that tears it." Sally hopped on one foot as she fussed with the other shoe. "Next time we go chasing after that idiot, I'm wearing men's trousers and boots. These stupid pumps about broke my ankle."

Sabina tried to suck air enough into her lungs to answer. Though what would she say? She didn't want there to be a next time—she just wanted Roman to live through *this* time.

Heavy footfalls sounded behind them, and they both spun around. Roman's partner—Cliff, wasn't it?—pounded to a halt a step away. He cursed, loudly and vehemently. "Tell me he wasn't with Detective Norton."

"Who's Norton?" Sally asked as she put her foot back onto the ground.

Sabina finally pulled enough air into her lungs to speak. "I don't know his name, but it was a cop. A few inches shorter than Roman, red face."

Cliff cursed again and jammed agitated fingers through his fair hair. "That's him. I just talked to his lieutenant, who just realized Norton's working for Manny. Someone saw him leaving the Mancari house this evening."

No. Sabina grasped Sally's arm. "That must be who Papa was talking to. We've gotta get where they're going. What's that way?" She nodded to the left where the car turned at the corner.

Sally and Cliff answered simultaneously. "Ava's Place."

Sally started off after them, Sabina leaped to keep up, and Cliff grabbed them both by the shoulders. "Huh uh," he pronounced in a definite cop's voice. "I don't know what the two of you are even doing here, together no less, but you're *not* heading into a gunfight. Sally, take Sabina into Roman's and stay out of the way."

As if expecting to be obeyed, Cliff took off at a run. Sabina exchanged an exasperated glance with Sally, and they both went after him.

Her feet hurt, her lungs burned, and the streetlights barely made a dent in the darkness. But she just focused on every circle of light and prayed with everything in her that Lorenzo had reached his brothers in time.

Lorenzo braked to a halt in the alley behind Ava's Place, killed his engine, and let his eyes slide closed. He'd tried the speakeasy first, but a cousin had opened the slide instead of Val and informed him that his brothers had been "promoted." To Ava's Place.

Vinny had written down the directions, and Lorenzo had taken two wrong turns as he navigated the unfamiliar streets. But he was here, finally. He didn't see anyone else in this alley, but hopefully that just meant he'd made it before anything went down.

Not that he was already too late.

Hands still gripping the wheel, he took one long breath to steady himself, forming the exhale into an impromptu prayer.

The stakes in this situation dwarfed him. So much could be lost—his brothers, or his relationships with them. O'Reilly. And Manny...who knew what *his* response might be if he discovered his future son-in-law interfered with his orders? He just hoped Sabina had made it home by now. *Please, God...*

Engine sounds filled the alley as an old jalopy turned in. Lorenzo watched in his rearview mirror as O'Reilly got out, turning and reaching as if to pick something up. He wasn't given the chance. The driver peeled away, nearly running over the agent's feet. O'Reilly spewed a stream of vehement curses.

Lorenzo hurried to get out of the car. If the plan was to have someone dump O'Reilly where they wanted him, then that meant they wouldn't give him any time to leave. His brothers would be right—

There.

The back door to Ava's opened as Lorenzo slammed his car door shut. In his periphery he saw the familiar gaits of Tony and Val, but he kept his gaze on O'Reilly.

The agent was focused on the Capecce brothers and the weapons that gleamed in their hands. First understanding, then fury, and finally resignation settled over O'Reilly's countenance. His hands dangled at his sides, proving he had no weapon. Perhaps that was what he'd been reaching for.

Then O'Reilly turned and spotted Lorenzo. His lips peeled back in a knowing sneer, as if there was some twisted victory in seeing that Lorenzo was on his brothers' side. The sneer faltered as Lorenzo moved toward O'Reilly rather than the opposite side of the alley.

"Enzo!" Tony's voice vibrated with pent-up frustration. "What the devil are you doing here? Go home, you *babbo*. Now."

He didn't answer—just stopped in front of O'Reilly and faced him squarely long enough to watch the questions flicker through his green eyes. Would he land one last punch before going over to his brothers, out of the way of the Betsy's aim? The gleam in his eye testified that his thoughts ran in that vein. But Lorenzo saw confusion flicker as he moved his feet slightly, then he turned to face his brothers.

His heart beat a frantic rhythm in his chest, pumping life and energy to every cell. His mind was clear, crystalline, every thought perfectly formed and held within a prayer. Senses on alert, he was aware of every shift Roman made behind him, and he shifted to compensate so that the agent remained fully blocked from his brothers' sights.

Tony growled out a low warning. "Enzo…"

O'Reilly shifted again. Lorenzo shifted to compensate. "Will you just stand still, you idiot?"

The agent stilled, but his voice was curiously similar to Tony's. "What the devil *are* you doing here, Capecce?"

"Trying to save your neck. My car's right there. We can move toward it together, and I can get you out of here."

O'Reilly snorted. "Why, so you can take care of me yourself?"

Lorenzo rolled his eyes, even if the *babbo* couldn't see it. "Yeah, that's it. You saw right through me."

"Well what am I *supposed* to—"

"Enzo." Tony held his gun raised, at the ready. He motioned Lorenzo out of the way with it. "Leave. *Now*. We have a job to do here."

Lorenzo crossed his arms over his chest, his feet shoulder width apart. He'd stand like this all night if he had to, a Colossus incapable of being moved. "I'm not going to let you kill him. You want to, you're going to have to kill me first."

Curiously, the same Sicilian expletive came from both in front of him and behind. O'Reilly shifted again, and Lorenzo moved to compensate. Tony's arms quivered, but he knew it wasn't from anything but anger.

Val, at least, lowered his Betsy. "Come on, Enzo. Get out of the way. There's no way he's leaving this alley alive, and you don't want to be here to see it."

Lorenzo's throat constricted. "You don't have to do this. You don't have to be like them."

Tony's nostrils flared. His gun was still trained on O'Reilly and, hence, on Lorenzo. He could feel the scorching circle boring through his chest. "This is our life. Our world."

Lorenzo raised his chin. "It doesn't have to be! It's *their* world, not ours.

Not if we choose something different. When are you two going to realize you can make your own choices? All I see right now is *Manny's* decision. He decides it's time for you to prove yourselves, and—"

"Enzo, I'm sorry." He didn't sound sorry. That could have been regret in his eyes but, absent repentance, it was black. "I know this hurts. But we can't all be you. You were born a saint. I was born a mafioso."

"That's crap and you know it."

Behind him, O'Reilly gave a small, humorless laugh. "Don't you get it, Capecce? This *is* their choice. This is how they prove they're ready to take over. You know very well they have to spill blood, take a life, to do that."

Lorenzo's fingers dug into his arm. He wanted to deny it, had always wanted to deny it, but the truth stared back at him. His brothers—his best friends—weren't content to just be in the Mafia. They wanted to run it. "Well they're not going to start with you."

"Who better?" Val angled his gun back up a bit, though he didn't level it at them like Tony. His usual cheerful, mischievous smile played on his lips, the boyish expression clashing with the deadly weapon. "It's bad enough he betrayed us. Betrayed *you* with Bean. Then he pursues a murder that's none of his business, and finally he was planning to steal your girl away before you could marry her. And I mean literally, whether she wanted to go or not."

"I know that." Lorenzo didn't budge. "It doesn't matter. Because this isn't just about saving *his* life—it's about saving *yours*. You kill a cop, and you can't undo that. You carry that with you the rest of your lives. You really want that?"

Tony cocked his head to the side. "Orders are orders, Enzo. Not my call. Val, get our *scioccu* brother out of the way."

"Try it and I'll knock you for a loop. Last time we tussled you lasted all of five seconds." Lorenzo glared at the baby of the clan, who nevertheless took a step toward him.

Tony's lips turned up in a merciless grin—a stranger's smile. "And while you're pinning him, I'll take my shot."

O'Reilly cursed behind him. "Just get out of the way, Lorenzo. All you're doing is prolonging this. Manny's signed my death warrant, and if they don't kill me now, they'll just follow me until another opportunity presents itself. Or if they don't, he'll send someone else, and then they'll be disgraced."

"I don't really care if they're disgraced." He raked a hand through his short hair. At least Val's advance had halted again.

Tony snarled. "Val!"

The youngest started forward again, and Lorenzo unfolded his arms and leaned onto the balls of his feet so he could pounce. He directed a low mutter to O'Reilly. "Please have the good sense to hit the ground or run."

"So they can shoot me in the back? I'd rather face it head on, thanks. I'll bet you a thousand to one they're not the only ones with guns around here. I run, I bite it anyway. Hate to render your heroics useless, but face it, Capecce. You're not going to outmaneuver the Mafia."

Maybe not. Maybe he'd not only fail to save Roman, maybe he'd die himself trying. But if so, then he would die fighting for what was right, die praying that God would use it to call his brothers to repentance. He would gladly lay down his life if it had a hope of saving their souls, even if he would much prefer living to see the change.

He drew in a long breath, closed his eyes for one moment. Put his life, his brothers' lives, O'Reilly's life, all in the palm of God. *Thy will be done.*

That was when chaos broke loose. Behind Tony, the door opened. Manny came out first, Franco and Father close behind. Then four other thugs joined the ranks, half of their faces not familiar. One was undoubtedly the man who had driven the car that dropped O'Reilly in the alley. He must have circled around.

All had guns and scowls and a look of bloodlust in their eyes, mingled with fury when they spotted Lorenzo in their way. Manny's query of "What's the problem, boys?" faded away into a low, drawn out, "Enzo…"

A new shout went up from the end of the alley. Lorenzo didn't take his eyes off the furious mafiosi, but O'Reilly called out, "Cliff!"

In his periphery, Lorenzo saw a tall man charge into the alley. Not good. The sudden shift in balance was guaranteed to rip apart the fragile net of inaction. Lorenzo heard that one moment of silence before the storm, smelled the electricity of coming disaster. Then it snapped.

Bullets rent the air.

One hissed by his ear, followed by another. He glanced over at the newcomer. Cliff had sought out cover behind an unmarked crate. Good. That only left O'Reilly. Lorenzo spun around with the intention of tackling him behind whatever they could find. But Roman was a second faster—he was already tackling *him*. They hit the ground with a thud that would leave some nice bruising on his ribs.

That wasn't what really knocked out his breath. A far too familiar voice screamed his name, growing ever closer as she charged down the alley. *Sabina*. Lorenzo jerked up, spotted her coming at him, and could manage only the most wrenching of prayers. "God, no!"

A bullet from a handgun rang out. And silence echoed in its wake.

Sabina's vision narrowed to Lorenzo. She couldn't have given any other description of the scene. There was only him, once again caught in a hail of bullets because his stupid, noble heart didn't want to see anyone else get hurt. What if this time it killed him?

For the first time in her life, fear didn't render her motionless; it spurred her into action. She flew down the alley, oblivious to the gunfire. "Enzo!" she cried, and then cried it again.

He looked up, mouthed something she couldn't hear. Terror filled his eyes, and he lurched forward, but Roman held him back, kept him behind the stack of boxes.

A different sound pierced the air. Still a bullet, but not as wild as a Betsy. Short. Loud. Effective. Silence immediately followed. She pulled to a halt only steps away from Lorenzo. She looked to the building, where the new shot had originated.

Papa still had his hand raised, his lips pulled back in a snarl. "You do not." *Bang.* "Shoot." *Bang.* "At my *children*!" *Bang, bang, bang.*

With each bullet, she flinched, shuddered, swallowed down bile. A Betsy clattered to the ground. Seconds later a figure slumped over it. The dirty cop, she was pretty sure.

"Bean." Lorenzo's arms closed around her before she was even aware he had moved. She buried her face in his chest and clung. Her eyes closed, every sound in the alley intensified.

Sally darted behind them, aimed at Roman. Tony spoke, obviously addressing Papa. "I'm sorry. Enzo was in the way, and—"

"You think you need to apologize for not shooting your brother?" Papa cursed and fired another round into the corpse.

"We'll take care of him now," Tony said.

Roman's curse echoed Papa's. Sabina pulled her face up so she could look at him over Lorenzo's shoulder. He didn't even seem to have heard Tony. Incredulous, he stared at Sally. "You mean to tell me all this is for *nothing*? He didn't even *do* it?"

Papa tore his gaze away from the body and aimed it at the pile of boxes. Bloodlust still colored his eyes, but contemplation narrowed them. "You care to explain that outburst, O'Reilly?"

Roman cursed again. "You didn't kill Eddie."

"I could have told you that, had you ever bothered to ask and been willing to listen." Papa finally lowered the arm holding the gun, and he lowered it right in front of Tony. A barricade.

He turned his gaze on Sabina and Lorenzo. He was angry, that was obvious. But it was tempered by the rush of fear for them. "I'm assuming the two of you didn't show up by happenstance. This cop means that much to you, Bina?"

Her arms tightened around Lorenzo, and she shook her head. "*He* doesn't, Papa. *You* do. I don't want him dead, but more, I don't want you to be guilty of his death. I love you too much. And Tony and Val."

A low growl sounded from Papa's throat. His head angled, and he swallowed hard. Without looking away from her, he aimed his words at Roman. "O'Reilly. If I let you live..."

"I'm done." A glance at Roman proved his face matched the crisp tone of his voice. "Call me what you want, but I'm an honest cop. You didn't kill him, I'm not going to frame it to look like you did. It was one of Torrio's boys."

Tony lurched forward, but Papa pushed him back. "Sabina, Enzo, escort him from the boxes, please, so I can look at his face and he can be assured Tony's not going to shoot him."

Lorenzo guided Sabina forward with a protective arm around her. Into her ear, he whispered, "You ever scare me like that again, I'll lock you in the apartment and never let you out."

She bit back a shaky smile. "Well, if you stop putting yourself in the path of bullets..."

Roman and Sally pulled each other to their feet and stepped out, careful to stay partially masked behind Sabina and Enzo. Their hands were linked. Cliff joined them from the other side.

Papa took a half step forward. His face had gone blank. He didn't quite look like her father, but neither did he look like the unfamiliar Mafia boss she had seen a moment before. "Explain how you've come to believe it was Torrio."

Roman shrugged. "Sally said so."

"Sally." Papa's gaze moved to the blond.

Tony scoffed and strained against the restraining arm. "And you believe her? Right."

"I have no reason not to."

Papa's smile was small and mean. "Don't you? She's been keeping Ava apprised of your investigation from start to finish with the promise of a room here for her troubles."

Sabina craned around to verify that Roman's smile was just as small, just as mean. "And she's kept *me* apprised of all she's told Ava, because I offered to pay off her debts to Torrio so she can get out altogether."

Papa grunted. "There's a reason girls like her end up where they do, O'Reilly."

"And it shouldn't matter to you if I waste my savings giving her another chance. The point is, I'm done with you. You call off your lap dogs, and I'll stay out of your way."

Tony tried unsuccessfully to step forward again. "Oh, please! He just saw you gun down Norton—"

"What he *saw* was me defending my daughter and future son. And, for that matter, *him*. Isn't that right, O'Reilly?"

"Unfortunately."

Tony finally lowered his Betsy to his side, though mutiny still erupted in his eyes. "He was supposed to be my—"

"Antonio. Stop. I have no shortage of enemies—you don't need to prove yourself with this one, when it will cost you your brother. Family first."

Tony rolled his shoulders back. Sabina hoped the spark in his eyes was relief. But it looked more like disappointment, and she knew Lorenzo would see it, too. She clung to him, knowing how it would hurt him.

He sighed but held her back, tight as could be.

Papa reached out and took Tony's weapon. "You want a challenge? Take care of Norton. You too, Val. I don't want any questions from the police on this." As the brothers bent down and picked up the limp body, Papa turned back to Roman and pointed a finger at him. "You. Stay out of my way. And try not to forget that I not only spared your life, I just saved it. Got it?"

Sabina looked at Roman again, met his deep green gaze. The emotion in them wasn't quite regret, but it was close enough to make her certain he had no problem agreeing with her father's terms. He nodded. "*Capisciu.*"

Papa turned to his lieutenants. "Inside, all of you. Franco, please re-assure Ava that all is well, she'll have been frightened by the gunfire." The men filed inside, taking all the weapons with them. Papa crooked a finger at Sabina.

She stepped forward, pulling Lorenzo along with her. As they neared, she tried to keep her eyes off the pool of blood and failed. The streetlamp's glow streaked the otherwise black puddle with red and reflected off the bullet shells littering the ground. Evidence that Tony and Val would undoubtedly remove by morning.

If only her memory could be swept as clean. If only she could sweep her family clean with it.

Lorenzo pressed his lips to her temple. "Look at me, *bedduzza.*" She tore her gaze away from the blood and fastened it on his face. There she saw life, filled with love and promise. It would be enough to keep the nightmares at bay.

They stopped in front of her father, and she looked up into his hard face. His anger still burned under the surface. She refused to be intimidated. Maybe if she let him see the light in her, it would lead him toward the One who lit it. If not tonight, then tomorrow, or next week, or next month, or next year. The job of a candle was to shine despite the fact that the darkness could never comprehend it.

She let go of Lorenzo so she could put her arms around her father, even straining up on her toes to kiss his cheek. "*Grazii*, Papa."

The muscle in his jaw ticked. "You shouldn't have been here. This is the third time I've seen you between my men's guns and my enemies. I won't see you there again." His words were stern, but his arms closed around her and held her close. "You scared a decade off my life."

"Papa..." She had no idea what she wanted to say. There were no words to convince him, so she just held on.

"Enzo is going to have his hands full with you. Running off to the Levee—what possessed you to do something so stupid, *principessa*? Don't you realize the danger you put yourself in?"

She pulled away enough to look into his face. It was on the tip of her tongue to point out that it was a danger he created, a danger he fostered every time he broke the law. She bit it back. He wouldn't listen. "Yes, I know. But I couldn't let you kill him, Papa, so I tried to convince him to leave. And please don't look at me like that. You were doing this for me. I had to prove you didn't have to. And I did. He promised to leave me alone. And with Sally's help, he realizes you're not guilty of Eddie's murder." A truth she was still thanking God for every time she thought about it.

"Sally." Papa's eyes narrowed. "And how, pray tell, did you meet up with *her*?"

Sabina drew her lip between her teeth and darted a glance at Lorenzo, who looked interested in the answer to that, too. "I, uh…took a wrong turn leaving Roman's. Found myself in a bad part of town, and—she saved me, actually. I owe her."

"Hm." Papa pulled away, darting a glance over her shoulder. "I'll see that she's thanked. Enzo, I trust you can get my wayward daughter home safely? I have ends to tie up."

Lorenzo accepted her gratefully back into his embrace. Worry had taken up residence in his eyes. "I'll get her home."

"Good. And you two?" They both looked up at him. He frowned. "I can't have you interfering in my business. It not only weakens my position, it puts you both in danger. You don't want to be involved, then stay out. *All* the way out. You're my children, and I love you. But I had better never see either one of you in the Levee again."

Sabina nodded. Then the blood caught her eye again, and her heart sank down into her stomach. He loved her enough to kill for her. But never enough to forgive for her.

"We can't change any of them," Lorenzo whispered into her ear as Papa disappeared into the building. "But we can pray for them every day. A light in the darkness."

"A path through the night." She hugged him tight, knowing he felt this sorrow for them as keenly as she. She looked up at the sky, where stars probably shone beyond the city's glow—and movement caught her eye. A curtain shifting, a silhouette at a window above them. A palm pressed to a pane of glass.

Ava was watching over them—another friend, praying in the darkness. She lifted her hand from the glass, pressed it to her lips.

Sabina pressed her own to her heart, over the pendant she wore.

Lorenzo turned her toward his car, his arm still around her. Roman, Cliff, and Sally were waiting behind it.

Roman spoke first, looking and sounding testy. "I owe you. I don't want to."

Lorenzo grinned. "You helped me get to safety. I think we're even."

Roman groused and jammed his hands into his pockets. "Yeah, but you were about to do the same for me. And even though you were stupid to get involved and weren't doing much good anyway, I can't deny nobility when I see it. My da would have liked to know you."

The convoluted compliment made Lorenzo chuckle. Cliff shook his head and started for the alley's exit, but Sabina held out her hands to Sally. When she gripped them, they shared a wobbly smile. "I count you as a friend after tonight. If you ever need anything, Sally..."

The blond squeezed her fingers. "Well, you can start by calling me Cecily. That's who I was before I came here."

"Okay. Cecily." She pulled her in for a brief hug.

When they separated, Lorenzo held out a hand to her, too. "You're really getting out of this life?"

Cecily nodded.

Lorenzo said, "Then you'll need a job. My boss mentioned hiring another secretary, so if you're interested..."

Wariness masked her face. "I'm not qualified."

"You can take a course. And Helen will take you under her wing. It's the least I can do. You saved my girl."

Cecily grinned at Sabina. "Best thing I ever did. And I might just take you up on that offer."

Roman reclaimed her hand. Irritation still rode on his shoulders, but there was a softer light in his eyes. "I'll go tomorrow and get the money to pay off Capone. You can be a new woman by Monday. *Cecily*."

Lorenzo cleared his throat and tugged Sabina toward the Nash. "Well. Not to run off, but Mama Rosa's going to be frantic."

The reminder put a spur under Sabina. She all but leaped through the driver's door, then scooted over to make room for him behind her. "She's going to be furious!"

"Mm hm." He slid in too and closed the door. "Lucky for you, you only have another week under her roof."

Sabina grinned and leaned over to kiss him. She whispered, "*Ti amu, me amari.*"

Lorenzo kissed her soundly in return. "We're going to make it, Bean. No matter *who* our family is, we're going to make a life together we can be proud of."

She snuggled close as he started the car and pulled out. Behind her lay an alley of shadows, the lone circle of light shining on a nightmare. She didn't look back.

Lights in the darkness. A path through the night. Immortal diamond. She looked down at the one winking on her finger and knew it would be enough.

AUTHOR'S NOTE

I first wrote this story when my son was six months old—I have all these lovely memories of being up at 4:30 in the morning with him, the Mafia on the screen before me, my foot bouncing him in his chair and willing him back to sleep. I thought, at the time, that this book would be my big break.

Yeah…thirteen years later, I finally reread it and rewrote it, and I'm so very glad I had those years of learning to really bring the depth to the story that it deserved! Sabina and Lorenzo don't just have a romance—they have a story of familial love in the worst of circumstances, and more importantly, the love that God shows for His broken, darkness-stained creation.

When I was doing my original research for *Shadowed Loyalty*, I read book after book on the Mafia in turn-of-the-century America. In those first few decades of the twentieth century, the Mafia was made up almost entirely of men newly arrived from Italy, who brought with them their prejudices against oppressive government and authorities, and their solution to the problem. At its start and its heart, the Mafia was about family—a way to protect one's own against the corruption around them, even if one had to resort to violence to do it.

In Chicago into the twenties, these old-world gangsters ruled the day, and they had their code, their rules. Family was precious. You could take out another mafioso, but you did *not* mess with their wives and children. All that began to change when Al Capone came on the scene from New York. In many ways, he singlehandedly rewrote what the Mafia was and what it stood for, stomping all over those rules and codes in the pursuit of power and money. The Mafia we know today from fiction is the Mafia he recreated. When I sat down to write a story about this shadowy organization, I wanted to capture their shifting world—where old and new first collided. That's why I chose the year I did, and that brief window of time when Capone was still clawing his way up but the old bosses were still ruling.

Of course, one of the delights for me of writing a book set in the Roaring Twenties was the fashion! Inspiration for Sabina's wedding gown, veil, and expensive bouquet were actually taken from the old photograph in the front of my own wedding photo album—my husband's great-grandparents. They arrived from Italy not long before they married, and I love hearing my mother-in-law's stories about them! Though bouquet and dress and veil have been lost to time, the beautiful triple-strand necklace this young Italian bride wore on her wedding day now sits in my own jewelry box—a reminder of how we're linked to the past.

And now, the portion of the program that involves my sincerest gratitude. First to my amazing family, who always support me and keep the world moving while I huddle away to write. To Stephanie, who first told me thirteen years ago that this book had something in it, and then sat on the couch across from mine during our writing retreat for my rewrites—our first one where we were writing the same setting! Three cheers for Twenties Chicago!

And to the amazing team at Chrism Press. When I sent you the book I hadn't opened in well over a decade, I knew it would need a lot of work. Your advice, brainstorming, and answers to my endless questions about how my Catholic characters would behave were invaluable! It's a true joy to work with you all—Marisa, Rhonda, Karen. You're the best!

And finally, to my readers, who follow me from America to England and back again. Thank you for always being excited for the next story. Thank you for every email, social media message, and card in the mail. Thank you for making it possible for me to answer this call to write.

I always love hearing from you! Be sure to sign up for my newsletter on my website, www.RoseannaMWhite.com, where you'll get all the latest news and blog posts. And never forget that whatever shadows seem to plague you, we are now what Christ is—we are His light. His hands. His feet. Immortal diamond.

DISCUSSION QUESTIONS

1. At the start of the book, Sabina feels lost and superfluous in her world after their family's circumstances had changed so drastically within the past couple years. Have you ever not known what to do with yourself? Have you ever struggled to find your purpose?

2. Lorenzo thought he was protecting Sabina but in fact hurt her deeply. Have you ever been in a situation—on either side—where people who love each other actually do the opposite of what the other needs, though their intentions are good?

3. Though Sabina always "knew" what her father did for a living, she doesn't truly see the reality until he's arrested. Have you ever had to confront uncomfortable truths about your family or friends? Did you find it difficult to love them afterward? Or was it perhaps difficult to accept the truth about them?

4. Roman O'Reilly is, from his point of view, fighting for justice and against corruption. Do you think he was right to use Sabina as a means of bringing down her father? Have you read or watched other stories where the hero does this—did you root for him or against him in that situation? How could he have acted differently?

5. Who is your favorite character? Your least favorite? Why?

6. Isadora and Mary react very differently to their mother's illness and their father's abandonment. Are you more likely to embrace distractions and turn to escapism when burdens are heavy or try to carry them all alone? Why do you think neither sister had told anyone how desperate their situation had become?

7. Lorenzo observes with sorrow how he and his brothers were all taught the same lessons about faith and God, but they still turned into very different people. Have you observed this in your own life or family or community? Why do you think these lessons sink deep into some hearts and are so easily ignored by others?

8. The vibrant immigrant community of Chicago's Little Italy provided the backdrop for this story; in American history, some communities clung to the ways they brought with them, and others abandoned their mother language and culture and embraced American traditions. How connected are you with your own family's history? Was it preserved? Do you know your family's immigration story (if you have one) or how they ended up in the particular community you grew up in? Do you ever wish your ancestors had done things differently?

9. How did you feel about Ava as the story progressed? What about how Sabina responded to her at the various points in the story?

10. Sally doesn't begin as a very sympathetic character. Did that change for you as you learned her history? Knowing that her father abused her in the name of God, what do you think it would take to show her the true beauty of Christ's sacrifice? What do you imagine the future holds for her?

11. What do you think Lorenzo's relationship with his brothers will look like in the future? What about Sabina with her family?

12. Were there any themes or scenes that resonated with you and made you view things in a way you hadn't before? Do you have any questions or thoughts lingering after you finished the book?

ABOUT THE AUTHOR

Roseanna M. White is a bestselling, Christy Award winning author who has long claimed that words are the air she breathes. When not writing fiction, she's homeschooling her two kids, editing for WhiteFire Publishing, designing book covers, and pretending her house will clean itself. Roseanna is the author of dozens of historical novels that span several continents and thousands of years. Spies and war and mayhem always seem to find their way into her books...to offset her real life, which is blessedly ordinary. You can learn more about her and her stories at www.RoseannaMWhite.com.

Be sure to check out her books, blog, podcast,
and shop for signed books and other bookish goodies at:
www.RoseannaMWhite.com

Sign up there for her newsletter, where you'll get
sneak peeks, deals, and weekly updates!

ALSO BY ROSEANNA M. WHITE

BIBLICAL FICTION
A Stray Drop of Blood
A Soft Breath of Wind
Jewel of Persia
Giver of Wonders
The Prophet's Songbird

STAND-ALONE NOVELS
A Heart's Revolution
Dreams of Savannah
Shadowed Loyalty
Yesterday's Tides

CULPER RING SERIES
Ring of Secrets
Fairchild's Lady (novella)
Whispers from the Shadows
A Hero's Promise (novella)
Circle of Spies

LADIES OF THE MANOR
The Lost Heiress
The Reluctant Duchess
A Lady Unrivaled

SHADOWS OVER ENGLAND
A Name Unknown
A Song Unheard
An Hour Unspent

SECRETS OF WAYFARERS INN
Greater than Gold
All the Inn's a Stage
There's No Place Like Holmes

THE CODEBREAKERS
The Number of Love
On Wings of Devotion
A Portrait of Loyalty

SECRETS OF THE ISLES
The Nature of a Lady
To Treasure an Heiress
Worthy of Legend

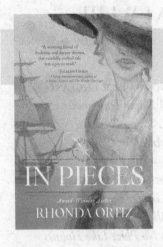

In Pieces - Molly Chase, Book One
by Rhonda Ortiz

Boston, 1793—Beautiful and artistic, the only daughter of a prominent merchant, Molly Chase cannot help but attract the notice of Federalist Boston—especially its men. But she carries a painful secret: her father committed suicide and she found his body. Now nightmares plague her day and night, addling her mind and rendering her senseless. Molly needs a home, a nurse, and time to grieve and to find new purpose in life. But when she moves in with her friends the Robbs, spiteful society gossips assume the worst.

Brother Wolf
by Eleanor Bourg Nicholson

For Athene Howard, the only child of renowned cultural anthropologist Charles Howard, life is an unexciting, disillusioned academic project. When she encounters a clairvoyant Dominican postulant, a stern nun, and a recusant English nobleman embarked on a quest for a feral Franciscan werewolf, the strange new world of enchantment and horror intoxicates and delights her—even as it brings to light her father's complex past and his long-dormant relationship with the Church of Rome.

Learn more about these and Chrism Press's other titles at
www.ChrismPress.com

Chrism Press ~ Anoint Your Imagination

CPSIA information can be obtained
at www.ICGtesting.com
Printed in the USA
BVHW030152030522
635912BV00024B/489